PRAISE FOR **IN THE I**

T0168491

2016 Foreword INDIES Bronze Awar

One of *USA Today*'s HEA Blog's Must-Read Romances of 2016

"Ms. Pack is a gifted storyteller who uses characters, plot, location and time to lay out the narrative. Definitely without a linear plotline, this book is nevertheless exciting to follow... *In the Present Tense* is one of the most unique books I've read in a long time."

—*USA TODAY*'s Happy Ever After Blog

"Four Stars... When Miles is betrayed in the worst way, *In the Present Tense* escalates to a frightening pitch right before reaching a happy ending."

—*RT Book Reviews Magazine*

"I'm definitely looking forward to the (as yet unannounced, but cross your fingers) sequel."

—Prism Book Alliance

PRAISE FOR **GRRRLS ON THE SIDE**

2017 Foreword INDIES Award Finalist (Young Adult Fiction)

2017 Bisexual Book Award Finalist (Teen/Young Adult Fiction)

"Like the riot-grrrl movement itself, unsubtle but full of heart."

—*Kirkus Reviews*

"...the universal themes of finding one's voice and community will resonate with all readers."

—*School Library Journal*

IN THE PRESENT TENSE

CARRIE PACK

interlude ✸✸ **press**™ • new york

interlude press • new york

For Lex.

"We have trouble with tenses emerging from time travel here. It might be more accurate to say that any action must will have existed."

—Brian Clegg, *How to Build a Time Machine*

CHAPTER ONE
MILES

At first, Miles thought he had imagined the scent of cinnamon in the air. Everything was wrong: the smell of the room, the feel of the sheet twisted around his legs, the hazy predawn light filtering through the window. Something was just off.

He rolled over to check the time, but instead of finding his phone on his nightstand where he had left it, his fingers came in contact with something silky and soft, almost like hair. Lifting it in his hand, he could just make out the shadow of it against the light blue of the wall—thick, glossy strands of an undetermined color. It *was* hair. And hadn't that wall been dark, striped wallpaper when he'd gone to bed?

As he let the hair drop from his grasp, a muffled groan startled him fully awake, and a distinctly female voice asked, "What time is it?"

Miles squeaked as he flopped backward onto his pillow, tugging the sheet with him.

The woman flew into a sitting position with a force so powerful her ebony hair flopped forward, completely obscuring her face. As she used her right arm to flip it back over her shoulders, she made eye contact with Miles.

"Ana?!"

"Goddamnit, Miles, you nearly gave me a heart attack."

She glared at him before lying down on her back and forcing long, even breaths in and out as if she were trying to calm herself.

Miles stared at her in disbelief. Before she could drift off again he asked, "What are you doing here? My parents—"

"Are asleep in the guest room." She yawned. "Go back to sleep."

"Why are they in the guest room?"

"You know I need my sleep or I'm an absolute bear," she groaned, rolling over and burying her face beneath a fluffy gray pillow.

"Why are the pillowcases gray?" he wondered.

"Did you fall on your head before you went to sleep or are you still drunk from last night?"

"Drunk?" Miles didn't remember drinking the night before. He hadn't had a drop since that unfortunate party last summer where he'd vomited all over Adam's shoes.

"Please just let me get twenty more minutes before you have a complete breakdown," she moaned.

"But—"

Her hand came up in front of his face. "Shut it, or I will smother you with this pillow."

"Just tell me why you're in my bed," he whispered.

"For fuck's sake, Miles."

"What?"

Ana rolled over with her back to him. "Go. To. Sleep."

Miles sat there and tried to make out shapes and colors in the dark room as he searched his brain for a memory of anything.

Nothing looked familiar. His desk, his drum set, the sheets—all gone. Not one thing looked the way it had when he'd fallen asleep, and Ana certainly hadn't been in his bed.

He tried to replay the previous day's events, but everything seemed fuzzy, like a fogged bathroom mirror that he couldn't wipe clean.

Why was everything so fuzzy?

Last night... What happened last night?

Adam had come over and they were watching TV together, and Adam had given him a small stuffed giraffe because Miles was scared about having surgery. He reached for his left arm, expecting to find the cast that had been there for the last two months, but it wasn't there. His heart began to beat so loudly he glanced over at Ana to make sure she was still asleep.

Unable to determine what had happened to his cast, Miles resumed his tally of the previous evening's chain of events. At around ten-thirty, his mom said Adam had to leave because they had to get up early to go to the hospital. He had taken his pain meds and gone to sleep with the phantom of Adam's goodnight kiss on his cheek. He'd been happy.

He'd gotten a text from Ana earlier in the evening, but she was only wishing him luck with the surgery. She hadn't come over. In fact, as far as Miles knew, Ana had been several hours away in her dorm room.

So how had she gotten into his bedroom? And who had changed his sheets?

He threw off the covers and stood up, noticing he was only wearing a tight-fitting pair of boxer briefs instead of his usual basketball shorts.

He looked around the room for anything familiar, but it was still dark out, and all he could see were shadows and vague shapes. On the dresser opposite the bed, he found a few framed photos. Squinting to see without turning on a light, Miles studied the images carefully.

As his eyes focused, he recognized a couple of the photos. One was from last year's prom: Adam wearing that ridiculous corsage Miles had bought him, Ana being dipped by her date, David, as all four of them smiled widely in front of a cheesy faux tropical scene. One of the frames held a collage of photos of his and Ana's friends. He recognized Adam, Lucky, Antonio, Dahlia and Brienne. But the last one, the largest of all the photos, was of him and Ana—her in a flowing white dress and him in a black suit, both wearing broad smiles and flanked by Miles's parents and a woman Miles had only seen once: Julia Espinosa, Ana's mother.

A loud clatter echoed through the bedroom as the frame hit the edge of the dresser and fell to the hardwood floor. This wasn't his room, and he didn't remember that photo being taken.

"Go back to sleep," Ana mumbled, her voice muffled by the pillow.

"Ana," he whispered, risking her full anger, but unable to stop himself, "we're married."

"Thanks for the update. Now go back to sleep before I divorce your dumb ass."

He dropped to the floor on his knees, barely even noticing the sharp pain of bare skin hitting the hard surface.

Married. To Ana?

What the hell had happened?

HE WASN'T SURE WHEN HE'D gotten up from the floor, but Miles found himself standing over Ana, watching the rise and fall of her chest with each breath, as he tried to figure out what was going on. Her hair was longer than she'd ever worn it, longer in fact, than it had been the week before when it had fallen just to her shoulders. Judging from the way her hair fanned out over her face and curled around her upper arm, he figured it must be twice that long now.

He could make out the edge of what appeared to be a tattoo peeking from behind the strap of her tank top. When had she gotten that? Miles didn't dare wake her again, so he sat on the edge of the bed and tried to make sense of something, anything. Running his left hand over his own face, he felt the coarse scratch of stubble where a light dusting of peach fuzz should have been. His hand shaking, Miles let gravity take over, and his hand fell into his lap. He jumped when he felt something heavy and cold strike his thigh. Even in the dim predawn light, he could see that it was a silvery ring—a wedding band.

Behind his eyes, a dull ache had begun to form, making it difficult to think. He paced back and forth between the dresser and the bed, trying to sort his thoughts.

Ana must be playing a prank on me, he thought. *She dragged me over here after I was asleep and changed my clothes and put this ring on me. She photoshopped that picture of us and—*

Even in his own head it sounded ridiculous. But what other explanation could there be? He had woken up in bed with Ana and had no idea how he'd gotten there.

Maybe it was the pain meds.

Miles paced the room as the sun rose. If he'd been able to form a clear thought about his situation, he probably would have searched the room for more answers, but he couldn't wrap his head around any of it. Nothing made sense. Why was he here... and where was *here*? And what had happened to his cast?

The harsh buzzing of an alarm next to the bed pulled Ana slowly out of sleep. She groaned as she turned it off and rolled over onto her back. Stretching her arms over her head and yawning, she sat up and pulled back the covers. Without looking at Miles or speaking, she shuffled past him into what he assumed was the attached bathroom. As the shower sputtered to life, he could only stand there staring.

"You should probably put some coffee on before your father has a fit," Ana called. "You know how he is without caffeine in him."

Miles stood frozen, glancing over his shoulder at the open bathroom door. How did Ana know what his father was like before his first cup of coffee?

"Oh and make sure he stays away from the last poppy seed muffin," she said, peering around the door. He could see that she was naked, at least from the waist up. "That shit is mine."

Ana disappeared again, and Miles began to shake. His legs felt as if they were about to buckle and his stomach swooped as if he were careening down the first big hill on a rollercoaster.

"Miles? Honey?" a voice called from the hallway. "Are you two up yet? I can't find the grinder for the coffee beans." His mother knocked softly three times. "Honey?"

Oh shit.

His mother was knocking on his door and Ana was naked in the bathroom, and he was standing there in his underwear.

"Just—" Miles's voice cracked on the first syllable. He cleared his throat and tried again. "Just a minute, Mom. I'll be right there."

"It's behind the coffee beans," Ana yelled.

"Thanks, sweetie," his mother replied, and her soft footsteps retreated from the door.

Okay, so his mom obviously knew Ana was in his room and wasn't freaking out about it, and Ana was acting as if this were all perfectly normal. Miles didn't like that he was the only one not in on the joke.

When he heard the shower shut off, he realized he was still standing in the middle of the bedroom in nothing but his underwear and he probably looked like a deranged person. He looked frantically for some clothes to throw on and spotted a pair of jeans draped over a chair near his side of the bed. He slipped them on quickly and realized they fit perfectly. He found a rumpled gray T-shirt underneath them and threw that on as well.

Just as he was leaving the bedroom, Ana came out of the bathroom wrapped in a blue towel; her hair was hidden beneath a polka dot shower cap.

"Poppy seed," she said pointing at him. "Property of me."

Miles nodded and closed the door behind him, then sagged against it as he let his breath out in a rush. His brain was working overtime trying to piece this puzzle together, and he was coming up blank. Maybe his parents would have some answers.

He followed the familiar voices he heard drifting down the hallway and found himself in a brightly lit, high-end kitchen. His parents were sitting on stools at a granite-topped island and sipping from oversized coffee mugs.

"Oh, you look awful," his mother said when she saw him.

Miles's words caught in his throat when he saw her dark hair was salt-and-peppered with streaks of gray. And its usual long weave had been traded for a close-cropped natural style. His father looked different too; his forehead was more lined and his hair was thinner on top and absolutely white where it had been simply graying the day before.

"Are you hungover?" his father asked, wincing. "You certainly had enough vodka last night."

"Oh, leave him alone, Mitch." His mother swatted at her husband's arm. "Do you want some coffee, honey? I made plenty."

She was up and out of her chair before he had a chance to respond. "You still take it with lots of cream and no sugar?"

Miles managed to give some indication that she was right, because his mother smiled and poured him a cup of coffee.

She placed it in front of him, and he tentatively took a sip as he glanced down at his father's tablet, which was still open to the *Orlando Sentinel's* news app. The headline on the first story read "Olympic team prepares for 2020 games." Thinking he'd read it wrong, Miles scrolled down to the next headline: "Tribute concert to honor 10th anniversary of King of Pop's death." He frantically dragged his finger across the screen until the top of the page was in the window. The date read March 28, 2020.

His mug shattered when it hit the granite countertop and coffee splattered all over his shirt, the tablet and every surface within a two-foot radius.

"Dammit, Miles!" his father snapped, grabbing the tablet from him and wiping it off with his sleeve.

"Don't move," his mother said. "I'll clean it up."

"Holy crap," Ana said from behind him. "I leave you three alone for five minutes and you're practically burning the house down."

"It's just a little spill, Ana. I'll have it cleaned up in a jiff. Why don't you help Miles? He looks like he could use a shower."

"Sure thing, Mrs. L."

Ana grabbed him by the elbow and tugged him toward the bedroom.

"God, you're a fucking mess," she said, yanking his soaked shirt over his head and tossing it in a hamper. "You suck when you're hungover."

"Ana, this is going to sound crazy..." He couldn't finish that sentence. She would have him committed.

"Try me," she said, crossing her arms and leveling a stern look at him.

He blinked, shivering now from the cooled coffee that had soaked through his shirt and still clung to his skin.

"Oh shit, it's happening again," Ana said, her eyes wide.

"What is?"

"The time travel thing."

"What time travel thing?"

"Oh shit, how young are you this time, Lawson? Don't tell me I got the version of you who hasn't figured it out yet."

He stared at her. *Time travel? Had she lost her mind?*

"Fuck me running," she said when he didn't respond. "Have a seat, Marty McFly. I've got a story for you that's gonna blow your mind."

As Miles sat on the edge of the bed, Ana disappeared into the bathroom and reemerged holding a clean towel that she tossed at him. While he was drying off, she opened a drawer and pulled out a fresh shirt, then laid it next to him on top of the duvet.

"Thanks," he muttered.

"Oh, so you *can* speak."

"I'm just really confused, Ana. Can you tell me what's going on? Why were we sleeping in the same bed and why do my parents look like they aged ten years overnight?"

She sighed and sat down beside him, then ran a soft hand down his cheek.

"What year is it?" she asked.

"Ana—"

"Humor me," she said softly. "What year is it for you?"

The question didn't make sense, but since Ana was the one with the answers, he decided to play along.

"Two thousand twelve."

"Okay then," she said with raised eyebrows. "That explains your parents."

"I don't follow."

"Of course you don't." Ana ran her fingers through her long hair and twisted it around her hand. "Okay, Cupcake, here's the deal. I'm going to explain things to you, but you can't interrupt me until I'm done. It's all going to sound completely crazy, and you need to hear me out before you go freaking out. Got it?"

Miles nodded.

"Have you been having like really vivid dreams? Things that feel real but can't possibly be?" Ana asked.

When Miles nodded, she smiled knowingly.

"Right on time," she said.

"What are you—?"

"Still talking," she said, holding up a finger to silence him.

Miles bit his lip to keep from interrupting. His vice-like grip on his own hands was cutting off the circulation to his fingers.

When Ana was satisfied he wasn't going to say anything else, she continued, "Okay, so when you were like sixteen or seventeen you started having these crazy dreams—dreams that would come true, but they were, like, really, really specific. Songs on the radio, what someone was going to wear the next day, what the teachers said before they said it. It was creepy."

She laughed. Miles didn't see what was so funny.

"When you and Adam broke up—"

"We broke up?"

"Just after your senior year of high school, yes." She punctuated her exasperated tone with an eye roll. "Jesus, Miles, let me get through this and then you can ask all the questions you want."

Miles took a deep breath as Ana rested a hand on his. He tried to smile reassuringly, but it probably looked more like he was in pain.

"When you broke up, it started happening more frequently. By the time you got to college, you were starting to get suspicious they weren't just dreams, but you were hesitant to tell anyone. And then you knew my date's name."

Ana laughed again.

"What's so funny?"

"*I didn't even know his name. He was a hookup. Or so I thought. Dan and I ended up dating for two years before we called it quits. But you acted like you knew him, like you'd known him for a while, actually. And I'd just met him the night before."

Shaking her head, Ana smiled at him fondly.

"I got you drunk that night and made you spill the beans about the dreams. I convinced you to see a therapist about it, and he referred you to a psychiatrist, but it kept happening. The doc thought it was a psychological disorder and put you on meds, but it started happening more frequently and you stopped going to the doctor. I think you were just content to deal with it. Until about three years ago."

"What happened three—?"

"Patience. I'm getting there."

She intertwined her tanned fingers with Miles's darker ones and stroked her thumb over his wrist.

"Three years ago you showed up on my doorstep insisting that we had to get married so you could hire a private research company to study your condition because you were time-traveling. Said you were from a year in the future."

"You must have thought I was crazy."

"Oh, I threw you out on your cute little half-black ass."

"I'm confused."

"I came around," she said, letting out a heavy breath. "You knew about Monica."

Miles furrowed his brow. "Your sister?"

"She was sick." Ana's eyes began to well up. "Shit. I didn't even know. No one did. She didn't want to worry us."

As the tears began to fall, Miles smoothed Ana's hair from her face.

"You told me she was going to die, and I didn't believe you. You gave me the exact date and time and everything. God, I was so fucking stupid. I should have gone to see her that same fucking day." She sniffed. "The doctors gave her nine months. She only lasted eight."

"Ana, I'm sorry."

"It's fine," she said, waving him off and swiping a finger under her eye. "It's been years now. Anyway, it took me a bit to come around, but when I did you told me that you'd split your trust fund with me if I married you. Otherwise, you'd have to wait until you were thirty to have access to the money."

"My grandfather made my dad put that clause in there."

"I know."

"So we got married?"

"Yep."

"You're my wife?"

"That's usually what married means."

"But I like *boys*," Miles said, his head throbbing.

"Well, we really got married out of convenience—at first."

"What do you mean 'at first'?" Miles asked.

She shrugged. "A lot changed after high school. You and Adam broke up; he ran off to backpack across Europe with a guy named Harry, and you started dating a girl... Amber, I think."

"So, I'm bi?"

Ana nodded.

"You said we got married out of convenience, though," Miles said. He took a deep breath as he steeled himself for his next question. "So what you're telling me is we fell in love after we got married?"

"Yes."

"Shit."

"It's a lot to take in, I'm sure."

"It's... But... I'm..." Miles curled into himself, his posture collapsing as he clutched at his own thighs. His breathing came in shallow, rapid bursts as he tried to wrap his head around the complete mindfuck Ana had just unloaded on him.

"Do you need to lie down?" she asked.

"No," he said, jumping up and patting his pockets in search of his phone. There was only one thing he could think of to do. "I've got to talk to Adam."

Ana raised a hand and gently grabbed his wrist. She looked up at him, her deep brown eyes full of empathy.

"Miles, you haven't talked to Adam in six years."

Miles couldn't speak; he sat on the bed without his body's consent. It was as if Ana's words had paralyzed him. What had happened to him that he no longer spoke to Adam? He couldn't imagine a world where they weren't at least friends.

"Miles, are you all right?" Ana's voice sounded tinny and far away, like a voice recorded on an old, scratchy record. "Shit, you look like you're going to pass out."

She disappeared into the bathroom, returning seconds later with a small paper cup of water. "Drink," she said, forcing the cup to Miles's lips as she sat beside him on the bed.

He complied like an obedient child. Staring at his bare feet, he said, "Tell me about Adam."

Ana exhaled slowly. "Are you sure you want to know?"

Breathing deeply, Miles nodded. "I just need to know why Adam didn't want to be with me."

"Miles," Ana said, resting her hand on his knee. "Honey, you broke up with him."

Miles felt his stomach lurch and his vision blur as tears began to sting his eyes. "Why?"

"No idea." Ana's eyes were beginning to swim as well. It was obvious she wanted to help him but didn't know how. "You just told me you two had a bad breakup and that it was over. I haven't seen him since Dahlia's wedding last year, and he wouldn't talk to me."

"He knows we're married?"

"Yeah, he knows."

"What did he say?"

Ana shrugged. "Not much. I think he expected it after all those years of flirting we did."

"We flirted?" he asked.

"I guess you wouldn't remember that," she muttered, almost to herself.

Miles felt queasy. "Ana, what is wrong with me?"

"Well, that part's a little hairy," she said. Standing up, she began to pace the small area rug at the foot of the bed.

"Just tell me," Miles said. "I need to know."

"You made me promise not to if I ever saw you before you figured it out," she said. "You said something about screwing up your timeline or some shit."

"The space-time continuum," Miles mumbled.

"God, you're such a nerd," Ana said with an eye roll. "Anyway, you said no. So my lips are sealed."

"How the hell do I get back?" Miles said, more to himself than Ana.

"You just have to wait for it to pass," she said. "Or you could go see Dr. Benson."

"Dr. Benson?"

"Yeah, she's your therapist."

Miles's mind was swimming with information, and his head was pounding. Unable to decide between finding Adam and calling this Dr. Benson, he looked up at Ana, searching her face for answers. But she only looked at him with sympathy.

"What do I do?" he implored.

Her eyes softened and she ran a hand across his cheek. "Just do the next thing, I guess."

Miles leaned forward and wrapped his arms around... his wife. The word even sounded strange in his head, but Ana was familiar and he needed a hug. "I'm so glad I have you," he said.

Ana hugged him back before clearing her throat and pushing him away. She shifted her weight and began to chew on a fingernail. "I uh... should check on your parents. And you... you should take a shower." She motioned to his bare chest and dirty jeans.

Looking down at his haphazard appearance, Miles realized how wonderful a shower sounded.

Ana left him alone, and it took him a few moments to find his underwear drawer and some clothes. He found a clean towel in a small cabinet in the bathroom and turned the faucet on as hot as it would go.

As the scalding water washed over his skin, he tried to clear the clutter from his brain, but only one thought echoed through his mind like a steady metronome of anguish. What if he never saw Adam again? They had just gotten into a groove and were starting to get serious. Miles was overwhelmed with wanting to go home just as it also occurred to him that he *was* home.

He watched the soapy water swirl down the drain and began to feel dizzy. The edges of his vision grew fuzzy and uncertain. He gripped the wall for stability, only aware of the water as it trickled down his back. The water seemed to have lost pressure and gone cold. Miles reached up to turn the tap marked hot, but everything went black, and he fell to the shower floor. His head struck the slick tile as his body crumpled beneath him.

MONDAY, OCTOBER 12, 2009 · 1:08 P.M.

"All I'm saying is, if you're willing to die for your country, it shouldn't matter who you're sleeping with." Adam's voice was firm and bold.

Miles turned in his seat to study his expression. He'd never heard Adam speak this passionately about anything. His glasses sat forgotten on his desk as he gestured and argued with some Neanderthal named Jake about Obama's announcement that he would repeal the military's "Don't Ask, Don't Tell" policy.

"But why do we need to know?" Jake asked. "Can't they just keep it to themselves?"

"Yeah, sure," Adam retorted. "If I used that logic, then no one could ever talk about their spouse or family at work. Even wearing a wedding ring would be out."

"That's different."

"How is it different?"

"Because being straight is the norm."

Miles thought Adam was going to come out of his seat. He flung himself back into his chair in exasperation as the class erupted in incoherent arguing.

Here we go again, Miles thought.

Their history teacher, Mr. Turner, was a decent enough guy, but he often brought up topics just to push their buttons. Miles always hated when the discussion turned to LGBT rights. Inevitably someone would say something like, "As long as I don't have to see it," and the class would devolve into bitter arguments that ended up with Mr. Turner flashing the lights to calm everyone down. Miles usually sat and watched it all unfold. But today he was emboldened by Adam's passion.

He cleared his throat and raised his voice to be heard over the din. "I think the purpose of 'Don't Ask, Don't Tell' is that it doesn't matter. It's just a backward way of looking at it."

The noise in the room fell to a dull roar, and Mr. Turner worked to shush everyone. "Mr. Lawson, that's an interesting point. Tell us more."

"Well, if you're saying, 'Don't ask me about my sexuality and I won't tell you,' isn't that the same as saying it's irrelevant? If it's relevant, why not talk about it?"

"Exactly," Jake agreed. "So we should keep it."

"Why don't you shut up about things that don't apply to you," Adam said.

"It does apply to me if some fudge-packer is watching my back. I don't want anyone checking out my ass while we're rooting out snipers."

"Oh, like anyone would want to check out that flat ass," Adam said.

"Gentlemen, let's keep it civil," Mr. Turner chastised. "And, Mr. Abernathy, we don't use slurs in my class. Do it again, and I'm suspending you."

Thankfully, the discussion ended there because the bell rang. As Miles packed up his books, Adam tapped him on the shoulder. Miles turned to see he'd put his glasses back on and carried his backpack slung over one shoulder. His arm flexed as he hiked the backpack higher, revealing thick veins across his bare forearm. Miles's breath caught.

"Thanks for backing me up," Adam said. "I was starting to think I was all alone."

Not wanting to look as though he was ogling, Miles focused his attention on his books. "Most of the class is pretty progressive," Miles said. "It's just that Jake is really vocal about his hate. He does that a lot, and everyone gets sick of arguing with him."

"Well, you can't argue with stupid."

Miles laughed. "So true."

"Still, it's always nice to know we have allies."

Miles looked up. "We?"

Adam tilted his head, forcing his crooked grin into an even more charming line. "Yeah, I thought you knew. I've been dropping hints for weeks." Adam inched closer, his extra height pressing in on Miles and making the room seem hotter.

"I just thought you were... Well, I don't know what I thought." Miles's heart began to race. He and Adam were the only ones left in the classroom, and they were only inches apart.

"I am so into you. I can't believe you didn't notice." Adam's eyes lingered on Miles's lips and then ventured down and finally across his torso.

"I—" Miles licked his lips. "I like you too."

Adam stepped closer, placing his hand on Miles's hip. "Is this okay?" Adam asked with his face so close, Miles could feel Adam's breath on his cheek.

Miles nodded, afraid of breaking the spell if he spoke. He closed his eyes and let himself sway closer, hoping Adam would finish the job. He'd been fantasizing about kissing Adam for weeks, and now it was really happening. His fingertips tingled, longing to grab Adam by the neck, but he balled his hands into fists at his sides, feeling his fingernails digging into his palms. He inhaled and caught the sweet scent of mint on Adam's breath. He'd planned this.

Miles relaxed his jaw and felt the barest hint of Adam's lips against his own mouth: a subtle graze that only lasted a second before it was gone, leaving Miles hungry for more. Feeling emboldened by the knowledge that Adam wanted to kiss him, Miles pushed forward, seeking Adam's lips again. They bumped noses, and Miles pulled back, embarrassed. But before he could retract the offer completely, Adam's lips covered his, firm and sure this time. A jolt of warmth shot straight through to Miles's core as a swooping sensation fluttered through his midsection. His hands flew to cup Adam's face and before he knew it, his tongue was pressing on Adam's bottom lip, tentatively seeking permission for more. Adam gasped, and his lips parted, giving off the impression that his own tongue was hungry for a taste of what Miles was offering.

Miles had no idea how long they stood there kissing, but when it was over, Adam pulled back, pressed his forehead against Miles's and sighed dreamily. "I've been wanting to do that forever."

Miles blinked at him, shocked. "Me too."

"Boy, am I glad. Otherwise this could have ended really badly."

Miles laughed; the nervous flutter in his stomach still drew his attention and his brain had stopped working. "We should get to band."

Adam stepped back and gave him a questioning look but didn't say anything. Without a word, they walked down the hall together, remaining inches apart but not quite touching. It was too new, too tenuous, and Miles was afraid of bursting the bubble. They could figure this out later. He just wanted to savor the moment. A refrain of "Adam kissed me" echoed through his brain. "Adam kissed me, and it was perfect."

SUNDAY, MARCH 29, 2020 · 10:45 A.M.

Miles woke from a dream in a cold sweat. A distant beeping that matched his pulse seemed to get closer the more alert he became. The beeping slowed as his breathing calmed. His left arm felt heavy; a dull ache radiated downward from his forearm and into his fingers. Through drowsy, unfocused eyes, he could just make out his surroundings: a hospital bed, heart monitor, television and a hideous mauve recliner with a thin, white blanket draped over it. A pillow rested on the windowsill. Someone must have slept in the chair.

He tried to remember what day it was—what year. The stabbing pain behind his eyes alerted him to a recent episode, but not even a shred of a memory would reveal itself to help solve the mystery. It happened like this often, an episode of which he had no memory, and he'd never figured out when or where he'd been. Perhaps his condition was worsening.

He looked to see if his phone was within reach—he should probably call Dr. Benson and let her know he'd had another episode—but his eyes only found an empty coffee cup with a smudge of bright red lipstick on the lid. Miles smiled, knowing that Ana had been there. Apart from Dr. Benson, his wife was the only person he had trusted with the truth of his condition.

As if his thoughts had summoned her, Ana, heels clicking sharply on the tile, breezed through the door to his hospital room.

"You're awake," she said, concern lurking beneath her forced smile.

Attempting to sit up, Miles hissed at the pain that shot through his left arm as he put his weight on it. "What happened?" he asked as he sagged against the pillows in defeat.

"You collapsed in the shower. Don't you remember anything?"

"Not since Friday night when my parents got in. We went to Bortello's for dinner, and I might have overdone it with the vodka tonics."

Ana nodded. "How's your head?"

"Fuzzy. I think I might have had another episode."

She leaned forward, brushing his damp hair away from his face. "Yeah," she said softly. "It was a bad one."

"Tell me."

Her brown eyes narrowed. "Are you sure?"

"I need to know."

The bed shifted as Ana sat next to Miles. Crossing one long, brown leg over the other, she reached for his hand. "You asked about Adam," she said solemnly.

Miles hadn't thought much about Adam since before he and Ana were married. The breakup had been painful, but over time Miles had moved on, and Adam had moved away. If he'd asked Ana about Adam, the version of himself that had showed up must have been quite young. As always, Miles felt guilty for subjecting Ana to his condition's side effects.

"I'm sorry," he said, resting his head on her shoulder as the scent of her hair enveloped him in wonderful memories. He tilted his head up just as a tear rolled down her cheek. He squeezed her hand tighter.

Ana wiped at the stray tear with her free hand. "I'm fine," she said. "You know me, made of razor blades and leather." She winked at him, but Miles knew she was lightening the mood for his sake. He decided to play along.

"So what did teenage-me have to say about us shacking up together? I imagine I was shocked."

"Honey, you were a fucking mess," she said with a laugh. "I thought you were still drunk."

They were quiet, and then Miles asked, "How long?"

"A couple of hours. You've been in the hospital longer than you were the other you, actually. I didn't want to call an ambulance, but your mother dialed nine-one-one before I could stop her. Anyway, I couldn't very well tell her the truth. 'Oh, he'll be fine, Mrs. L. He'll just wake up with a shitty headache after he's done time-traveling.' Besides, you broke your arm when you fell."

"Shit, I'm really sorry," Miles said, lifting his heavy arm and noticing the cast for the first time.

Ana shrugged. "Comes with the territory. But now that you're awake, you can make it up to me because I am not dealing with your mother when she comes by this afternoon. That's all on you."

"You got it." Miles motioned for Ana to lean back against the pillow with him.

She laid her head next to his, her forehead to his temple. Miles could feel her breath hot and feather-light against his cheek. He listened to her slow, even breathing and tried to piece together a reasonable explanation to give his mother.

Ana's hair tickled his neck as she tilted her head to look at him. "I didn't tell you anything about Adam," she said. "Other you, I mean. The younger you."

Miles twisted his neck awkwardly to try to see her face. He could see that her eyes were closed.

"You wanted to know why you haven't spoken to him in so long, but I did what you told me. I didn't say a word." Her voice was barely audible over the steady whirring of the monitors and the periodic noises from the mechanical compression socks Miles wore.

"Maybe you should have," Miles muttered. "Saved me some heartache."

"But you said—"

"I know what I said. You did the right thing." Miles stroked Ana's ebony hair and twirled a lock around his index finger. "It's just sometimes I wish I'd known. Maybe then you and I would have gotten together sooner."

"Not a chance, dork face," she said, playfully swatting his arm. "I was way too cool for you in high school."

"This is true."

Ana had been homecoming queen, an honor student who was friends with everyone. Miles had Adam, a chip on his shoulder and music—the only reason he knew Ana at all. They were in marching band together. Ana played clarinet; Miles played percussion. But they rarely spoke outside of their mutual circle of friends, until Ana's senior year when they became best friends, and by then, he was already dating Adam.

"So you really don't remember waking up in bed with me when you were seventeen?"

Miles shook his head. "It's weird. You'd think I'd remember something like *that*."

"You used to remember the big things."

"Dr. Benson thinks it might be the medication she has me on."

"Maybe that means it's working."

Miles shrugged. He had no idea if it was working or not. His episodes were coming more frequently since he'd started the new medication, but they didn't last as long. Unfortunately, he no longer kept his memories from his trips. His younger self's time-traveling exploits were a mystery. Maybe the seventeen-year-old version of himself didn't remember waking up next to Ana. There was no way to tell what effect the medication was having on his body or his mind.

"Do you have my phone?" he asked. "I should probably set up an appointment with Dr. Benson. She said she wants to see me after an episode."

"It's in my bag," she said. "Want me to get it?"

"In a minute. Could you just stay here? I hate hospitals." He pulled Ana closer and rested his head on her shoulder.

"Sure thing, Irving."

FRIDAY, APRIL 21, 2017 · 2:16 P.M.

Miles panted heavily as he scaled the steps to Ana's apartment. The moment he'd realized what year it was, he had jumped in his car and driven the two hours to Gainesville. He needed Ana's help and he had to warn her about Monica. She would believe him if he could predict what was to come. Or so he hoped.

He knocked three short raps and heard a voice call out, "Hang on a sec!" Composing himself, Miles ran his sweaty palms over his thighs and hitched his pants up an inch.

The seconds stretched on for what seemed like an eternity before Ana, dressed in only a sports bra and a pair of shorts that might as well have been underwear, swung the door wide. Miles swallowed hard. Before he had a chance to speak, she'd engulfed him in a strong hug.

"Miles!" she said into his shoulder. "What on earth are you doing here?"

He inhaled the scent of her. She had obviously been sweating, but she still smelled faintly of citrus, a light, girlish scent she'd worn since high school. She'd even worn it to Monica's funeral. He bit his lip to fight back the tears threatening to spill.

"Can I come in?" he asked, pulling away from her slowly. He now noticed that her hair had been cut short into a choppy bob that was longer in the front than in the back. It suited her.

"You look great," he said as she stepped back to allow him to step inside.

"I'm a hot, sweaty mess," she said. "I had hot yoga this morning and haven't showered yet. Too busy studying for finals, and it's like Satan's armpit out there anyway."

"I thought you graduated," Miles said, forgetting momentarily that it was a year earlier than it had been when he woke up that morning. Ana didn't seem to notice, though.

"Law school." She beamed proudly before rolling her eyes. "I'm such a glutton for punishment."

"Evidently. Doing hot yoga in Florida in this heat? You always were smart."

She slapped his arm playfully at the jab. "Well, I had the grades, and you know I like to argue."

"That you do."

She sat down and gestured for Miles to sit next to her. "So what brings you to the swamp on this fine humid day?" She exaggerated the word fine and drawled out the full sentence with her best Southern belle accent.

Miles's face fell. He couldn't keep the smile plastered to his face any longer. He'd come to see Ana on very serious business and he didn't know how much time he had.

"Marry me," he said.

Ana widened her eyes and then started laughing.

"I'm serious. If I don't get married, I can't access my trust fund until I'm thirty."

She looked at him as if he had two heads. "No really, why are you here?"

He could see this was getting nowhere, so he changed tactics. After clearing his throat, Miles asked a question to which he already knew the answer. "When was the last time you talked to Monica?"

"My sister?" Ana asked, incredulous.

Miles nodded.

"Uh, I guess it's been a few months. We had a fight about abuela's living situation. Monica wanted to put her in a home; Mom refused, and I sided with Mom. Monica was furious and hasn't called either of us since."

"Call her," Miles implored.

"You drove all this way to make a joke about getting married and to meddle in my personal business?" Ana said. "Are you high?"

"I'm serious," Miles said. He swallowed hard. There was no easy way to say this, so he just blurted it out. "She's dying."

Ana looked shocked and then burst out laughing. "Nice try, Lawson. You almost had me."

Miles placed his hand on her knee. Her skin was warm and smooth. "Ana, I'm serious."

"You barely know my sister. Why would she tell you and not me?"

"She didn't," Miles said. He looked at his feet; his whole body tingled under the weight of what he was about to say. "I'm from the future."

The silence that followed was overwhelming, but still Miles hoped Ana would believe him. When she finally spoke, it was as she was crossing to the door.

"Get out," she said, swinging the door wide and holding it open. Her eyes flashed with rage.

"Ana—"

"OUT."

Miles rose. He'd done all he'd come to do. As he walked past her, he let his hand brush hers. Ana jerked away sharply, refusing to make eye contact. Before he crossed the threshold, Miles quietly uttered, "July twenty-second, twenty-eighteen. Early morning."

By the time he turned to catch her expression, Ana had slammed the door in his face. He hoped it was enough to get her to believe him. At any rate, he was out of time. The throbbing behind his eyes was back and he barely made it to the car before his vision blurred and the world went black.

MONDAY, MARCH 30, 2020 · 10:52 A.M.

Ana tapped her fingers on the faux mahogany surface of her desk. It was a nervous habit that stretched back to her childhood, much like twirling her hair around her finger when she was thinking. Whenever something was pressing on her mind, she tapped out a sharp rhythm on whatever surface she could find. Miles always teased her about it because it was a drummer's habit and one they didn't share. Miles never tapped. No, when her husband became preoccupied, he time-traveled. If only he could tap out his worries instead of hopscotching through time and leaving chaos in his wake.

She cupped her hands over her mouth and blew warm breath over her icy fingers. It was always so damned cold in her office. It made her fingers ache, which made the tapping painful—a bad combination. Worrying gave her headaches, which made her neck tense. Between that and the freezing cold temperature of an air-conditioned office, her body was one tiny ball of tension. Stretching her arms high over her head, Ana heard a few small pops but nothing that would give her the relief she craved. She searched her desk drawers and when she found a bottle of ibuprofen, she knocked back a couple of the bright orange pills with a swig of her now ice-cold coffee.

Miles's episode had been rough on both of them. She knew he had started seeing Dr. Benson again regularly, but she thought the episodes were decreasing. Either that or he was hiding the truth from her. The thought made her gut flutter with anxiety. A tight knot of tension nestled just below her solar plexus, like someone twisting a spoon around her insides. Maybe she should start seeing someone to talk about this whole thing. Where was the rule book for a time-traveling husband?

A sharp rap at her office door pulled her from her scattered thoughts, and Ellen's round face peered through the opening. Ana's assistant was a middle-aged woman with graying hair that she tried to cover with bright red hair dye. But Ellen never managed to keep up with it, so her mismatched roots were always showing. Ana had once given her a gift certificate to a fancy salon for Christmas, but Ana suspected she never used it.

"Tim Evans is here for his deposition," she said.

"Show him to the conference room," Ana replied. "And—"

"Get him some coffee," Ellen added with a smile. "Already done. Steno is on her way and Mr. Beekman's attorney called from his car. He'll be a few minutes late."

"Thanks, Ellen."

Ana tugged her feet out of the warm slippers she kept under her desk and back into her high heels.

Ellen was about to leave when she stopped short. She turned around and studied Ana with kind eyes; her bottom lip was caught between her crooked teeth.

"Yes?" Ana inquired.

"You look tired. Or worried," Ellen said as she cocked her head to one side. "Something wrong at home?"

Ana sighed, feeling the tension in her shoulders as she tried to relax them. A half-truth tumbled from her lips. "I haven't been sleeping very well. Miles broke his arm and he tosses and turns a lot."

Concern flitted across Ellen's features. "Oh, I didn't know."

"He's fine," Ana said. "A few weeks in a cast, and he'll be good as new." The false cheeriness in her voice was so obvious to her own ears.

"You should sleep in the guest room," Ellen said. "When I had surgery last year, I spent two months as a single lady. Took over the whole gosh darn bed like I was the Queen of Sheba while Mr. Fussypants sweated it out on the bottom bunk in the boys' room. I never could figure out why it gets so hot up there. Probably because it's over the garage. Never seemed to bother our boys, but the way Hank carried on you'd have thought he was sleeping in a sauna. I even got him one of those box fans, you know, from over at the Walmart, and cranked the A.C. way down to sixty-eight degrees. I had to put an extra blanket on the bed... in June!" Ellen's eyes went wide as if she were the first person to ever need to do such a thing.

Ana huffed out an awkward laugh.

Ellen winked as she pushed her glasses up the bridge of her nose. "Anyways, what I'm saying is, dear, one of you needs to sleep in another room."

"Noted."

"Tell that adorable husband of yours I hope he feels better soon."

"I will."

Ana smiled to herself, but with Ellen gone, the nagging feeling in her gut returned. Ana set a reminder on her computer to call Dr. Benson—maybe she could recommend a therapist—and went down the hall to the conference room.

"ALL I'M SAYING IS, WE both might sleep better if one of us stayed in the guest room."

Miles rolled his eyes at her. "Ana, you know how I feel about that. I told you what happened to my parents after they started sleeping in separate beds."

"It's only temporary," she pleaded. "Until your arm heals."

"No, absolutely not."

Ana pressed two fingers to the bridge of her nose. "Fine. But you're taking the medication they prescribed at the hospital. Otherwise, you'll toss and turn all night and neither one of our asses will get any sleep."

"Deal." Miles's smile shone brightly. It made Ana's heart melt a little.

THURSDAY, FEBRUARY 14, 2019 · 6:29 P.M.
"Will you marry me?" Miles beamed at her expectantly.

Ana could feel the tears welling up and fought to keep them from spilling over. She hated the way she looked when she cried, all snotty and red-faced. She blinked a few times and lifted her gaze to the ceiling. "But we're already married," she said, unable to meet Miles's gaze.

He grabbed her hands, forcing her to look at him. "Technically, yes, but this time for real. I love you and I want to marry you. Stay married to you, whatever. You know what I mean."

The laugh came out choked and abrupt, making it sound more like a sob.

"Is that a yes?" Miles asked.

Ana couldn't do anything but nod.

Miles stood and swept her off her feet, spinning her in a sweeping hug. He looked happier than he'd been in ages. She hoped he always would be, but a small part of her, even then, knew that happiness could be fleeting, and that the biggest drop on the rollercoaster always comes after the highest climb.

CHAPTER THREE
MILES

APRIL 1, 2020 · 9:59 A.M.

Dr. Benson's office was in a complex that had big, leafy maple trees—a rarity in Central Florida, and a feature that went out of style in the latter half of the twentieth century along with the stark architecture that distinguished the building from its surroundings. For that reason, Miles had chosen Dr. Benson out of the short list of psychiatrists covered by his insurance, even though he now had the means to choose any doctor he wanted. Miles had lucked into her willingness to believe in time travel and research his condition extensively while also helping him find a private research firm to look into it even further.

The red-haired receptionist, Darlene, stared at him from behind the desk as he shivered in the air-conditioned office. "Good morning, Mr. Lawson. Dr. Benson will be ready in just a moment."

Miles took his usual seat across from the door leading to Dr. Benson's office. He watched under the nondescript gray door for shadows that would indicate the doctor's approach. As the minutes ticked by, he fidgeted, first tapping his foot, then adjusting the magazines on the table to his right. He checked his phone, then went to the water cooler in the corner. The cups were tiny, so he drank two as he paced. Scratching underneath the edge of his cast, he glanced at the clock. Dr. Benson was running late. He looked at Darlene, who gave him a sympathetic smile.

"I'm sure she'll just be a few moments," Darlene said unconvincingly.

Miles sighed and checked his phone again. His lock screen was a picture of him and Ana from his last birthday. She was laughing so hard her eyes were practically closed, and Miles was making a silly face, as he so often did. It was his favorite picture of the two of them. He'd never thought he was photogenic until he'd discovered that silly faces made him less aware of the size of his nose or the gap between his front teeth.

Adam had loved that gap; Ana still teases him about it.

Without thinking about what he was doing, Miles opened Facebook and typed "Adam Lange" in the search bar. The picture that greeted him when he found his ex-boyfriend's profile made his heart flutter. Adam's eyes were bright, and his lopsided grin was as charming as ever. The dark-haired man kissing his cheek had an almost possessive grasp of Adam's chin. They looked happy. That made Miles unexpectedly angry. He closed the app and pocketed his phone before he did something stupid like send Adam a friend request.

He'd promised long ago he'd never speak to Adam again. Not after what happened. Not after Adam had betrayed him so spectacularly. It was too painful—even after nearly a decade, he couldn't face him. The only reason he'd even thought about Adam was that Ana had mentioned his younger self asking about him.

Besides, he was happy with Ana.

Searching for Adam on Facebook seemed like a betrayal of Ana's trust and hardly worth feeding his mild curiosity.

He had just pulled out his phone with the intent of texting his wife when Dr. Benson appeared at the door and beckoned Miles toward her office. She offered him a warm smile as Miles rose to follow her.

As he crossed the waiting room, a strange but all-too-familiar feeling overwhelmed him. The swirling pattern on the carpet told him he was going to black out. The deep blue concentric circles became bright pink and the edges of his vision went out of focus. He glanced up to Dr. Benson for help, but it was too late, her back was turned and the fuzziness was already giving way to blackness. His legs crumpled as he lost consciousness.

MILES FELT THE COLD LEATHER beneath his body before he was fully aware of his surroundings. The smell in the air reminded him of something familiar—jasmine, he recalled—but he couldn't quite place it. Knowing he was not in gym class as he had expected, he slowly opened his eyes, unsure of what he might find.

An unfamiliar blonde woman stood over him, calling his name. Her blue eyes were framed by laugh lines, and her smile was warm. She looked motherly in a Hollywood sort of way—older but undeniably pretty. She also had the taut look of someone who'd had a facelift.

"Where am I?" he muttered, realizing as he spoke how cliché it sounded.

"In my office," the woman said.

Miles bit his lip, deciding if it was safe to be honest with this woman. She seemed nice, but he couldn't be sure if she could be trusted with a secret like the one he carried. Something on his face must have alarmed her because her eyes went wide, and her mouth fell open just enough to reveal her shock.

"Miles, this might sound a little strange, but bear with me." She paused and fixed her gaze on his, and then studied his face. Miles nodded.

"How old are you?"

Miles's stomach dropped. He laughed nervously. "What?"

"Play along," the woman said. "How old are you right now?"

"How old do *you* think I am?"

"I know how old you are," the woman said with a laugh. "I want you to tell me."

He tried to glance down at his hands; maybe they would give something away, anything to tell him where or when he was. But this kind-looking woman would not let him break her gaze. She gripped his chin gently and spoke again. "Miles, you can trust me. I know about your secret. Just tell me how old you think you are right now."

Miles cleared his throat. "I'm um, well..."

She nodded encouragingly.

"Ebbentim," Miles mumbled.

"How old?"

"Seventeen," he whispered.

Her eyes lit up. "This is utterly fascinating. This is the first time you've switched while you were visiting me."

"Huh?"

"Oh, perhaps I should introduce myself," she said. "I'm Dr. Eleanor Benson. Your psychiatrist."

"My... what?"

"I've been helping you cope and also heading up the research on your disorder."

"My disorder?"

"The thing that causes your episodes. We've actually started experimenting with medication."

"Okay," Miles said. His head was swimming.

"We're tentatively calling it Dissociative Chronology Disorder."

"Dissociative Chronology Disorder? What does that mean?"

"Think of it as a close cousin of Dissociative Identity Disorder."

"Like schizophrenia?"

"No, that's hearing voices. DID is alternate personalities. In your case, you revert to alternate versions of yourself—from different points in your life—instead of distinct alternate personalities."

"So I'm time-traveling?"

"Well, for lack of a better term, yes."

Miles began to chew on his thumb, a habit his mother often chided him for. Time travel.

He could feel Dr. Benson's eyes on him, but he refused to look up. He was afraid if he made eye contact she might be looking at him with pity. So while Miles stared at his feet and ripped the skin of his right thumb to shreds, Dr. Benson spoke.

"We think it's your brain's way of self-equalizing. Certain emotions seem to cause a greater likelihood of an episode. Something traumatic probably triggered this episode and your body took you out of your current state and into another. It's as if your body senses the heightened emotion, and to protect you from a panic attack, you disassociate."

"So instead of dealing with what I feel, I time-travel?"

"That's more or less how it works. The rest is pretty complicated and not necessary for you to understand."

"Why did I travel forward? Do I sometimes travel back in time?"

"We think so. All we really know is when your brain chemistry evens out again, you come back, more or less."

"More or less?"

"Well, I'm not one hundred percent sure that's how it works, but process of elimination and all that. Extreme emotion, especially stress, seems to exacerbate it."

"Okay," Miles said, still unable to fully process it. "How do we fix it?"

"Well, as I said, we've been trying medication, but there are side effects. There's also therapy, especially if a related event caused an adjustment disorder."

"How do you mean?"

"Have you experienced any major life trauma?"

"You mean besides the time travel?"

"Perhaps it hasn't happened yet," Dr. Benson said, almost to herself. "Well, at least not to *you*. I've asked older you, but memories of your childhood are scarce."

Miles's head began to pound; a sharp pain burned behind his eyelids that made him feel as though he might vomit. He closed his eyes to try to focus his thoughts and stop the room from spinning, but the loss of orientation only made it worse. When he tried to open his eyes, his eyelids felt too heavy to lift. Dr. Benson's voice suddenly sounded very far away—as if she were speaking into a pillow. He tried to respond to her questions, but his mouth felt stuffed with cotton, and his lips wouldn't move. Just when he thought he couldn't take the pain in his head anymore, he felt himself slipping out of reality and into nothingness.

"How long was I gone?" Miles muttered. His voice sounded thick and raspy.

"Only a few minutes," Dr. Benson replied. "Do you remember anything?"

"Just some fuzzy memories. Feels a bit like déjà vu."

"I'd like to run some tests if you're up for it, Miles. I never thought I'd have the luxury of being present for an episode. This might be our only chance."

Miles sat up, gripping his head. "Whatever you want, doc. I'm your ever-willing guinea pig."

"Take it easy," Dr. Benson said. "I'll get you a glass of water, but the aspirin will have to wait until after I draw some blood."

Miles swallowed hard. "Do we have to? I hate needles."

"I'll make it painless, I promise." Her smile didn't reassure him the way it should have. Instead his heart began to beat faster. He focused as best he could in order to avoid another episode. He wasn't sure he could fend it off, but he had to try.

Squeezing his eyes tight, he braced himself for the familiar prick of the needle.

"Relax and breathe, Miles." Dr. Benson's voice was soft and close.

He tried to breathe deeply and slowly. Behind his eyes, a dull throbbing formed.

"Just another second," Dr. Benson said.

Miles squinted his eyes tighter and squeezed his free hand against his thigh. Even with his eyes closed he could feel that he was starting to shift.

"There now, that wasn't so bad was it?"

Miles opened one eye and saw Dr. Benson smiling at him. She took off her gloves and laid them on the tray with the rest of the supplies.

"That's it?" he said.

"All done."

A dull ache remained behind his eyelids, but otherwise, Miles felt fine. Maybe he was getting over his fear of needles. He watched as Dr.

Benson dropped the used needle in a bag marked biohazardous material. His stomach lurched violently. He had to swallow to keep from vomiting.

Maybe not.

ANA TOOK A DEEP BREATH and exhaled slowly. "You had *another* episode?"

"Don't worry," Miles said, "I was with Dr. Benson. This is a good thing."

Through the phone Miles could hear Ana tapping her nails on her desk, an indication that she was worried and didn't believe him for a second.

"I should come home," she said.

"No, baby, I'll be fine. Really."

Because of his condition, Miles hadn't been able to hold a steady job in years. Ana supported them both and, as a result, worked long hours. As an attorney, she made more than enough, but because most of Miles's trust fund had gone to pay for his treatment, he picked up odd jobs whenever he could.

"Are you sure? I could get Ellen to—"

"Ana, I said I'm fine. I'm going to be sitting here on the couch when you get home. Promise."

"I know you hate it when I fuss over you, but I'm worried."

"I know," Miles said. It wasn't that he hated her concern; it was the nagging guilt he felt whenever Ana left work to take care of him after an episode. "Look, I need to get this piece done. Can I call you later?" Lately Miles had been doing some copyediting for a friend's blog that had taken off.

Ana sounded reluctant when she said, "Sure," but Miles didn't push, mostly because he didn't want Ana asking him about his episode in Dr. Benson's office. She'd been so worried since his last one, and he didn't want to add to her already stressful situation. The thing is, he knew his wife would ask about what was going on right before the episode, and he didn't want to tell her he'd been thinking of Adam.

"I love you," he said.

"I love you more."

MONDAY, AUGUST 31, 2009 · 1:25 P.M.

Miles traced the pattern of tiles with his left foot while he waited for the bathroom to clear out. A urinal flushed and then the faucet sputtered to life for a second before it was silenced, followed by the telltale sound of paper towels being wound off the roll and torn haphazardly. There was a muffled cough, the creak of the door and then nothing. Miles counted to ten before undoing the latch. Peering out from his stall, he could see he was finally alone. His heart raced, as it did every time Matthew Butler walked by, or smiled or existed. Miles had just barely managed to duck into the stall before half the basketball team caught him gawking at their star forward, and he had waited until they all left before revealing his presence.

Miles nearly jumped out of his skin when he heard the toilet two stalls down from him flush. The door slammed open to reveal a skinny Asian boy with jet black hair and glasses wearing a Fitz and the Tantrums T-shirt. White earbuds hung from his ears and disappeared into his right jeans pocket. He gave Miles a cursory glance and smirked.

"You look like your mom caught you whacking off," he said, pulling out one of the earbuds.

Miles rolled his eyes. "You just startled me," he said. "I thought I was alone."

"Do you need to be alone?"

The boy's quirked eyebrow made Miles realize how creepy he sounded.

"No!"

"Settle down, dude. I was just teasing. Name's Adam."

"I'm Miles. You new here?"

"Transferred from Texas. Land of excellent Mexican food and questionable politics."

Miles laughed. He liked this kid.

"We should hang out or something. I can show you around."

"Cool."

The bell rang and both boys realized they were late for their next class.

"Where you headed?" Miles asked.

Adam pulled a wrinkled slip out of his pocket. "Uh, room 347, Mr. Hathaway."

"You're in band? Me too! What do you play?"

"Drums. You?"

Miles grinned widely. "Living the drumline dream."

"Don't ever say that again," Adam said, holding the door open for Miles to walk through.

"If you can't handle that, you're gonna hate the chants Mr. H makes us do."

"Kill me," Adam said with an exaggerated eye roll.

"Not on your first day."

CHAPTER FOUR
ADAM

SATURDAY, APRIL 4, 2020 · 7:58 P.M.

The porch swing creaked with each movement as the breeze tickled Adam's face. He closed his eyes and inhaled Anthony's scent, a bright mix of citrus and musk that smelled like home.

"I can't believe our vacation is over and we have to go back to real life tomorrow."

Anthony shushed him. "You're spoiling it."

They watched the sun sink behind the tree line until there was nothing but a pale pink glow to show where the sun had once been. Adam sighed, his mind drawn back to his everyday worries: work, bills, the band.

He and Michaela were starting a new round of tests on Monday, and they still needed to get approval for the extra equipment. Had he remembered to put in the correct paperwork?

"You're thinking so loud, I bet they can hear you down the hill." Anthony nodded at the tiny cabin at the base of the hill, at least half a mile away. A lone light in the front window twinkled brightly in the burgeoning darkness. They had come to Anthony's family cabin in the Smoky Mountains, simply because they couldn't afford to take a vacation anywhere else. Adam felt drunk with relaxation, but he knew the hangover would be severe.

Adam threaded his fingers through Anthony's and brought their joined hands to his lips. Maybe this was what true happiness was. It had been so long since he'd felt anything beyond a dull ache that anything better than the status quo made him impulsive. So when he looked into Anthony's eyes a whisper escaped his lips, almost unbidden. "Marry me?"

At first Anthony's only response was a raised eyebrow as his pale blue eyes searched Adam's face. "Are you serious?" he asked. "You better not be shitting me. I will end you."

"I'm completely serious," Adam said, although he hadn't planned to propose. Now that it was out, he was all in. "Let's get married. Say yes." He smiled and waited.

Anthony smiled back, his eyes already brimming with happy tears. "Yes! Yes, yes, yes!" He grabbed Adam's face and kissed him firmly. He pulled back, but left his hands framing Adam's face. "Oh my God. We're getting married," he whispered.

"We're getting married," Adam parroted.

MONDAY, APRIL 4, 2011 · 4:21 P.M.

"Let's get married," Miles said, his chocolate brown eyes dancing with mirth. "We could run off to California or Vermont—one of those states where it's legal already."

"Florida won't recognize it," Adam said matter-of-factly.

"So? We can still do it."

Adam stopped flipping through his history notes and side-eyed his boyfriend. "Miles, we're still in high school."

The look he got in return told him the logic had been lost on Miles.

"I have a history test tomorrow." Adam returned his attention to his notes. "And band practice."

He could feel Miles nudging his knee, but he refused to look up. He bit his lip to keep from grinning.

"Come on, don't you want to marry me? I want to marry you," Miles said. His voice was the childish singsong of a dare, and he inched forward on the bed to press his lips to Adam's neck, just below his ear.

A sharp exhale escaped his lips.

"We could do it this summer," Miles added, following his words with the tip of his tongue down Adam's neck. He paused to press light kisses where the neck and shoulder met. Adam began to squirm.

"You're distracting me."

"I know."

"But... history test." Adam had a hard time finding his words; the air tickled where his neck was damp from Miles's kisses. His heart beat a heavy rhythm. He could feel the bed shift where Miles leaned on his hand to support his weight, and Adam followed the strong line of his arm up to Miles's shoulder and across to his face. He was smirking, eyes wide with lust.

"It's not until fifth period," Miles said. He traced a finger up the inside of Adam's thigh, barely grazing his now semi-hard dick through his jeans. "You can study during lunch." The whisper of his words sent shivers down Adam's spine.

Adam, suddenly not at all concerned about the test, twisted quickly and pinned Miles to the bed. They were both breathing heavily already.

"You are in so much trouble, Lawson," Adam teased.

"Oh yeah?" Miles licked his lips in anticipation.

Adam didn't make him wait, though. He dove in and captured Miles's mouth in a bruising kiss, using his nose to nudge Miles into the perfect position.

When they pulled apart, panting and sweaty, Miles simply looked up at him and said, "I love you."

"We're still not getting married."

"Fine," Miles said with an exaggerated pout. "But can we at least get naked?"

Adam didn't answer; he simply yanked his shirt over his head and bent to kiss Miles again.

CHAPTER FIVE
MILES

WEDNESDAY, APRIL 15, 2020 · 10:02 A.M.

"When was your last episode?" Dr. Benson asked.

"That one I had in your office, actually," Miles said with a smile. After nearly two weeks, Ana's constant vigilance faded, and Miles was starting to feel normal again, hopeful that Dr. Benson had found the right combo of meds this time.

"Have you given any thought to what might have been the catalyst?"

Miles inhaled deeply and exhaled a rush of air. "I think it may have been Adam."

"That the boyfriend you told me about? From high school?"

"Yeah," Miles said, rubbing his eyes with his thumb and forefinger, bringing them to a pinch at the bridge of his nose. "When my seventeen-year-old self showed up, he was asking about Adam. I hadn't thought about him in years, not really. So when Ana mentioned his name, I think I got curious." Miles paused, focusing on his hands in his lap. He began picking at the edge of his cast where it had frayed. Truth was, he had thought of Adam, a lot, just not in the way his younger self thought of Adam. It was normal to think of old friends after you lost touch. Nothing wrong with that.

"And?" Dr. Benson leaned forward in her chair with her elbow resting on her crossed legs.

"I Googled him, looked him up on Facebook, thought about calling him."

"And how did that make you feel?"

Miles looked up at her, scowling. "You know I hate it when you ask that question. It's so cliché."

"It's overused because it works," she insisted. "Now quit stalling and tell me more about what you were feeling before your episode. What memories came to the surface? The way Ana might feel about you looking up an ex-boyfriend? Perhaps the reason you broke up?"

Miles's face flamed hot. "I told you before I don't want to talk about that," he said through gritted teeth.

Dr. Benson gave him a pointed look, one that said everything without a word. A look that said, "You're going to have to talk about it eventually."

But not today, he resolved.

When the silence stretched out over a few moments, Dr. Benson conceded defeat. "Okay, then, why don't you tell me what you found out about Adam? What's he up to?"

"I think he's in a band. He works for a pharmaceutical company or something and he's obviously dating someone. It's nothing... really." Miles shrugged it off. "Just normal life stuff. I don't know how any of that could've set me off."

"Maybe because it represents the road not taken."

Miles gave her a questioning look.

"What I'm saying is, it's natural to be curious when our life takes a path we hadn't expected."

Miles considered her words. "Well, I certainly never thought I'd end up married to a woman."

"Tell me more about that," Dr. Benson prompted.

Miles rolled his eyes but continued, "I'm not sure if I told you, but until college, I assumed I was gay. I never considered girls an option, which is funny because most of the guys I knew were the opposite; they never thought about anything but girls. Anyway, all my early crushes were on boys, so I just assumed I was gay. Girls never factored in. I planned my life around that: only looked at colleges in gay-friendly communities, came out to my folks, dated Adam. When that ended, and I eventually started dating again in college, I hit the gay bars."

"When did you realize you were bisexual?"

"Her name was Amber," Miles said with a wistful smile. "She was naturally blonde but liked to dye her hair crazy colors, and I liked that about her. She was fun." He shrugged. His relationship with Amber had been superficial. Lots of sex, lots of beer and pot, the occasional concert. Very little substance. It worked for him. He had no interest in repeating what he'd had with Adam, and with his condition, it was just easier not to get attached.

"Did you Google her when you looked up Adam?"

"No."

"Why do you think that is?"

"I told you. I was thinking about Adam because younger me brought him up."

"But not Amber?"

"Well, he... I mean *I* hadn't met her yet."

"I see."

"That's kind of how time travel works."

"Right. Yes, of course," Dr. Benson said, pushing her glasses up on her nose and recapping her pen. "I think the dosage we put you on is working, so maybe we'll keep you at that level for a while. See how you do, okay?"

Miles nodded. "Any luck on that lab work? Think we might be close to curing me?"

"Let's just take this one step at a time, okay?"

Miles nodded again, his frustration growing. He'd been paying Dr. Benson and a team of researchers for two years, and they were no closer to curing his condition than on day one.

As Miles was leaving Dr. Benson's office, the phone in his hand buzzed, and he instinctively glanced down, even though he expected it to be Ana calling to check up on him.

Instead, the face staring up at him from his phone made him smile.

"Darius," Miles greeted. "What up, man?"

"Just checking on the legalization piece."

Darius and Miles had met in a coffee shop right after one of Miles's episodes. He'd helped him get home and never asked any questions. Miles liked that about him. When Darius had found out Miles needed sporadic work, he'd offered him freelance gigs as often as he could. For reasons neither of them could discern, Darius's music blog *JAMM On* had suddenly taken off, and was now profitable enough to pay them both to write about their shared love of music and pop culture. They'd been working nonstop on a series of articles on marijuana legalization, and it had just been legalized in Florida. *JAMM On* had landed an exclusive with Governor Blankenship, who had championed the cause.

"It's almost done," Miles said. "I just need to fact-check a couple more stats."

"Sweet. I was worried the arm might slow you down some."

"It makes typing tough, but otherwise, I'm almost back to full speed."

"I swear, man, you're like a walking disaster. You're in the hospital more than anyone I know, and my nana is on dialysis."

"I'm just clumsy I guess," Miles said mechanically.

Ever since he'd started having his dissociative episodes, he'd had to make excuses for the injuries he sustained when he blacked out. Most of his friends and family thought he walked into a lot of doors. Adam had affectionately called him Mr. Magoo. Ana, of course, knew the truth and called him things like Marty McFly. He'd just learned to go with it.

Miles hadn't realized the line had gone silent until Darius spoke. "You sure you're all right, man? You sound out of it."

He stared down at the keys in his hand. "Yeah, sure. Just tired I guess." He had gotten home on autopilot with no memory of having driven there. His head was clear, or he might have been worried it was another episode.

"Well, I can let you go," Darius said. "Let you catch a few z's?"

A nap sounded wonderful. "Thanks." Miles threw his keys on the counter. "Hey, can I ask you something?"

"Shoot."

"Do you believe in fate?" He plopped down on the sofa and leaned back against the cushions.

"Like, win the lottery, run into a hot chick who turns out to be your soul mate kind of fate?"

"Yeah, I guess."

"Sure, why not? Don't you?"

"I'm not sure," Miles said, kicking his shoes under the coffee table. Ana hated it when he did that.

"You're not cheating on Ana, are you?"

"No, nothing like that!"

"Because you know I'd be happy to help her ease her broken heart."

Miles laughed. "I'm sure she'd love that." It was no secret Darius found Ana attractive. Both Ana and Miles found it flattering, mostly because Darius was harmless and a good friend. Miles liked the reminder that Ana—beautiful, smart, funny Ana—had chosen to stay with him even after they'd gotten the money from his trust fund. "It's just that I wonder if I made the right choices in my life."

"But this isn't about Ana?"

"It's about me," Miles said. "I just feel... lost."

Darius laughed. "Man, everyone feels that way. That's just growing up."

"Yeah, maybe."

"Listen, I gotta go. Someone just walked in. Talk later?"

"Sure thing, D."

Miles hung up and grabbed his laptop, but instead of working on the piece Darius needed, he Googled Adam's name again.

The first result was a page for a band: Harper's Bell. Intrigued, Miles clicked it.

There he was, eyes narrowed with determination. Tattoos and a close-cropped haircut made him look different than he had in high school, but there was no mistaking him. Adam was the drummer. His arms had filled out in the years since Miles had known him, and his boyish charm had given way to masculine allure.

Miles felt his heart flutter with airy nostalgia that quickly morphed into the telltale twinge of attraction. Up until that moment, he had been able to convince himself that he'd simply been curious about Adam's current life. Knowing he still felt something when faced with the reality of Adam, Miles felt guilt begin to inch into the corners of his mind.

He needed to get out of the house.

He slammed the laptop shut, grabbed his keys and took a few steps before his vision began swimming and the floor came up to greet him like an old friend.

The cool air smelled faintly of cinnamon. Miles opened his eyes and took in his surroundings. He lay on a stiff, moss-green sofa, a pair of shoes kicked off under a mahogany coffee table, a laptop sitting closed beside him; his left arm was in a cast—had been for a few weeks from the look of it. The house around him was quiet, no signs of others in the vicinity, but he closed his eyes and listened to be sure. The gentle whir of air conditioning stuttered to life and drowned out any other possible sounds.

Miles opened his eyes and began scanning the room. What year was it? What day?

The clock beneath the TV read 11:44 and the sun was out, so it was definitely a.m. He felt around the sofa cushions for the remote—twenty-four-hour news channels were always a safe bet for knowing *when* it was. His hand struck something cold and metal. The laptop.

He nearly smacked his forehead with the absurdity of it. Why hadn't he thought of that first? The Internet was infinitely better at finding precise information than TV. The laptop was lighter than he expected—his first indication that he was in the future. The one constant in his life was that technology either got smaller or lighter, sometimes both.

As the machine whirred to life, he prayed his older self still used the same password. But he didn't need it. The logon screen indicated he should swipe his index finger over the trackpad. As he did so, the desktop popped into view.

"Sweet."

He guided the cursor to the menu at the top of the screen and clicked the time to bring up the drop-down: April 15, 2020.

Doing the math, he figured he was twenty-five. He ran through the list of things he knew about his twenty-five-year-old self: married to Ana, no children, living in Winter Park, working freelance as a copyeditor.

Miles patted his pockets for his phone. The model was unfamiliar, but he figured it out quickly enough. He still had no contact information for Adam, but a quick check of his browser history on both the phone and his laptop revealed he had recently searched for him. Adam's Facebook page was still up on Miles's phone, in fact. Without considering the repercussions, Miles tapped "Add As Friend" and began browsing the few public photos on his page.

He'd only gotten through half a dozen or so profile images when the alert came through: Adam Lange has accepted your friend request. He held his breath, and tapped the "About" tab. His heart fell when the address field was blank, but just below it, in blissful clarity, was Adam's phone number.

Careful not to dial it just yet, Miles entered the number into his phone and added Adam as a contact. Within a few minutes, Miles had Adam's address, employer and the names of a few close friends. It was amazing how easy it was to find someone once you had a little bit of personal information, like a phone number or middle name.

Miles quickly jotted Ana a note on the back of an envelope that he found on the kitchen counter: "Went to run some errands. Be back soon. –M"

He wasn't sure how he and Ana usually handled this sort of thing, but he hoped the note would suffice. Adam lived at least two hours away, and he might not be back before Ana got home.

On the drive, he had a lot of time to think, time to go over what had gone wrong. Time to worry that Adam had forgotten him. Time to worry that, at twenty-five, he'd forgotten Adam as well.

THURSDAY, MAY 31, 2012 · 6:28 P.M.

Adam looked at him with furrowed brows. "Miles, what you're saying is crazy. Time travel?"

"I know it sounds nuts, but it's like I'm seeing things that haven't happened yet. Other times I feel like I'm reliving things that have already happened to me. The other day, I woke up in a strange house and I was married to Ana!"

"Espinosa?" Adam asked, incredulous.

Nodding, Miles continued. "Apparently you and I had broken up, and she wouldn't tell me why. But she said I'd been time-traveling and that's why we got married. I needed—"

"Miles, honey," Adam interrupted, "I think you probably just had a very vivid dream."

Miles considered it. Even now, the memory was fading, slipping through the cracks and falling into the abyss that consumed the outer edges of his mind most days. "Maybe you're right," he said.

"Could be the pain meds," Adam offered, gently tapping Miles's cast. "When I had my wisdom teeth taken out, the stuff they gave me was wicked. I dreamed I was a masked wrestler named Pablo Picante."

Unable to help himself, Miles roared with laughter.

Adam grinned, his deep amber eyes sparkling in the afternoon light. "I know. It was crazy. A Korean masked wrestler. Can you imagine?"

"I think you'd look good in a unitard," Miles said, leaning in and kissing the tip of Adam's nose lightly.

"Yeah?" Adam's grin turned to a smirk full of desire.

Miles wrapped his hands around Adam's waist, careful not to bump his cast. "Yeah."

"I think Antonio would let me borrow his singlet," Adam purred as he bent to press his lips to Miles's.

As he parted his lips and Adam's tongue slipped through, all thought of time travel and wrestling singlets was lost. All Miles could think of was getting naked and tasting the salty tang of Adam's skin.

"Skip it," he said. "You don't need it."

CHAPTER SIX
MILES

WEDNESDAY, APRIL 15, 2020 · 11:31 A.M.

Miles hit the highway in that rare pocket of time when fewer cars were on the road. It wasn't empty—never was—but it was clearer than usual, so he made good time. According to his limited research, Adam now lived near Merritt Island, a swath of seaside Florida known for its proximity to Kennedy Space Center and its tranquil setting. Sixty miles east and a few turns and he'd be in Adam's arms. He hoped.

The last time he'd shown up in his twenty-five-year-old body, he'd been shocked. This time he was prepared. Knowing that he and Adam had been apart for the better part of seven years, he planned to reconnect. If Ana wouldn't tell him what had happened, he'd just have to find out from the source. Now that he'd told seventeen-year-old Adam about his time travel, surely the older version knew all about it as well.

Still, part of him worried that the whole thing was in his head. Maybe he was just crazy. Maybe the time travel was just a hallucination.

The more he thought about it, hallucinations were far more likely. He could only remember snippets of his trips and sometimes nothing at all—only a throbbing headache to let him know he'd gone anywhere. The things he could remember were hazy, and he had to repeat details like mantras to remember them. When the trips started happening more frequently, he had started keeping a journal. Whenever he had a headache, he wrote down anything he could remember. He now had three composition books full of notes, none of which made much sense, but for some reason he kept traveling back to this time, when he was twenty-five and married to Ana. By now he'd pieced together enough details to realize he'd manipulated history to get her to marry him. He'd gone back to tell her that her sister would die. That was in his first journal. But what he hadn't been able to suss out was why he and Adam had broken up. He knew they had broken up some time after their senior year of high school, but the reason was unclear.

So he'd decided to ask Adam himself. His hands itched as they gripped the steering wheel; the tickle of the unknown forced his foot down harder on the gas pedal. The sun traveled as he did, but in the opposite direction, as if it were running away from him as he ran toward Adam.

Miles felt his phone buzz in his pocket, but he didn't take it out. He was focused on the road, on his future. On Adam.

FRIDAY, JUNE 7, 2013 · 8:32 P.M.

"It's the next left, I think," Miles said, leaning forward in his seat as he looked for the street name.

"Are you sure you're okay to go to this thing?" Adam asked. He glanced over at Miles in the passenger seat and rested his hand on Miles's thigh. "We can still hang at my place instead."

Miles, feeling exasperation at his boyfriend's concern, rolled his eyes. "Yes, I told you. Everything is normal."

"Except for the time travel part," Adam mumbled, moving his hand back to the steering wheel.

"Look, I said let's drop it."

"I'm just worried about you. It's not every day your boyfriend insists he's twenty-five and married to some chick."

"Ana," Miles muttered.

"Whatever," he said. "What scares me is you can't remember any of it."

"I told you—"

"Yeah, time travel. Makes perfect sense."

Miles sighed but didn't respond. As they waited for the light to change, he listened to the click of the turn signal, each staccato beat punctuating the uncomfortable silence. He had hoped confiding in Adam would make him feel like less of a freak, but now he just wanted to forget the whole thing. He wanted to feel normal again. He wanted to shake the idea of a breakup looming over his head. Besides, he couldn't actually be time-traveling. Could he?

Anyway, he had an appointment with a psychiatrist on Monday. He'd get on some medication, and the dreams would stop. Simple as that.

"I just want to go to this party, get trashed and have a good time with my boyfriend before we have to think about college or summer jobs or any of it. Okay?" Miles held out his hand and felt his shoulders relax when Adam lifted his hand from the steering wheel and threaded his long fingers through Miles's own.

"Okay."

Miles smiled at him as they turned onto Dahlia's street. A throng of cars in the cul-de-sac framed the two-story blue house, and a Mylar balloon on the mailbox read "ConGRADulations!"

"Promise me you won't get too drunk this time," Adam said over the top of his Acura. "I'm wearing my good shoes."

Miles closed the passenger door a little harder than was necessary. "I'm never living that down, am I?"

"Not on this timeline." Adam grinned at him.

"Very funny, asshole."

Adam threw his arm over Miles's shoulder and pulled him close. "Maybe they have a hot tub," he said. "We can go back and meet your teenage mom."

"How about before we met?" Miles said, nudging him in the ribs. "I could stay in that bathroom stall and avoid all this."

Adam gave him an exaggerated pout. "Oh, come on. You know you adore me."

"I do, but I think twenty-five-year-old me had other plans." Miles laughed, but something in his words caused Adam's expression to darken. It was only a second before he started to laugh too, but Miles had seen it, and it scared him.

THE SMALL RANCH HOUSE WHERE Adam lived was neatly kept. A large queen palm bowed gracefully over the front lawn, perfectly framing the walkway that led to a deep teal front door. Next to it, on the front porch, sat two white Adirondack chairs. A pair of brown clogs like the kind his mother wore for gardening sat by the front door.

It's a *home*, Miles thought to himself. Suddenly the idea that Adam had a life without him hit Miles like a freight train. Could he go through with it? Could he upend Adam's life by suddenly reappearing in it? Would his appearance even faze Adam?

"This was a mistake," he muttered under his breath.

Miles had turned to walk back to his car, when he heard a deep voice inquire, "Can I help you?"

A tall, dark-haired man wearing a Harper's Bell T-shirt had opened the door. He looked familiar, but Miles couldn't place him.

"Look, if you're selling something, we're not interested," the man said.

Miles opened his mouth, but he couldn't make words form. He suddenly remembered where he'd seen this guy—kissing Adam in his Facebook profile pic.

"Also, we're gay and we're atheists and we only give to charities we've researched extensively so if you're trying to 'save' us or want a donation, you're wasting your time."

"I'm not... I mean... I don't—" Miles swallowed heavily and then cleared his throat. "Is Adam here?" he finally managed.

"Oh shit," the man said, running a hand through his unruly dark brown hair. "You're probably a fan, right? He's not here."

"I'm not a fan," Miles said, starting to feel a little annoyed. "I'm an old friend."

The man's face broke into a warm smile. "Well, why didn't you say so? Any friend of Adam's is a friend of mine. You wanna come in?" He gestured behind himself into the house.

"I don't think so," Miles said. "Could you just tell him I stopped by?" He turned and started toward his car, stuffing his hands in his pockets.

"Wait!"

Miles pivoted and almost tripped over his left foot.

Adam's boyfriend stifled a laugh. "It would help if you told me your name."

"Oh, uh... it's Miles. From high school."

"Nice to meet you Miles from high school," he said. "I'm Anthony, Adam's partner. You sure you don't want to come in? Adam should be home in a couple hours. I'm sure he'd love to see you."

Had Adam mentioned him?

A dull ache began to form behind Miles's eyes. He felt the edges of his vision begin to recede. The urge to get away from Anthony was overwhelming.

"I gotta go," he blurted, turning quickly and stumbling to the car. A searing pain took over his vision and his head swam. Just as he reached for the door, everything went black.

MILES RUBBED HIS TEMPLES AS he sat in a well-worn recliner. A glass of ice water dripped condensation on a stone coaster on the table next to him. He'd woken up outside, laid out on the concrete with a large, dark-haired man looming over him. He recognized the guy from Adam's Facebook profile and immediately felt sick to his stomach.

"Are you okay?" The same man was now standing across the room from him, looking at Miles with concern.

"Fine," Miles mumbled. "What did you say your name was?"

"Anthony."

"Right. Well, thank you, Anthony, but I should head out." He stood up and felt himself sway, his head throbbing and his stomach threatening to show its contents. Somehow Miles managed to keep his footing and take a few wobbly steps. The skin beneath his cast itched.

Anthony's pale blue eyes widened slightly; his eyebrows rose to form a questioning gaze. "Don't you want to wait for Adam?"

"It's really not necessary."

"I texted him a second ago," Anthony offered. "He's on his way home now."

"This is so embarrassing," Miles said. He needed to get out of there before Adam saw him. "I don't know why I came by."

"It's all right, really. I know what it's like to wonder about your ex."

Miles felt his cheeks burn with shame. "It's not like that," he said. "I just... I've been going through some shit and I..." Miles shook his head. "Never mind. I'm sorry I bothered you."

"No worries." Anthony looked as if he wanted to say something else, but he closed his mouth.

"Tell Adam I'm sorry," Miles said and headed for the front door.

Anthony said something but Miles couldn't make it out. He needed to leave before he lost it completely.

He was fifteen miles away in a Target parking lot when he finally let go. The tears came hot and fast; his anger seared through him like wildfire. Beating the steering wheel with tight fists, Miles felt his fury begin to subside, but his body still ached with humiliation.

He couldn't remember how he got to Adam's house, but he damn well knew who had gotten him there. Why couldn't his younger self leave well enough alone?

THE TRAFFIC WAS SO BAD that, by the time he got home, Ana's car was already in the driveway. He took a deep breath and hoped she wouldn't ask where he'd been.

Ana's bag was sitting on the kitchen counter; her running shoes had been kicked off haphazardly beneath it. Her keys were on top of a note in his handwriting, so she'd seen it. It didn't say where he'd gone. Venturing farther into their home, he saw that their bedroom light was on and he heard the shower running.

"Hey," he called out, trying to sound as nonchalant as possible.

"Hey yourself," she called back. "You wanna order something from Ling's? I'm starving."

"Sure. You want the usual?"

"Yeah, and get an extra egg roll."

As he scrolled his contacts for the number to their local Chinese hole in the wall, he finally felt his shoulders relax. At least he wouldn't have to explain himself to Ana.

Just as he hung up, Ana appeared with a towel wrapped around her head. An old Florida Gators T-shirt with multiple holes in it barely fell to her upper thighs, revealing a pair of lacy black panties. He had always loved seeing her this relaxed.

"Food should be here in ten," he said.

"Great," she said, leaning over to pick up her shoes. "Did you pick up laundry detergent?" She had headed back to the bedroom, so she didn't see the look of confusion that was plastered on his face until he collected himself and remembered that the note said he'd been running errands.

"I forgot," he called out. "I'll get it tomorrow."

"Where were you then?" she asked. She was using the towel to soak up some of the water from her hair and tilted her head as she spoke.

"Last-minute meeting with Darius. He wanted to go over that legalization piece we've been working on." Not a total lie, he rationalized.

She scoffed and tossed the towel over the back of one of their bar stools. "Meeting... yeah right." Miles felt a momentary panic rise up, but then she continued. "I know what you boys are like when you get together for coffee. Gossiping and cutting up. You're as bad as a couple of teenage girls."

Miles laughed. "Well, you know Darius."

Suddenly she leveled a hard gaze at him.

"You're sweating," she said. "What's wrong?"

"Nothing." Another lie.

She studied him. "No, something's wrong."

"I'm fine," he said. "Really."

She shook her head. What if she didn't believe him? Could he tell her that he'd had another episode? Just be honest with her and hope she didn't go ballistic?

"Don't tell me that idiot took you out drinking when you're on new medication. I swear to God—"

He stroked her cheek in what he hoped was a soothing gesture. "Honey, I'm fine. It's just really hot outside. You're worrying over nothing."

She sighed and sagged into a kitchen chair.

"You have no idea what it's like worrying about you all the time," she said, looking up at him with watery eyes. "I got home and you weren't here and if I hadn't seen that note..." She trailed off and started picking at her cuticles.

Before Miles could say anything, the doorbell rang. "I'll get it," he said. His voice was shaky and raw.

The smell of the food reminded Miles he hadn't had anything to eat since breakfast, and he didn't think his younger self had thought to grab lunch on the way to Adam's house. His stomach growled loudly enough that Ana heard it and laughed.

Miles loved her laugh.

"You wanna take this in the living room and watch a movie?" he asked. "Your pick."

Ana smiled warmly. It seemed her earlier concern had passed, and for that, Miles was grateful. But something niggled at the back of his mind, an errant thought of what Adam would think when he came home and found out that Miles had been there and gone. A wave of embarrassment washed over him, and he had to hide his face so his wife wouldn't see his shame. Once he started shoveling Kung Pao chicken in his mouth, though, his worries subsided, and he spent the evening curled up on the sofa with Ana's feet in his lap.

CHAPTER SEVEN
ADAM

WEDNESDAY, APRIL 15, 2020 · 1:35 P.M.

Adam drove home as fast as he could, wondering the whole time what on earth had made Miles want to see him. The last time they had spoken, Miles had said he never wanted to see Adam again, and he meant it. They hadn't spoken in years and now, on the same day, Miles friended him on Facebook and showed up unannounced on his doorstep. The Miles he had known when they were kids was impulsive, doing whatever struck him in the moment. But Adam had learned through friends that Miles had settled into a quiet suburban life, married Ana and was working for a pop culture blog. Not that Adam had looked him up; it was just they had a lot of mutual friends. No, Miles had been firmly left in the past. Adam still thought of him fondly, but rarely. And this was out of character for settled, married Miles.

The driveway was empty when Adam pulled his blue hatchback into his usual space. Anthony, his feet bare and a sweaty bottle of beer in his right hand, sat waiting on the porch. He stood when Adam killed the engine and opened the door.

"Where's Miles?" Adam asked.

"He left. Totally freaked out on me and took off like a crazy person. I couldn't get a word out of him. He didn't look good."

"Did he say why he came by?"

"No, nothing. Just said he had been going through some shit and told me he was sorry he bothered us."

"It's so strange," Adam said, sitting in one of their porch chairs. Anthony sat next to him, offered him a sip of his beer. Adam declined. "I haven't seen him since high school and then out of the blue, he's on our front porch in the middle of the day."

"I think he was curious about what happened to you. I know I would be."

"There is a thing called Facebook," Adam said.

"You know, I think I've heard of it." Anthony refused to get a page, or use any social media for that matter. Apart from helping Adam with some stuff for the band, he resolutely remained disconnected from hashtags and memes.

"I'm just saying he could get all of that without leaving his house. Why drive all this way only to turn around and leave without seeing me?"

"Search me. Was he always such a weirdo?"

Adam thought about it before shaking his head. "He was a sweet kid. Great boyfriend as first loves go. We broke up just after senior year, and that was the last I've seen of him."

"Why haven't you mentioned him before?" Anthony picked at the label of his beer in a way that made Adam realize he was feeling out the situation, and probably wondering how Adam felt about Miles.

"Honestly, I haven't thought about him in years. Until today, it hadn't occurred to me to ask. We grew up, moved on, you know?"

"Was he that hot in high school?"

Adam laughed, and it echoed off the stucco. "He was cute in a boyish way. Good to know he turned out hot, though." He nudged Anthony's knee with his own.

"I have eyes, babe. Just call 'em like I see 'em." He paused, and his expression turned more serious again. "Are you going to call him?"

Adam picked at a hangnail and looked out over their front lawn. It was in need of a mow. "I don't know," he answered. "If something's wrong. Do you think I should?"

Anthony shrugged. "Beats me. He looked pretty messed up. The question is, do you want to get involved if it's drama? What if he had a fight with a boyfriend or something?"

Adam couldn't help himself, he laughed again. "I don't think that's it."

"It's not out of the realm of possibility."

"It kind of is. He's married." Adam paused for dramatic effect. "To a woman."

"Oh."

"Yeah, I guess he figured out he was straight after high school."

"He's probably bi," Anthony corrected.

"As far as I know he's only dated girls since me."

"If he's still attracted to dudes—and you don't travel halfway across a state to see a guy if you aren't—he's bi. It's a real thing, Adam."

"I know it's a real thing, dumbass. I just..." He trailed off. It was such a simple thing and yet Adam had never considered that Miles might be bisexual. He hadn't minded being Miles's first and only boyfriend.

Anthony stood up. "You've had a rough day. How about I grill us up some steaks and you open a bottle of wine. We'll have dinner on the patio."

"That sounds great, but do you mind if I sit here for a bit? I need to think."

Anthony looked uncomfortable, worried even, but he nodded and went inside, leaving Adam with his thoughts.

FRIDAY, JUNE 7, 2013 · 11:47 P.M.

The liquor had dulled Adam's senses; he was sitting on a rusty lawn chair in Dahlia's backyard watching the clouds shift and change over the starry sky. The air was thick with humidity, but no rain was in sight. Nearby, someone was smoking pot, but he was already too relaxed to care about finding them and bumming a puff or two.

The crunch of leaves to his left caused him to turn, coming face-to-thigh with Danny Dubrow, a sophomore from the trumpet section who also happened to be a huge gossip.

"Lange," he said. "You look like you could use another beer." He handed Adam a lukewarm can of cheap, watery beer and took a seat on the grass facing him. Danny's shaggy, blond hair fell in his eyes and he jerked his chin back to flip it out of the way. "Heard you and Lawson had a fight. Thought you could use some cheering up."

"I'm not in the mood for your kind of cheering up, Danny."

Danny had gone through every guy in school except Miles and Adam. They had a bet on whom he would hit on first. Looked like Miles might have won the bet.

"Christ, Lange, I'm not always trying to get in someone's pants. I just thought you might like to talk."

"I'm sick of talking," Adam said. He and Miles had argued again after they'd both had a few drinks, and Miles had gotten a ride home from Brienne. Adam stayed and had a few more shots and now he was nursing a warm beer.

"That bad, huh?" Danny knocked back the beer in his hand and cracked open another one. The foam sputtered out of the opening and he sucked on it loudly.

"Let me ask you something." Adam's words slurred together a little, but he was still just sober enough to remember what a player Danny was.

"Sure, dude."

"Have you ever been in a serious relationship? One that lasted longer than it took the guy to zip up his pants?"

"Nah, man, too messy. I prefer to love 'em and leave 'em."

"And that works for you?"

"I've never had any complaints."

"I don't think that means it works for your, uh, conquests."

"The way I see it is we both get what we want. I get off and they get to say they've been with Danny Dubrow. It's a win-win."

Adam spat out a sarcastic laugh. "Whatever." He drained his warm beer and belched, the sound echoing off the live oak branches above them.

"You want another?"

They finished an entire six pack together, just shooting the shit, Danny gossiping about their mutual friends, Adam trying not to think about Miles. And then he did the unthinkable.

"Do you believe in time travel?" he asked.

"Like *Back to the Future* kind of shit?"

"Sort of. Do you think it's possible? That we could just move through time the same way we drive down the highway?"

Danny shrugged. "Maybe. I mean, I guess it's possible. Sure, why not?"

Adam finished the last of his beer. "Miles thinks he's time-traveling." Adam paused, leaving his words hanging between them.

At first Danny didn't react, as if he hadn't heard what Adam had said. Then he tilted his head and his eyes went wide.

"No way! Seriously? Dude that's crazy!" The grin on his face stretched into pure glee as he started laughing. "That is some *X-Files* fucking shit, man. See, this is why I don't do boyfriends. Too fucking messy."

"Stop it, man; it's not funny. He's really messed up about it."

Danny squinted at Adam. "You don't believe this shit, do you?"

"I don't know," Adam said, dropping his head back and staring at the stars. Miles had been pretty adamant that he thought he was time-traveling, and Adam was beginning to question everything. Maybe he and Miles weren't meant to be together. "We're going to different colleges in the fall anyway. Maybe it's better if we break up now and save ourselves the drama."

"I couldn't agree more, man. Just kick him to the curb. You can't be with the same guy the rest of your life. Don't you want to taste what's out there?"

"That's what I'm saying." Adam could feel the buzz of alcohol blurring his senses as he gestured wildly. "I need to be free to get my thing on, you know? To fly free." He stood up, stretched his arms wide and swayed as he ran circles around Danny, flapping his makeshift wings. Danny was laughing and following Adam's movements with his head.

"I feel dizzy," Danny said. "Stop spinning."

At that moment Adam started to feel it too. He lost his balance and tripped over a root, stumbled and landed on top of Danny. They both fell into peals of laughter.

"Ow, your elbow is digging into my ribs," Danny said.

"Sorry," Adam pulled back, resting his weight on his hands, hovering just over Danny. They were both panting. As he leaned in, Danny's beer-scented breath heated his face just before he pressed his lips to Adam's. Danny's kiss was so different from Miles's. He was rough and clumsy, where Miles kissed softly and sensually, but Adam didn't care. Right now he just wanted to feel anything but the pain and anger he felt any time he thought about Miles. He pulled back to see Danny's pupils were now dominating his blue irises, probably mirroring his own desire. He was just about to dive back in for round two when he heard a high-pitched, "Oh my God!" and turned to see Dahlia, barefoot and mouth agape, as she took in the scene before her.

Adam scrambled to get up, but she had already seen. Dahlia ran back in the house before he could get to his feet.

"Shit." Adam sat down hard on the damp grass, not caring if it ruined his shorts. He ran his hand through his sweaty hair.

"Sorry, dude," Danny said. "Guess I should, uh, probably go."

Danny stood and brushed off his cargo shorts; a streak of mud clung to the left leg. He stood there, probably wondering if he should say something else, but eventually he just walked back to the house, leaving Adam alone and feeling sick to his stomach.

CHAPTER EIGHT
MILES

Dr. Benson didn't speak at first. She sat patiently waiting for Miles to speak, just as she always did. But for some reason, Miles couldn't find his voice. He didn't know what to tell her first: that he'd gone to see Adam or that it had been a result of another time-travel episode.

This time, Dr. Benson broke the silence first. "You get that off soon?" she asked, nodding at his cast.

Small talk was one of her methods for getting him to open up when he wasn't talkative. Miles cleared his throat. "Later today, actually. As soon as we're done here."

"I bet you're ready for that."

Miles didn't acknowledge her remark. Instead he blurted, "I had another episode. Wednesday morning."

Dr. Benson didn't reply; she simply raised an eyebrow.

"It was only a few hours, but I went to see Adam and made a complete ass of myself."

"Did you talk to him?"

"Adam? No, he wasn't home. But I met the boyfriend." The word tasted like bile on his tongue.

"How'd that go?"

"I came to in their driveway. I just got out of there as fast as I could. I couldn't face Adam like that—a complete basket case. 'Oh, hey, remember me? The psycho guy you dated in high school? I'm back and guess what, I'm still time-traveling!' Can you imagine? He'd probably call the cops."

"What did Ana say?"

Miles looked down at his lap. "I haven't told her."

"Why not?"

"She worries too much." Miles scratched at his cast, hoping the skin beneath could feel the attempt despite the inch of plaster. "It's not like I actually *saw* Adam."

"Is that what you think would upset her? Not that you time-traveled, but that you went to see Adam?"

Miles shrugged.

"You might want to think about your reasons for keeping things from your wife," Dr. Benson said, pushing her glasses up on her nose. "Also, I think it might be a good idea to get Ana back in here for another chat."

"Is that necessary?"

"Well, as I told you the last time, it's totally up to you. If you don't want Ana to meet with me, you have that right. But I think it can be very beneficial to your progress if I got an idea of how you're doing at home these days." She watched Miles expectantly, but he didn't reply. "Why don't you think about it and let me know next week, okay?"

Miles shifted in his seat. "Sure," he mumbled.

"Now, let's talk about what you were doing right before this most recent episode. Do you remember what you were doing in the moments preceding the event?"

"I was working, I think. Editing a piece for Darius's blog, normal stuff."

Why was he lying again? Could Dr. Benson sense it?

"That's all?" she asked. "That doesn't seem like something that would trigger you. Had you done anything else that morning?"

She wasn't going to let this go. The way Miles saw it, he had two options: one, continue to lie, or two, tell her the truth and hope she didn't judge him too harshly.

"You know I'm not here to judge," she said gently.

"I know." Miles took a deep breath. "I was searching online for Adam. Nothing major. I just wanted to know what was going on with him, if he was happy. Stuff like that."

"And what did you find?"

"Not much. Website for his band. A picture. But then I closed my laptop and was going to go for a walk to clear my head."

"And that's when you switched?"

Miles nodded. He hated when Dr. Benson called it switching. Even though he'd technically been diagnosed with a dissociative disorder, he hated the terminology that went along with it and had asked Dr. Benson to refer to his dissociative states as "episodes." She usually complied. Since his condition, which Dr. Benson had dubbed Dissociative Chronology Disorder, wasn't a true psychiatric diagnosis, they were stuck with the mental illness terminology accepted within the community. Didn't mean he had to like it.

"And the next thing you remember is waking up in Adam's driveway?"

"Yep."

"Have you had any contact with Adam since then?"

"God, no," Miles said. "I can't even bear to tell my wife, why in the hell would I seek out someone I barely know?"

"That's a very good question, Miles. I think you need to think about that." She looked at the clock on the small table next to her. "Looks like our time is up for today."

"HOW'D IT GO WITH DR. B?" Ana asked when Miles walked through the door later that night. She was sitting at the kitchen counter working on her laptop, reading glasses perched low on her nose.

"Okay I guess. She wants to see you again."

"Oh?" she said, without looking up.

After getting his cast off, Miles had gone for a long drive to think about what Dr. Benson had said and parked near the Orlando Eye, watching the giant Ferris wheel spin until he had sorted through his broken thoughts. Not only had he decided to take Dr. Benson's advice, he'd also decided to tell Ana everything. He leaned against a wall and watched her. "Can we talk?"

"Sure thing, Irving," she said. "Just let me save this file and then I'm all yours." Ana made a few more keystrokes, a couple clicks of the mouse, and smiled at him. "Should I get a bottle of wine, or is this more of a beer talk?"

"Neither," he said.

"Vodka?"

"No, I need a clear head for this," he said. "And so do you."

Ana slid off her stool and crossed the room to him. "Now you have me worried," she said, sliding her long, slender arms around his waist. She smelled like Dove soap and citrus. He inhaled deeply in case one of them was sleeping in the guest room tonight. "Does this have anything to do with why Dr. Benson wants to see me?"

"I'll get to that," he said. "Just listen."

"Okay." Ana sat back down, this time on a kitchen chair.

Miles pulled out the chair opposite her. He folded his hands together on the table between them and stared at the skin around his wrist where the cast had been. His arm felt strangely light and disconnected from his body. Come to think of it, so did his mind.

"You remember last Wednesday, when I came home late and you asked if something was wrong?"

Ana's eyes narrowed. He could see her jaw clenching as she managed a terse "yeah."

"I told you everything was fine," he said, taking a deep breath that he exhaled slowly. "But I wasn't totally honest with you."

Ana was silent. That might be a good sign. No yelling, no pacing, no exaggerated arm movements. But Miles couldn't help but think it was the calm before the storm.

"I had another episode," he said. "Younger me showed up and took himself to see Adam."

"All the way to Merritt Island?"

"How did you know Adam lived in Merritt Island?"

Ana began picking at the edges of the bamboo placemat in front of her. "Never mind," she said. Guilt clung to her like a wet blanket.

"You knew?"

"Not that you went to see him, but I checked the GPS." She looked up into his eyes. "I'm not proud of myself."

Miles stood up, began pacing the kitchen floor. "You were checking up on me?" He pivoted, and his shoes squeaked on the tile.

"I was worried!" she shouted, now out of her chair too. "And with good reason apparently!"

"You barely give me room to breathe. I feel like a patient in my own home. Every time I so much as yawn, you act like I'm having a mental breakdown."

"You usually are!"

It was a low blow. Miles felt his rage surface and flood his veins with heat. He balled his fists at his sides to keep from throwing something. Ana recoiled.

"Oh, for fuck's sake, Ana. I'm not going to hit you."

"I never know what you're going to do these days, or who you are," she said. "It's like being married to two different people."

"You knew when you married me—"

"That was different, and you know it. We weren't in love then, and neither of us was planning on staying together."

"I didn't plan on a lot of things," Miles muttered.

"You don't get to do that," Ana shrieked. "You don't get to shirk responsibility just because you have a mental disorder. That's not fair to me, and it's not fair to yourself. You think I want to go through life wondering if today's the day my husband won't come home and I'll be stuck with a seventeen-year-old boy for the rest of my life?"

"I think he'd age eventually."

"Ugh, that's so *not* the point."

"I know," Miles said softly. He crossed the floor to his wife and took her in his arms. "Can we try to talk about this like adults?"

"I don't know, *are* you one?" Her pout was exaggerated and her eyes wide as she looked up at him through her lashes.

Miles wasn't ready to make up, but he was trying to be honest. "For the moment, yes."

She rested her head on his shoulder. "Did Adam freak?"

"I left before he got home," Miles replied. "I met the boyfriend, though. He seemed nice."

"Oh, shit, how embarrassing."

Ana knew him so well. "God, I love you," he whispered into her hair.

"I love you too," she said. "But you need to be honest with me. You need to trust me."

"I do trust you," he said. "It's me I don't trust."

SATURDAY, JUNE 8, 2013 · 7:42 A.M.

Miles was bleary eyed and numb the morning of graduation. He'd managed to avoid Adam so far, but when they lined up in alphabetical order, there was no avoiding the dumb luck of being a Lawson, who had just been betrayed by a Lange.

The night before, he'd had his phone in his hand to text Adam an apology when Dahlia called and told him what she'd seen between him and Danny. And his whole world had shifted. How was he supposed to deal with that?

Keeping his head down, Miles followed Emily Lattimer toward the end of the tunnel that led onto the field. The last time he'd been here, Emily had reprimanded him and Adam for not being able to stay in the right order. Today she smiled at him.

"I can't believe this is it," she said.

Miles grunted and tried to focus on anything but the person he saw approaching from his left. He tried to pretend to be lost in conversation with Emily, but Adam grabbed his arm.

"There you are. I've been looking all over for you. We need to talk."

Unable to look at him, Miles said, "I don't want to talk to you." Emily gave him a weak smile and turned away, taking his safety net with her.

Adam ducked down into Miles's sight line and Miles's stomach lurched at the sight of him. Or it could have also been the beer still rolling around in his gut.

"I made a mistake," Adam said softly. "You have to believe that it was a simple, drunken mistake."

Emily glanced over her shoulder at them. Adam tugged on Miles's arm and shuffled them away from the rest of their classmates.

Miles yanked his arm back as he leaned against a concrete pillar.

"Look, I know you're upset," Adam said. "You have a right to be."

"You don't know how I feel." Truth was, Miles didn't know how he felt. Betrayed? Hurt? Sad? It was a lot to process.

"Miles, baby, we'd just had a fight and—"

"And you think that excuses anything?" Miles glared at him, anger taking over all other emotions.

"No." Adam's gaze shifted, his eyes welling up. "I was upset and Danny asked me if I was okay. We got to talking, had a few beers and…"

"I don't want to hear this." He took a step away, and Adam reached for his hand. Miles looked down at it as if they'd never touched before. Something was different this time.

"Nothing happened," Adam reassured. "We kissed once. Once. That was it, and it will never happen again. You know how Danny is."

Miles took a deep breath. "Yeah." Danny was a jerk and a player, and he'd probably been working his way through all the guys in school. Maybe Adam was on his list.

Adam smirked. "If you can believe it, he was trying to comfort me about our fight."

"I'm sure that went over well." Despite the sting of betrayal, Miles felt his resolve softening. Adam must have sensed it, because his shoulders relaxed and he leaned against the pillar, too.

"He was more concerned with whether I believed you about the time travel."

It took a second for the words to register, and when they did, Miles reeled back, his blood cold. "You didn't?"

"What?" Adam stumbled as he shifted his weight back to his own feet. Miles's anger had caught him off guard.

"I can't believe you told that halfwit Danny about my dreams!" Miles shouted. "That was private information!"

"I was drunk," Adam said, panic evident on his face. He rubbed his temples. "I think I still am."

"I don't give a flying fuck about your hangover! That moron is a bigger gossip than Dahlia. It will be all over town by tomorrow morning."

"Oh my God! I said I was sorry."

"I don't think that's enough," Miles said. He raked a hand over his shaved head.

"What's that supposed to mean?"

Miles looked up at him and saw the pain in his face, but he had to focus on his own pain right now. "I need some time," he said. "I'll call you."

He could feel Adam's eyes on him as he got back in line behind Emily, but he didn't turn back. He couldn't.

THURSDAY, APRIL 30, 2020 · 6:22 A.M.

Miles awoke with a splitting headache. His muscles felt taut and heavy, as though he'd been lifting weights all night instead of sleeping. He kicked off the covers. The room was far too warm, and his mouth felt dry and thick. He rolled over, hoping to find the glass of water he usually kept beside his bed, but came face to face with a snoring Ana instead. The shock nearly made him shout, but he slapped his right hand over his mouth just in time. He eased himself to the edge of the bed as silently as he could, taking care not to wake Ana. He didn't need a repeat of the last time he woke up like this.

The rest of the house was bathed in early morning light and was blissfully quiet. It gave him a few moments to gather his thoughts and figure out when in his life he'd shown up. After a quick check of a cell phone lying on the kitchen counter, he learned it was only a few weeks after the last time he'd visited and embarrassed himself in front of Adam's new boyfriend. It occurred to him that he didn't know how long they'd been together. Was he new? Were they married? So far in the future, surely same-sex marriage was legal.

Maybe none of that mattered. If Adam was happy, should he try to upset that? His own desire to find out why he and Adam had broken up was not nearly as strong as his need for comfort. The only problem was that Adam could provide him with both. Even though Miles knew that his older self was in love with Ana, he didn't feel the same connection and was in desperate need of... something.

He was so completely overwhelmed that he sat on the sofa and buried his face in his hands. The tears came unbidden, like a waterfall over a cliff. The dam had broken, and his emotions were laid bare. He hadn't cried this hard since his grandmother died when he was fourteen. Sobs wracked his body like rolling waves.

"Honey?"

Miles opened his eyes to see Ana's perfectly manicured feet next to his own. When he looked up into her eyes, they were nearly black with worry. He crumbled into her arms. The tears came again.

"Miles, baby, what's wrong?" Ana stroked his head and let him cry it out, waiting patiently for his answer, but Miles didn't have one.

"I don't know why I'm crying," he said. "I just feel so lost."

"Why do you feel lost, baby?"

"I don't know," Miles lied. He wanted her comforting caresses to last a little longer. He feared if he told her he was the seventeen-year-old version of himself she'd treat him differently.

"It's okay," she said, her voice a soothing lullaby of familiar sounds. It reminded him of his mother. It was that thought more than anything that caused him to break.

"I'm not me," he sobbed. "I'm never me. It's all so confusing, not knowing who I am or where I am."

Ana pulled back, just as he had feared. "How old are you?" she asked with an urgency that Miles hated.

"Seventeen," he said, and when he saw the disappointment in Ana's eyes, he added, "and I've got a calculus test tomorrow!"

To her credit, she didn't laugh. She simply stood up and walked to the kitchen counter. "I'm calling Dr. Benson," she said as she picked up the phone.

"No, I don't want to see her," Miles pleaded. "I want to see Adam."

"Well, that's not happening," she muttered, putting the phone to her ear. "Yes, hello, this is Ana Espinosa-Lawson. I'm Miles Lawson's wife. Yes. Would it be possible for us to see Dr. Benson today? It's urgent." She paused, listening to the person on the other end. "No, it's not an emergency. Just important. I'd appreciate it if she could work us in. Yes, I'll hold." She tapped her fingernails on the granite countertop as she waited. Miles started to speak, but Ana held up a finger to silence him. "Yes? Thank you so much. We'll see you then."

Ana hung up the phone and gave him a sympathetic smile. "Get dressed," she said. "She's working you in before her first patient. We have to hurry."

MILES DIDN'T ARGUE ABOUT SEEING Dr. Benson. Instead, he tried to bide his time. Ana refused to let him drive, so he was more or less trapped. He tapped out a dull rhythm on the arm rest and watched the scenery roll by out the window.

"Do you have to do that?" Ana asked.

Miles stopped tapping. "Sorry. Drummer's habit."

"You haven't done that in years."

Miles shifted in his seat. The seatbelt pulled at his neck.

"The other you, I mean."

"I know," he said.

The silence was overwhelming. Miles didn't know what to say, and the tension radiated from Ana like heat from a campfire. He couldn't tell if she was angry or just worried, and he didn't dare ask.

He wasn't paying attention to where they were going until she made a sharp right turn and steered them into a Walgreens parking lot. She cut the engine and sat there with her hands on the steering wheel. The car began to heat up quickly, and Miles was just about to ask her what they were doing when she spoke.

"Why did you go see Adam?" she asked.

Caught off guard, Miles stumbled over his words, only managing a few "ums" and "ahs" before she cut him off.

"I'm not angry," she said softly. "I just want to know. Even though I know you're dating him in your time, my Miles is happy and never talks about him. So I'm just wondering why you're so obsessed. Why is it that your sole focus when you take over my husband's body is to see an ex-boyfriend that you know he has had zero contact with? What's the point?"

Miles took a deep breath. The truth was going to hurt, but he owed her that much. Still, he couldn't face her while he said it. Turning to look out the window, he focused on a bright blue recycling bin overflowing with beer bottles. It calmed him to know that people were still enjoying themselves despite his world being in complete chaos. It gave him hope.

"Because I love him," Miles said on a heavy exhale.

He heard Ana's sigh, and knew from the muffled echo of it she was also staring out her window. They sat there like that for several minutes, neither of them speaking. Miles finally got the courage to look at his friend. Tears silently streamed down her face, but she held her head high.

Without looking at him, Ana asked, "Do you think he still loves Adam too?"

"I don't know," Miles answered honestly. "I can tell you that Adam has moved on."

She nodded, sniffling and rubbing the back of her hand across her nose. "I'm sorry if I scared you," she said.

"You didn't."

"Still."

Ana put the car in gear and pulled out of the parking lot. Her face was a perfect mask of composure by the time they arrived at Dr. Benson's office.

THURSDAY, APRIL 30, 2020 · 7:45 A.M.

Ana watched Miles intently, looking for even a small sign that he might have come back to himself, but the way he tapped his foot and chewed the skin around his thumbnail practically screamed nervous teenager. He was still seventeen.

"Stop fidgeting." She hated that she sounded like her mother.

"Sorry," Miles mumbled. "I'm just nervous."

"Don't be. You trust Dr. Benson. Or you will. You know what I mean."

"Can't we just wait until I'm back to normal?"

Ana sighed. "When is that ever going to happen? And besides, this appointment isn't technically for you. So it doesn't really matter, does it?"

"I guess not."

Miles looked as if he wanted to add something, but the red-headed receptionist called their names, preventing him from frustrating her further. As much as she loved Miles at twenty-five, she was beginning to understand why she had disliked him so much when they were kids.

DR. BENSON'S OFFICE, DESPITE CONTAINING comfortable couches and lush carpeting rather than an examination table and cheap linoleum, still had the cold, sterile feel of a doctor's office. She didn't understand how Miles could be comfortable here. It also smelled strange. Something floral and sweet that reminded Ana of spring. Honeysuckle, maybe? Or jasmine. Either way it was overpowering and seemed to linger around Dr. Benson in an invisible cloud, wafting from her in pungent waves that clung to the inside of Ana's nose. She sniffed, but it only drew the scent in deeper.

"Well, hello, Ana. I wasn't expecting to see you." Dr. Benson's smile revealed a row of bright white teeth, too perfect to be natural. She had a small speck stuck between her incisors that looked like a poppy seed. Ana sucked on her own teeth in sympathy while shaking the doctor's hand.

"Miles said you wanted to talk to me about his treatment, and he's well..." Ana motioned to Miles, who had his hands in his pockets and was scuffing his foot on the carpet.

"Why don't we have a seat and you can talk about what's bothering you." She raised her voice on the end as if it were a question, but her movements indicated that she expected them to agree. While Miles and Ana exchanged nervous glances, she uncapped a pen and rested her legal pad on her lap. She motioned for them to sit, and when they didn't speak, she prompted, "How are things at home?"

How could a woman whose business it was to understand the inner workings of the human mind be so oblivious to their discomfort?

Miles was picking lint off his left sock, so Ana decided to answer for them. "Um, good I guess."

"How so?"

The pen scratching on the paper made Ana's heart leap. What was she writing?

"Well, as I'm sure you know, Miles's episodes have been increasing again. So we're dealing with that. And he just got his cast off, so we're actually sleeping now. I don't know. Just normal stuff, I guess."

"Miles, do you want to add anything?"

Miles looked up, startled. He glanced from Dr. Benson to Ana and back again. "I don't really feel like talking today."

"But I thought this was urgent." Dr. Benson stared at Ana.

Ana glanced at Miles, who looked panicked, and even though she found his seventeen-year-old indignation frustrating, Ana couldn't stand to see the frantic look in his eyes. She decided her initial panic in getting him to Dr. Benson could wait.

"False alarm," Ana said with a nervous laugh. "Maybe the two of us could just talk and you and Miles can chat during his regular appointment next week?"

"That's fine," Dr. Benson said, looking caught off guard. She reached around her to put the notepad back on her desk. "But I'm here if you change your mind." She tilted her head to one side, trying to catch Miles's gaze.

Miles shifted in his seat and mumbled something that sounded like "thanks." He stood up. "Do I need to sign something or... ?"

"We have a signed release on file, so a verbal confirmation is all that is needed for today." She paused. "Do I have your permission to discuss your diagnosis freely with your wife?" Dr. Benson asked. "I won't reveal anything you've said to me about your relationship. Just the basics of your condition and what she can expect from your treatment."

"Sure, I guess." Miles's posture and tone were undeniably childish, but Dr. Benson didn't seem to notice or care.

"Is that all right with you, Ana? If we talk alone?"

Ana nodded. She suspected that Miles shared pretty much everything from his sessions anyway, but perhaps Dr. Benson could explain it better than he could. It couldn't hurt to try.

Dr. Benson smiled and turned back to Miles. "Well, why don't you have a seat in the waiting room so Ana and I can have a little chat, hmm?"

Miles rose, but didn't leave. His gaze fixed on the carpet as he opened his mouth, almost as if he had something to add, but he caught himself on an inhale and he didn't speak.

Dr. Benson spoke softly, almost too quietly for Ana to hear. "As I said, just information about your treatment and diagnosis. Nothing personal." He didn't look up.

"Thank you." He gave Ana a weak smile before leaving her alone with Dr. Benson. Ana's heart began to race.

She kept her eyes trained on the door as if she expected Miles to appear suddenly. So when Dr. Benson spoke, her words caught Ana off guard.

"I'd like to adjust his diagnosis; I don't think he's time-traveling."

"What?"

"Time travel. I don't think that's what is happening. I think it's switching to a dissociative state, just with a younger version of *himself* rather than an alternate personality."

Confusion washed over her. Why would Miles lie to her? Why would he make something like that up? Did he know what Dr. Benson was telling her?

"What do you mean he's *not* time-traveling?"

"Surely you don't believe that nonsense. Isn't it more likely to assume that he's just dissociating and reverting to a child-like state?"

This woman was so condescending. It seemed preposterous to be sitting across from her, listening to her uproot their lives again. Ana felt positively indignant.

"But my sister. How could he have known about my sister dying?"

Dr. Benson shrugged. "Lucky guess, perhaps? Look, I'm not saying he doesn't *believe* he's time-traveling, but I do think there are other factors at play here."

"What other factors?"

"Well, that's between me and your husband, but what you need to know is we have a diagnosis. He has Dissociative Identity Disorder... with a few caveats."

"Such as?" Ana raised an eyebrow.

"I'd like you to keep this particular diagnosis between us. I'm not sure it's appropriate telling you, but since I think it's in the best interest of the patient, there is some leeway." She was almost talking to herself, which was just as well, because Ana had stopped listening.

"You want me to lie to my husband?" she asked.

"No, not lie. Simply help with his treatment. It's important that he think we believe he's time-traveling."

"How is that *not* lying, exactly?" Ana asked, even though she did believe him. "Keeping his treatment from him, I mean?"

Dr. Benson looked confused. "His treatment will remain relatively unchanged. I just thought you'd like to know you have an ally in this.

I assumed you knew his time travel was psychosomatic. Or at least guessed."

"Yes, of course." Ana couldn't help but try to save face. "I simply meant, is that good for him? For us to pretend."

"Well, it's not common practice, no. But I think in Miles's case it might help us get to the root cause. So far it's been effective in our sessions. One thing I'm sure you've noticed is he refers to his switching as an 'episode' rather than what it is, a dissociative state that brings about an alter. I've been trying to use his terminology for his comfort. Ultimately, we'll talk to him about his actual condition, but for now, I think it's necessary to indulge the time travel fantasy a bit longer. He's started to open up about some of the things that may have led to the dissociation in the first place."

Ana nodded, still reeling from the news that Dr. Benson didn't believe Miles was time-traveling. She cleared her throat. "Uh, so what's—what's next? Do I need to do anything?"

"I'd like you to keep a journal of any 'episodes' and let me know if you notice a change, good or bad, in Miles's mental state."

"That feels so dishonest."

"I've already told him I may ask you to monitor his behavior. He's okay with it."

The sofa beneath Ana's legs squeaked as she uncrossed and recrossed her legs. Her left thigh burned a little where it had been stuck to the leather. She rubbed it while considering her words. If Miles had consented, she supposed it wouldn't be wrong for her to keep tabs on her husband. What if he asked to see the journal, though? Should she tell him he needed a new therapist?

"Ana, I know this is a lot," Dr. Benson said, interrupting her racing thoughts. "But I want you to know I have Miles's best interests in mind here. He's deeply troubled and he needs to get well. The only way he can do that is to face whatever trauma led to his dissociation and face it head on. Addressing that behavior is much more important than focusing on a diagnosis. That way he can integrate with his alters fully and function like a normal, healthy adult."

There was no doubt in Ana's mind that she wanted Miles to heal so he could stop time-traveling, and even Miles was convinced that it was a form of dissociative disorder. If this was the way to make it happen, maybe a little white lie wouldn't hurt. Maybe she could go through with it if it meant Miles would be healthy finally. And, she reasoned, if it got to be too much, she could always tell him, and they could find a new doctor, together.

"Okay," she said. "I think I can do that." As soon as the words were out of her mouth, she felt queasy, but she refused to take them back. She'd have to see it through to whatever conclusion was to come. For Miles's sake.

THE DOORBELL SHATTERED THE UNCOMFORTABLE silence that had fallen between Miles and Ana in the hours after their visit to Dr. Benson's office. Ana couldn't bring herself to say anything to him, even though he had to know she was frustrated that he was young Miles yet again. She could see it in the tension in his shoulders, hear it in the uneven way he breathed. It was unbearable.

"I'll get it," Miles said.

Ana barely acknowledged him, continuing to type away at her laptop. She had been feigning work for the past hour. She considered going for a walk, but she didn't want to leave Miles alone.

Ana didn't expect what she heard next.

"Adam! You're here!" Before she could get up, Miles had wrapped Adam in a passionate hug, only retreating when he must have realized Adam's arms were firmly at his sides.

Adam ran his hand through his hair. "I hope it's okay that I dropped by."

"Of course it's okay," Miles said. "I've missed you so much." He looked as if he wanted to touch Adam again, but he didn't. For that, Ana was grateful, even if just a little bit.

"Hello, Ana."

It seemed Miles hadn't realized Ana had gotten up from the sofa, but when he turned around, the look on his face showed a mixture of fear and anger.

Ana didn't need to ask why Adam was there; she could see it in his eyes. He was worried about Miles. If Adam knew what was going on with his old friend, he'd probably run as far away as he could get. Because it wasn't something that was easily blurted out, Ana simply turned on her hostess smile and invited Adam into their home.

"How was the drive?" she asked, ignoring what the three of them knew was the time-traveling elephant in the room. She wondered if that was what had brought Adam two hours from home on a Thursday night.

"Traffic was a nightmare," he said.

"Always is."

"Yeah."

Adam looked nervously from Ana to Miles and back again. He started to speak several times, but stopped himself. Ana watched Miles fidget, expected him to say something, but he didn't speak either. Finally, she could bear it no longer.

"Looks like I'm going to have to be the one to start this ball rolling," she said. "Miles, Adam is here because he is worried about you after you showed up uninvited on his doorstep. Adam, Miles wants to sit in your lap because he thinks he's in love with you. Is that about right?"

Adam's jaw was slack, and Miles had begun sweating. The looks on their faces were comical, or they would have been if the entire situation weren't a complete disaster.

"I'm going to pour myself a glass of wine and take a bath," Ana said. "You two do whatever the hell you want."

She left them staring after her as she grabbed an open bottle of cabernet and headed for the master bath. She didn't care what Miles did or didn't tell Adam, she needed to consider her own mental health for once.

Neither of them came after her, so she filled the tub with scalding hot water and bubble bath and let herself soak and get very, very drunk.

CHAPTER TEN
ADAM

"I've missed you so much." Miles's face was filled with emotion.

"Yes, you said that already." Adam ran a hand through his hair. It was probably a total mess by now. "Shouldn't we check on her?" He was incredibly uncomfortable and didn't understand what was going on with Miles and Ana. He wasn't sure he wanted to know.

"We should probably let her cool off," Miles said. "It's been a *day*."

Adam glanced in the direction Ana had gone and then back to Miles before deciding that was probably the best course of action for now, even though he wasn't too keen on being alone with Miles.

"You want to sit down?" When Miles gestured toward the sofa, Adam could see he was shaking. It was unnerving, so Adam took a seat in a chair across from the sofa. Miles looked him up and down. "God, you look so amazing."

Never one to be comfortable with a compliment, Adam found this one even more disconcerting. "Thanks," he mumbled.

They sat in silence before Miles finally spoke. "Why did you come here?"

"Why did you come to see me?" Adam retorted. The sudden realization that he was angry with Miles caught him off guard. "Sorry. I just— Miles, you haven't even so much as called me in almost eight years and I'm just trying to understand what is going on here."

"I'm sorry too," Miles said. He rubbed his hands on his knees, then flexed his fingers. "I think I got a little carried away but I couldn't resist. I needed to know what happened to you."

"You could have called first. Or sent me an email, a text. You scared the shit out of Anthony."

"Anthony?"

"My fiancé. You met him at the house. He called me at work in a panic because some guy had passed out in our driveway. Who does that? Were you drunk?"

"No, I wasn't drunk." Miles's voice was small and shaky.

"Then what, Miles? What could possibly make you drive all that way, pass out and then leave without talking to me?"

"You won't believe me."

"Try me."

Miles closed his eyes and took a deep breath that he held for what seemed like an eternity. "It's me," he said, as if that explained everything.

"What about you?"

"I mean, it's the me you dated. In high school. I'm seventeen."

"Miles, this is crazy; you're twenty-five. I'm twenty-five."

"My body is twenty-five, but this is me, I swear. I'm here from two-thousand twelve, and I've been time-traveling for years. You have to believe me."

Adam stood and paced the floor as panic began to creep in. "This is crazy," he said. "You're crazy. I don't know what I'm doing here. It's like a bad dream; it has to be a dream. You *can't* be doing this again."

"I told you? When did I tell you?"

"Now I know why Ana was so pissed. You must have been spouting this shit since... well, since whenever, and here I am showing up all worried that your mom had died or something. I'm a fucking idiot." He crossed to the door, ready to leave, when he heard Miles's voice, small and scared.

"Please don't leave, Adam. I love you."

He turned around. A single tear streaked down Miles's cheek, and was then followed by several more. As Miles's tears continued to fall, Adam felt his resolve crack. Maybe Miles really needed him. He closed the distance between them and wrapped his arms around Miles in a comforting hug. Miles collapsed into his arms and began to sob.

"I'm so scared," Miles said.

Adam led him back to the sofa and took a seat beside him. He eased Miles away from him and looked into his eyes. "Start from the beginning," he said. "Tell me everything."

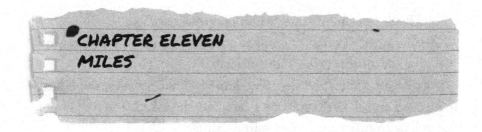

CHAPTER ELEVEN
MILES

THURSDAY, APRIL 30, 2020 · 7:22 P.M.

When Miles had finished telling Adam about his time travel, he felt lighter, but he needed to know what Adam was thinking. "Say something," he said. "Anything."

Adam shook his head. "I don't know what to say. It's—"

"A lot, I know."

"Do you remember telling me all of this before?"

"No, when did I tell you?"

"Twice actually. The first time we both thought you were having these really vivid dreams, crazy ones, but just dreams. The second time, you were convinced it was time travel. It was the day before graduation, and we got in a big fight about it."

"Well, that explains why I don't remember it," he said. "It's the summer between sophomore and junior years for me. Just after we, *you know*, for the first time."

"Oh my God." Adam dropped his face into his hand.

"Don't be embarrassed," Miles said. "It was wonderful."

Adam glanced over at him and began to roar with laughter.

"What's so funny?"

"I'm sorry. I can't help it," Adam said between laughs. "You really think you're seventeen, don't you?"

"I *am* seventeen," Miles insisted. "My birthday was last week."

"It's April. Your birthday is in June."

"Well, it's June in my time," Miles said with a shrug.

Adam sighed. "Look, I'm going to go. I need some time to think and you should probably go be with your wife."

At the word Miles recoiled. She didn't feel like his wife, and it hurt to hear Adam call her that. "Can I call you?" he asked. The thought of not talking to Adam made him start to panic.

"Um, I guess that would be okay," Adam said.

As he walked to the door, Miles couldn't help himself, and he called out, "I love you." Adam didn't reply; he simply walked out the door, leaving a broken Miles to his racing thoughts.

Unable to face Ana just yet, he began to replay the conversation in his mind. Obviously Adam didn't believe him, and knowing that Ana did only made the rejection hurt worse. He wondered what had happened when his older self had shown up while he was at Adam's if it had scared Anthony so much. Miles could picture Anthony's gorgeous face and perfect body as if he were looking at a photograph, and he suddenly felt queasy. And then another thought came. Did he say Anthony was his fiancé? Adam was getting married.

The throbbing behind his eyes began so suddenly Miles barely had time to register it as it radiated outward and everything went black.

"Are you okay?"

Miles woke to the sound of Ana's voice. Even in those few words, he could tell she was exhausted. She was standing over him with her long hair falling around her face like a waterfall.

"My head hurts a little, but I think I'm okay."

"I came out of the bathroom, and you were passed out on the couch. What the hell happened? Where's Adam?"

At the mention of Adam's name Miles sat up; it caused his stomach to lurch. He had to close his eyes to keep from vomiting. "It's me." The thought of forming more words than that seemed impossible.

Ana's face was a mask of confusion until Miles's words registered.

"Oh, thank God," she said, sitting down beside him on the couch. She began to rub the back of Miles's neck, and he immediately relaxed into her touch. "You were gone for a whole day this time."

"Shit," Miles said. "Honey, I'm so sorry."

Ana waved him off. Her fingers made delicate circles at Miles's hairline; he felt himself falling under their soothing spell.

"That feels nice," he said.

They were silent as Ana soothed Miles's aching head. He could sense that Ana's breathing was shallow and harsh.

"What's wrong?" he asked, realizing as soon as he said it, it was a stupid question. *Everything* was wrong.

"Adam was here," she said softly. "That's not what's wrong, not really. But you were so excited to see him, and I felt like I didn't matter."

"Of course you matter," Miles said, turning to face her. Ana's hand fell from his neck into her lap. He captured her face in his hands. "I love you, Ana. Never forget that."

"I know," she said. "Just sometimes it's hard. When you were seventeen, you and I were *just* becoming friends. This version of you treats me like the enemy."

"Well, can you blame me? You were terrifying in high school." Miles's attempt at levity fell flat. Ana's expression remained pained. "I'm sorry, honey. I'm just trying to lighten the mood a bit. I wish I could remember what I did so I could make it right."

Ana looked at him and smiled. "It's okay," she said. Miles noticed the smile didn't reach her eyes. "You're here now, and that's what matters. Are you hungry? I could make something." She stood up and crossed to the kitchen. The sounds of her opening cupboards and drawers soon drifted from the other room.

Miles could tell she needed to keep busy, so he let her putter. He dropped his head to the back of the sofa and closed his eyes as he waited for his headache to subside. He wondered what had happened since his younger self had shown up, but realized it didn't matter. It was obvious he had left chaos in his wake, and Miles was left to pick up the pieces.

MONDAY, JANUARY 22, 2001 · 9:07 P.M.

The darkness closed in around him, as the sound of footsteps came closer and closer until he could see the shadowy outline of feet beneath the door. Miles closed his eyes tight, hoping tonight would not be one of those nights, that tonight he would be spared the embarrassment. He held his breath and waited. After what seemed like an eternity, he heard the telltale scrape of metal on metal as the doorknob twisted and the door creaked open, an ominous click of the door closing and then silence.

Miles's whole body tensed as he braced himself for what was coming. He could feel his heart beating at a manic pace; his palms began to sweat, and then blackness came. Nothing. Only peace.

WEDNESDAY, MAY 6, 2020 · 10:06 A.M.

"So you said you think you had a flash of a memory?" Dr. Benson's head tilted so that her short, bottled-blonde hair fell unevenly to her shoulders. It made her look much younger, and that made Miles feel vulnerable. "Something that you hadn't remembered before?"

Miles nodded. "I was in a dark room on a bed. I was staying with my aunt and uncle, and I think my parents were on vacation or something. Wow, that just came back to me. They were in Bermuda, second honeymoon. I was staying with my dad's sister." He paused. The memory was fuzzy, and the more he tried to pull it into focus the harder it became to make everything line up properly. "I was so afraid." His voice sounded tinny and distant in his own ears.

Dr. Benson sat up straighter. "Of?" she prompted.

Miles shook his head. "I... "

When he didn't continue, Dr. Benson prompted him. "Take your time. Just let yourself feel it."

But the memory was vague. He remembered the darkness and the panic but little else. Sweaty palms, perhaps, and a sense of not wanting to be left alone in the spare bedroom all night. He could suddenly see the creepy taxidermied animals—ducks, rabbits and other small game—and there was the stale smell of... something. No, that was somewhere else. The bed in the dark room was in another place. Or was it?

"I think I was afraid of the dark," he said with a shrug. "It's a little fuzzy, like déjà vu or something. You know, like when you wake from a dream and you can remember the feeling but not the details. It's like that."

She nodded. "It's not uncommon for someone to only remember bits and pieces at first, but what's important is your mind is allowing you to access your repressed memories. Whatever your younger self is protecting you from is surfacing. It may only be a matter of time before we know what it is."

The thought terrified him. As much as he wanted to be cured of his time travel condition, Miles was worried about what might be uncovered. If it was so awful he had blocked it out, why should he be so keen to remember it? His focus turned to the sole of Dr. Benson's shoe, scuffed and worn. From the pattern of wear, it was obvious she walked on the outside of her feet and put more weight on her right foot. It helped to think of her as a person with flaws when he was vulnerable like this. Miles looked up and took in her expectant expression.

"I'm not sure I can handle that," Miles said.

Her face softened, and she let her pen rest on the notepad across her lap. He liked her better when she wasn't taking notes or studying him intently. "Miles, human beings are amazing creatures. We can handle a lot, but sometimes we develop unhealthy tools to deal with the traumas of life. Those tools can work for a time, but then we need to learn *new* tools that will help us to become the people we were meant to be. And it's important to remember that you can consciously work through all of that, and the good news is, I'm here to help you. All of you."

Logically, Miles knew what she was saying was the truth, but the idea of facing whatever his mind had blocked from his consciousness was something he wasn't sure he was prepared for.

FRIDAY, MAY 8, 2020 · 11:54 A.M.

Ana had been unsettled since Miles had returned to himself. Even though his younger version hadn't made an appearance in over a week, she found herself waiting for the other shoe to drop, for her world to come crashing down around her once again, leaving her broken and alone.

Since Adam had shown up, she and Miles had had no contact with him and had settled into the idea that maybe that was the end of the story. For his part, Miles had become even more obsessed with finding a cure. He had doubled his sessions with Dr. Benson to twice a week and took weekly trips to the research lab in Gainesville to get updates from the genetics professor whose research had devoured most of Miles's trust fund.

Once they had decided theirs was no longer a marriage of convenience, Ana relinquished her claim on the promised half of Miles's inheritance. She considered it *their* money now and they both had equal access to it. Of course, Miles dipped into it most frequently, paying doctors and researchers and psychics to tend to his mental state. She'd never begrudge Miles his treatment, but she couldn't help but resent where all that money was going.

The long hours she worked were for her own peace of mind rather than a financial need, but she also knew one day Miles's trust fund would run out, and her career might be the only thing saving them from financial ruin.

"Ahem."

Ana shook off her wayward thoughts. "Oh, Ellen, I didn't see you there. You startled me."

"My apologies, but you weren't answering your chat messages." She nodded in the direction of Ana's computer, where she was logged in but hadn't noticed the blinking icon showing her that a new message had come in.

"I was just thinking, and I must have zoned out. What did you need?"

"Your mother is here," Ellen said, leaning in conspiratorially and lowering her voice to a whisper. "I didn't know if you were expecting her so I told her you were in a meeting."

"Let her in," Ana said. "We're having lunch."

Ellen looked disappointed there wasn't more to it than that, but she escorted Ana's mother into the office and offered her a drink.

"I tell you before. Nothing for me." She turned to Ana, but then realizing how brusque she had been, added, "Thank you."

Ana's mother, Julia, had a deep, rich voice that was thick with her native Colombian accent: her consonants flowed musically; her vowels were soft and lilting. She never missed an opportunity to correct anyone who mispronounced her name with the Americanized hard J sound, telling them firmly, "In my country, the J make the H sound. Hoo. Hoo." When they were children, Ana's older sister had always giggled and said, "*Mami*, you sound like an owl." Monica would then flap her wings and hoot around the room while Ana laughed and egged her on.

"*Mija*," Julia said, using the endearment that Miles always found so amusing. His own mother only called him by his name, or when he was younger, my baby boy, but endearments other than the occasional "honey" were not something that were tossed around lightly in his family. Everyone in Ana's family was referred to by an endearment and a nickname, as well as their own name.

"Hey, Mom. I'll just be a few minutes." She knew her mother hated being called Mom, but Ana had agreed to lunch before Miles's most recent episode, and now she wished she had canceled. She busied herself with menial tasks, hoping to steel herself for her mother's inevitable barrage of questions. *How is Miles? When are you going to give me little ones? Why you work so much? The husband should work.* It never ended.

Eventually she had to face reality, and they walked to a café around the corner from Ana's office.

Her mother, however, was unusually quiet, taking careful bites of salad and watching Ana intently. After several minutes of silence, Ana could no longer bear it. "Okay, what's up? You haven't said a word and you keep staring at me like I have mustard on my face."

"Nothing, Ana. I am enjoying my lunch."

Ana raised an eyebrow and leveled her gaze. "Come off it. There's something you're not saying. Out with it."

Her mother exhaled an exaggerated sigh. "*Mija*, you look so *flaca*. It is not healthy to be this skinny if you want to have babies."

"Oh my God." Ana covered her eyes with her hand. "You are unbelievable, Mother. This is about grandchildren?"

Julia reached across the table and stroked her daughter's forearm. "When I was your age Monica was already three years old and I was pregnant with you."

"Things are different now, and anyway, Miles and I don't want children."

That wasn't totally true. They had never talked about it; nearly every conversation they had was about his dissociative disorder and how soon it would be cured. Ana never brought it up because she knew that while Miles's future was uncertain, neither of them could properly care for a child.

Julia waved her hand in the air. "Eh, you will change your mind."

"Mama, that's not—"

But Ana didn't get to finish her rebuttal because her mother nudged her shoulder and pointed toward the door.

"Is that your friend?"

Ana looked around, but didn't see anyone familiar; the waiter at the next table was blocking her view of the hostess station. "Who?"

"You know, the flower one."

Ana turned back to her mother. "What flower one?"

"Her," Julia nodded in the woman's direction. A short, plump blonde-haired woman was walking toward them, listening to the loud woman she was with.

"Dahlia!" Ana cried.

The woman turned; her long, wavy hair fanned out behind her, and she smiled when she recognized them. She had put on weight since the wedding, but still looked exquisite. Ana stood to hug her.

"Mrs. Espinosa, it's so good to see you!"

"Hello, dear." Julia went back to her salad and gave Dahlia a sideways glance.

"You look great! I haven't seen you in so long!" Dahlia said. She had a way of making every sentence sound like an exclamation even when she wasn't excited. "How is Miles these days? Still being treated for—"

Ana made a throat-slitting motion, but it was too late; the damage had been done.

"Is Miles sick?" her mother asked, turning to Ana.

Ana glared at Dahlia, who mouthed a pained "sorry."

Her heart began to race. She had confided in Dahlia last year at her bachelorette party, after one too many cocktails, that Miles was seeing a therapist for depression. It was a half-truth, but she had needed to talk to someone and it was at least truth-adjacent. She was not about to tell her mother that her husband had serious emotional problems, so she told her the "other" truth. "He broke his arm, *mamá*. Nothing to worry about."

Julia speared a tomato and chewed thoughtfully. Ana knew that wouldn't be the end of it.

"I should get back to my friend," Dahlia said, still looking contrite. "But call me, we should grab drinks! The boys can come too! It'll be fun. Bye, Mrs. Espinosa!"

They hugged again, and Ana sat down, draped her napkin across her lap and took a sip of her water.

"Why did you not tell me that Miles was sick?" Ana's mother had placed her fork beside her plate and folded her hands on the table in front of her.

"I told you, it was nothing. Plus, his parents were in town, and work was crazy. It just slipped my mind." She tapped a haphazard rhythm on the table, flicked at her straw wrapper, wiped a crumb to the floor. Then she returned to tapping.

"I would have sent a card."

"It's fine, really."

"That is not the point."

"Then what is the point? That I don't call you with every little problem? That my husband is clumsy? That I'm so stressed I can barely remember my own name? What?"

"I will not be talked to this way." Julia stood and dropped her napkin over her plate. "You call me when you can be respectful."

"Mama," Ana said, turning in her chair. But it was no use. Julia walked away quickly and left Ana with her guilt and the beginning of a dull headache.

TUESDAY, JULY 24, 2018 · 3:46 P.M.

Ana stroked the blade of the knife with her index finger. The cold, unyielding steel caught the light and flickered brightly, causing her to squint. All it would take was a couple of simple cuts; the blood would flow out of her like a river, and then peace would come.

Her sister's funeral had been beautiful; family had come from Colombia, and all of their friends had been there, but still Ana felt empty and alone. Everything seemed pointless without Monica. Something had to give.

She raised the knife slowly to her thumb and pressed down. She ran her skin across the blade and watched as the thin line turned red, as her blood pooled in an elegant curve around the cut. The knife was freshly sharpened.

The bathroom floor was cold beneath her bare legs. She had rolled up the bathmat so she wouldn't get blood on it and left her black dress draped across the bed in her childhood bedroom. Now, in only her bra and panties, she sat and stared at the fading linoleum and let the tears fall. She didn't bother wiping them from her cheeks. What did it matter how she looked? Soon her eyes would be dead and cold like the rest of her. Like Monica.

Leaning against the side of the tub, she laid her arm on her thigh with her palm facing up. She could just make out the veins beneath the surface, blue and pulsing with life. She turned the knife over in her right hand, bringing the blade in line with her arm.

A knock at the door startled her, followed by her mother's voice. Ana froze with the knife hovering just above her skin. "I'll be out in a minute," she called.

She let the knife fall to the floor.

FRIDAY, MAY 8, 2020 · 9:13 P.M.

"Ana, are you in there?" Miles's voice sounded tinny and hollow through the bathroom door. She had been soaking in the tub for, well, she'd forgotten how long, but the sun had long ago set, and her feet had finally stopped aching.

"I'm in the tub, babe. Come on in," she called out. She pulled herself up so her neck and shoulders were out of the bubbles and felt her joints crack and pop as she shifted.

Miles peered around the door. "Lunch with your mom didn't go too well, huh?"

Ana motioned for him to come in.

"Not really, but it was a rough day over all. What about you? How did your session with Dr. Benson go?"

He sat on the edge of the tub and dipped his hand into the water, swirling the bubbles around with his fingers. "She thinks I'm remembering stuff, which is good I guess."

"Honey, that's great," Ana said. If Miles was remembering that meant they were one step closer to being finished with this whole mess. She wondered what they'd do with all their free time. Maybe travel through Europe as they'd always wanted or take a cruise to Alaska. See the Great Wall.

"Earth to Ana," Miles said, nudging her with his damp hand.

"Sorry, I must have zoned out. What did you say?"

"Just wanted to know what you wanted for dinner."

"Oh, I'm not hungry. Can we just curl up and watch some bad TV?"

"Sure, babe. Just let me get changed."

"Not yet," she said, reaching out a hand. The air felt cool on her warm, wet arm. Her fingers slid across Miles's cool skin. "Keep me company?"

"I'll do you one better," he said, tugging his shirt over his head to reveal his well-toned midsection. "Room for one more?"

Ana smiled; a familiar heat built in her stomach as Miles continued to undress. With each inch of skin she felt the day's stress melting away until there was nothing but skin on skin amid bubbles and heat.

FRIDAY, MAY 8, 2020 · 7:18 P.M.

The kick drum pedal squeaked as Adam pumped it with his foot, just hard enough so that it wouldn't strike the bass drum. Practicing in suburbia had its drawbacks, but all in all, his life was good. He and Anthony had made a life for themselves, and he loved it. He loved Anthony.

So why was he daydreaming about Miles? The firm cut of his jaw, where he used to have baby fat. His neatly cropped hair that always grew faster than he could manage. Those deep brown eyes that held more promise than one could imagine from such a dark sea. He looked taller, more filled out. Perhaps he was; it had been years after all. Seven long years that were quickly turning to eight that he hadn't heard from Miles, only been given glimpses into his world through friends or the occasional group text, which had gotten rarer in recent years. Seeing him had been like a punch to the gut and a deep inhale all at once. He didn't know what to make of what he was feeling.

On top of that, Miles still believed he was time-traveling. How could that be?

Between troubling thoughts, Adam tapped out a rhythm on practice pads, mimed cymbal crashes and squeaked out the bass line with a worn pedal.

"That sounds pretty good," Greg said. "Something new?"

"Nah, just fucking around." He rested his sticks on one of the snares. "You're here early."

"My bird kicked me out. Book club or some shit. Like I can't sit around watching football while she and the other birds talk about Fifty Shades of Whatever. Fucking bullshit, mate. It's just some excuse to get pissed and talk shit about their husbands."

"You do realize you sound even more English when you're pissed off?"

"Whatever. I'm getting a beer. Anthony at home?"

"Yeah, and he's sleeping, so be quiet. He's back on nights again."

"Quiet as a fucking mouse, mate," Greg said, pressing a finger to his lips and walking backward in an exaggerated tiptoe.

By the time he came back with his beer, the rest of Harper's Bell had arrived: Tony, guitar and lead vocals; Greg, bass and ugly rock faces; and Joe, pretty much anything he could make noise with, including a hundred-year-old mandolin he'd found in his grandparents' garage.

Practice proved to be an excellent distraction, and Adam fell into bed that night exhausted but no longer thinking about Miles.

And then his phone rang. Even with the words "unknown number" flashing on the screen, something in his body knew it was Miles before he answered it.

"Hey," the familiar voice said. There was no preamble, no introduction. It was as if they'd talked on the phone the day before.

"Hey," Adam replied. "You feeling any better?"

"Am I myself, you mean?"

Adam didn't respond. What could he say? *I'm sorry you're "time-traveling" again*, with the air quotes audible in his voice as they both tried not to think about how and why they'd broken up?

After an uncomfortable silence, Miles cleared his throat. "Look, I just wanted to call to apologize. My younger self can be pretty overzealous, and I probably should have warned you that he had resurfaced and was asking questions about you."

"You can't be held accountable for the actions of an alternate-universe version of yourself, can you?"

"That's not—Never mind. I just wanted to apologize for showing up unexpectedly and also for freaking you out."

"I wasn't freaked out."

"Well, whatever it was that caused you to drive halfway across the state to see me. I'm sorry."

Miles sounded agitated and embarrassed. He was probably chewing on the skin around his fingernails. Sure, Adam hadn't expected the time travel thing to come up again, but he wasn't scared or disgusted. He didn't want Miles to think that he was.

"I was worried about you," Adam said before he could chicken out.

The silence on the line stretched out for what seemed like hours.

"I'm fine," Miles said finally. His voice was quiet and barely audible.

"I'm glad to hear it."

"Yeah, well anyway, I just wanted to apologize. So..." He trailed off.

"Miles, it was good to hear from you."

"Bye, Adam."

The phone beeped twice, indicating Miles had terminated the call, and Adam sat staring at his phone until the screen went black and he was in complete darkness. He didn't remember falling asleep.

SATURDAY, MAY 9, 2020 · 10:47 A.M.

After the fifth ring, Adam hung up, chickening out for the third time in the last hour. But this time, the phone rang back. He glanced at the screen to see it was the number he had just called.

"Shit."

Against his own better judgment, he swiped his thumb across the screen. Before he got the phone to his ear, the voice on the other end screeched, "Listen, asshole, if you don't quit calling me I'm going to look you up and key your fucking car!"

Startled, Adam struggled to respond.

"Did you hear me?"

"Ana, it's me," Adam said finally.

"Adam?" she asked, her voice suddenly much more calm and at a normal pitch.

"Sorry. I was... Well, I don't know, but I'm sorry."

"Is everything okay?"

Adam ran a hand through his hair and lay back on his queen-sized bed. The pillows still smelled of Anthony, and the bed was unmade, but the sheets were cool and comforting.

"Yeah, I um... is Miles okay?"

Ana's breathing was the only sound that indicated she hadn't hung up. Adam waited for her to speak, not wanting to push her.

"How much do you know?" she asked finally.

"He told me about the time travel when we were kids. He brought it up again last week when I came by."

Ana sighed, weary and resigned.

"He's such a mess, Adam," she sobbed. "I probably shouldn't be telling you any of this, but it's so hard with no one to talk to, and the doctor? She thinks he's making up the time travel stuff. I just feel so alone, you know? And my mom, my fucking mom. She keeps asking about grandkids, like that's the only thing I have to worry about. Meanwhile, I'm supporting us almost entirely, and Miles is stuck on getting back in touch with you. I just can't fucking deal anymore."

She broke off in muffled sobs; the line crackled with each breath she took.

"Hey, hey... it's okay," Adam soothed. He knew it was far from okay, but what else could he say? His words could do little to soothe the pain that was obvious in Ana's voice. "Can I do anything?"

Another sigh. "I don't know."

"Does he have a diagnosis?"

"Yeah, Dissociative Identity Disorder. You know, alternate personalities? The doctor says the time travel is just how his manifests."

"Well, you have to admit, the time travel thing seems kind of far-fetched."

"But how could he know stuff, Adam? Remember in high school? He did it all the time. Don't you remember?"

He remembered. "Could be lucky guesses."

"Maybe. It's not important, anyway. I just want him to get better."

"Me too. I'm sorry if I upset you."

She sniffed. "You didn't."

"I'm here if either of you need anything, you know." He thought he heard Ana hum in acknowledgment. "Miles called me yesterday to apologize," he added as an afterthought.

"Miles called you?" Her tone had changed; she no longer sounded vulnerable.

"Just to apologize. I thought you should know." Adam traced the edge of the sheet with his finger and watched the color change in the shifting sunlight pouring in through the blinds.

"How did he sound?"

Nervous. Wonderful. "Good. He sounded good." Adam paused and took a deep breath. "Ana, are *you* seeing anyone? I know Miles has a therapist he sees regularly, but do you?"

"I'm just so busy. And anyway, it's Miles who has the serious problems."

"Therapy can be really helpful," he said. "It can help you figure out ways to cope and even protect yourself from further trauma."

"You sound like you have personal experience."

"Actually I've been in recovery for about five years. Sober for most of it, and the therapy really helps when I am struggling with feeling... I dunno, like I'm not good enough. Or when I feel out of control. It doesn't have to be about some psychotic episode. Depression, anxiety, normal everyday stress—getting counseling for that? Nothing to be ashamed of."

"You sound like a walking twelve-step program," Ana said with a sarcastic laugh.

"Not far from the truth."

His addiction had been insidious; at first he would do a line before a show, throw back a few beers. Then he'd have enough energy to perform. Over time it became more frequent, and then he'd started needing something to wake him up the next day, just to get going in the mornings for his internship at the lab. Then he started on the synthetic stuff because it was cheaper and easier to come by. He'd overdosed and spent a week in a coma before he agreed to go to rehab.

"I didn't know. I'm sorry," Ana said.

"I'm fairly open about it," Adam said. But that was only partially true. He talked about his addiction, but feared revealing the full spectrum of what had happened to him. In fact, he'd never even told Anthony the whole truth. He knew Adam had some trouble with drugs in the past, but he didn't know how bad it had been. If he did, he probably wouldn't keep beer in the house. He also probably wouldn't have let him see Miles.

The heavy drinking had started only a few months after they broke up and continued well into his college years. That was where he picked up pot and eventually coke. He barely managed to graduate from college, and jobs came sporadically. The band was his only other solace. He used the drugs to numb the pain of having fucked up the only good relationship he'd ever had. Because he'd lost Miles.

When he'd finally gotten into treatment, the doctors and counselors made him face those demons, but having Miles back in his life could only mean trouble.

"I just wanted to be on the up-and-up with you, Ana. No secrets. I want you to know I don't share Miles's counterpart's sentiments on our younger days. I am happy with Anthony; Miles has you, and, whether his alternate versions believe it or not, he loves you. It's going to be okay."

"I really hope you're right," she said. "It was good hearing from you."

"You too, and please call me if you need to talk. Even if you choose not to see a therapist."

"I will," Ana promised.

After he hung up, Adam rolled onto his side and inhaled the scent of his fiancé, smiling to himself as the comforting familiarity washed over him. He hoped Miles and Ana were as happy as he and Anthony were. But something poked at the back of his brain, a tiny worrying thought that he hadn't heard the last of Miles yet, and that something big was coming.

SUNDAY, OCTOBER 11, 2015 · 2:48 P.M.

Adam's mouth felt fuzzy and thick, as if he'd been sucking on cotton balls in his sleep. Nearby something beeped just loudly enough to be irritating, but he couldn't find the source of it. As he shifted in the bed to get a better view of the room, the stiff sheets scratched at his bare calves. When was the last time he'd washed his sheets?

His eyes blinked in the blinding light; a vague awareness that he wasn't in his own bed broke the surface of his thoughts, and a millisecond later he realized that was because he was in a hospital bed.

"He's awake!"

"Mom?" His voice sounded scratchy and weak.

"Dad's here too. Don't try to speak," she said, pushing his hair away from his forehead and kissing his brow. "We were so worried, sweetie."

Tears shone in her deep blue eyes; her mousey brown hair fell around her face and shielded Adam from the blinding fluorescent lights. Because he had been adopted when he was just a baby, his parents' features had always fascinated him. What would a mix of their biology have produced if they had not adopted him and his sister from South Korea? Their biological child certainly wouldn't have looked like him. And yet, he had his father's love of spicy foods and his mother's sense of humor. His sister's voice sounded so much like his mom's that he often had to ask who it was when they answered the house phone.

"What happened?"

His mother shared a knowing look with his father that said everything and nothing all at once.

"What happened?" he asked again, trying to sound as forceful as possible without being able to lift his head or raise his voice above a whisper.

"You overdosed," his father finally said. His wire-rimmed glasses sat low on his nose, and he pushed them up before running a hand through his hair. Adam got that from his dad too.

Adam rolled his head away from his father's judgmental glare. He saw his mother shift on the balls of her feet.

"I'll go get the nurse," she said. "Someone should probably check you out." She paused over his bed and kissed his forehead again. "I'm so glad you're back."

"I love you, Mom."

"I love you too, sweetie."

He couldn't bear to look his father in the eye. So he counted the mismatched tiles on the floor and waited for his mother to return.

CHAPTER FOURTEEN
MILES

MONDAY, MAY 11, 2020 · 2:26 P.M.

The road stretched out in front of Miles, straight and gray, lined by acres of longleaf pine. Cars zoomed past; their passengers, focused on reaching their destinations, never noticing the surroundings. But even as a child, Miles had found the towns and scenery rolling by far more fascinating than wherever he and his parents were going. The journey was where he found joy; the destination mattered little. This time, he was in the driver's seat and was on a mission. Because whatever memory he had suppressed was entwined with memories of his father's sister, Miles knew the only way to fill in the blanks was to talk to his parents.

Ana had begged him not to go. Her concern shone brightly in her deep brown eyes, but Miles pleaded with her, told her it was vital to his mental health and to call Dr. Benson if she didn't believe him. In the end, she had relented. She couldn't go with him because she had to work, and he assured her that his parents would call should anything out of the ordinary happen.

Miles hadn't told his parents why he was coming, simply that he wanted to see them. They were probably wondering why he was visiting now, when in the past he had refused to drive to Jacksonville to see them. His parents had wanted to retire near the ocean and left central Florida for the coast just after Miles and Ana married. They lived in a high-end golf-course community that had guards at the gates and identical mailboxes in front of each house. Street signs were low to the ground and inconspicuous so as not to ruin the perfect landscaping. Anyone who entered the community either lived there or had been invited and would know where they were going. The labeled streets were merely a formality, a necessity for mail delivery and emergency vehicles.

Miles wouldn't have told his parents he was coming if he hadn't needed their authorization to get through the gate. A fat, balding man eyed Miles suspiciously as he pulled up to the guard station and gave his name. The shield on the man's sleeve gave him an air of false authority; his paunch revealed his inability to do anything other than dial 911 should Miles be a threat. When he found Miles's name in the computer, he handed Miles a paper pass and smiled at him as the arm lifted and Miles was allowed entrance.

He'd never understood the point of a gated community. The gates only allowed for a feeling of security. Truth was, anyone with a lawn mower in the bed of a truck could gain entrance by pretending to own a lawn service. Cars were still broken into, locked or not. And residents still had to lock their doors, and many of them opted for high-end security systems to protect their high-end lives.

His parents were standing in the driveway when he pulled up, his father's arm around his mother's shoulder. If it weren't for their differences in race, they'd be the perfect picture of white suburban America. Miles never understood why his parents hadn't moved to a more progressive place, but his dad loved to golf and his mother loved the beach. One of his dad's business partners had talked them into buying an older home and renovating before they retired, which turned out to be a great idea because the housing market had spiked, and their house was now worth almost twice what they had paid.

"It's so good to see you," Miles's mother said, pulling him into a tight hug before he was all the way out of the car.

"Let him breathe, Gabrielle. We just saw him a few weeks ago."

"Oh, let me smother him a bit, Mitchell. The last time we saw him he was in the hospital."

Miles's dad slapped him on the back. "Looks like I lost this one, son. You're going to have to endure it."

"I think I'll manage," Miles said, forcing his mouth into an uncomfortable smile.

"I'm makin' lasagna," Gabrielle said. "I know how much you love home-cooked food, and I just know that Ana doesn't have time to cook for you."

"Mom, Ana works really hard supporting us, you know that."

"It wasn't a dig. I just meant—"

"Miles knew what you meant, dear. Let's not argue." Mitch Lawson never did like conflict. He swept away disagreements and feelings the way most people swept crumbs from the kitchen floor: sometimes pushed under the rug, sometimes placed in the trash, but never let anyone know there was a mess in the first place.

Miles's mother disappeared into the kitchen, and his father led him to the living room where they sat opposite each other while Miles stared at his shoes and his father stared at him.

"Here you go, sweetie," Gabrielle said, handing him a cold beer. "Use a coaster, okay?"

He nodded and set the beer down atop one of the dozen coasters that his mother kept on various tables throughout the house.

She took a seat next to his father and smiled warmly at Miles, her eyes expectant. Miles thought it best to cut right to the chase.

"Mom, Dad, what can you tell me about the time I stayed with Aunt Carla and Uncle Bob?"

They exchanged nervous glances.

"What on earth made you think of that?" Gabrielle asked as her hand floated up to tug on her earring. "It was so long ago."

"Well, you know I'm still seeing Dr. Benson. She is helping me recover some of my lost memories." It was best if they didn't know everything, but he figured a little truth couldn't hurt.

"I don't know why you insist on seeing that head-shrinker," Mitch said, his lip curling in disgust. "There's nothing wrong with you. You come from a good family."

"Dad, I didn't come here for a lecture."

"Of course you didn't, sweetie," Gabrielle said. She reached out a hand to Mitch's knee and began stroking soothing circles. Suddenly it came back to him. She used to do that when he was a child. She'd rub circles on his back and sing to him. Miles smiled at the memory.

Focusing on his mother and ignoring his father's harsh glare, Miles tried again. "Would you please tell me what you know about that visit?"

Gabrielle glanced at her husband and took a deep breath. "Well, we don't know much because we weren't there."

"Just tell me what you remember."

She pressed her lips together and met Miles's eyes. "Your daddy and I never got a real honeymoon. He was still in school when we married, and it didn't make much sense to spend what little money we did have on a trip when we had other expenses to worry about. So we waited, and when you were about six we were able to take a cruise. It was after your granddad died, and we'd inherited the money."

"Get to the point, Gabrielle."

"Sorry," she said, patting Mitch's knee. "I always think it's best to start a story at the beginning."

"Miles knows about the damn trip. He wants to know what happened to him at my sister's house." He turned to Miles and raised his brows. "Don't you?"

"Yes, sir." Miles could feel his hands shaking as he raised his hand to his mouth. He nervously chewed on his thumb. He could see his mother restrain herself from chastising him for it, but to her credit, she didn't say anything.

"I don't know if you remember this or not, but you used to have dreams about time travel as a kid."

Miles felt his lips go numb. They knew.

"I remember." His voice sounded raspy and distant.

His parents exchanged a quick glance, but his father continued. "I had told Carla about it at her wedding. We were all drunk as hell and I— Well, there's no excuse. I told her about your dreams." Mitch hung his head; his cheeks had gone pink, and Miles could have sworn he saw his father wipe away a tear. When he didn't continue, Miles's mother picked up where he had left off.

"Well, you see, Bob's brother worked for this company called ChronoCorp that has been researching the possibility of time travel since World War Two."

"I've never heard of it." With all the years of research he'd done, Miles had never even caught a whiff of company called ChronoCorp.

She nodded. "From what I understand it's a very private company. They're not even publicly traded, and it's all privately funded research."

"What does that have to do with my missing memories?" Miles asked.

"Your Uncle Bob called his brother while you were staying with them. Apparently, you had one of your dreams while you were there, and he freaked. Chuck, that's the brother, he had them bring you into the lab and they ran some tests."

"What kind of tests?"

"Um, blood tests, I think," she said. "Sleep studies. I think they watched you sleep a lot and asked you a lot of questions. Bob insisted it was all pretty harmless."

His father took his wife's hand. She gripped it so tightly his dad flinched.

"When we found out about it, though, I was furious," his dad said, his voice sounding strained and rough.

"We threatened to sue," his mother added proudly.

"They offered us a settlement, and we took it. Added it to your trust fund." Mitch was subdued and would not meet Miles's gaze.

"We figured it was for the best," Gabrielle reassured. "Of course, as you know, we haven't spoken to your Aunt Carla or Uncle Bob in about twenty years."

"After that, the dreams stopped and things returned to normal," Mitch added. "But you had lost a lot of memories, and we were worried. So we took you to see Dr. Forsten. He said you'd be fine and that as long as you continued to develop normally, we shouldn't worry about the... what was it he called it?"

"Dissociative amnesia," Gabrielle interjected.

"Right. The doc said it was a normal response to trauma and that you'd outgrow it, or suppress it, but that it wasn't a big deal."

Miles felt his face flush hot. "Not a big deal?" Dad, I've been trying to uncover those memories since I was seventeen, and now you're telling me you knew and you did *nothing* to help me?"

Miles stood up, towering over his parents and wanting to run, but unable to move his feet as his rage burned through him.

"Sweetie, calm down," Gabrielle said. Her eyes were swimming with tears when she looked up at him.

"I will not calm down, Mom. You have been lying to me. My aunt and uncle sent me to be poked and prodded by needles and you didn't think it was important for me to deal with that? And Mom, you *knew*. You knew I was still dissociating in high school and you said nothing."

His father shifted his glance to Gabrielle. "What is he talking about?"

Gabrielle stammered as she wrung her hands. "I took Miles to see a psychiatrist because he was complaining about having vivid dreams about the future. I didn't want to worry you. But he's fine now. Aren't you, honey?"

"Oh, I'm just peachy fucking keen! I can't believe you hid all this from me!"

"We were just trying to protect you," Gabrielle cried. "I didn't want to hurt you."

Miles laughed. It sounded hollow and filled with rage. His mother recoiled, and his father stood to face him at eye level.

"Say whatever you need to say, son, but I'm not going to apologize for doing what I thought was best for my family. And neither is your mother."

"Mitch, please..."

"No, Gabrielle. If Miles can't understand that we did this out of love, then he can leave. I will not have us screaming at each other over the dinner table."

Miles shook his head and looked at his mother, who was now studying the carpet. His father had won. His mother would not defy his wishes.

"Fine," he said. "I'll leave." He leaned down and kissed his mother's head. "I'm sorry about dinner."

Just as he was about to close the door behind him, he thought he heard his mother release a gut-wrenching sob. Miles paused, contemplating going back, but then he heard his father say, "He'll be back," and his pride wouldn't let him. He closed the door softly and headed for his car.

The headache didn't hit him until he was on I-95, headed south. He barely had time to pull off the road before everything went black.

MILES FOUND HIMSELF AT AN unfamiliar gas station on a very busy road. He had no idea how he'd gotten there, but could only surmise that he'd once again traveled to a different year, and this time, he was inhabiting his younger body. A glance at his credit cards and driver's license told him it was some time before 2021, so he was still in his mid-twenties. The memories came back in a flood. He'd been to see his parents and was on his way home after finding out about the early ChronoCorp experiments. That meant he didn't know everything yet and was only beginning to scratch the surface. The knowledge of what was to come and what it would do to his younger self, and everyone around him, made his stomach churn. The nausea hit him so suddenly he barely had time to open the car door before he was vomiting into a storm drain.

It had been years since he'd felt the jolt of leaping through time and slamming down inside another version of his own body. He'd almost forgotten what it felt like. He didn't miss it at all.

It only took him a few minutes to devise a plan. If he had shown up in a younger body, that probably meant he was here to change something or set events in motion. He had little time to waste, though. His twenty-something travels were volatile and unpredictable. There was no way of knowing how long he might be here or how much he could accomplish, so he had to be judicious. He needed to find a way to pique Miles's curiosity that wouldn't seem out of the ordinary. He considered leaving a note, but there was no guarantee his younger self would follow through once he was back in his own time. Still, it was a quick option that would at least capture his attention.

As he was searching for a pen, the car's Bluetooth system alerted him to an incoming phone call. Darius.

"Perfect," Miles said to himself. He answered the phone with an overly bright, "Hey, man!"

"Yo. Sorry to bug you. I know you were headed to visit the folks, but I can't find that email you sent me with your final edits. Could you resend it?"

"Uh, yeah sure. No problem," Miles said. He had no idea what email Darius was talking about, but he figured it would get taken care of one way or another. "I was actually about to call you with a small favor."

"What kind of favor?"

"Research. Easy stuff; just a bit of Googling."

"Then why can't you do it?"

"Um, my parents have shitty Internet service, and my phone battery is almost dead. I forgot the charger like an idiot."

It amazed him how easy it was to fabricate a lie. Although, his parents did have shitty Internet. He remembered a long-ago conversation with his dad bragging that his service cost half what the cable company was charging.

"I understand, dude. My auntie won't even pay for it. Must be the generation."

Miles laughed mechanically. He needed to hurry; the dull ache behind his eyes was returning. "I need you to research a company called ChronoCorp." He spelled it out for Darius and told him what little his younger self would know about the company, giving him an excuse about wanting to do a piece on time travel for the thirty-fifth anniversary of *Back to the Future*.

"Sounds like it could be a cool story. Want me to email you whatever I find?"

"That would be great. Thanks, man. I owe you one."

"Nah. It's cool. I don't mind. Just don't forget to send me that story."

Miles promised to send the story, even though he knew it wouldn't happen, and disconnected the call. He took a deep breath, resting his head on the back of the seat. His temples throbbed as he tried to fight off the nausea. It would be only moments before both he and his younger self returned to their own times. He only hoped Darius's research would be enough to get himself to the right place at the right time.

SUNDAY, FEBRUARY 3, 2013 · 3:06 A.M.

The cold steel table reflected the stark fluorescent lighting and the blue-green of the hospital scrubs, giving the whole room an eerie undersea glow. The sterile smell invaded Miles's nose as he tried to focus. He felt unnaturally cold, but unable to move to cover himself. The only thing between him and the rubbery surface beneath him was a thin layer of cotton with a blue and purple crosshatch pattern. A woman with a surgical mask covering all but pale green eyes hovered over him. A wisp of light brown hair poked out from beneath a cap that matched her scrubs. She stroked his brow gently, but the gesture seemed empty through the layer of blue latex covering her hand.

Miles couldn't speak, but he sensed that it wouldn't matter. His body felt small and helpless, a sensation that was familiar to him, though when he tried to think why, the memories skittered away from him.

The woman standing over him spoke words that he couldn't quite make out, but he knew they were soothing. He allowed his eyes to close as he was lulled into a peaceful sleep.

When he awoke Miles was back in his own bed and his proper body, but the memory of the operating room and the fear that had inhabited his body remained.

CHAPTER FIFTEEN
ADAM

It took Adam a few moments to realize the muffled buzzing sound he heard was his phone. He found it wedged between the couch cushions; he'd already missed two calls. When the ring tone stopped, he realized they were all three from the same person: Miles.

The inevitable panic set in—someone had died; Miles was missing and Ana was using his phone; Ana was missing; someone was playing a trick on him. A voicemail alert sounded, and a moment later the phone began to ring again. Adam stared at the device as if it were a completely foreign object, something he'd never seen before. In stunned silence, he listened to the digitized tone that he'd never bothered to change from the factory setting and debated letting it go to voicemail for a fourth time. Instead, he swiped his thumb across the screen and waited for Miles to speak. He worked to calm his breathing, only then realizing that his heart was racing.

"Oh my God, you answered," Miles said, panic radiating from each syllable. "Please don't hang up. Please. Oh my God, I need you." He broke into choked sobs; the phone line crackled as his breath blew out the speaker.

"Shit, Miles, what's wrong? Is Ana okay?"

"I don't know," he choked out between sobs.

"Okay, calm down. Just breathe. Come on, breathe, Miles."

"I can't. Oh my God. I don't know where I am."

Adam hadn't heard Miles this panicked since... since high school. "Miles, you can figure this out. Just think. You've obviously got your phone, right? Use the GPS. It will tell you where you are and how to get home."

"Okay. Yeah, okay. Hang on a sec."

Adam heard some rustling and a muffled beep followed by a relieved sigh.

"I'm in Jacksonville," he said. "I know where I am."

Relief flooded his senses. "Good. Are you going to be okay?"

"Can you stay on the line with me for a bit? I don't want to hang up."

"Uh..." Adam wasn't sure that was the best idea, but what choice did he have? He couldn't leave Miles alone in this state. He was obviously having an episode. He'd never forgive himself if something happened to Miles. "Sure, I can do that."

"I don't know how I got here," Miles said. His voice was barely audible, but Adam could still sense his embarrassment.

"Shh, it's okay. You're gonna be fine."

"I'm glad I called you. I don't know what I would have done if you hadn't picked up."

"Probably called a fifth time," Adam said. Miles's responding laugh sounded strained. Adam let the silence breathe. "Miles, can I ask you something?"

"Of course."

"Why *did* you call me?"

"Honestly, you were the first person that came to mind when I showed up here."

"What do you mean, 'showed up'?"

"In this time. Whatever time it is. I mean..." Miles paused. Adam could hear the road noise over Miles's breathing, so he knew they were still connected.

"I know what you mean," he said finally. "How old are you?"

"Almost eighteen. We're graduating soon."

Adam swallowed hard. He felt as if a golf ball were lodged in his throat.

Miles continued to ramble on. "Dahlia's throwing this big blowout at her place. I guess her parents caved after she got a twenty-one hundred on her SAT."

"I remember that," Adam said, staring off into the distance. They'd all been so worried about their scores, Dahlia most of all, and then she'd blown them all away.

"Yeah?" Adam could picture Miles's smile from the sound of his voice. He couldn't help smiling in return. "What else do you remember?"

Adam's smile fell; the golf ball was back. He couldn't tell Miles what he remembered. It hurt too much—fighting with Miles, kissing Danny, Dahlia finding them, graduation, the phone call when Miles broke it off permanently a week later. He couldn't tell Miles what he remembered because what he remembered was screwing up everything. He cleared his throat.

"Do you really think we should mess with the fabric of time like that?" Adam tried to sound lighthearted, but he knew it sounded halfhearted.

"Do we break up?" Miles's voice was deadpan, resigned, as if he already knew the answer and just wanted Adam to confirm it.

Adam pinched the bridge of his nose between his fingers. He wanted a drink so badly; he tried to level his breathing and said, "I think you should wait and find out for yourself."

"What good is fucking time travel if I can't stop the bad shit from happening?"

Adam didn't have an answer. He didn't think Miles wanted one. "Look, uh... I should probably go. Will you be okay?"

"Yeah, I think so. I have the GPS pointed toward 'home'... whatever that means."

"You're going to be fine."

"I wish I could be sure."

When Adam hung up he could do nothing but stare at the mirror above the fireplace, the ceiling fan reflected on its surface. He watched it go round and round until he could pick out the individual blades. He and Anthony never turned it off, so he couldn't remember how many blades there were. Four? Five? Maybe it didn't matter. Each one was important, all working together toward the same goal, but he couldn't help but notice how each blade was stuck on the same repetitive loop. That fan would continue to spin until they turned it off or the damn thing broke. He wondered which would happen first.

MAY 2012

They visited Miles in the hospital in shifts for the entire two weeks he was there. Dahlia and Lucky took the early afternoons, right after school. Brienne, or sometimes Antonio, would swing by after dinner, usually bringing gossip. Other less loyal friends dropped by once or twice, but Adam never left unless someone forced him out. He got to know the night nurses on a first-name basis—Marie usually brought him ice chips around eleven; Shanay came by with coffee at six, just before he left to get ready for school.

It was supposed to be a relatively simple surgery. A few metal pins in his arm, and Miles would be good as new. But he had stayed comatose far longer than expected. The doctors couldn't figure out why. He should have come out of it when the anesthesia wore off, but he was unresponsive.

Later Miles wouldn't remember being in the hospital, let alone being unconscious for twelve days, so Adam never mentioned it. But he never forgot.

MONDAY, MAY 11, 2020 · 6:07 P.M.

"Babe, you okay?" Anthony's face carried the look of worry like a heavy weight as Adam blinked his eyes open. Anthony was standing over him, and the room was dim and hot.

Adam sat up and ran a hand through his hair; it was damp with sweat. "Just tired, I guess."

Anthony felt Adam's forehead. "You never nap in the middle of the day. You sure you feel all right?"

Adam shrugged off his hand and pushed back the sheet that was tangled around his legs. He must have fallen asleep after Miles called. "I'm fine. What time is it?"

"Just after six. You hungry?"

"Yeah, a little." More than anything, though, Adam's head hurt. For some reason his brain was throbbing as if he had the worst hangover of his life. How could a two-hour nap make him feel this bad? He stood up, and his stomach lurched. Swaying on his feet, Adam took a few stumbling steps into the bathroom and rooted through the medicine cabinet for aspirin.

Anthony appeared in the doorway. "You sure you're okay? You look flushed."

Adam dropped two aspirin in his palm and cupped his palm beneath the running tap. He swallowed the bitter tablets and wiped the water from his face. Anthony was blocking the doorway; his pale blue eyes searched Adam's face. There would be no escaping this. Adam sat on the edge of the tub.

"Miles called."

Tilting his head, Anthony said, "What happened?"

Leave it to Anthony to jump to a reasonable conclusion. He never thought the worst of Adam, or anyone else for that matter; it was one of his best qualities and something that Adam found completely infuriating at times.

"He had another episode. A bad one. He was in Jacksonville with no idea how he got there, and I was the first person he thought to call."

"Whoa," Anthony said. He crossed his arms and leaned against the counter. "Is he okay now?"

"I think so. I told him to use the GPS to get home. I just wish I knew why he did this. And why he keeps contacting me. I'm not encouraging it, I swear."

"I know you're not." Anthony rubbed Adam's shoulder. "He's a troubled guy. Something in him needs comfort, and for whatever reason his brain thinks it's seventeen and so that means you're the one who comforts him."

"Where on earth did you get that psychobabble?"

Anthony shrugged. "I did a little research."

For Anthony, "a little research" usually meant several hours combing websites and forums for information. He loved to research everything from pop culture history to rare medical conditions. Once he looked up a character actor's name online and ended up becoming a minor expert on the Apollo program. That's just how he was, always looking for answers. It was no surprise he had looked up Miles's condition.

"How many books did you buy?" Adam asked.

"Just one," Anthony said with a laugh. "How do you always know?"

"You can't help yourself. It's like you took those stupid high school classroom posters seriously or something: Knowledge is power. You with a little bit of information is like a bodybuilder on steroids. Nothing can stop you."

"I just like to know what I'm up against," he said. "And a little knowledge can help you cope. Did you know that people with DID have alters that reflect their fears? Like if they were abused as a child, they might have an alter that is big and tough, like a bully to defend themselves when they feel threatened. Or if they need to be comforted, they might revert to a child-like state." He paused, making full eye contact with Adam.

"Seventeen's hardly a *child.*"

"My point is, something about you and your time together reassures him. If he was feeling scared or stressed, maybe his brain remembered that and brought out his youngest alter."

"And that doesn't bother you?"

"No," Anthony said. "It's pretty harmless... and kind of sweet." He grinned. "His inner child is pining away for you. Can't say that I blame him."

Adam rolled his eyes. "Stop it. You're being silly. This is serious."

Anthony's expression turned serious. "Does it bother you?"

Adam leaned forward, resting his elbows on his knees. He let his head drop. "Kind of. I mean, it's a lot. You didn't hear the panic in his voice. He *sounded* like a kid. And what if it's not just his inner child that's obsessed with me? Doesn't that mean that a part of him is still in love with me?"

"Okay, honey? You need to calm down. We don't know that he's in love with you. It could just be about comfort. And he's married, like really married. To a woman. This is not your problem, and it's definitely not mine. We don't need to insert ourselves in this. Just because he called you a couple of times, that does not mean it's going to happen all the time."

Adam looked up and smiled, even though it was halfhearted. "You're probably right," he said. "I'm probably overreacting."

"I'd say you're just worried about someone you used to care about."

"I still care," Adam said. "I want him to be happy."

Anthony knelt in front of him and rested his chin on Adam's lap. His eyes held a look of empathy that Adam knew went to his core. "I know you do, babe."

Adam caressed Anthony's cheek. "Thank you for understanding. I swear I don't know how you put up with me."

"Well," he said, drawing out the syllable as he trailed a hand up Adam's inner thigh. "You could make it up to me by cooking dinner."

"I'll do you one better. Let's go out."

"Ooh, big spender," Anthony teased, rising to his feet. "I like the way you think."

"Just put on some shoes, asshole." He swatted at Anthony's rear as he turned, and smiled to himself when Anthony stuck out his tongue. He didn't know why he had been so worried. Anthony was right, this was none of their business. Miles would be okay. He had Ana and his therapist. There was nothing Adam could do, nor was it his responsibility. The only thing he needed to do was take his fiancé to dinner. His stomach growled to accentuate the point. Dinner... and then he'd call Ana to tell her what had happened.

MONDAY, MAY 11, 2020 · 8:12 P.M.

Miles came stumbling through the front door looking disheveled and nervous. His eyes darted about the room as though he were scanning it for threats. Ana immediately recognized that he was having an episode and rushed to him.

"Miles, sweetie, are you all right?"

"I—I think I've been time-traveling again."

"How old are you?" The question sounded so silly, and yet it was always the question she started with because it was the only way to know for sure which version of Miles she was dealing with.

"Seventeen," he replied in a robotic tone. "I remember this place." His eyes took in the room, resting on Ana's face after a moment.

"You were here a few weeks ago," she said.

"It's been months for me," Miles replied. "Nearly a year."

"Shit." Ana led Miles to the sofa and eased herself down beside him. "What happened?"

"I don't know. I was in chem lab and then suddenly I was in a car, parked at a gas station. I'd never been there before."

"You were headed to see your mom and dad—the older you, I mean. Did you ever get there?"

"I don't know. Do they live in Jacksonville?"

"How did you—?"

"That's where I was. I called Adam and he said to use the GPS. He calmed me down and everything. He's so sweet."

Miles got a dreamy look in his eyes and grinned at her. It made her sick to her stomach.

"What else did Adam say?"

Miles shrugged. "That everything is going to be okay."

"Boy, is he way off base," Ana mumbled.

"What?"

"Never mind. If you want, we could try some techniques Dr. Benson taught me—to try to get you back to your own time, that is."

"That couldn't hurt. What do we do?"

"We need to try to get you to integrate your different selves," she said, looking him square in the eyes. "I need to talk to my Miles. The one who lives here and is twenty-five years old. Can you ask him to come out to talk to me?"

Miles looked at her in confusion. "He's not here," he said. "That's why I need your help."

"He's not here," she said. "But he's in there." She pointed to his head, hoping he would understand. She knew that Miles and this alter believed he was time-traveling, but Dr. Benson said that it was possible for them both to exist in his head at the same time. "Just work with me," she implored. "I think you may have just shoved him to the side when you showed up."

"Like he's in here with me?" Miles rolled his eyes up as if he were trying to see into his own head.

Ana tried not to laugh.

"Sort of, I mean, where does he go when you come here. Does he end up in your body?"

"I—I guess I never thought about that. But I'm usually unconscious during episodes, so I don't think he's in my body."

"Well, then it's possible he's still here with us, isn't it?"

Miles looked thoughtful. "I guess that's possible."

Ana felt a small satisfaction and smiled reassuringly. "Okay, then. Close your eyes and see if you can reach him. Imagine you're in a quiet room together—just the two of you—talking. Can you see him?"

"Uh, I think so?" Miles opened one eye and quickly closed it again.

"You're not taking this seriously."

"I am. I just don't know how to contact someone who isn't here."

"Ugh, I give up!" Ana stood and threw her arms up.

"I'm sorry, Ana. I want to go home. I promise I do."

She suddenly felt guilty and wanted to reassure him. "I know you do, sweetie." She stroked his head gently. "Are you hungry? I could order a pizza."

"That sounds great. I don't think I've eaten."

She dug her phone out of her purse and took it into the other room. But instead of dialing the pizza place, she called Dr. Benson.

"Hello, Dr. Benson? It's Ana, Miles Lawson's wife. Do you have a moment?"

"Hello, Ana. Yes, of course. I told you you can call me at this number. What's the matter?"

"Younger Miles is back," she said. "I tried some of the techniques we discussed but I couldn't even draw my Miles out. I don't know what to do."

"It's frustrating, I understand." Her tone was condescending. "But Miles must feel safe to return. If he thinks you are angry with him, or frustrated, he may retreat further. Something triggered his dissociation, and if this is the younger alter, he probably needs comfort. Go talk to him. Reassure him. Then try the technique again."

"And if that doesn't work?"

"I may have another solution," she said. "An inpatient facility that specializes in DID."

"A facility? You mean you want to commit him?"

"It would only be temporary, but it would give him around-the-clock care and therapy. It might help him work through the trauma faster, especially if something is regularly triggering his switching."

Ana felt her stomach lurch. Committing her husband seemed like a betrayal. What if he hated her for it?

"I know this is overwhelming," Dr. Benson said. "But please understand that inpatient care is a last resort. I don't want to play our trump card unless we have to. Miles should return to his host personality soon. In the meantime, be patient and make him feel safe… loved."

"I think I can do that."

"I know you can."

Ana wasn't so sure.

TUESDAY, MAY 12, 2020 · 7:35 P.M.

Ana had taken the day off work to make sure Miles didn't do anything reckless. Or maybe it was for her own sanity. His younger self had never stayed this long before and she was practically climbing the walls with anxiety. They spent most of the day working on the therapy techniques Dr. Benson had suggested, and Ana was exhausted. Miles was a fidgeting mess of nerves, tapping relentlessly and pacing whenever Ana tried to talk to *her* Miles. Nothing worked.

After dinner she had convinced him to take a shower and was now sifting through Miles's emails trying to make sure her husband didn't come back to a mess of work from Darius and a bunch of unanswered messages. A lot of it was junk mail, but there were three emails from Darius. And one from his mother. Ana opened the first message from Darius, a request for a file to be sent to him. Easy enough. Miles was pretty good at filing and naming his files so she found it quickly and sent it off. The second email was a follow-up to the first, but the third made her lean forward in her chair.

"Info on ChronoCorp," she said to herself. "What the hell is ChronoCorp?"

It proved to be a moot question because the answer, parts of it anyway, was right in front of her.

"Dude, this company you had me look into is crazy. The only things I could find on the Internet came from fringe conspiracy theory groups. It's some X-Files, Area 51 shit, man. ChronoCorp has been studying time travel since WWII, but hardly anyone has heard of them. They operate in secret, hiding behind a parent company called Tempus Labs that studies the long-term effects of transcontinental travel on aging. Crazy, right? There's no major media coverage on them, but some blogs track them and post spec and rumors. According to this one blog, TimeNet (they've been online since 1992), ChronoCorp is based right here in Florida. So I used some of my connections with the university to dig up some more info. Apparently, they have a lab in Merritt Island that is disguised as a research facility. It's previously been a..."

"I can't find anything to sleep in," Miles muttered. His eyes were downcast, and he was self-consciously holding a towel about his waist.

Ana slammed the laptop shut.

"I'll find you something. Miles usually sleeps in his underwear, but I guess..." She trailed off. She couldn't talk to a seventeen-year-old about underwear. Even if he was in the body of her twenty-five-year-old husband.

Ana followed him into the bedroom and dug an old pair of sweatpants out of Miles's bottom drawer. She laid it on the bed.

"If you want a T-shirt, there's a whole drawer full of them. Take your pick."

She turned to go back to the kitchen.

"Thanks," Miles said.

Ana offered him a weak smile. "I'll sleep in the guest room tonight."

"You don't have to do that. I'm the guest. You should have your bed."

The night before, Miles had fallen asleep on the sofa after sobbing in her arms for an hour, so Ana had left him there. He'd slept in his clothes and she'd taken a long, hot bath before retreating to their bed. But tonight, she didn't want to sleep there again without Miles.

"This bed is more comfortable," she said. "And if my Miles comes back, I don't want him thinking I made him sleep in the guest room."

Her tone was firm, and she knew she sounded far more harsh than she intended, but she was too tired to care. Besides, she wanted to get back to that email and find out why Darius was researching some lab for her husband. Was he hiring more researchers?

"Goodnight, Ana," Miles said. His voice was soft and sweet in a way that made her heart ache. Ana missed her husband. This version was a cheap copy, a false idol of the man she loved. If she didn't stare too long or listen to the timid cadence of his voice, she could almost fool herself into thinking he was there, instead of... Well, she didn't know where her husband was, but this unwanted twin was not him.

"Goodnight."

When the bedroom door clicked closed, she leaned against it and listened to her own breathing. Why would Miles have Darius research a time travel company?

WEDNESDAY, JUNE 3, 2020 · 10:11 A.M.

"Miles, how do you feel about undergoing hypnosis?" Dr. Benson's smile was cautious, making Miles uncomfortable under her expectant gaze. He was already feeling as though he had no control over his body. The idea of being hypnotized was not appealing in the least.

"Is that safe?" Ana asked.

Miles had refused to let Ana leave his side. She might not love him the way she loved his older self, but at least she made him feel safer than he felt when alone with Dr. Benson.

"It's controversial among the psychiatric community," she said. "But I think Miles might benefit from it, especially in this altered state." She shifted her smile from Ana to Miles and then back again. As usual, her demeanor suggested that their permission was merely a formality, and that she knew best regarding Miles's treatment.

"It couldn't hurt," Miles said finally. "What else have I got to lose? I'm already out of my time, and it has been three weeks."

Ana gripped his hand. "If it gets you and my Miles back in the right body, I'm all for it," she said.

Out of the corner of his eye, Miles thought he could see Dr. Benson give Ana a peculiar look, but he couldn't be sure.

"Are there other options?" Miles asked.

This time Ana and Dr. Benson shared a look. Ana quickly looked way, but Dr. Benson shifted her cautious gaze to Miles.

"We could look at other options, but I'd like to try this first," she said. "I promise I won't make you do anything strange like pretend you're a chicken."

Ana laughed, but it sounded forced. She turned to Miles; her eyes softened as she spoke. "I can stay right here and hold your hand if that would make you feel better."

Miles nodded reluctantly. "Okay, if you stay with me," he said to Ana.

Ana squeezed his hand and turned to Dr. Benson. "Okay, let's do this."

"Okay, Miles, I want you to relax. This will be a pleasant and helpful experience. If anything you are wearing or have in your pockets is too tight or weighing you down, I want you to remove it and get yourself into a comfortable position."

Miles emptied his pockets and took off his belt. "Okay," he said, gripping Ana's hand more lightly.

"Close your eyes and inhale deeply. Hold on to that breath for five seconds and then exhale as slowly as you can."

Miles's eyes drifted closed, and he did as Dr. Benson asked.

"Keep doing that five more times."

He felt Ana squeeze, but it was less noticeable.

Dr. Benson continued, "With each inhale, you bring more oxygen into your body. With each exhale, your body relaxes more and more."

With each breath, Miles felt his muscles go slack, felt his mind drift pleasantly without conscious thought.

"As you continue to breathe easily and freely, feel yourself becoming more calm and peaceful." Dr. Benson's voice was like a cloud of peace. He'd never noticed how soothing it was.

"I can see that you are moving into a very deep, peaceful state of relaxation. With every word that I say, you will keep relaxing more peacefully, not caring how relaxed you are, just happy that you are becoming more calm, more peaceful and more at ease. Your breath is easy and free.

"As you relax, I want you to know that your subconscious mind will always be aware of what I'm saying to you, so you will not need to consciously listen to my voice in order to hear my words. Your subconscious mind, and all of your inner mind, can hear and receive everything I tell you, and your conscious mind can relax completely."

Dr. Benson's words were coming to him only as feelings. He no longer registered each word as she said it. His body felt relaxed; Ana's hand rested firmly in his own.

He wasn't sure if it was real or not, but he thought he could hear birds chirping and feel a cool breeze on his face. In the distance, a stream trickled between the trees, falling over rocks and branches.

"Now I want you to imagine yourself lying in a comfortable position. You are outside and it is a clear, perfect day."

The sunlight shining through the trees hit his face, and it was warm, although the breeze was keeping him cool. Miles began to feel sleepy.

"You are feeling calmer, more relaxed and more secure." Dr. Benson's voice sounded far way, but he knew what she was saying, even without hearing her words. An overwhelming feeling of positivity washed over him, a feeling he hadn't experienced in a very long time.

"I am calm, secure and relaxed," he thought. "Comfortable, at ease. I am in control of myself, responsible for my body."

Dr. Benson's words returned, far away as if through a tunnel, but Miles felt safe and secure; there was no anxiety, no distress.

"Your subconscious mind, and all aspects of your mind, can now review and examine what has caused you to dissociate, and you can assess that information and work out a solution that is pleasing to you."

Miles saw a flash of something in the corner of his eye; he could feel his heart rate increasing, but he was still lying on the ground in the woods, wasn't he?

The stream stopped flowing. The birds were silent, but he could still feel the cool earth beneath his body. Or was that a cold, metal surface?

"I want you to visualize a screen where you can watch yourself and replay your trauma. You are safe. There is no danger here, only the visual of a memory. This screen can go forward or back; it can go at a normal pace or very quickly. You can control the emotions at any time by listening to my voice and anchoring yourself to the present. Nod if you understand me."

Miles nodded.

"Now, I want you to view the screen and go back to the trauma you experienced as a child. I want you to view this experience from the first moment you experienced it."

Miles felt his arms stiffen. The relaxation began to fade.

"Remember, this is only a memory," Dr. Benson soothed. "You are simply feeling the experience. Allow yourself to be aware of its various elements. What are the sounds, smells, tastes and touches? Don't be afraid of the fear you feel."

He could see an elderly man in a white coat looming over him. The man smelled antiseptic, almost too clean, like bleach. It burned Miles's nose. His gray hair stuck out from beneath a blue cap; his face was covered by a mask that only revealed watery hazel eyes that were partially obscured by wire-rimmed glasses. Miles recognized this man, but could not remember his name. They had spoken on several occasions, enough that Miles could remember his thick, southern accent—a drawl that made him sound as if he were misplaced in time, as if he were from another era. He leaned close, and Miles could smell the tobacco on his breath. It made him nauseated. Miles sensed another person in the room but could only see a glimpse of hospital scrubs and a flash of metal instruments. His eyes darted around the room but it was too bright; everything looked faded. His heart began to race; his palms grew sweaty.

Even through his fear, Miles felt safe, as if he knew the experience was only a dream and would soon be over. He allowed himself to feel the fear and realized it could no longer harm him. And then it was gone.

Suddenly the birds returned, and the stream began moving again. He heard Dr. Benson's words sneak in at the edge of his consciousness.

"When your inner mind understands what has caused your trauma and realizes that it is okay for you to get rid of the problems it caused, one of the fingers on your right hand will lift toward the ceiling and will remain up until I tell it to go back down."

Miles didn't move. He still wasn't sure what he was seeing.

After some moments, he heard Dr. Benson speak again. "Okay, Miles, I want you to picture your current life on that same screen. Can you see it?"

Miles saw Adam sitting on his bed, laughing at something. He was wearing a lightweight gray sweater, and his hair was disheveled. They were completely in love and content. It made him smile. His body felt warm down to his bones.

"Good," Dr. Benson said. "I want you to remember that feeling. Hold on to it. Protect it. I'm going to count from zero to five now. With each number, that feeling will become more and more a permanent part of you—a happy, safe memory that you can access whenever you are feeling scared or anxious. And when I get to five, you will be completely awake, feeling refreshed, content and very aware of what we've talked about."

Miles let the feeling wash over him and when he awoke, he saw Ana and Dr. Benson looking at him expectantly.

"Where's Adam?" he asked.

Ana pulled her hand away and choked back a sob. Dr. Benson looked frantically between them.

"Miles, how old are you?"

"Seventeen," he replied mechanically. The disappointment was evident on both their faces, but the warmth in his bones remained.

Ana's face was anguished. Miles tried to comfort her, but she recoiled at his touch.

"Miles, why don't you wait in the lobby while I chat with Ana for a moment?"

"Okay." He left them alone, looking over his shoulder before he passed through the doorway. He was about to go to the waiting room when he heard his name. He stepped back and pressed his ear against the door.

"Do you really think that's necessary?" Ana asked. She sounded scared.

"I think an inpatient facility might be our best option at this point. He's clearly not capable of facing his trauma in a therapy setting. We may need to take more drastic measures."

"But committing him? I don't know if I can do that!"

He heard Ana sniffle and then muffled words he couldn't quite make out. An inpatient facility? They were going to throw him in a psychiatric hospital. He couldn't believe Ana would betray him like this.

"... Call me next week and we'll go from there."

He could tell by the increased volume of Dr. Benson's voice that they were nearing the door, so he hurried to the waiting room, giving Darlene a cursory smile as he sat down and waited for Ana. His hands were shaking, so he sat on them and shuffled his feet, hoping the movement would hide his nerves. His efforts were unnecessary, though, because Ana wouldn't look at him.

"ADAM, IT'S ME, MILES. UM, I'm sorry for calling like this again, but I don't know who to talk to." He paused for a breath, scratching the back of his head as he tried to find his words. "I hate leaving this on voicemail. It's so impersonal. Could you call me back? Ana wants to commit me. She thinks I'm crazy." He paused again, took another breath. "I'm not crazy, Adam. I'm not, and I think you know that. Just call me back, please. I don't know what to do." He paused again, looked at the picture of him and Ana on the dresser and added, "I love you."

Miles hung up the phone and dropped it on the bed. He and Ana had driven home in silence, her posture tense and unyielding, Miles's emotions in turmoil. He was unsure if he wanted to confront her about what he'd overheard or simply let it go. From the sound of it, nothing had been decided, and *he* would eventually leave. Did it matter if his older self was committed? That wasn't exactly his problem. At least not yet.

If only Adam had picked up.

"Miles," Ana called, knocking on the door. "Are you okay?"

"I'm fine. I think I'm going to take a nap," he said. "Dr. Benson's session really took it out of me."

"Okay. Let me know if you need anything."

Her footsteps echoed down the hall, and he heard the door close on the spare bedroom, Ana's room for the time being, and he let his muscles relax, his body molding to the soft mattress beneath him. He felt so betrayed and so alone. He wanted his mom, or just to go home and be in his own bed.

As if his body knew exactly what it needed, he began to feel the familiar ache behind his eyes that preceded an episode. He closed his eyes and curled into a ball, waiting for the ache to turn to blackness and take him home.

WEDNESDAY, JUNE 3, 2020 · 1:41 P.M.

Adam hung up after listening to Miles's message and stared at the blank screen on his phone, hoping for some sort of clarity amid the chaos. All around him the lab equipment whirred as he shivered from the frigid cold of the air conditioning. It was unusually chilly in the lab today. The outside temperatures were soaring to the high nineties, and the humidity made it nearly impossible to breathe. As a result, someone had turned the thermostat below sixty-five, and most of the women were wearing bulky sweaters under their lab coats. Michaela even had a scarf wrapped around her slender neck. Adam usually appreciated the brisk temperature, but today he felt chilled to his bones, and it wasn't just the cold.

He'd listened to that voicemail three times, and he still didn't know what to do. Should he call Miles back? Should he call Ana and find out what was going on? Should he tell Anthony?

"What's the matter, doll? Trouble with Steve?"

Miles looked up to find Michaela standing over him. Her burnt orange scarf clashed with her strawberry-blonde hair.

"Why do you keep calling him Steve? His name's Anthony. You've known him for three months."

"Adam and Steve... get it?" Michaela grinned broadly, giving him an exaggerated wink that revealed perfectly winged eye liner.

"You are too much," he said.

"So what's the deal, you guys fighting?"

"No, nothing like that. Just an old friend asking me for help. I'm not sure if I should do it."

"Old friend, eh? Like an old boyfriend?" She sing-songed and waggled her eyebrows for effect, causing Adam to roll his eyes.

"That's irrelevant."

"Then what's the problem? He want you to rob a bank or something?"

Adam laughed. "No, nothing like that. It's just a personal problem, and I'm not sure I want to get involved in the drama."

"Ah. Well, that's never fun. What does Steve say?"

"I haven't told him yet."

"So it *is* an ex-boyfriend. I knew it!" Her ID badge swayed on her lapel as she jumped excitedly. The logo turned from its lounging sphinx shape to a blur of green and gold. Michaela had only worked at Tempus Labs for six months, but she had already declared herself Adam's "work wife," ignoring his protests that he was gay and explaining that a "work wife" was simply a good work friend that you talk about all the time outside of work. She had a way of presenting herself that made it impossible to say no, especially when she turned on her Julia Roberts smile. So they had become fast friends, even if their chatter often got in the way of their research.

"Look, I haven't told Anthony yet because I haven't *talked* to Anthony yet. I'm not hiding anything."

She stopped her girlish giggling and sat down next to him; the crinkles around her golden eyes softened as she turned serious. "Well, without specifics I can't offer much in the way of advice, but if you're this broken up about a voicemail, you already know what you want to do; you're just afraid to do it." She stood up and tightened her scarf. "Just my two cents." She shrugged and walked back to her station, glanced over her shoulder at him and offered a friendly smile.

He hated to admit it, but Michaela was right. He knew what he wanted to do; he just had to find a way to tell Anthony.

SATURDAY, JUNE 15, 2013 · 7:16 P.M.

"I wish you'd pick up." Adam sniffed and dragged the back of his hand across his nose, bumping his glasses askew. "I'm sorry. Please call me back."

He hung up and let his arm fall limp to his side. He'd left Miles six messages and a dozen or more texts and he still hadn't responded. He'd even sent him flowers on his birthday. He didn't know what he would do if Miles never called him back. It had been a week since Adam had kissed Danny and everything had fallen apart. He wondered if he could ever make things right.

Danny had called, though, making everything more difficult. Adam wanted nothing to do with him, but Danny insisted on apologizing and asking him if he wanted to hang out—just as friends. Adam knew that would only make matters worse, and yet, he needed someone to talk to. Someone who wasn't also Miles's friend, who could listen to Adam bare his soul without judgment. Dahlia refused to speak to him; Brienne and Antonio had taken to replying in single syllables. Lucky, in his need to be liked by everyone, refused to "take sides," insisting that he was friends with both of them and would not discuss their breakup with either of them. And then there was Miles.

They'd fought again at graduation, and then Miles had refused to look at him, even though they were seated practically next to each other; an alphabetical lottery win they'd been so excited about the week before was now a painful reminder of all they had lost. When the principal had called Adam's name, he'd looked back to watch Miles receive his diploma, but when he offered a smile as Miles descended the steps, Miles had raised his chin and made a sharp turn to walk back to their seats. After the ceremony, Adam had tried to catch up to him, hoping Miles's parents would force him into politeness, but Miles disappeared so suddenly, Adam couldn't find him amid the sea of blue graduation gowns and identical gold tassels.

His sister was the only one who had noticed that Adam wasn't quite himself. She'd cornered him at dinner and made him spill the beans. But instead of offering her brother a shoulder to cry on, she'd chided him for his behavior and told him if she were Miles, she'd never want to see him again. He had no one, and that's why he found himself sitting in a nearly empty Starbucks, spilling his heart out to Danny Dubrow.

"*If he'd just call me, I could explain,*" Adam said.

"*Dude, you've said that three times. I get it.*"

"*I'm sorry. It's just—I know I fucked up, but you think he'd at least let me try to apologize or something.*"

"*I think you may get your chance.*"

Adam sat up, a hint of optimism pecking at the corners of his mind. "*What do you mean?*"

"*He just walked in.*" Danny pointed over Adam's shoulder and nodded in the direction of the door.

As Adam turned, his heart sank. Miles and Dahlia were standing near the counter, glaring at him. As he stood up, he heard Miles say, "*Let's go.*" Adam somehow managed to get to the door before they did and blocked their way. Miles wouldn't make eye contact, and Dahlia just glared.

"*Will you let us by?*" Dahlia pursed her lips and tilted her head.

"*I just want to talk to Miles.*" Adam looked at him, but Miles was focused on the floor with his arms crossed firmly across his chest.

"*He doesn't want to talk to you,*" Dahlia said.

"*Miles, please,*" Adam begged.

Dahlia stepped between them. "*You honestly think he'd talk to you when you're here with Danny? After what happened? Grow up, Adam. It's over.*" She shoved him out of the way and grabbed Miles by the arm. "*Let's go, sweetie.*"

"*But... Miles, please.*" Adam's voice cracked on the last word. He couldn't let Miles go. His body ached with fear that he'd never see him again. "*I love you.*"

Adam's words were cut off by the door closing, and he watched as Miles got into Dahlia's car and buckled his seat belt. He thought he saw Miles wipe a tear from his cheek, but the lights from the coffee shop were causing a reflection on the windshield.

Adam's shoulders sagged, and his arms hung at his sides, as he felt Danny's hand on his shoulder. "*Come sit back down,*" he said.

"*It's over,*" Adam whispered. "*It's really over.*"

Danny stroked his arm; the comforting gesture was awkward and out of character for him. He often slapped people on the back and was obviously comfortable making out with them, but the stuff in between, the little intimacies, those were lost on Danny.

"You wanna go to that gay bar downtown?" Danny asked. "Flirt with some college guys? I'll pay the cover."

"No thanks," Adam said, still looking out at the now-empty parking space. "Can you just take me home?"

"Forget him. One day you'll wonder why you were so hung up on Miles Lawson. I promise."

"No, I won't."

THURSDAY, JUNE 4, 2020 · 6:20 P.M.

Before he even opened his eyes, Miles knew he was in his own bed. The familiar scent of the apple-cinnamon air freshener, the feel of the six-hundred-thread-count sheets, the softness of his down pillow—all of it added up to create an environment he knew well. He reached for Ana, hoping to run his hand through her soft hair, but found empty, cold mattress instead. Opening his eyes, Miles could see the fading sunlight coming in through the blinds, and he realized it was early evening. He stretched, kicking the sheets from where they were stuck to his sweaty legs. Unsure of what day it was, or even the year, he went in search of Ana. He found her in the living room, nose buried in her laptop as she furrowed her brow and mouthed the words of whatever she was reading.

"Hey," he said. He scratched his head nervously as he waited for her to look up.

Her expression was harsh for a moment before her lips stretched into a warm, inviting smile.

"Is it really you?" she asked. Miles nodded as Ana stood, leaving her laptop on the coffee table and rushing across the room to him for a hug. "I thought I had lost you!" She squeezed him tighter, and he could feel her body shake with sobs.

"It's me, I promise."

"You were gone for so long," she said, her words muffled by Miles's own chest.

"How long?"

"Three weeks, two days." Ana lifted her head to reveal tear-stained cheeks and a lingering shadow of exhaustion.

"I'm so sorry," Miles said. He hugged Ana tighter and stroked her hair. "What happened? The last thing I remember was leaving my parents' house."

"You switched on your way home and stayed like that," Ana said, finally allowing some space between them. She tilted her head up and took a step back, still clutching Miles's hands. "What happened with your parents?"

"Later," he said, unable to tell her the betrayal he had suffered at his parents' hands. He needed to find the right way to tell her that their actions might have exacerbated, if not led to, his condition. "Tell me what I missed."

Ana groaned. "You should probably sit down for this."

Ana led him to the couch and recounted everything that had happened since Miles came back from his parents' house, including Dr. Benson's attempt at hypnosis. She paused and squeezed Miles's hands, which she held firmly in her own, laid across their laps as they sat with knees touching.

"Dr. Benson wants to send you for inpatient treatment."

Miles blinked mutely as he tried to absorb what Ana had just said.

She leaned in to his eye line. "You okay?"

Miles recoiled and pulled his hands away. "It's just... inpatient? You mean, she wants to commit me? *You* want to commit me?"

"Now hold on! I never said that. I am just relaying information here. Nothing's been decided." She reached for him, taking his hands between hers again. "I wanted to talk to you about it first. I wouldn't feel right having you wake up in some facility and not know how you got there. I wouldn't do that to you—any of you."

Miles tried to smile, but it came out crooked and broken. "Do you think I need special treatment?"

"Honestly, I don't know. Dr. Benson said this place specializes in DID and could help you. You'd have daily therapy and monitoring of your episodes. They would adjust your medication as needed, and you'd be able to focus on getting better, rather than worrying about me, work and whatever."

"What do you want?"

"I want what's best for you. Whatever that is. I'm willing to try whatever *you* think will help you, but Miles, we have to do something. What we've been doing isn't working. You were gone for three weeks. I was a mess, and I tried to cover for you with Darius, but I think he suspects something. And your mom called last Sunday wanting to talk to you, I guess about what happened at their house, but I told her you were in the shower, and she said you're probably still mad at her. She left you six messages; texted you twice. I didn't know what to do."

Miles wrapped his arms around her, letting her fall limply into his embrace. "God, honey, I'm so sorry."

His condition was getting out of control. Something in him knew that he couldn't fix it on his own, but the thought of entering a psychiatric facility where he would be monitored like a lab rat sent his anxiety into overdrive. He hated hospitals; the thought of being poked and prodded made his skin crawl. He wanted to jump out of his skin.

For the first time in his life, it occurred to Miles that he was having the feelings that often preceded an episode: this feeling of wanting to be somewhere else, or someone else, even if just for a while. Was that what was causing his dissociation? Could it really be that easy?

"Honey, if you think I should try inpatient therapy, then I will."

"Miles, you don't have to—"

"No, I'm serious. If we think it might help, even a little, we have to try it. Why else did we dip into my trust fund if we're not going to use it to help me find a cure?"

"Are you sure?"

Ignoring the fear that was clamoring to be heard, Miles uttered a quiet "yes" as he stroked his wife's hair. He felt her body go lax in his arms as she exhaled, every bone in her body sighing with relief.

MONDAY, JUNE 15, 2020 · 8:15 A.M.

The Monday after his twenty-sixth birthday, Ana and Miles drove to Winter Haven to check him in to the inpatient facility that Dr. Benson had suggested. From the outside, the building looked modern, but the hallways had pale pink walls that were lined with a hideous floral wallpaper border. The furniture, mismatched and outdated, was like something out of the mid-nineties. And the entire place smelled of an orange-scented disinfectant, sickly sweet and sharp at the same time. The interior certainly looked like a hospital, and even though the name—Longleaf Retreat—was designed to make its residents feel comfortable, Miles found himself wary. Despite Dr. Benson's reassurances, Miles couldn't shake the overwhelming fear that he was placing his fate in the hands of people who would do him unspeakable harm.

The rooms were small: just a bed, a desk and a small wardrobe each for the two patients who would live there. There was none of the warmth portrayed on the glossy brochure full of smiling faces and sun-dappled courtyards that Dr. Benson had shown him in her office the week before. Well, there was a courtyard, but it was hidden in a cloud of cigarette smoke and hotter than the surface of the sun. Miles didn't see himself using it for the leisurely reading depicted in the brochure. Everything inside seemed sterile and practical, no nonsense or extraneous comfort. And perhaps that was for the best. Miles was here to work through his mental health issues, not for a vacation.

When he arrived, he was placed in a room by himself, but the empty bed taunted him with the possibility of a roommate at any time. He woke up every day expecting to find a stranger on the lumpy twin mattress across from him, but the only other patient he had met so far was a dark-haired girl who looked to be about twenty and had piercing gray eyes. Her long hair hung in loose waves that covered her face when she wasn't pushing it out of her eyes. Her skin was so pale it seemed to reflect the light, as if she hadn't seen the sun in years.

Miles first caught a glimpse of her when she eyed him suspiciously on his first day. She stood in the doorway to what he later learned was her room, peering from beneath her shaggy bangs and biting her nails. Ana gave her a sideways glance as they passed her room, but Miles turned and smiled at her. Her eyes narrowed, but she responded with a lopsided, close-lipped grin before closing her door and disappearing. When Miles saw her at breakfast, she offered him the same lopsided smile and then sat at a table by herself on the other side of the room. He didn't expect to make friends, so it didn't bother him much, but something about her intrigued him. She seemed lonely and timid, but confident in a way he couldn't quite put his finger on.

The other residents steered clear of both of them as if someone had labeled them as lepers, so it became even more obvious that she would not meet his eye.

Three days later, he learned the girl's name.

"Bethany, I'm not having this argument with you again," a tall, slender nurse called Kathy said. "You need to take your medication. Do I need to call Dr. Branagan?"

At this, Bethany's eyes went wide, the dark circles under them turning pale just before her hair fell in her face. She took the paper cup from Kathy's hand and knocked back the medication, swallowing it in a loud gulp and without the aid of water.

"Thank you." Kathy's voice was firm but kind. Even so, Miles watched as Bethany glared at Kathy as she walked away.

"I need a new job. Seven years is too long to deal with Miss Attitude," Kathy muttered to herself as she passed Miles.

He glanced at Bethany who was now draped over an oversized green chair reading a dog-eared book. If she had lived at Longleaf for seven years, she'd probably been there since she was a child, a fact that Miles found troubling.

"It's not polite to stare," she said without looking up from her book. Her hair covered her face so that only the tip of her nose and her mouth were visible. She chewed on her lip and turned a page.

"Sorry," Miles said. "I was just sympathizing. I don't like the medication either."

Bethany made a sound caught between a huff and a laugh.

"It makes me sleepy," Miles added.

"Do I look like I care?"

When she didn't move her head, he assumed she was still reading. "I just thought—"

She lifted her head and regarded Miles with cool eyes. "You aren't good at taking hints, are you?"

Miles took the eye contact as an invitation and moved to the chair nearest her. "Not especially, no."

Bethany dropped her book to her lap and turned to face him with her mouth open.

"I was just wondering," he said, "if you noticed that no one talks to either of us—just us."

"No, I hadn't noticed. I did, however, notice that you insist on talking to me despite the fact that I gave no indication of wanting to talk to you."

"But you *are* talking to me." Miles laughed.

"Under protest."

"My name's Miles." He stuck out his hand.

"Bethany." She looked at his hand and sneered.

"What are you in for?" he asked, rubbing his hands together self-consciously when he realized she had left him hanging.

"The usual," she said. "Crazy."

"I have DID," he said. "Or something like it. Except instead of multiple personalities, I time travel."

He waited for her shocked reaction but Bethany's disinterested expression suddenly turned to terror. She stood. The book in her lap fell to the floor.

"What's wrong?" Miles asked. He reached for her arm, but she yanked it away.

"Don't touch me!"

She took off in the direction of her room; her black sneakers squeaked on the floor as she picked up speed. Her hunched posture gave the impression that she was trying to fold in on herself and disappear. Miles started to follow her, but she turned to enter her room, tears streaking her face, and he stopped short. Something deeper than their conversation was bothering her, and he didn't want to intrude. Not yet anyway.

FRIDAY, JUNE 19, 2020 · 8:50 A.M.

Miles woke up in an unfamiliar place. A pungent citrus-y smell burned his nostrils and the air was unnecessarily cold. He lay on a twin bed, lumpy and hard; the sheets were a rough, hospital issue, stiff from bleach and hundreds of washings. The room contained another small bed, stripped and empty, two small desks and two identical wardrobes. The light coming through the window behind him left an angled pattern across his thin blanket.

Was he in the hospital again?

A knock at the door startled him, and he barely had time to sit up before a tall woman in hospital scrubs stepped into the room.

"Good morning, Miles," she said, a friendly smile on her face.

"Uh, hi." Miles fidgeted with the edge of the sheet and leaned forward to read her name tag. "Kathy."

"Dr. Branagan wanted me to tell you he had to move your therapy session up to nine-thirty. So you need to get out of bed, sleepyhead." She gestured for him to get up, and he stood, letting her tug the sheet over the mattress.

"You'll have to hurry if you want to shower," Kathy said. She fluffed his pillow and pulled the blanket taut.

Miles nodded, although she wasn't looking at him. Then he realized he didn't know where the shower was.

She turned around, tilting her head when she saw him standing there, unmoving.

"What's wrong, sugar?"

"Where am I?" he asked. The linoleum felt cold beneath his feet, causing him to shift uncomfortably.

"Longleaf Retreat. Your wife dropped you off four days ago." She studied him carefully. "Oh dear, it's happened, hasn't it?"

Miles looked at her in disbelief. He'd been committed. Immediately his mind shifted to Adam. Did he know Miles had been committed? Probably not if he had a "wife." He hoped it was still Ana.

"Oh, honey," Kathy said, "you must be terrified. Here, have a seat and let's get you some water." She pulled out the desk chair and motioned for him to sit.

"I'm fine," Miles said, sitting on the bed. "Could you just tell me why I'm here and when I can go home?"

Kathy's shoulders sagged.

"Well, you voluntarily committed yourself so we can treat your dissociative disorder."

Miles shook his head firmly. "No, I want to leave."

"I'm sorry, sugar. You're here until Dr. Branagan discharges you." Her voice was soothing but the words stung.

That couldn't be. How could he be stuck here? "No," he said again.

Kathy sighed and gave Miles a sympathetic look. "I know it's scary, but I promise you're in good hands." She patted his shoulder.

"I need to make a phone call."

"Well, there's a phone in the lounge for personal calls, but there's always a wait. You get your cell phone once a week for private calls, but that's on Sundays."

Miles stood and began to pace. "This is insane. I need to use the phone. You can't keep me here!"

Kathy walked to the bed and pushed a small button on the wall behind Miles's headboard. A tinny voice came over the intercom. "Nurses' station, can I help you?"

"It's Kathy. I have a situation."

"I'm on my way."

Miles continued to rage as he paced, using his hands in exaggerated motions, demanding to use the phone.

"Miles, I need you to calm down," Kathy urged.

"I'm calm!" Miles shouted. "I just want to use the fucking phone!"

Another woman in scrubs burst through the door. She was much larger than Kathy, thicker through the middle and solid as a bodybuilder. Her short, sandy blonde hair carried wisps of gray and stuck out in odd directions. Miles noticed she carried something in her left hand that looked like a small leather belt with thick fleece padding. His eyes darted from her hand to her face and he caught a determined expression.

"Dr. Branagan is on his way," she said. "He said we should restrain him."

Miles suddenly realized what the "belt" was for. "Restrain me?" he said. "You can't!"

"Grab his arm," the new nurse said.

Kathy took his arm gently, but Miles jerked it away.

"Don't make this any harder, Miles," she urged.

Miles struggled and fought, but eventually they wrestled him to the bed. The stocky woman held him down while Kathy attached the restraints to his wrists and ankles. He continued to thrash, but it was useless. He was firmly strapped to the bed with no means of escape. Over Kathy's shoulder he caught a glimpse of a dark-haired girl in the doorway. She hugged a ragged paperback novel to her chest as she chewed on her lip, taking in the scene before her. Miles pleaded with his eyes for her to do something; she regarded him, tilting her head as if she were contemplating how she could overpower two nurses and get Miles out of the bed. Suddenly, something in the hallway caught her attention and she took off in the opposite direction, barely sparing Miles a second glance.

Moments later, an older white man in a lab coat strode through the door. His wire-rimmed glasses were perched low on his nose, magnifying the liver spots on his cheeks and the deep-set wrinkles around his eyes.

"Good morning, Miles, I'm Dr. Branagan."

When he smiled, his overly white teeth gave him a sinister air, making Miles's heart flutter anxiously in his chest.

"I want to go home," Miles said. His voice wavered, but he balled his hands into tight fists to give the appearance of bravado.

"I'm afraid I can't do that," Dr. Branagan said, his voice dripping with false compassion. His dentures clacked when he talked, a dull sound that was only audible as he came closer to Miles's bedside. "You signed yourself into my care, and until it's been determined that you've been cured, you can't be released."

Miles struggled against his restraints. "Who decides that I've been cured?"

"Well, I do, of course." There was that smile again. "Now, why don't you lie back and try to relax."

He pressed firmly on Miles's chest with one of his frail hands, but Miles resisted, tugging on the straps holding his wrists to the bed frame.

Dr. Branagan frowned. "Have it your way, then." He turned to face the nurses. "Looks like Mr. Lawson needs to calm down from his anxiety attack. Get me ten milligrams of diazepam and an IV."

Kathy nodded and disappeared, but the larger nurse remained. Dr. Branagan leaned closer and studied Miles's face. "Welcome back," he said wryly.

Narrowing his eyes, Miles studied the man's features. Something about him looked familiar, but he couldn't fully form the memory. It was as if he'd seen Dr. Branagan in a dream, the edges of it fuzzy and malformed. A thick fog rested over the finer details, but the doctor's voice and demeanor remained. Miles's pulse raced as he tried to place it, but despite his best efforts, the memory remained hazy.

When Kathy returned with several needles and an IV drip, Miles began to panic. He struggled even harder against the restraints, arching his back for more leverage. "Let me go!" he cried. "Please." He caught Kathy's gaze and pleaded with his eyes. Her expression was sympathetic, but she didn't budge.

"Hold him down," Dr. Branagan instructed the second nurse. She and Kathy each grabbed a leg and an arm while Dr. Branagan prepared the injection. Miles felt the needle pierce his skin, but didn't immediately feel the effects of the drug. He started to laugh, a low rumble in his chest that made his whole upper body shake. It occurred to him that the medication wasn't going to work on him. Surely they had given him some sort of sedative, but he felt nothing.

He felt another sharp prick in his arm and the telltale sensation of blood being drawn, a loose discomfort that lingered on the edge of pain but never quite arrived. He'd never liked that feeling; for his entire life, any time a doctor had needed to draw blood, he had looked away. As he felt the blood leave his arm, Miles closed his eyes and let his head drop to the pillow. He'd wait for them to leave and then he'd start working on those restraints in earnest.

IT WASN'T UNTIL MILES AWOKE in the late-afternoon gloom with his arms and legs still firmly pinned to the bed that he realized he had indeed been sedated. An IV line was sticking out of his left arm; the bag hung beside the bed, but it was not attached to the line.

They must have needed to draw blood again, he thought. The idea made his stomach churn. What else had they done while he'd been sleeping? An IV line meant they wanted to be able to administer drugs quickly. He'd learned that when he was in the hospital for his broken arm.

Outside, an afternoon thunderstorm raged. He lay there listening to it, trying to decide what to do, when the dark-haired girl appeared in his doorway. Her arms were empty, but she still gave the impression that she was hugging something tightly to her chest. She shifted from one foot to another and glanced over each shoulder before entering the room.

"Hi," she said. Her voice was soft and scratchy, as if she wasn't used to speaking.

"Where am I?"

"Longleaf Retreat," she said. "Don't you remember?"

The girl studied him as she moved forward, her feet making barely a sound on the tile floor.

"They told me I committed myself," Miles said. His memory was foggy but he vaguely remembered how he had gotten tied to the bed. And he remembered Dr. Branagan.

The girl nodded. "Is that all?"

"My name is Miles," he said, attempting a shrug. The restraints stopped him from drawing his shoulders up too high.

"Yeah, I know," she said with a crooked grin. "We've met before."

Miles raised an eyebrow. "I don't remember you. Well, unless you count you creeping in my doorway earlier."

"That could be the drugs."

"Or the time travel." Miles laughed sardonically at his own joke, but the girl didn't. Her eyes narrowed as she peered into his face. Her gaze shot back and forth before she reeled back.

"Whoa. You weren't making it up."

"Making what up?" Miles asked. "And who are you?"

"I'm Bethany," she said. "And you really can time-travel."

Her face carried a look of shock, but not in the way Miles was used to. She believed him, and what's more she was surprised not that time travel was possible, but that Miles himself could do it.

"Can *you*?" he asked suddenly.

As she slowly nodded, Miles felt his face flush. His heart rate increased and his palms began to sweat.

"Are you serious?"

"Since I was a kid," she said, walking to the foot of his bed and staring out the window. "I've been here at Longleaf since just before I turned twelve. My parents committed me because of my hallucinations. But I think my doctor knew I didn't just have schizophrenia. He wanted me under close observation."

"How old are you now?"

"Nineteen. You?"

"Seventeen," he said. "Well, *I* am, but the body's twenty-five."

"Ah yes, the problem with personal pronouns and verb tenses," Bethany mused. "Neither was made for time-traveling teens, were they?"

"No, not really." It felt good to laugh, but more importantly to have someone to share this with.

Bethany sat on the edge of the bed, one knee bent against Miles's hip. Her other leg dangled over the side. "Can you control it?"

Miles wished he could sit eye-to-eye with her, rather than looking up her nose.

"Do I have a booger or something?" she asked, wiping the back of her hand over her nose.

He must have been staring. "No, sorry. I was just thinking I'd rather sit face-to-face than study your nose hairs."

"Could have fooled me," Bethany said. Her hand was still covering her nose self-consciously. "Although, I could untie you, I guess."

"Won't you get in trouble?"

"Nah, Kathy just went on break and the doc left hours ago."

"What about the other nurse?" Miles asked. "The big one."

"Diane? Her shift ended at two, and J.D. won't leave the nurses' station unless he's called. It's just you and me for a bit."

"Well, what are you waiting for, then?" Miles tugged at the restraints for emphasis.

"Right, sorry."

Bethany untied his right wrist first, so he could help with his left while she moved down to his feet. When Miles was free, he yanked the IV from his arm and immediately regretted it. Blood poured out of the open wound and it hurt.

Rolling her eyes, Bethany pressed the edge of the sheet against Miles's arm. "Hold that there," she said and dashed out of the room. A few moments later, she returned with a cotton ball and some tape. "You can't just pull out an IV like that."

Her words were accusatory but her hands soft as she dressed Miles's wound.

"There," she said. "Now don't do anything else stupid, like run with scissors or anything."

"Thanks." Miles was so grateful for her help, he didn't know what else to say, so he sat there staring at her.

The scrutiny must have made her uncomfortable because she let her hair fall in her eyes, obscuring most of her face from his view.

"Don't get any ideas," she muttered. "I've got a girlfriend."

"Don't worry. I have a boyfriend *and* a wife. My plate is full." He started to laugh at his own joke, but he realized something. "Wait, I thought you said you'd been in here since you were twelve."

"I have."

"Then how—?"

"I sneak out." She said it so matter-of-factly that Miles wondered if she didn't just walk out through the front door, right past the nurses and doctors as if she owned the place. "And before you go getting any ideas, no, I can't sneak you out right now. It has to be at night."

Miles nodded. That made more sense. Besides, he could wait.

"Could you at least show me where the phone is?"

"The one in the lounge is always being used. But I know a staff phone that's usually unguarded." She jumped to her feet. "Come on."

Miles rose and followed. His arm still throbbed, but the bleeding had stopped. He pulled his T-shirt sleeve down, but it wouldn't cover the bandage.

"It's fine," Bethany said. "No one will notice. They take blood here almost every day."

"Is that normal for a loony bin?"

Bethany shrugged. "It is for this one."

She peered around the doorway, looking up and down the hall. She must have decided it was safe because she motioned for Miles to follow her. He tried to match her soundless footsteps, but his sweaty feet stuck to the cold floor, making a squelching sound he was sure could be heard in every corner of the building. Why hadn't he thought to put on shoes?

"We should be clear to that corner up there." Bethany pointed to where the hallway made a left turn and glanced back at Miles. "But when we get to the second door on the right, there will be a small lab that usually has three or four researchers in it. We need to duck down and be extra quiet. Can you do that?"

Miles didn't have a choice. He had to get to the phone. "Let's go."

Bethany walked purposefully down the hallway, looking completely nonchalant until they reached the corner. She held up a hand in front of

Miles's face and a finger to her own lips. She peered around the corner, just enough so only her eye would be visible if someone was in the corridor. She grabbed Miles's shirt and tugged him forward, rounded the corner quickly and pointed to the door to the research lab. She got on her hands and knees as they approached the door and crawled. Miles followed suit, keeping as close to her scuffed sneakers as he could without being kicked in the face. The tops of their heads were just below the large window that must have overlooked the lab. Pure white light poured out of the opening and flooded the section of hallway in brightness. This part of the facility seemed much different from the residential area. It was eerily quiet and far colder and reminded Miles of something from his nightmares. It gave him the creeps. He suppressed a shiver and focused on keeping up with Bethany.

When they had passed the lab, Bethany jumped to her feet but motioned for Miles to remain quiet. They hurried to the end of the hallway, ducked into the last office and shut the door softly behind them. The room was pitch black with no windows, but Bethany must have been there before, because she quickly found the light switch and brought the room to life.

There on a counter, below a printed sign that read "Staff use only," sat their prize: a nondescript, outdated beige telephone. Two of the lights were blinking red and another was solid. The last light on the phone was dark. Bethany pointed to it.

"Use that one," she said. "Dial nine for an outside line. It's not like a cell phone. So if you're calling outside of the area, you'll have to dial one before the area code."

He picked up the handset and started to dial before he realized he had no idea where he was.

"We're in Winter Haven," she said. "Where are you calling?"

"It's an Orlando number."

Bethany punched the number nine and then the one. "Now enter the full number."

Miles hoped Adam hadn't changed his cell number since the last time he had visited. It was his only hope. He dialed the number and waited.

"What are you doing here?"

They turned to see a man in a white lab coat standing in the doorway. He had close-cropped brown hair, and his skin was almost as pale as Bethany's, as if he hadn't been outside in nearly as many years.

"Miles needed to use the phone," Bethany said.

"Patients use the phone in the lounge. This one's for staff only." He pointed to the sign as if they hadn't seen it.

"We know," Bethany said, her voice becoming sickeningly sweet, "but it was in use, and Miles here, dumb ass that he is, forgot his grandma's birthday. He was all panicked that she'd disown him or something so we popped in here for a quick phone call. Surely that's not against the rules."

Miles couldn't see her face, but he imagined Bethany was batting her eyes at him, trying to look as seductive as possible.

"I don't think Dr. Branagan would like that," he said. His voice sounded unsure. Miles turned away and continued dialing. "Hey, I said no." The man's arm shot out as if he were trying to knock the phone out of Miles's hand.

Bethany stepped between them, but the man's body weight knocked her partially off-balance. She bumped Miles's hand, and he hit a wrong number. He quickly hung up and began to dial again. This time, he didn't break concentration, letting Bethany handle the lab coat.

"Please, sir," Bethany pleaded. "He just needs two minutes. We won't tell anyone. Just go back to the lab and pretend you never saw us."

Miles heard the first ring.

"I don't know," the lab coat said.

Second ring.

"Come on." Bethany had moved closer, her hand trailing down the lapel of his lab coat.

Third ring.

Bethany and the lab coat were backing out of the room. Miles hoped he could finish his call before Bethany had to go any further with this.

Fourth ring.

"Hello?"

Adam's voice sounded like music to Miles.

"It's me," he said. "Don't hang up."

"What do you want?" Adam sounded annoyed, but Miles couldn't worry about that now.

"Ana had me committed," he said.

"What? Where?"

"Some place called Longleaf Retreat." Miles could hear arguing outside. Through the crack in the door he could hear Bethany's voice, lab coat's and another much deeper one. "It's in Winter Haven. Just come get me please." He hung up the phone before Adam could respond.

Knowing Bethany needed his help, he swung open the door. Standing next to her and the researcher was Dr. Branagan; his watery eyes fixed on Miles with anger.

"Mr. Lawson, you should be in bed." His voice dripped with false concern.

"I was just telling him that," Bethany said. "I think he was having an episode."

Miles grabbed his head, feigning a headache. "I don't feel so good," he said, allowing his eyes to roll back in his head and swaying on his feet. The lab coat grabbed him under the arm as he started to fall. Miles forced his body to go limp, and his eyes fell closed.

"See?" he heard Bethany exclaim.

"Help me get him back to his room," Dr. Branagan said. "Miss Carter, you should return to your room as well. I'm sure Miles is grateful for your help."

Bethany didn't reply but Miles sensed she was gone. Two pairs of arms gripped him and lifted him from the floor. With difficulty, Miles remained limp. When he was finally back in his room, laid out across the bed, Dr. Branagan buckled his restraints and re-inserted the IV. And this time when he left, he locked the door behind him.

Miles tugged on the straps binding his wrists, but he was losing focus. His vision grew hazy, and a headache bloomed behind his eyes, signaling an oncoming episode. Relief washed over him. He was going home. He didn't have to be stuck in this awful place. He could see Adam.

Miles smiled and let himself slip into oblivion.

FRIDAY, JUNE 19, 2020 · 4:25 P.M.

Dumbfounded, Adam stared at his phone. The sun beat down on his neck. It was hot to the point of stinging, and he'd probably be sunburned tomorrow, but he didn't care. Right now he needed the warmth of the sun to chase away the icy fear that shot through his veins. Miles had hung up so abruptly, Adam couldn't tell if he was in his adult state of mind. Had Ana really committed him? He sounded so panicked.

"You okay?" Michaela asked. "You look white as a sheet." She sat next to him on the bench outside their office building. They often sat here on breaks to get warm; she must have been really cold because she was still wearing her sweater, a fuzzy peach thing nearly the same color as her hair.

Shielding his eyes from the sun, Adam turned to face her. "Remember the old friend asking for help?"

"The 'not-an-ex-boyfriend' old friend?" A smile was breaking through her serious expression; laugh lines formed around the outer edge of her sunglasses.

"Miles," Adam supplied. "And yes, he is an ex-boyfriend... from high school. A very long time ago."

"And he called again asking for help."

It wasn't a question but Adam answered it like one. "Yes. He says his wife had him committed." He glanced back at his phone. The screen was still black, but it felt burning hot in his hand.

"Like to a mental hospital?" Michaela's eyebrows shot up when he nodded. "Well... you probably shouldn't get involved in someone else's marital problems, but you *definitely* shouldn't get involved in their mental health emergencies." Michaela had a knack for pointing out the obvious, but sometimes the finer points were lost on her.

"It's more complicated than that," Adam muttered, shifting his phone between his hands.

"It's *more* complicated than your ex-boyfriend's wife had him committed and now he wants your help? Damn."

Adam didn't say anything. He just sat there staring at his phone, wondering what the hell he should do.

"Do you need me to cover for you so you can beg off early? Say you ate something that didn't agree with you?"

Adam checked the time. It was four-thirty.

"No, thanks," he said. "I can make it. I need time to think anyway. I can't go off half-cocked."

Michaela snickered, and Adam couldn't help but smile. She could turn anything into innuendo and did so frequently.

"Sorry," she said, trying to keep a straight face. "Is there anything I can do?"

"Nah, thanks." He stood, ready to go back inside and finish his day when a thought occurred to him. "Actually, could you drive me to Winter Haven?"

"Now?"

"Whenever. I think I should at least go see him."

"And you want me to drive you?"

Adam shrugged. "Your car is more reliable than mine, and I don't think I can ask Anthony to borrow his truck."

"Yeah, I can see how that would be awkward. Um, I think I could go tomorrow?"

"Thank you," Adam said. He leaned down and kissed her cheek. "You're the best."

"Easy there, Casanova, what would Steve say? Running off to rescue your ex and kissing me on the cheek in the same day!"

"I just want to talk to him," Adam said, sulking. "I didn't say I was going to rescue him."

Michaela held up her hands in mock surrender. "Sure, whatever you say. I'm just the wheel man."

MONDAY, OCTOBER 12, 2009 · 3:28 P.M.

The movie was awful; dinner was practically inedible, and yet it turned out to be the best night of Adam's life. It was their first official date—they'd been making out in Miles's bedroom for weeks, but they'd only made it official just before band practice that day. When the section leader, Jake, saw them holding hands on their way to the football field, the drumline had started to tap out a simple cadence. It was a tradition Jake had started whenever a new couple started in band, and Miles's smile went ear-to-ear when he heard it.

"Is that for us?" he whispered in Adam's ear.

"I don't think anyone else got together this week," Adam replied. He looked around to see half the band staring at them. A group of flute players was cheering and a couple of the guard girls started chanting, "Adam and Miles sitting in a tree..." Adam turned to face Miles and smiled back. "Oh, it's for us."

"Should we give 'em a show?"

It took Adam a moment to realize what Miles meant, and by the time he did, he had already decided. He spun Miles on the spot, dipped him and planted a kiss firmly on his lips. In front of everyone.

Another whoop and cheer went up from the girls and someone started applauding, causing everyone else to quickly join in. It was a sweet kiss, just a dramatic peck, but Miles wasn't kissing back. Worry began to creep into Adam's thoughts. He pulled Miles back to his feet and tried to get a read on what he was feeling.

"Oh my God, it's just like a movie," Miles said, breathless. His mouth broke into a timid smile.

"Oh, thank God," Adam said. "For a second there—when you didn't kiss back—I was worried I had embarrassed you."

"Not a chance. That was so freaking romantic. You just caught me off guard." Before Adam could respond, Miles kissed him. He took his time, as

if he were trying to prove that he most definitely wasn't embarrassed to be kissing his boyfriend in front of all their friends.

When they finally parted, Adam took his time opening his eyes. He knew everyone was watching them but he wanted to be alone with Miles in their little bubble for a while longer.

"Look who's caught off guard now," Miles said.

Adam opened his eyes to find Miles beaming. He glanced around at their mutual friends, taking in their dazed expressions. "Well, we certainly gave them something to talk about."

"Yeah, I bet no one's still talking about Jenny falling in the mud after that." Miles snorted with laughter.

"You're such a dork," Adam said.

"Yeah, but I'm your dork." Miles kissed him gently.

Before Adam could say anything else, the drum major blew his whistle, signaling the start of practice. It was hot and humid—Adam's shirt stuck to his back and his hands were so sweaty he kept dropping his sticks. He was dying to get Miles alone again and kiss him until neither of them could breathe, but the afternoon dragged on. They ran the same sequence at least six times, until Adam thought he might scream out of frustration, and yet it was the best practice ever. Miles couldn't stop smiling at him, and during breaks they were never more than a few inches from each other's side. It was perfect.

SATURDAY, JUNE 20, 2020 · 11:15 A.M.

The drive to Winter Haven wound through desolate stretches of road where the only company for miles was the occasional bird or snake. The trees dripped with Spanish moss that hung far over the road in places. Michaela sang along loudly to the radio, giving Adam plenty of time to think. What was he going to say when he saw Miles? He didn't have any idea what condition he was in. Would Miles even want to see him? Maybe it was an alter that had called him. Then again, maybe he was being held against his will. There were a lot of unknowns.

Michaela turned down the volume on the car stereo. "Penny for your thoughts."

"I was just wondering if Miles really wants my help."

Michaela looked confused even in profile. "He called you didn't he?"

"Well, like I said, it's complicated."

"We've got some time to kill," she said. "Why don't you fill me in."

The low hum of music blended into road noise as Adam tried to decide where to begin. The delicate rhythm lulled him into a sense of security and peace.

"We met in high school," he began, weaving an intricate tale of young love and the complications and inexperience dealing with emotions that led to their breakup. He left out the time travel stuff at first, opting for the more simplistic explanation of, "We had a fight and I got drunk and made out with another guy." But when he got to the present day and how Miles had appeared out of nowhere, he had no choice. He had to tell her about Miles's mental condition. He braced himself for the look that said "whoa, your ex is nuts," or at the very least the sympathetic feigning of interest that would let him know she thought he was equally crazy. But it didn't come. Michaela simply listened as he finished the story, only speaking when he stopped talking.

"So, where does Anthony think you are?"

Brushing his hair away from his face, Adam looked out the window. "A conference for work. He knows I'm with you."

She hummed in response, but Adam couldn't tell if it was in agreement or in judgment.

"So?"

"So what?" She glanced at him, an unreadable look on her face.

"I just told you my ex-boyfriend time-travels and you have *nothing* to say?"

"I'm just trying to absorb it, that's all. It's... different."

"I told you it was complicated." Adam turned to stare out the window again, watching the road race by in a blurry flash. As a kid he was fascinated by the difference between looking out the side windows and looking out the front or back windows. His sister got car sick, but he could watch the grey streak of road go by for hours. His favorite was the symmetrical rows of pine trees that lined the tree farms. Open spaces slashed through the green at parallel intervals, creating order where there should have been chaos. He wished it were as easy to get his life in order, to plant everything in neat rows, and he could grow and change without leaving the neatly designed parameters he had set. But everything changes— even tree farms had the occasional sprout that hadn't followed the rules, shooting up defiantly and hoping to grow tall enough before someone noticed and chopped it down. Kind of like Miles.

"So tell me," Michaela said. "Do you believe him? Is that why you're helping him?"

Adam thought about it. Did he believe? Was it possible that Miles was actually time-traveling and not just dissociating?

"You know, I think anything's possible," he said. "I believe that he believes it, and that's enough for me. He's not a liar. So I have no choice but to believe him."

Michaela patted his hand. "You're a good friend. He's lucky to have you."

Adam wasn't so sure, but he nodded. "I just want to make sure he's okay."

Even as the words were leaving his mouth, Adam realized he had already decided to help Miles no matter what. He refused to let him be chopped down before he reached his full potential, even if that meant sacrificing his own neat rows for a forest full of chaos.

Adam leaned forward and turned the radio back up. He just wanted to get there and find out what was going on. Michaela seemed to understand, because she went back to singing and left Adam with his thoughts.

SATURDAY, JUNE 20, 2020 · 4:45 P.M.

Dahlia's big blue eyes searched Ana's face as she recounted how Miles had voluntarily committed himself the week before. Dahlia furrowed her brow at all the right places, placed her icy, perfectly manicured hand on Ana's to comfort her, even dabbed at the corners of her eyes at precisely the right moments, and yet Ana still felt empty. Nothing had changed. Miles was still in that horribly cold and uncaring place, sleeping in a room that smelled of oranges and Lysol. And it was all because she had suggested it.

"I should have known he'd do anything to make me happy," she said. "He's always been so, so.... Well, that's just Miles, you know?"

Dahlia squeezed Ana's hand. "I know, sweetie, I know. How long is he there for?"

Ana shrugged. "The doctor said he'll keep me posted, but that it would at least be a few weeks, maybe months."

"Oh, that's awful! I can't imagine being away from Christopher for that long!" She twisted her enormous diamond ring as she spoke, as if she were rubbing a talisman for good luck, wishing away the kinds of misfortunes that plagued Ana's and Miles's lives. "How are you holding up?"

Ana scoffed, as if the bags under her eyes weren't visible from space. "I'm getting by, I guess. Work keeps me distracted."

"That's good!" Dahlia's broad smile was blocked by the wine glass she brought to her lips. The deep red liquid gave her teeth a sinister look, as if they were coated in blood.

Normally Dahlia's perky personality didn't bother her, but Ana was exhausted, and it was getting hard not to let her annoyance show. "Dahlia, look, I know you're trying to be helpful, but could you just stop with the theatrics for a minute and just let me vent?"

Dahlia set the wine glass on the table. Her smile was gone, a flash of hurt blinked across her face before her expression turned neutral. "I'm just trying to help," she said sheepishly.

Ana pinched the bridge of her nose. "I know you are, sweetie. But you're helping by just being here. I promise." She patted Dahlia's hand and earned a gentle smile in return.

"So tell me more about this facility," Dahlia said, brightening a little. "Are there straitjackets and men in white coats?"

Ana took sip of her wine and relaxed a little, knowing that Dahlia's false optimism would not make another appearance that night. "Yes to the men in white coats—at least the doctor wears one—but I didn't see any straitjackets. Miles's therapist says inpatient therapy isn't like that anymore. Not the stuff you see in horror movies."

"Well, that's a relief." Dahlia popped a grape in her mouth and cut herself another piece of cheese.

"I don't think I could have convinced Miles to go if the brochure hadn't been so 'Weekend At the Spa.' You remember how terrified he is of doctors and needles."

"Still?"

"Yeah, even with all the broken bones and trips to the hospital, he still has to close his eyes and hold my hand whenever they draw blood." Ana shook her head and laughed. "You know, once he practically fainted when I cut my leg shaving. I asked him to get a Band-Aid and he fucking swooned."

Dahlia giggled. "Really?"

"Yep. Swayed on his feet just like a lady in a Victorian novel."

Still giggling, Dahlia asked, "Did you have to get the smelling salts?"

"Stop," Ana said, fighting back her own laughter.

"Yeah, we probably shouldn't be picking on the guy who's been committed, should we? At least not until he's here to defend himself." Dahlia's expression remained mischievous, however.

It felt good to be silly like this. Ana had almost forgotten that Miles was stuck in that awful place. Almost.

When Dahlia changed the subject to her own fledgling marriage, Ana appreciated the distraction, listening to Dahlia drone on about trying to get Christopher to let her paint the living room pink. She laughed when she was supposed to and acted shocked when Dahlia expected it, but even so, Ana's mind kept wandering. Was Miles lonely? Was therapy working? She longed for his phone call on Sunday afternoon.

"I swear it's like he thinks Target is the height of home décor." Dahlia paused and waited for Ana to agree.

"Oh, I know what you mean," Ana said. "Miles has this awful throw that..." She trailed off, imagining her husband wrapped in the ratty blue blanket that he'd had since college. She'd tried to throw it out on several occasions, arguing that the holes were bigger than the surface area of the blanket itself, but he wouldn't give it up. Ana had jokingly referred to it as his security blanket, and whenever Ana caught him wrapped up in it, she called him Linus and teased him relentlessly. Suddenly she couldn't picture him without it and tears began to sting her eyes.

"I'm so sorry," she said. "I just got to thinking about Miles and that stupid fucking blanket and I lost it."

Dahlia's hand rubbed her back; she'd switched chairs so she sat next to Ana. "It's okay. I'm surprised you held it together this long."

Ana dabbed at her eyes and took a few deep breaths. "I think I should go," she said.

"Of course, sweetie. But you call me if you need to talk, okay?"

Ana stood, dropping her napkin on the table. "Thanks for this. I'll call you."

FRIDAY, AUGUST 23, 2019 · 10:11 P.M.

Ana had had three rum and Cokes and was beginning to get the floaty feeling that preceded being really and truly drunk. It felt good. She glanced over at the rest of the group, dancing around Dahlia in her long, white veil. They were singing along to some eighties song she couldn't quite place. Dahlia threw her head back and belted out a line, catching her ridiculous penis tiara just before it slipped off her head.

"Don't want to lose my crown o' dicks," she said, her words slurring together just enough to show she was well on her way to becoming absolutely trashed.

The group laughed, one girl named Hayley—one of the six sorority sisters at the party—slipped and spilled her drink on the dance floor. The girls scattered, leaving Dahlia and Ana to claim the mess.

"I'll get someone to clean that up," Ana shouted over the music.

"I'll come with you," Dahlia shouted back. "It's hot in here." She fanned herself for effect.

They inched their way back to the bar, dodging drunk frat boys and the occasional cougar. While they waited for one of the bartenders to notice them, Dahlia wrapped her arms around Ana.

"I'm so glad you came," she said.

"I wouldn't miss it." Ana stroked the arm that was practically choking her as she tried to pry it off. "Besides, I really needed the night out."

"Trouble in paradise, finally?"

Dahlia always assumed Miles and Ana had a perfect marriage. They'd never corrected her assumption, not even when their marriage was one of convenience.

"Just be glad you're marrying someone normal." As soon as the words were out of her mouth, she thought the rum must have liquefied her brain. What the hell was she doing?

"Miles is normal," Dahlia said, rolling her eyes. She paused and pulled back to take in Ana's face. "Isn't he?"

Ana had a terrible poker face. She rushed to pull her expression together but the effort forced her to fumble for her words. "Uh, yeah, uh... Of, of course he is. Perfectly normal."

"Oh, no... I know that look, Ana. Something's up." She tugged on Ana's arm and led her to the bathroom. It had a lounge area with a large round banquette that served the dual purpose of being semi-private and drowning out everything but the thumping music from inside the club. "Spill." Dahlia yanked her arm so they were sitting side by side.

"Dee, it's complicated. You don't want to ruin your bachelorette party with this shit."

Dahlia waved her hand in front of her face. "Don't be silly. It will ruin my bachelorette party if I know you're sad when I could have done something about it. Not to mention, I have the benefit of being the only one of your friends who knows you both. I'm like a Miles and Ana expert or something!"

Ana still wasn't sure, but the drinks had made her freer with her words than normal, and she needed someone to talk to. Dahlia was looking at her expectantly, so Ana took a deep breath and said, "Do you believe in time travel?"

SATURDAY, JUNE 20, 2020 · 10:02 A.M.

"How are you liking it here at Longleaf, Miles?" Dr. Benson sat at the edge of Miles's bed, obviously trying to keep her legs crossed in a professional manner, or maybe it was to keep her skirt from hiking up. Even though she no longer treated Miles in weekly therapy, Dr. Branagan thought it would be best if she continued to check in with him in order to transition him to the facility's therapists. Miles couldn't figure out why Dr. Benson had come dressed for a meeting on Wall Street. They were meeting with a therapist called Jamie, who wore ratty old Converse and oversized sweatshirts that looked as if they were last washed during the Bush administration. Therapy at Longleaf was laid-back, more like talking to a friend than a doctor.

"It's fine," Miles said. "Kind of quiet."

He considered calling Dr. Benson by her first name. He rolled the name around in his brain: Eleanor. It didn't feel right. He looked over at her, sitting prim and proper on the edge of the bed, her ankles delicately crossed as she held her purse in her lap. Why hadn't anyone reserved them a therapy room where they could be more comfortable? This seemed like an awkward, sick first date.

Miles cleared his throat. "We could sit in the lounge," he offered. "The chairs look kind of gross but they're actually pretty comfortable."

"Um, if that's what you want, sure." Dr. Benson stood, tugged her skirt down to her knees and followed Miles down the hallway.

He found a spot in the corner where they could speak without being overheard. The lounge was oddly quiet for a Saturday afternoon.

"I had an episode the other day," Miles said. "They had to restrain me."

"Restrain you?" Dr. Benson looked shocked.

"Well, I assume that's what happened. I woke up as me and I was strapped to the bed. Took me a while to convince them I was back to my normal self, but they finally untied me."

"That must have been scary."

"At first, but I realized pretty quick that they had left the call button within reach. I pushed it, and one of the nurses showed up. At least I had someone to talk to until they sorted things out."

"You seem pretty calm about the whole thing," Dr. Benson said. She looked impressed.

"I am. I'm here to get better, right? So I figured I can't fight it. I just need to go with the flow."

Bethany waved to him from the other side of the room before settling into an oversized chair to read.

"Who's that?" Dr. Benson asked.

"Her name is Bethany. I don't know much about her. We've only talked once, but she seems nice. Even if she is a bit of a loner."

"A loner? What do you mean?"

"I told her about my DID and how it manifests itself as time travel, and she freaked."

"So that means she's a loner?"

"Well, she skulks around a lot, not talking, and it was like pulling teeth to get her to talk to me..."

"Maybe she's just shy, or didn't want to talk to you, specifically. It could be a million things."

"I suppose you're right. I mean, maybe people around here just mind their own business," he said. "No one else has said five words to me, apart from the nurses."

"What about the therapists?"

"Well, yeah, but they only come on certain days. I'm talking about the people I 'live' with."

Dr. Benson hummed noncommittally.

"Don't you think that's strange?" Miles asked.

"What I think isn't important. If you're comfortable here, then I'd say that's a step in the right direction."

"I think—"

"Hello, Miles."

It was Jamie. She was missing her usual ratty ensemble. Today it was combat boots and a floral skirt.

"And you must be Eleanor." She reached out her tiny hand to shake Dr. Benson's.

As she rose, Dr. Benson towered over Jamie, who couldn't have been taller than five-one, even in her boots. Miles could see her nervousness as she glanced from him to Dr. Benson and back.

"Should we get started?" Jamie asked, her smile more cheery than usual.

Dr. Benson looked unconvinced, but she followed as Jamie led the way to an empty room. Miles glanced over his shoulder at Bethany who was studying him over the top of her paperback. When he smiled, she ducked her face behind its pages. So strange.

THROUGHOUT THE SESSION WITH DR. Benson and Jamie, Miles kept thinking about the strange look Bethany had given him. She looked as though she knew something he didn't, as if she were studying him to see if she could uncover something. What was she looking for?

He sat at the tiny desk in his room, trying to write in the journal Jamie had given him, hoping to tap into some repressed memory or something significant, and all he could think to write was, "We had peas with dinner."

"Those peas tasted like ass."

Miles looked up to find Bethany standing over him. Her face was pale, her cheeks hollow, but she smiled at him. Her clothes were a nearly identical variation on everything else he'd seen her wear: T-shirt, jeans, hoodie, sneakers. As usual, her hair covered most of her face, and she carried a book; this time it appeared to be a notebook or journal.

"Still it was better than the chipped beef. What the hell was that?" Without waiting for an invitation, she walked over to Miles's bed and sat cross-legged on it, facing him. She put the notebook in her lap. "I know you're not you, or you *are* you. Whatever. I met your alter yesterday. He's way less uptight than you are."

"Yeah, well, he's seventeen."

"And you're what, sixty-seven?"

Miles laughed. "So what did my alter want?"

"He wanted to make a phone call."

"Who did he want to call?"

"He didn't say. But I helped him sneak into an office in the research wing to use a staff phone. We almost got caught but he faked an episode and saved our asses."

"Research wing?"

"Yeah, this place is a fucking labyrinth. This is the residential area, but there's research and medical. And there's a rumor of a lab on the coast near the space center." She thumbed over her shoulder as if the beach were just outside the window.

Miles's head was spinning with all the information.

Bethany looked at her feet; her hair concealed her face and muffled her voice. "I read up on you, you know."

"Read up on me?"

"Yeah, you're like famous around here. Miles Lawson, boy wonder. They've been studying you since two-thousand five."

"Who's been studying me?"

She looked up. "Dr. Branagan, the researchers, the whole shebang." Bethany motioned around her as if these people were all in the room with them.

"I'm sorry, but you're going to have to fill me in. I have no idea what you're talking about."

"Time travel. They've been studying you. Us."

"Us?"

"Yeah, I can do it too."

"You can?" Excitement bubbled up at finding someone else like him. Maybe he was that much closer to a cure.

"Yep, although I'm not able to control it."

"Neither can I," Miles said with a shrug.

"Well, according to your files you can." She chewed on her fingernails, picking at the remains of black polish. "Or at least you used to be able to."

"Okay, wait," Miles said, turning in his chair to face her fully. "Start at the beginning. How do you know all this?"

She took a deep breath and recited information as if she were reading from a script. "Okay. My name is Bethany Carter. I've lived here at Longleaf since I was twelve years old; I'm nineteen now. I have experienced episodes of time travel since I was about seven, which my mother assumed were me playing with imaginary friends. When these 'friends' didn't go away, she took me to a therapist who diagnosed me with schizophrenia. He said the 'imaginary friends' were actually hallucinations, and that I needed to be on medication. So he referred me to a psychiatrist who put me on several antipsychotic drugs. But, when the medication only made things worse, mom took me to *another* psychiatrist who said she knew of a facility that specialized in my condition. She referred me here. That was six years ago, and I've been here ever since."

"How can they do that?"

"What? Keep a minor locked up against her will?"

"But you're an adult now," Miles protested.

"Who's been deemed mentally incompetent. I'm not stable enough to sign myself out. So here I sit." She gestured to the bed. "And anyway, at least these people actually believe that I can time-travel."

"What do you mean?"

"To most people my travel looks like hallucinations, seeing things that aren't there, hearing voices. Most people just assume I'm nuts. This place might suck, but it beats the fuck out of getting looked at like you have two heads."

"So then why do you sneak out?"

"How do you know I sneak out?"

"I don't know," Miles said, shocked at his own response. "I just sort of *knew* it all of the sudden."

"Cool," she said. "You might be getting control over it."

Miles gave her a quizzical look.

"The time travel. I told you when you were seventeen that I sneak out. Maybe you remembered it. Do you usually remember when you travel?"

Miles shook his head.

"I didn't used to either. But every now and then, I get flashes, nothing concrete really, but little bits of information here and there. You?"

"Dreams sometimes. Mostly just feelings of déjà vu."

Bethany nodded. "Yeah, I get that too."

They sat in silence. Miles tried to let it all sink in. He really was time-traveling. He'd always believed it but lately he'd started to question his own sanity. Even Ana had started to waver in her belief in his condition.

"Dr. Benson thinks I have Dissociative Identity Disorder."

"But it's like my schizophrenia?"

Miles nodded. "Instead of switching to an alternate personality, I switch to a different age."

"Younger or older?"

"Usually younger, but my older self used to visit when I was a teenager. I don't know if he's been around lately."

"Mine's all over the place too. I basically go into a trance or something when I time-travel. But I saw my daughter the other day. She's fucking blonde. Can you believe it? Makes her own soap or some shit."

"My younger self keeps trying to hook me up with my ex-boyfriend. I think my wife is a little freaked out."

"That the hot Latina who came with you on your first day?"

Miles nodded again. "Ana."

Bethany whistled. "Nicely done, sir. She's lingerie-model hot."

He laughed but felt a sudden pang of loneliness coupled with worry about his wife.

"So tell me more about what goes on here," Miles said. "Is this place legit or is it as creepy as it seems?"

"Well, I'm sure you noticed the other patients steer clear of us?"

"Yeah, what is up with that?"

Bethany shrugged. "My guess is they've been told we're dangerous."

"Why would anyone tell them that?"

She leaned in and whispered, "Because we're part of a top-secret experiment."

Miles rolled his eyes.

"I'm serious," she said. "Dr. Branagan is totally off the grid."

"Oh, come on. How could you possibly know that?"

"Do you want to hear what I know or not?"

Miles mimed zipping his lips together and folded his hands in his lap dramatically.

Bethany giggled at the gesture, but continued. "Longleaf is a legitimate inpatient mental health facility. That much I know. However, it's connected with ChronoCorp."

Miles's jaw dropped. Could it be the same ChronoCorp his parents had told him about?

"You've heard of it?" Bethany said, eyebrows raised.

"You could say that. Tell me what you know."

"I've pieced some stuff together, and the best I can figure is they've been researching time travel for a freaking long time, like since World War Two." While she talked, Bethany opened her notebook and flipped the pages. When she found what she was looking for, she handed it to Miles, pointing to a paragraph at the bottom of the page. "Read that," she said.

In 1976, ChronoCorp relocated its offices from the Cape to an undisclosed location in Florida. That same year, Dr. Emil Branagan disappeared, confirming TimeNet's suspicion that he was involved in the time travel experiments with ChronoCorp. Branagan's last known location before his disappearance was within 90 miles of the most widely accepted location of the ChronoCorp facilities, Winter Haven, Fla. In 2005, his son, Dr. John Branagan, also disappeared under mysterious circumstances. Although his family never reported his disappearance, his pediatrics practice was closed and his staff indicated they did not know where he had gone or if he was still practicing medicine.

"Whoa."

"No kidding. So I started snooping around on the computers whenever I can find one unattended and unlocked, which isn't often. But I managed to find a few policies and stuff. One of them says that no one can disclose the nature of their work here."

"That doesn't seem too strange. I mean it's patient privacy right?"

She shook her head firmly. "It's more than that. It's not just, 'Don't talk about patients.' They're not allowed to tell people what they do. Not even if all they do is empty the trash."

"Okay, that's kind of strange."

"Exactly."

"What's 'TimeNet'? Miles asked.

"Some blog that tracks time travel freaks, conspiracies, whatever. Point is, they've uncovered a shit ton about time travel but almost nothing about ChronoCorp. What do you know about a company called Tempus Labs?"

"The name sounds familiar but I can't figure out why."

She took the notebook back and turned the page. She handed it back to Miles.

He read the passage she pointed to.

1971 -- Mary Dupree, brief period of time travel w/out machine. Tempus Labs created ChronoCorp to study her.

Miles lifted his eyes from the notebook. "Is she here too?"

Bethany's face turned grim. "She died in 1997," she said, "while living here."

They were both silent. Miles couldn't think of a thing to say. He had lost hope for a cure. He was nothing more than a guinea pig at Longleaf. They had no intention of curing him. He'd been betrayed.

"Oh, God, I need to tell Ana."

"Tell her what?" Bethany asked. Her tone was sarcastic and biting. "That you're part of some huge time travel conspiracy? That you're in the care of a man who doesn't care if we live or die?"

"I thought you said you liked it here?"

"I don't *mind* it here. There's a difference." She ran a hand through her hair and tugged on it at the nape of her neck. "If I could get out of here and be sure Dr. Branagan wouldn't find me, I'd be gone tomorrow."

"How can he—?"

"With this." Bethany thrust her arm at Miles and pointed to a small dot. It looked like a freckle, or even a mole. "He put a tracking device in my arm. Whenever I sneak out, they always find me within eight, maybe ten hours. Once I got as far as Atlanta before they nabbed me."

Miles looked at his own arm, studying it for new marks or blemishes. Just an old scar from his arm surgery.

"I don't think they got you yet."

"They strapped me to the bed. Maybe when I was unconscious—"

"Nah, they'll take you to the research wing for stuff like that. Here they like to keep up the charade. No funny business in the residential area."

Miles raised an eyebrow, challenging her.

"Okay, yeah, they tied you to the bed, but that's not completely out of the question for a guy having a psychotic episode, right?"

He didn't want to believe her, but Miles knew she was right. Everything he'd seen so far indicated that Longleaf was a legitimate mental health facility. "So what do we do now?"

Bethany looked thoughtful. "Any idea who your younger self might have called?"

"Why?"

"Well, I think you asked whoever it was to come get you. Maybe they're on their way."

Who would he have called? He could have smacked himself for ignoring the obvious. "Adam."

Bethany tilted her head to the side, her dark hair falling in a diagonal across her face. "Who's that?"

"Remember the ex-boyfriend I told you about? I'd bet anything me-at-seventeen begged him to rescue me."

"That's perfect!" she said. "When he gets here, we can tell him what's going on and he can help you break out."

"What about you?"

She held up her arm. "I'm practically a homing pigeon," she said. "I'd lead them right to you."

"I can't leave you here."

Bethany sighed. "Why don't we just see if Prince Charming shows up first, okay?"

Miles agreed, but somehow he knew Adam would show. The question was, would Adam believe him?

TUESDAY, JANUARY 23, 2001 · 9:04 P.M.

Footsteps echoed through the hallway as they came closer and closer until he could tell someone was standing just outside the door. As he had every night for the last week, Miles closed his eyes tight, hoping the doctor would go away, that tonight they wouldn't poke him with needles and ask him a million questions. He wanted his mommy; even daddy would be better than the mean doctor and his sour-faced staff. He hated them. The way they stood over him so he could see all the way up their noses. The old doctor smelled like cigarettes and Listerine. It made him want to puke.

Miles held his breath and waited. He willed the doctor to go to another room, visit someone else. But then he heard the doorknob turn and he could sense the light on his face even though his eyes were still closed. The door clicked shut and it was dark again.

"I want my mommy," he whispered into the dark.

"Shh, it's okay, little man. We're not going to hurt you," the doctor said.

But Miles knew that was a lie. "You're going to poke me," he cried.

"But you'll get a lollipop after. Don't you want a lollipop?"

"No," Miles said, "I wanna go home."

He felt a cold, papery hand on his arm. "We need to make you all better first."

"I don't feel sick. I feel fine. I want my mommy!"

He started to cry. He didn't want to. Miles wanted to be brave like his daddy, but he was so scared. They were going to hurt him. The white room was so bright and cold. He hated it.

"Where's the nice lady?"

"She's in the lab," the doctor said. He sighed. "I don't have time for this, Miles. Now stand up and put on your slippers. We need to go to the lab and run some tests."

"No! I don't wanna."

The doctor crossed to the door and stuck his head into the hall. "Deb, can you help me out in here?"

"What do you need, doctor?"

When Miles heard her voice, he looked up. It was the nice lady. He smiled.

"Hi, kiddo. What's wrong?" She used the edge of her white coat to dry his tears.

"I don't wanna go to the white room," he said.

"Well, if you don't go with me and Dr. Branagan, you can't have a sucker. Don't you want a sucker?"

Miles nodded excitedly.

"What's your favorite flavor?"

"Grape."

"Mmm, that's mine too." Deb smiled. "Tell you what. If you go with us and let Dr. Branagan do a couple quick tests, I'll give you two grape suckers."

"Two?"

She nodded. "Just for you. How does that sound?"

Miles was about to agree but then he saw the doctor's wrinkly old face. "NO!" he shouted, crossing his arms and dropping his chin to his chest in an exaggerated pout.

"I don't have time for this. We're going to have to restrain him."

"Do you think that's necessary?"

"Don't question me, nurse. Now please, hold him down for me so I can sedate him." He reached into his pocket and pulled out a syringe.

"NO! HE'S GONNA STICK ME! DON'T LET HIM STICK ME!"

"Shh, Miles. It's okay. I promise. Shhh."

Deb's voice was drowned out by Miles's wailing. She held him tightly, and soon the drugs began to take effect. Miles felt his head grow heavy and his limbs grow weak.

"I feel funny," he said.

"Shh, go to sleep, little one."

SATURDAY, JUNE 20, 2020 · 1:33 P.M.

"Guess this is the place," Michaela said. They pulled up outside a nondescript complex of buildings that reminded Adam of his middle school in Texas. She put the car in park and they stared up at the sign over the door. "I gotta say, I was expecting something a little more... ominous."

"I know what you mean. It looks like a bunch of sixth graders are going to come bounding out of that door at any minute."

"Do we just go in or?" She craned her neck, following Adam's eye line to the door.

"There has to be some procedure for visitors," he reasoned. "Let's just walk through the front door and find out."

"Well, when you put it like that, it sounds so easy." Michaela laughed, which reassured Adam a little. She looked so relaxed, but she had to be as nervous as he was. Without her usual sweater and scarf bundled around her, Michaela looked much smaller, younger somehow.

Adam took a deep breath. "Come on," he said, opening the passenger door.

Michaela unbuckled her seatbelt and followed. She reached for Adam's hand, and he gladly took it as they made their way up the ramp and to the door. It took every ounce of courage Adam could muster, but he grabbed the door handle and pulled. The air conditioning hit them in the face. He hadn't realized he was sweating. Michaela shivered next to him.

Inside the door, a plump older woman wearing Mickey Mouse scrubs greeted them from behind a reception desk. "Welcome to Longleaf," she said. "If I can get you to sign in." She pushed a clipboard and a pen forward.

Michaela and Adam exchanged a look. Adam's laugh came out in a rush, and when he tried to stop it, he snorted. Michaela held her hand in front of her face to cover her responding giggle. Adam felt stupid for being so nervous.

The woman at the desk raised an eyebrow, and Adam cleared his throat. "Thank you," he said. He wrote their names on the list and handed it back.

"I'll just need your driver's licenses and the name of the patient you'll be visiting." Her words came out mechanical and rote.

"Sure." Adam pulled his license out of his wallet as Michaela did the same. "We're here to see Miles Lawson."

She took their licenses and typed something into the computer in front of her. A nearby printer whirred to life as she opened a drawer and took out two plastic clips. "Make sure you wear these at all times while you're here and please stick to the common areas and the patient's room. No wandering about." At the last part she looked at Michaela who gave her best "who me?" look. "And don't forget visiting hours end promptly at six." She handed them their visitor's passes, twin laminated badges that read "visitor" in bold letters with Miles's name and a six-digit number printed below. "We'll hold on to your driver's licenses until you turn those in." She pointed to the badges. "Any questions?"

"Where do we go?"

"Follow the hallway and make your second left, go all the way down to the nurses' station. They'll help you find your friend." She smiled, but instead of reassuring him, it brought back Adam's nerves.

"Uh, thanks," he mumbled.

Michaela nudged him in the back and he stumbled forward. When they were out of earshot, she whispered, "God, I thought I was going to puke before we walked in here, and then it was just like when I visited my sister when she had the twins. Easy peasy."

"You think so?"

Michaela smiled and threaded her arm through his. "Relax," she said.

Adam glanced around. The hallway was bright and sterile, and the entire place looked as though it hadn't been updated in decades. Michaela's hair had taken on an unnatural orange glow under the fluorescent lights, the same shade he saw every day in the lab. He felt safer somehow.

When they approached the nurses' station, Michaela spoke, which Adam was thankful for. "Can you tell us where to find Miles Lawson?"

Before the nurse could reply, Adam heard his voice.

"You came," he said.

Adam turned. Miles's face was ashen; his cheeks were hollow, as if he'd lost at least ten pounds, but Adam knew instantly he was the adult Miles. There was something in his eyes, a dark resignation that he and Adam were no longer friends, that gave it away. When the younger version of Miles visited, his eyes sparkled with adoration, the way they had when he was a teenager. When he was in love with Adam.

"You asked me to come get you. I was worried."

"I'm glad you came." Miles lifted a corner of his mouth, but didn't fully smile. He glanced at Michaela.

"Hi, I'm Michaela." She held out her hand.

"I asked her to drive me," Adam said. "Didn't want Anthony to worry."

"We work together," Michaela explained.

Silence stretched out between them, an uncomfortable, impenetrable wall. And yet, somehow, Adam found the courage to scale it.

"Are you okay?" he asked.

Miles fidgeted, picking at the skin around his left thumb, and as he spoke he stared at the floor. "Yeah, I'm fine. Well, I mean apart from being in a mental health facility. Sure, I'm fine."

"Miles, tell me what's wrong." Adam leaned down to meet his gaze.

"I'm sorry you had to drive all this way," Miles said. "I can pay you back for the gas when I get out of here." He still wouldn't meet Adam's eyes.

Adam grabbed him by the shoulders. "I know it wasn't you who called me, but I've got to tell you, your younger alter sounded really upset. So I need you to tell me if there's anything to worry about."

After a moment, Miles looked up. He glanced over Adam's shoulder toward the nurses' station. He whispered, "Let's go to my room. I'll explain there."

THE ROOM WAS SMALL AND held only the barest of necessities. One bed was stripped of any sheets or blankets, and on the other sat a girl with dark hair that fell in her face. She was biting her nails.

She waved at them. "You must be Boy Wonder's ex-boyfriend," she said. "My name's Bethany."

"This is Michaela," Miles added.

"Hey."

Bethany seemed to be in her late teens, maybe early twenties, but her mannerisms were far more childlike. At the mention of Michaela, her posture shrank and she began playing with her hair.

"Miles, what's this all about?" Adam asked. "I drove all this way, and I want some answers."

"God, at least shut the door," Bethany said.

Miles obeyed, which only confused Adam further.

"You probably want to sit down for this," Bethany said.

Why was she calling the shots? Adam looked at Miles and waited. Finally Miles gestured to the empty bed. Michaela sat next to him and crossed her legs. Adam continued to stare at Miles.

"I don't think I can stay here," Miles said. He sat in the chair next to the small desk closest to them. "It's not a good place."

"What do you need me for?"

"You can get me out of here."

"Why not just call Ana? She knows you're here, right? Call her. She's your wife."

"I don't think she'll believe me."

"Believe *what*? You're talking in riddles." Adam's voice was louder than he intended, but he was growing frustrated.

"I think what Miles is trying to say is that Ana helped put him here. She may not be too keen on getting him out so soon," Bethany said. She gave Miles a sympathetic look.

"Have you even tried?"

"The phone in the lounge is always in use," Miles said. "And we don't get our cell phones for personal calls until tomorrow. I think my younger self was trying to help me by calling you. He could have called Ana but he chose you. I think there's a reason."

Adam dropped his head in his hands. "This is fucking nuts," he said.

"I know it's a little crazy."

Adam looked up. "A *little* crazy? Can you fucking hear yourself?"

Michaela patted him on the leg. "Adam, I think—"

"No, don't try to soothe me, Michaela. My fucking ex-boyfriend, who has refused to talk to me for seven years, suddenly reappears in my life, introduces himself to my fiancé, passes out in my driveway, calls me in a panic... twice, and then begs me to bail him out of a nut house. I think I have a right to be a little upset!"

"I just think you should hear him out," Michaela said, her voice soft and gentle. "We drove all this way, and I know you'll hate yourself if you don't at least find out why he called."

"Listen to her, man. She's a smart chick." Bethany smiled at them, but when Michaela glanced over, she dropped her head and began picking at the edge of one of her sneakers.

"Fine," Adam said, taking a deep breath. "I'll hear you out, Miles."

"Thank you," he said.

"Don't thank me yet," Adam said. "I agreed to hear what you had to say. I didn't say I'd help you."

SATURDAY, JUNE 20, 2020 · 2:02 P.M.

When Miles finished telling Adam what he knew about ChronoCorp, Longleaf and Dr. Branagan, the four of them sat in silence. Finally Adam made eye contact with him.

"Now you see why I have to leave," Miles said.

"I don't get it," Michaela interjected. "If you're here voluntarily, why can't you just sign yourself out?"

"I can't. My voluntary commitment is conditional. I need a doctor's approval to go home."

"And guess who's the only one who can do that?" Bethany said, rolling her eyes.

"Branagan," Adam replied.

Bethany tapped her index finger to her nose and pointed at Adam. "We have a winner, ladies and gentlemen."

Adam ignored her comment and grew serious. "Okay, we need to think about this strategically. If we try to walk out the front door with you in tow, we'll definitely be seen. There's a lot of open space around this place."

"And that lady at the front desk has our IDs," Michaela added.

"Right." Adam furrowed his brow the way he used to when learning a particularly hard drum combination. He was thinking.

"I know a way out," Bethany said. "But you'd have to go at night."

"I could sneak out and meet you somewhere," Miles offered.

"I know a bar on the edge of town," Bethany said. "I go there sometimes when I want to pretend to be normal."

"That could work," Michaela said. "We could wait until it gets dark and then meet you there."

"I'm still not sure this is such a good idea," Adam said.

Everyone turned to face him. He seemed to be the only one not on board, and Miles felt a pang of disappointment.

"We came all this way," Michaela said. "Don't you want to help?"

"First of all, you used that argument already to convince me to hear him out. Second, of course I want to help. I just think we need to think this through. Miles voluntarily committed himself here and his wife and therapist agreed to it. It feels wrong to go off half-cocked."

Michaela and Bethany both snickered.

"Stop. This is serious." Adam gave them both a chastising look, but Miles could see that even after they stopped laughing, they were still looking at each other and turning red.

Adam was growing visibly frustrated, and this was getting them nowhere.

"Ladies, do you think you could give us a moment to talk alone?" Miles asked.

Bethany was out the door before Miles could say another word. Michaela, however, looked to Adam for reassurance, and when he nodded, she followed Bethany into the hall.

When the door clicked shut, Miles crossed the room to sit beside Adam on the bed.

"I know this is complicated for you," he said. "But I wouldn't ask you for help if it wasn't a life-or-death situation, you know that right?"

"Yeah, but you didn't ask me for help. *He* did."

"True," Miles said. "But he's still me. He's just the me who's in love with you."

Adam turned and looked out the window, his eyes watery. "How long do you think he has before he hates me?"

The words hit Miles in the chest like a cannonball. All the pain of losing Adam when they were eighteen came rushing back, filling his body with tension and regret. He cleared his throat.

"I think, uh, probably a few weeks at the most. He said it was almost time for graduation."

"Dahlia's party."

"Yeah."

"Did you ever think—?"

"About warning him?"

Adam nodded.

"I did. But I told Ana not to. I needed to experience that to be who I am today. I couldn't take that away from her."

Adam's jaw tightened. "You could have warned me," he said.

"Would you have believed me?" Miles tilted his head to catch Adam's gaze. "You couldn't even believe me about the time travel. And Danny Dubrow? You'd have laughed in my face."

Adam laughed. "True." He rubbed his left eye. "I'm sorry about that, you know."

"I know," Miles said. He grabbed Adam's hand where it lay between them on the bed and squeezed. "It's in the past. We have to move forward."

Adam looked at their hands, his expression frozen between confusion and anger. "I loved you so much," he said. "I fucked up so bad and I just kept fucking up. I couldn't forgive myself." He pulled away and folded his hands in his lap. "Because you couldn't forgive me."

"It wasn't just kissing Danny. I felt betrayed because you told him about the time travel."

"That was pretty shitty of me. I'll give you that. I was so fucking drunk, though. And… " He paused, and Miles held his breath. It seemed as if he'd waited eons to hear why Adam had betrayed him. "I thought I'd lost you."

The answer left him feeling empty. Only after hearing it did he realize he didn't know what he had expected. That Adam had hated him all along? That Danny was the love of his life? That he'd temporarily gone insane? He had planned for a million and one scenarios. Everything but the perfectly ordinary "I was afraid of losing you."

"And you lost me anyway," Miles said. "Ironic isn't it?"

"I think it's what you call a self-fulfilling prophecy."

"So what now? Are you going to help me?"

Adam took a breath so deep he tilted his head back, and Miles felt the mattress shift beneath them. "Miles, please understand. I want to help you. I'm just uncomfortable doing anything without talking to Ana first. She is your wife, after all."

"I know she's my wife," Miles said bitterly. "But she's not here."

"Only because you haven't called her. She loves you. You don't think she'd be here as fast as she could if she thought you were in danger?"

Miles shrugged. "Maybe. I think she's overwhelmed with my condition and just wants me to get better."

"You don't honestly think she'd leave you in here if you told her what you told me."

"I don't know what I think anymore, Adam. I feel like my life is falling apart." Miles dropped his head in his hands and fought back tears. Adam began to rub gentle circles on his back. He tensed at the touch.

"Sorry," Adam mumbled. "I thought you liked that."

"I did," Miles said. "Not anymore."

"I guess it really has been a long time."

"I'm sorry I haven't talked to you in so long," Miles said. "I was hurt, but I shouldn't have just cut you off like that."

"It's in the past. I don't like playing the 'what if' game."

"It's not a game," Miles said. "I have the chance to fix it."

Adam looked confused. "I think it's a little late for that."

"I can time-travel. Or do you still not believe me?"

Adam stood. He crossed the room in three steps and stood at Miles's desk. He looked down at the journal and one pen that sat on it. "You know, I've given that a lot of thought." He turned to face Miles. "I know I teased you about it when we were together, but you have to see it from my perspective. Time travel? It's insane. How was I supposed to know it was real?"

"And now?"

Adam picked at a rough edge on the desk, unable or perhaps unwilling to make eye contact. "Yeah, I believe you," he said, looking up and meeting Miles's gaze, his soulful brown eyes brimming with tears.

Miles went to him and wrapped him in a tight hug. Adam's arms folded around him and he squeezed. They stayed like that for a while, and Miles realized they hadn't been this close in years, not like this. Not physically and emotionally at the same time. A familiar swooping feeling in Miles's stomach caught him off guard, and he pulled back suddenly.

"I'm sorry, was it okay that I did that?" he asked.

Adam wiped a tear from his cheek. "Uh, yeah. It's okay."

Miles shifted nervously on his feet, wondering what to say next. "So will you help me?"

Adam closed his eyes and nodded slowly.

Before Miles could thank him, Bethany burst through the door. "You guys need to wrap it up quickly. Dr. Branagan is on his way, and who knows what he'll do if he sees us all in here talking."

"Shit, okay. Give Michaela the name of the bar and then go back to your room," he said. "I'll set everything up with them and fill you in at dinner."

"Okay," Bethany said, beaming. "We're breaking you out."

When she was gone, Adam turned to face Miles. "She's not coming with you?"

"She can't," Miles said. "That bastard Branagan put a fucking tracking chip in her arm."

Miles hadn't noticed that Michaela had returned until she said, "So let's cut it out." When the guys looked at her incredulously she said, "What? In for a penny in for a pound, right?"

"You know, I think I like this girl," Miles said.

"So, I HEARD YOU HAD some visitors." Dr. Branagan appeared at Miles's doorway, ghostlike and stern. It was less than five minutes after Michaela and Adam had left, and Miles was still sitting at his desk, trying to piece together his feelings about his conversation with Adam. He jumped at the sound of the doctor's voice. They'd only met once, the day he'd come to Longleaf.

"Good to see you're back to yourself again."

Okay, so they'd met while he was time-traveling. Still, it unnerved him to have the doctor suddenly in his personal space. Even though he'd only been at Longleaf a few days, he had started to make a place for himself, and his room had started to feel more like his.

"Did we have an appointment?"

Miles turned to watch Dr. Branagan work his way into the room and sit on the empty bed facing him.

"I thought we could chat a little, maybe I could answer some questions for you. I'm sure you have a lot of them."

"About?"

Dr. Branagan took off his glasses, revealing that his eyes were much smaller than the lenses made them look, and cleaned them on the edge of his lab coat. "Questions about me, Longleaf, the work we do." He paused and put his glasses back on. "Maybe about ChronoCorp."

Miles's blood ran cold. How could Dr. Branagan know what he and Bethany had talked about?

"I assume you've talked to Miss Carter about it," Dr. Branagan offered. "A regular Sherlock Holmes, that one. We've had to up our security here since she's been a resident." He smiled, his perfectly straight dentures looking unnaturally young compared to the rest of him.

"Don't be shy, Mr. Lawson. I know everything that goes on here. You can't shock me."

"How long have you been studying me?"

"You know more than I thought." He looked impressed. "Um, since you were a child. Your Uncle Bob's brother used to work for me and he brought you in. I think you were about six."

His heart racing, Miles couldn't think. His brain misfired every time he thought about that trip. Memories flooded his mind, drowning him in panic. He fought to control his breathing as he felt the headache start to bloom behind his eyes.

"Stay with me," Dr. Branagan said. "Focus on the here and now. Take deep breaths and don't let the panic take over. You can fight the urge to time-travel."

Through the fog of his episode, Miles could hear Dr. Branagan's words and he tried to focus on them. Breathing in and out as evenly as he could, Miles focused on his shoelaces. He felt the fake leather of the chair he sat in, smelled the citrus odor from the hallway, heard the whir of the air conditioning. His headache started to fade and his body felt more secure. The fog lifted and the only evidence that remained of the episode was a sheen of sweat on his forehead.

"Good, good." Dr. Branagan sounded like a cartoon villain. Miles half expected to see him steepling his fingers beneath his chin.

"How did you know that would work?" Miles asked, his voice thin and weak.

"I told you, I've been studying you for a long time. And a lot of other people too."

"Like Bethany?"

"Yes, Miss Carter is a special case. We've been treating her for quite a while. She has quite a bit of difficulty controlling her time travel."

"I can't control it either," Miles said.

"You just did."

As much as he wanted to argue, he knew Dr. Branagan was right. He had stopped an episode as it was happening. How could that be possible?

"If I can control it, then you can release me," Miles said.

Dr. Branagan laughed. "It's not that easy."

"But you just said—"

"You controlled it *once* and it was under my guidance. That's hardly enough to warrant releasing you." He stood and crossed to the window. "I need you to understand, Miles, that what we do here is vital to the future of mankind. Your condition is unique. There are fewer than a hundred cases on record today. Only six hundred or so since I started my research. We have to make sacrifices sometimes for the greater good."

"Like Mary Dupree?"

"That was an unfortunate situation," he said. Even with his back to Miles, Dr. Branagan had obviously tensed at the question. "She was... not well and did things that went against my recommendations." He turned to face Miles. "That's why it's crucial that you remain in my care until we have established that you are capable of controlling your time travel episodes."

"Then what do we need to do so I can control it?"

A menacing grin crept across Dr. Branagan's face as he placed a hand on Miles's shoulder. "I'm glad you're seeing reason, Miles. We'll set up a treatment plan and get started on the necessary tests first thing tomorrow. How does that sound?"

The idea of being poked and prodded made Miles sick to his stomach, but he reminded himself that he would be gone by then. He only needed to make it through dinner tonight and then he'd be free. Adam was going to save him.

"I'm ready. Let's do it."

"I knew you were a smart man. I'll see you tomorrow morning Miles. I'll send Kathy for you after breakfast."

When he was gone, Miles felt a lingering chill. He took the blanket from his bed and cocooned himself within it. A shiver rolled up his spine. Midnight couldn't come soon enough.

SATURDAY, NOVEMBER 3, 2012 · 9:56 P.M.

"No, no... NO!" Miles's own shouts caused him to wake, and it took him a second or two to figure out where he was. The road noise surrounded him and the hard back of the bus seat was digging into his right shoulder. An arm reached around him in a comforting embrace.

"It's okay, shh. You're fine." Adam's voice was soothing, and his arms cradled Miles gently. "It was just a bad dream."

Miles glanced around, taking in the bus full of band kids. His memory came flooding back. They were on their way back from a day-long competition in Tampa, and everyone was exhausted. The near-silence told him most of the bus was still asleep. He exhaled and relaxed into Adam's body.

"God, it was so real," Miles said. "I was in, like, an operating room. It was so bright. And this old man stood over me. He had those abnormally perfect dentures, like my gramps. Made his face look out of proportion. He told me to relax and take deep breaths, but I couldn't slow down my breathing. I couldn't. And I felt so small, Adam. Like a little kid. I couldn't stop it. I tried but I couldn't."

"Couldn't stop what?"

Miles thought. "I'm not sure," he said. "It's fuzzy, but I think they were running tests on me and I didn't want them to touch me. I hated all the needles, and there was this IV bag and I was strapped to the bed. I couldn't move."

Miles could see Danny and Max from the trumpet section looking back at them, but Adam told them to mind their own business. He stroked Miles's cheek gently and spoke softly.

"It's fine," he said. "You're safe now. I won't let them get you."

"It just felt so real," Miles said. "Like I was really there."

SATURDAY, JUNE 20, 2020 · 10:03 P.M.

The tea steeped while Ana watched the steam roll over the edge of the mugs. "Do you take honey?" she asked.

Darius sat down heavily in one of their kitchen chairs and draped his messenger bag over the chair next to him. "Yeah, that's fine."

"Thanks for coming over so late. With Miles gone..." Ana trailed off. She brought the honey to the table and sat down facing Darius. She knew what was coming and yet she couldn't start the conversation. She waited for Darius to speak.

"Will you please tell me what's going on?" Darius's hazel eyes were full of concern. "I haven't heard from Miles in weeks. That's not like him. A few days, maybe, but weeks?"

Ana twisted her hair into a loose bun and tied it at the nape of her neck. She stirred her tea and took a sip. She was stalling. "He didn't want me to tell you," she said finally.

"Tell me what?"

Ana took another sip. She stared into the mug and felt the warmth pour into her hands. "He's in an inpatient psychiatric facility."

"Wait... what? For how long?"

"He's been in therapy for a few years now. Those fainting spells and all the clumsy injuries? It's because he has a dissociative disorder, and it's been getting worse lately. His psychiatrist thought he would be better off in inpatient care for a while."

"He's in the loony bin?"

"Please don't call it that."

"Sorry, I'm just in shock, I guess. I didn't know he... Is he going to be all right?"

Ana broke down. "I don't know," she said. "I just don't know. Oh God. What if he's not okay?"

Before she knew it, Darius had moved his chair closer and wrapped his arms around her. It felt so good to simply be held. When was the last time someone held her like this? Tears rolled down her cheeks, landing on Darius's shirt in misshapen splotches, like a pathetic Rorschach test that she was definitely failing.

Pulling back, Ana suddenly felt ashamed. "I'm so sorry, Darius. I shouldn't have unloaded on you like that." She wiped at her eyes with the back of her sleeve.

"No worries. That's what friends are for, right?"

"We're not exactly friends, Darius."

"The way I see it, Miles is like family. You're his lady, so that makes you family too. Just how it is." Darius's smile was infectious. Ana couldn't help but return it.

"Thanks," she said. "I've just been so lonely with Miles gone. This house feels huge and I got in a fight with my mom."

"When it rains it pours."

"Exactly." Ana twirled the mug between her hands. "Meanwhile, I just want Miles to get better. He's been so strong up until now, and lately things have just been falling apart."

"You know, now that you mention it, he has been acting kind of weird lately."

Ana sat up straight. "What do you mean?"

"Okay, so like a couple weeks ago, I call him to check on an email he was supposed to send me, and he's rambling about time travel and wanting to do a story on *Back to the Future* or something. So he has me look up this corporation, Chromo-something, and it turns out that it's some top secret company that's been off the grid for years. Real creepy shit, right? But the more I keep digging, the more this company turns out to be harder to find information on. It's a black hole."

"Weird," Ana said. "I wonder why he had you looking into that."

"To be honest, I'm still not sure I know. It's crazy, man."

Ana nodded. "I just never know which Miles I'm going to get." She was being intentionally vague, but she needed to talk to someone and not have it turn into a discussion on whether they believed in time travel. "I mean, he's always been kind of all over the place, but lately... Well, you know."

"I kind of like that about him, you know? It keeps things interesting. But I can see how it might not be as appealing in a husband."

"That's an understatement." She took a drink of her tea, which had gone cold. "You want another cup?" She walked to the sink and poured hers out. The kettle still had some water in it, so she turned the stove on to re-heat it.

"No, I'm fine," he said. "Why don't you come sit back down?"

"I need something to do with my hands," she said. "I've done so much sitting lately. You want a sandwich or something?" She opened the fridge. It was empty except for a few cans of Diet Coke and a half dozen or so takeout containers. Shopping hadn't been a priority lately, and cooking for one was just depressing.

"Ana, please sit down."

She sighed. "What if he doesn't come home? What am I going to do?"

Darius stood and pulled her into another embrace, reaching around her to turn off the stove. "He's going to come home. That man would move mountains for you. Don't you know that?"

Listening to Darius's heartbeat as he held her, Ana felt herself relax. She tried to remember when she last felt protected by Miles. She looked up into Darius's handsome face, tracing the line of his jaw framed in dark stubble. She tried to remember her husband's face, but as soon as she brought it into focus in her mind, the image floated away.

Darius's face came closer, his full lips beckoning, and she felt herself lean in to the pull of his orbit. Her face tilted upward to meet his. Just as their lips were about to meet, the doorbell pierced the intimate bubble that surrounded them. The sound was like cold water being thrown in her face. Ana jumped back and clutched her chest.

"What is wrong with me?"

"You're under a lot of stress. Don't worry about it."

"I'm married. You're practically Miles's boss. This is sick."

The doorbell sounded again.

"You should go," she said. "Out the back."

"Don't you think you're overreacting to—?"

Ana shoved his bag at him, corralling him toward the lanai. "Just close the sliding door behind you. I'll lock it later."

But Darius stood firm. Ana shoved again, trying to edge him toward the door. "Please," she said. "I just can't deal with this right now. I'll call you."

"I'll hold you to that," Darius said.

Ana waited until she saw him disappear around the side of the house before going to the door. She was so rattled by their almost kiss, she forgot to look out the window before swinging the door wide.

"What are you doing here?"

Torn between excitement and terror, Ana couldn't understand why her husband was standing in the doorway beaming at her like Christmas morning. Over his shoulder she could see Adam and a pretty young woman with strawberry-blonde hair whom she didn't recognize. What the hell were they doing here?

Miles looked hurt. "Aren't you glad to see me?"

"I am... I just—Shouldn't you be at Longleaf? How did you get here?"

"Adam broke me out. Let us in and I can explain everything." He said it as if it was so obvious and gave her this look that said, *How can you doubt me?* Ana felt sick.

"You have to go back," she said.

Miles's face fell. "I'm not going back. That's what I came to tell you. Please let me in, Ana. This is our home."

Ana stepped aside reluctantly and let the three of them in.

"I still say we should go back for Bethany." The redhead was taking off a lavender sweater and making herself at home. "That poor girl."

"Who's Bethany?" Ana asked.

"Another patient at Longleaf," Miles said. He turned to the redhead. "But we can't go back for her, Michaela. You know that."

"Miles, I'm really confused. I'm calling Dr. Branagan." As she reached for the phone, all three of them shouted, "NO!"

Ana startled, dropping her cell phone on the floor. Her hands were shaking as she bent to pick it up.

Miles rested a hand on her shoulder. "Let's just sit down and talk, okay?" He seemed so calm. How could he be so nonchalant? He'd broken out of a psychiatric facility. He was supposed to stay at Longleaf until Dr. Branagan signed him out, until he was cured. What the hell was going on?

The couch cushion sagged when Miles sat down next to her. Ana hadn't realized she'd sat down herself. "Will someone please tell me what's going on?" Her heart was racing; her body was flooded with adrenalin.

She looked at each one of them, but Michaela was the only one making eye contact.

"That place isn't what you think it is," she said.

"And who the fuck are you?" Ana asked. Rage bubbled up inside her like molten lava.

Michaela's face flushed pink. "I'm uh, Michaela McDonald. I, um..." She swallowed.

"Michaela's my work colleague," Adam said. "Ana, I know this must be a huge shock to you, but we do have an explanation. Please?"

She nodded slowly, but held her phone tightly in her hand. If she didn't like this explanation, she was going to call Dr. Benson and maybe even Dr. Branagan.

"First of all," Miles said, "and I know this is going to be hard to believe, but time travel is one hundred percent real. I've been time-traveling since I was a kid."

"But Dr. Benson said—"

Miles took Ana's hand and caressed it gently. "Dr. Benson was wrong. She didn't have the whole story."

"And you do?" Ana knew she sounded petulant, but she couldn't help it. Her words came out sharp and angry before she could stop herself.

"I know more about my condition than I did a week ago—and certainly more than Dr. Benson."

Ana remained unconvinced. She turned her phone over in her hand, wondering if she could get the number dialed before one of them stopped her.

"That place, Longleaf? It's a front for another business. A corporation that has been studying time travel for a long time. Dr. Branagan has been monitoring me since I was six, and he manipulated you and Dr. Benson to get me to Longleaf. So he could study me."

Ana stared at him. His words made sense individually but she couldn't fully grasp what he was saying. She couldn't believe it. The place she had taken Miles to was a *nice* place. It had a real brochure and real patients. It was real.

"That's not possible," she whispered.

"It's true," Adam said. "Bethany told us all about it."

Ana glared at him. "Oh, and so we're just supposed to believe this random girl who's in a loony bin? Yeah, that sounds fucking brilliant, Adam."

"Ana, please." Miles reached out for her hand again, but she yanked it away. His eyes welled up when she met his gaze, and her heart broke a little.

Ana stood up. "I need to use the bathroom," she said.

She could feel their eyes on her as she left the room, but she kept moving. When the bathroom door was safely locked behind her, she allowed herself to fall apart. She choked back sobs, trying to keep quiet, as tears fell. Her body shuddered with each inhale, every inch of her feeling the anguish of Miles's betrayal. He'd promised her he'd see this through, and now instead of finishing treatment, he'd concocted some crazy story about an evil corporation. Worse still, he'd convinced Adam to help him, making her look like a fool.

He had to go back. He had to. Ana lifted her phone and dialed.

WEDNESDAY, AUGUST 1, 2018 · 12:07 P.M.

"I am worried about my Ana. She is not herself since Monica died."

Ana sat on the stairs, eavesdropping on her mother talking to their neighbor, June, an older woman who had babysat Ana and Monica when they were little girls.

"Sugar, she'll come around. Those girls were thick as thieves. I'm sure she misses her sister a lot."

It had been a week since the funeral, and Ana was still sleeping in her childhood room with the One Direction posters over the bed. She only had a few vacation days left, so she knew she'd have to go home eventually, but she just couldn't bear to be away from things that reminded her of Monica. Their rooms were joined by a bathroom, and every night, after the house went quiet, Ana would open the pocket door and sneak into Monica's closet. When they were girls, they would sit in there and tell each other scary stories. Somehow it seemed as if Monica might still be there if she closed her eyes and told a story to the old toys and blankets that now filled the musty space.

"She is going to put me in the early grave. I already lose one daughter and then Ana pulls that stint in the bathroom."

"I think you mean stunt, dear."

"Eh, you know what I mean," Julia said.

Despite her grief, Ana had to bite her cheek not to laugh. June was always correcting her mother's English and she was the only one who could get away with it. If Ana or Monica ever tried, they would get a speech about how hard it was to move to this country without knowing the language, and how she'd learned English from television. "If my English is so bad," she would say, "then it is because the Americans mess it up in the television." God help them if they tried to tell her it was "on the television." The worst part was, her English always got worse when she was angry or upset.

"Pardon me for asking, Julia, but what stunt did she pull? Why are you so frazzled?"

Ana could picture June's plump face growing soft with concern and her tiny hands resting on her mother's while they sat at the kitchen table drinking homemade sangria.

She couldn't make out what her mother said next, but soon, she heard muffled sobs followed by June's soothing shushing. Something in her exploded. She jumped up from her spot on the stairs and burst into the kitchen.

"It was an accident!" she shouted. "I was NOT trying to kill myself. Stop telling people I have a death wish!"

"You had a knife," her mother cried. "You slit the wrists like you were cutting through chicken. I find you in a pool of your own blood!" She collapsed into her own arms, folded in front of her on the table.

"June, I didn't try to kill myself." Ana's voice was restrained, and tears streaked her face. "I just miss Monica so much."

"I know, dear."

Ana fell into June's arms, leaving her mother to cry it out on her own. She wanted to wallow in her anger a while longer. Even the guilt she felt for yelling at her mother wasn't enough to make her apologize. Not yet.

CHAPTER TWENTY-SIX
MILES

SATURDAY, JUNE 20, 2020 · 10:26 P.M.

Ana was in the bathroom for a while. Miles could tell that Adam and Michaela were starting to feel uncomfortable. His own heart beat heavily in his chest as he stared at the door leading to their master bedroom.

Adam's hand was warm on Miles's arm, his fingers just barely grazing his skin where his T-shirt ended.

"Should you go talk to her?" Adam asked.

"She'll be fine," Miles said, without making eye contact. "Maybe you guys should go."

Adam tensed behind him.

"Are you sure you're okay alone?" Michaela asked.

"I'm not alone. Ana's here." Miles smiled at them, but he doubted that she was fully on his side. "I'll be fine, really. She'll come around." He hoped.

"Promise you'll call if you need anything," Adam said. He looked skeptical.

"I will," Miles said, trying to smile. He wanted Adam to stay, but couldn't bring himself to ask.

Adam and Michaela left, and Miles contemplated going to talk to Ana, but she must have been listening because she came out almost as soon as Miles closed the door behind them.

"You okay?" Miles asked.

"Yeah."

"I'm sorry if I scared you."

She stared at him with dull eyes. Something was missing.

"Miles, will you tell me the truth? Why did you leave Longleaf?"

He didn't understand. "I told you. That place isn't safe. It isn't normal."

"Is this about Adam? How old are you?"

"I'm twenty-six," he said. "What the hell, Ana? It's me."

"How can I be sure? Tell me something only *my* Miles would know."

He recoiled at being called *her* Miles, but he knew what she needed to hear. "Our wedding was in your mother's backyard. It poured down rain immediately after the ceremony was finished and we couldn't take the photos for an hour. The cake was ruined."

"You could have watched our wedding video," she said.

Miles sighed. "Okay, you have a freckle on your left butt cheek that I named Hector, and you said you hated that name because it reminded you of your grandfather."

She looked thoughtful, studying Miles's face as if trying to read his thoughts.

Then the doorbell rang. Without a word, Ana went to the door and opened it. There, under the porch light, and looking far less put together than Miles had ever seen her, was Dr. Benson.

"Hello, Miles," she said.

"What are you doing here?" he asked.

"I could ask the same of you. Does Dr. Branagan know where you are?"

"Does he know where *you* are?" Miles retorted.

"There's no need to be hostile, Miles. I'm here because Ana called me."

Miles stared at her in shock.

"I'm so sorry, honey." Ana's eyes were already swimming in tears. "I didn't know what else to do."

"I'm not going back there," he said. "I'm not."

Ana stepped closer to him. She reached out to touch his arm, but he pulled back. She folded her arms across her chest. "Miles, I know this is hard to hear, but you don't have a choice. You signed yourself into Dr. Branagan's care."

"Surely there has to be a way around that." Miles looked from one to the other, begging them silently to take his side.

"I'm afraid not," Dr. Benson said. "I've come to take you back. I thought that might be less threatening than someone from Longleaf. I promise you this is for your own good. Don't you trust me?"

He couldn't trust anyone. "I'm not going," he said again.

"Ana, could you leave us for a few moments? I'd like to talk to Miles in private."

Ana nodded and went to their bedroom. When the door clicked shut, Dr. Benson led Miles to the sofa.

"Let's have a little chat, shall we?"

Without makeup, Dr. Benson looked older; her features were washed out and her color was just a little off. Her eyes seemed smaller. It reminded him of Dr. Branagan.

"Fine, tell me what you know about Dr. Branagan and ChronoCorp." He challenged her with a raised eyebrow, but her expression remained neutral.

"Dr. Branagan is the head psychiatrist at Longleaf, and I've never heard of ChronoCorp." Her bottom lip twitched. She was hiding something. She knew more than she let on.

"I don't believe you."

"Miles, when have I ever been dishonest with you? I would not be taking you back there if I thought you were in any kind of danger."

The truth winked at him from within the lie. She knew what was going on, but she truly believed Miles wasn't in danger.

"You weren't there," Miles said, focusing on his hands. He chewed his nails. "Dr. Branagan is not a good man."

"Don't be silly, Miles. He's a doctor, no more, no less."

"Even so, I'm not going back."

She took off her glasses and pinched the bridge of her nose. "I'm not negotiating with you, Miles, but if you wish to be a full participant in your own life—a husband, a son, maybe one day a father—you must accept the reality of your life as it is now, with all your struggles, before you will be able to heal. Accepting it means getting treatment."

"I can continue treatment with you."

"No, Miles. I've done all I can for you. You need someone who specializes in your condition. Dr. Branagan is that person."

"He specializes in time travel. Did you know that?"

She didn't flinch. Not even a blink. She knew.

"You told Ana you didn't believe I was time-traveling."

"I did what I had to do in order to get you in treatment." She looked vindicated. "I did my job."

How many times could he be betrayed in a lifetime? "You lied to me," he said softly.

"It was for your own good."

Miles felt numb. He was alone; Ana was against him and Dr. Benson had betrayed him. His head began to throb, and his vision grew fuzzy.

"Not now!" he shrieked. He tried to remember what Dr. Branagan had told him about controlling his travel, but panic overcame reason.

Dr. Benson reared back in shock as Miles fell to the floor, slipping into unconsciousness.

MILES OPENED HIS EYES TO find Dr. Benson standing over him. It only took him a few seconds to confirm that he'd landed exactly where he had wanted. He craned his neck to see Ana standing behind the sofa, staring down at him with a strange look on her face. If only she knew.

"Are you all right?" she asked.

Miles sat up slowly, making careful, deliberate movements to keep his stomach from lurching. No matter how well he learned to control his time travel, it always made him nauseated. His mouth was sticky and tasted sour.

"I could use some water," he said.

"Miles, can you remember what we were talking about before you passed out?" As he worked his way to the couch, he tried to remember the exact conversation he'd had with Dr. Benson. It was such a long time ago.

"I think so," he said. "You wanted to take me back to Longleaf."

"You were pretty angry with me."

"I know," he said. "I felt like you betrayed me."

Ana returned with a glass of water. She offered it to him and then took a step back. She wasn't sure which version of him it was.

"It's me," he said. Miles hated lying to her, but he needed them both to believe he was the Miles from this time. "I just passed out. I didn't have an episode." Even calling it that seemed strange. He hadn't had to couch his language in vague terminology in years.

"You seem much more calm than you were before you fainted. Are you sure you're yourself?" Dr. Benson studied his face carefully, looking for any indication that he wasn't telling the truth. He had to be careful.

"I think I overreacted. I'm at least willing to talk to Dr. Branagan about my release. Maybe we can come to a compromise."

"Well, that's certainly very wise of you," Dr. Benson said. She still looked doubtful.

Ana, however, had inched closer. "Are you angry at me?"

He shook his head and stood. He held out his arms to her, and she fell into his embrace as if it were the easiest thing in the world. Tears began to sting at his eyes. He turned his face away from Dr. Benson and blinked rapidly to keep the tears from falling.

"I love you," Ana said. "I just want you to get well."

"I know, and I will."

When he finally released Ana, Dr. Benson picked up her purse from the coffee table. "We should get going," she said. "I bet they're wondering where you got off to."

"Can't he at least stay the night?" Ana sounded like a child asking her parents for a slumber party.

"I think it's best if we get him back tonight," Dr. Benson said. "That way we don't risk another episode."

Ana wiped a tear from her cheek and tried to smile.

"I'll see you Friday," he said. That was the day they'd set aside for family therapy.

"I'll be there," she said.

But I won't, he thought.

CHAPTER TWENTY-SEVEN
ADAM

SUNDAY, JUNE 21, 2020 · 1:49 A.M.

"I don't think she believed us." Michaela looked sad, reflecting what Adam already thought. "Do you think Miles is okay?"

"I'm sure he's fine," Adam said. "Anyway, it's none of our business, right?"

Michaela took her eyes off the road and gave him a sideways glance. "You don't really believe that."

"What? She's his wife. I'm just an ex-boyfriend, from a long time ago. We did what Miles asked, and the rest is, well, it's just not something we need to concern ourselves with." He stared out the window, watching the blackness roll by. It was almost two in the morning, and Adam was beyond exhausted. He'd probably never get to sleep.

"Can I stay with you tonight?" he asked. "I don't want to be home when Anthony gets in from his overnight."

"Won't he wonder where you are?"

"I'll tell him I had to go into work early. He won't question it."

"It's Sunday."

"Oh, right." Adam fluffed his hair. He was sure it looked like a greasy mop by now. "Well, we could tell him you had car trouble and spent the night on the road. I should have told him it was a two-day conference."

"Why can't you just tell him what actually happened? Drop the conference cover story. I'm sure he'll understand."

"No, I'm too tired to explain it all. He'll just be getting in from work and he'll be all jacked up on coffee like he always is, and he'll want to know where I've been, and then I'll have to go through the whole ChronoCorp, time-travel-is-real conversation again. I won't get any sleep and I'll be an absolute bear at work tomorrow."

She laughed. "Well, we can't have that." Her eyes darted in his direction again. "Fine, you can stay with me. Just promise me you'll tell Anthony. You'll regret it if you don't."

"Yeah, I know."

She raised an eyebrow without taking her eyes off the road.

"I will, I promise," Adam said. "Jeez. You're as bad as my sister."

"I didn't know you had a sister." Michaela turned down the music and yawned.

Adam sat up straighter. "You need me to drive?"

"Would you? I'm just getting so sleepy, and we need gas anyway. Good time to switch."

Adam slipped his shoes back on as Michaela exited. By the time the tank was full and they were back on the highway, Michaela was asleep, and Adam had time to think about what had happened with Miles.

Time travel. Such a simple concept, but the situation Miles was in was far from simple. And yet, Adam could only think of the way Miles's eyes crinkled at the edges when he smiled, the way he chewed on his nails when he was nervous, the way he'd looked at Adam when he'd agreed to help him.

Michaela began to snore softly. It was a strange sound coming from such a tiny person, but with her head back and her mouth open, she barely looked like herself. Maybe she *had* changed a bit. Adam knew he wasn't the same person he had been that morning when he still thought Miles might be crazy. Oddly enough, the strangest thing to happen that day wasn't finding out that time travel was real; it was learning that Miles trusted him again. It felt good being needed by Miles again, and that scared the shit out of him.

Just as they exited near Michaela's apartment, Adam's text alert sounded. Michaela stirred, rubbing her eyes and sitting up straight. "Oh, we're almost home," she said, massaging her neck. "I can't wait to get into my own bed."

Adam's phone buzzed again.

"You want me to check that?"

"Sure."

She swiped the screen, the light reflecting off the windshield. "Shit."

"What?"

"It's from Ana."

"What's it say?"

"Miles is back at Longleaf. Please don't contact him again."

SUNDAY, JUNE 21, 2020 · 1:47 P.M.

Adam had finally fallen asleep around nine that morning, after he had quieted his brain and convinced himself it would be impractical to drive all the way back to Winter Haven. Michaela had fallen asleep quickly; her muffled snores drifted from her bedroom to the living room, where Adam lay on the sofa.

He woke around two in the afternoon to find Michaela trying to be quiet while she made coffee and looking as if she had slept a full eight hours.

"You look like hell," she said.

"Your couch is lumpy."

"Haven't you ever heard the saying 'Never look a gift horse in the mouth'?"

"It's too early for riddles. Are you a horse now?"

"Never mind." She set a mug in front of him. "Cream?"

"Please."

"I'm all out of sugar. I don't usually keep it around." She opened a cabinet full of spices and baking supplies. I might have some Splenda in here somewhere."

"Just cream is fine," he said. "How did you sleep?" He pulled out a stool at the counter.

"Barely. I was up all night tossing and turning." She leaned on the counter across from him.

"Could have fooled me with all that snoring."

"Shut up, I do not snore."

He didn't have the energy to argue. "What was on your mind?"

"I couldn't stop thinking about that whole ChronoCorp thing. How is it that no one knows about them?"

"Wouldn't be much of a secret organization if they had a Twitter or something."

"I guess, but there's nothing. Well, not *nothing*. A few blogs here and there." She picked up her phone and scrolled while she talked. "The name pops up in some old newspaper articles, but nothing beyond business licenses and conspiracy theories. And check out this logo I found for ChronoCorp." Michaela turned her phone toward Adam.

On the screen was a resting sphinx, just like the one they both wore on their ID badges at work. Only this one faced left instead of right and was deep red rather than green.

"That looks just like the Tempus logo," Adam said.

"I know, and it gets way creepier. Listen to this: Project Sphinx was renamed Tempus Labs in order to continue ChronoCorp's research with private funding and to establish a non-government entity for the purpose of time travel research." She looked up, eyes wide. "This is one hell of a coincidence, don't you think?"

"Are you saying we work for the same company that has practically kidnapped Miles?"

"Well... yeah."

"Michaela, Tempus Labs recruited me. I had an internship with them before I even graduated from college. Have they been watching me all this time?"

She shrugged. "I suppose it's possible."

"And you didn't know anything about this?"

Michaela shook her head. "My advisor at Miami actually advised against working there. She said it was an old boys' club. I doubt they were out looking for me. Why would they?"

Adam sipped his coffee and let his mind mull it over. Had he been part of this conspiracy all these years and not even known it? Looking back, it had been kind of odd that Tempus Labs had sought him out during his undergrad years. He'd missed so many classes thanks to his addiction that he wasn't even sure he'd graduate. That spring, his advisor asked him if he had considered his post-graduation plans, and he mentioned his interest in time travel research.

"My grad school advisor encouraged me to apply for the internship," Adam said. "I was obsessed with relativity and time travel. Probably a holdover from what happened with Miles in high school. I always wondered if he really could time-travel. Anyway, he said he knew of a lab that was looking for interns to study aging and travel. He thought it might get me interested in things again."

"You think he was in on it?"

"No, I remember that the guy I interviewed with was not a fan. I thought I'd blown it, but about a week later I got a call from the president of the company asking me to come back for a follow-up. They offered me the internship on the spot with a promise of a job after graduation. I've worked there ever since."

"Adam, this is eleven kinds of crazy."

"No kidding." He rubbed the back of his neck, trying to ease the tension from stress and sleeping on Michaela's couch. "Well, we obviously can't go to work tomorrow."

"Why not? The way I see it, they don't know you've caught on, and we could use the opportunity to dig up some dirt and maybe figure out a way to get Miles out of that place for good."

"Do you think there's a chance it's not all bad?" Adam stared into his coffee mug. "Maybe they could cure him."

"Maybe he doesn't need curing." She poured herself a second cup of coffee. "Regardless, he's there against his will, and he asked for your help."

"Why do you think Ana told me to stay away?"

"Well, I'm not a mind reader, but if I were her, I'd probably feel threatened if my husband's ex showed up out of nowhere and 'White Knighted' him."

"But she knows I'm engaged to Anthony. I was just trying to help."

"Still, you have a history with Miles, and that's always threatening. Even under normal circumstances, but in this case, well, she's under a lot of stress."

"I just wish she believed Miles." He finished off his coffee. "Can I ask you something? How were you able to believe it so easily?"

Michaela studied her coffee. "We've been studying the effects of aging for months together, Adam. We've seen first-hand how cells break down, helpless against the passage of time. I guess I just like to believe that it's possible to have some control over that."

"It's not exactly the fountain of youth."

"No, but if humans are capable of time travel, it might as well be. Think about it. What if we could revisit our favorite memories, or travel forward and see our grandchildren? It would give you the benefit of immortality without the side effects. You could live a dozen lifetimes without aging a day."

"You are such a disgusting optimist, you know that?"

"One of my many ways to annoy you." She winked at him. "I'm going to go get dressed and you're taking me to brunch. Mama needs her eggs Benedict."

CHAPTER TWENTY-EIGHT
MILES

"Look what the cat dragged in."

Bethany, her hair uncharacteristically pulled up into a loose bun, stood in the doorway to Miles's room.

"Good thing you're holding a book or I might not have recognized you."

"And he's got jokes." She stepped into the room, easing her way closer as she studied Miles's restraints. She shook her head. "I had such high hopes for you, kid. And now look at you. What happened?"

"I trusted the wrong people." It was true. No matter how he looked at it, Ana had betrayed him.

When he'd finally come back to the right time, he was already in the car with Dr. Benson on his way to Longleaf. He probably would have made a break for it when she stopped to get gas, but when he'd looked for his phone, he found a note in his pocket—in his own handwriting.

Don't panic. Adam will come back for you and get you out. For now you'll have to play along. Dr. Benson doesn't know you time-traveled, so you're safe. Learn all you can at Longleaf. It will come in handy.

At the bottom of the scrap of paper, crammed beneath the cryptic message were four more words: *Take Bethany with you.*

"People went crazy around here looking for you," she said. "Dr. Branagan questioned me for an hour. He was like something out of an episode of *Law & Order*."

"I'm sorry," Miles said.

She waved him off. "It was nothing. Kept me entertained for a while at least."

Miles laughed.

"What's so funny?" Bethany sat on the edge of the bed, careful to avoid sitting on his IV.

"I suddenly just had this image of you sitting there handcuffed to the table refusing to talk without your lawyer."

"Take away the request for a lawyer and you wouldn't be that far off." She held up her arms to reveal two dull red marks around each wrist.

"That asshole. I could wring his wrinkly old neck for doing that to you."

"That could be kind of difficult in your current condition." She tapped the IV line. "I'm surprised they don't have you sedated."

"They did, but when Dr. Branagan realized I was here voluntarily he finally backed off a bit. I convinced him I had been another version of myself when I escaped."

"Smart."

"I might have picked that one up from you," he said with a wink.

"So what's the plan?"

"I'm not sure, but I have it on good authority that Adam will come back for me."

"On whose authority?"

"Mine." He tried to sit up, but the restraints only gave him leeway of about three inches. "An older version left me a note, Bethany."

"Shit."

"That's not all. I'm pretty sure it was deliberate, and I think that in the future, I can control it completely."

"Oh my God." She jumped up from the bed and began pacing the room. "Oh my God."

"So you see, I had to come back so I could learn more from Dr. Branagan."

"Miles, that's crazy. He could kill you. Mary Dupree—"

"I'm not Mary Dupree and neither are you. We're both getting out of here. I promise."

"You know I can't leave. He'll find me."

"Yes, you can, and you're coming with me." He held out his hand. Bethany walked over to him and placed her hand in his. "Promise me you'll do everything you can to cooperate with Dr. Branagan until Adam comes back. We have to learn everything we can if we're ever going to take back our lives and get out of here."

"But the tracking device..."

"Leave that to me. I have a plan."

BY DINNERTIME HE HAD CONVINCED Kathy to remove the restraints, and Miles was free to feed himself, although he wasn't hungry. He and Bethany sat at a corner table, filling each other in on what had transpired since Miles's jailbreak. Bethany had been digging for more information at Longleaf, no longer caring if she got caught. Dr. Branagan already knew that Bethany was snooping. What was the point in trying to hide it?

"The staff in the research wing are studying our biology—blood work, brain scans, genetics. They're looking for any kind of abnormality that can link us. From what I could gather, they think it's for general mental health research. Either that or Branagan has them well-trained because no one's saying a word about time travel. They're all technically employees of Tempus Labs, but they know their research is different than what Tempus is working on at the Cape. As far as I can tell, that research is one hundred percent legitimate, but I can't be sure what's off the books, you know? What about you? What did you find out?"

"I think your day was far more productive than mine." Miles twirled his spaghetti around with a plastic spork, watching the watery sauce form puddles on the plate. "All I found out is my wife doesn't trust me. I tried to tell her what we know and she sent me back here without even asking me."

"Oh, Miles." Bethany laid her hand over Miles's free one. "She probably thinks she's helping you. Don't take it personally."

"Is that what you tell yourself about your parents doing the same thing to you?"

She pulled her hand away. "That's not fair."

"Does it make you feel better, though? To tell yourself that your parents locked you up here for your own good?"

She focused on her tray and began picking at a stale dinner roll. Tears formed along her bottom eyelid. She sniffed. "Not really, no. But you're much more optimistic than me." A smile poked through her sullen expression.

"I think at this point I may be just as jaded as you are."

Bethany gasped, feigning shock. "Alert the media. Blabbers McTalksALot has finally decided he's a normal human being."

Miles flicked a pea at her. It hit her on the chin. Without missing a beat, Bethany glared back at him and flung a wad of dinner roll right at him. He ducked out of the way just in time and it ricocheted off his left shoulder.

"Missed me."

Bethany grabbed what was left of her roll and pulled back to throw. Miles ducked out of the way, but when he looked up she was still holding the bread in her hand. Before he could adjust his maneuvers, she chucked it in his direction, hitting him square between the eyes.

Miles held up his hands. "I surrender."

Smiling triumphantly, Bethany said, "It's for the best. I have more food left anyway. You'd never have stood a chance." She took a bite of her salad, the only thing that looked remotely edible on the plate, and said, "So are you going to tell me about this grand plan of yours, or do I have to guess?"

"Oh, please guess. I'd love to hear what you think I would come up with."

She looked annoyed but when Miles didn't give in, she said, "Okay, I'll play along." She made a show of looking as though she were deep in thought, rolled her eyes skyward and pursed her lips. "Military rescue?"

Miles shook his head.

"Body doubles? We'll put dummies in our beds at night and sneak out like in a bad teen movie."

"Get serious."

She rolled her eyes. "Fine." This time her "thinking face" was less dramatic; she was giving it serious thought. "Well, you said Adam's coming back. Soooooo... I guess that Michaela chick could pose as your wife or something and just sign you out."

"Not exactly."

"I give up. Just tell me."

"We're going to get Dr. Branagan to release us."

Bethany's face was unreadable.

"Well, say something."

"You really are a nut case, aren't you? You're absolutely batty, and for a second there I actually believed you were going to get me out of this joint." She slammed her hand on the table. "This fucking sucks. The only other person I've ever met who's capable of time travel and he's a fucking lunatic."

"Bethany, I'm serious. I think we can convince him."

"And I'm the Queen of England."

"No, really." Miles shoved his tray out of the way and leaned across the table so he could speak more softly. "He needs us alive, right? He told me there are fewer than a hundred known cases, and we're obviously the only ones here."

"Go on..."

"So we're valuable. No us, no experiments."

"And that's supposed to get him to release us how?"

"We threaten suicide."

Bethany leaned back in her chair and crossed her arms over her chest. She looked on the verge of tears. "You are, in fact, insane."

"I'm really not. Think about it. He needs us alive to do the tests, but if we threaten to kill ourselves unless he releases us, he's in a catch twenty-two. If we stay, we kill ourselves, and his research is over. But if he lets us go, then we live, and he is left with a shred of hope."

"That's really fucking risky, Miles. What if he calls our bluff?"

"We won't be bluffing."

She leaned forward. "So your grand plan is to *actually* kill ourselves?"

He nodded, waiting for her reaction.

"That is quite possibly, the dumbest thing I've ever heard. And I used to watch a lot of reality TV, so that's saying something."

She looked as though she wanted to leave, so Miles grabbed her arm. Bethany's eyes darted to his hand, so he let go, but he kept his hand resting on her sleeve.

"Wouldn't you rather die than spend another day here?"

For a second he thought she might slap him, or even turn her chair over and run back to her room. But in an instant, her face shifted, and Miles could see she agreed with him. He had been desperate after just a few days at Longleaf. He could only imagine how Bethany might feel after seven years.

"If we do this," she said, "we do it my way or not at all. I will not have you fucking up my suicide attempt and getting me strapped to the bed like your dumb ass."

"Fair enough."

Miles held out his hand, and Bethany shook it, pumping twice. She smiled in a way that Miles found unfamiliar. Her sly, crooked grin was replaced by something that he couldn't quite put his finger on. And then he met her eyes. There, highlighted by tears that she refused to let fall, Miles saw something he'd never seen in her eyes before: hope.

ON THE WAY BACK TO his room, Miles saw a man he didn't recognize sitting in the same oversized chair Bethany liked to use for reading. He wore a faded blue robe over pajamas that looked as if they were from another era. His chestnut brown hair was thinning and peppered with gray. Something about him seemed familiar, but Miles couldn't place it.

"Do I know you?" he said.

The man turned to face him, revealing watery hazel eyes that struggled to focus.

"I know you," the man said. He slurred his words and had the movements of someone who was intoxicated. He was sedated.

"How do you know me?" Miles asked, squatting to be at eye level with the man.

"You're like me," he said. "You're different."

"How am I like you?"

The man tapped his right temple. "It's here."

"What is?"

"All of it. Everything. It's all there."

Miles was about to ask him what he meant, but the man's attention had shifted. He was staring at a spot over Miles's shoulder. Miles turned to see what had caught his attention. It was Kathy.

"Time for bed, John."

The man stood and shuffled down the hallway away from them. Kathy picked up the magazine he'd been reading and laid it on the stack beside the chair.

"You too, Miles," she said. "Bed time."

"All right." He started in the direction of his room, but he could still feel Kathy's eyes on him. When he turned, she looked away and pretended she hadn't been staring. Miles watched her as she pretended to straighten the magazines. "Kathy, who was that man?"

"That's John," she said without looking up. "Dr. Branagan's son."

FRIDAY, JUNE 26, 2020 · 6:32 A.M.

The sound of the rain on the roof lulled Ana into a light doze. She lingered on the verge of sleep, taking in the gentle rhythm of it as she tried to will herself out of bed. She rolled over and shoved her face into a cool spot on the pillow. The early morning light filtered through the blinds and illuminated the room in a warm glow.

"I don't wanna get up," she groaned.

"Call in sick," Darius said.

The bed shifted next to her and he was up against her back, wrapping his warm body around her. His leg hair tickled her calf.

"I can't," she said. "I have to be in court at one."

"Your job is the worst," he said.

"Well, we can't all blog about sex, drugs and rock 'n' roll all day."

"You could try." Darius trailed kisses down her neck and onto her shoulder.

Ana pulled away to keep from getting sucked into something she wouldn't have time to finish. Also, she was going to visit Miles later, and it didn't feel right to visit her husband on the same day she slept with his boss. Not that it absolved her of sleeping with Darius, but she could deal with that later.

"I have to take a shower," she said, pulling back the covers.

Darius held her tight. "Five more minutes."

"No," she insisted. "Five minutes will turn into twenty. And I overslept already."

"You're no fun," he said, releasing her. "Can I see you tonight?"

"I can't. I have plans with my mother."

When she turned to face him, he was giving her an exaggerated pout. She leaned over and kissed the tip of his nose.

"I'll see you tomorrow. We can go out to that new sushi place on Davis or maybe a movie?"

He folded his hands behind his head and leaned back on them. "Or we could stay in." The smirk on his face almost drove her back to bed, but she had to resist.

"I'll think about it." Ana still wasn't sure she would continue this affair with Darius. The first time she'd slept with him was after telling him about recommitting Miles. She'd gone to him for comfort and had crossed a line she could no longer see. The solace she found in his bed erased the guilt she felt for betraying her husband—temporarily at least. She'd spent every night at his place since then, simply allowing herself to forget everything in her life that wasn't work, but also because she was unable to face the bed she and Miles shared. She didn't want to think about Miles. She just wanted to feel safe.

"You know where to find me, babe."

Darius rolled over and was back to snoring before Ana's feet hit the tile in the bathroom.

ANA SAT ACROSS FROM MILES and watched him shift in his seat, crossing his legs and uncrossing them. Finally he chose to sit on his leg and crossed his arms over his chest. He looked as uncomfortable as she felt.

Ana cleared her throat and picked at her cuticles. She couldn't look at him. "I know you're still mad at me," she said. "But I had to call Dr. Benson."

"You have no idea how I feel." Miles's words were laced with bitter venom, and when he finished speaking he clenched his jaw.

"You're right. I don't. But you have no idea what I'm going through either."

"At least you have your freedom."

"Miles, you agreed to come here. You said it was for the best." She finally looked up and met an angry gaze.

His eyes burned through her. "Why didn't you believe me?"

"You weren't yourself, sweetie. You brought Adam with you. What was I supposed to think?"

"You were supposed to believe me!"

Ana turned to look out the window. A cardinal landed on the crepe myrtle. He was only there for a moment before something startled him and he flew away. It reminded her of Miles—bright, temporary flashes of his true color, and then he was gone. He might return, but she couldn't be sure when or how long he'd stay, or if he'd be the same. She suddenly felt the exhaustion of the last few months bearing down on her.

"Miles, I'm out of my element here. I've tried to be understanding and I've always been supportive, but you can get care here that I can't provide. Don't you think it's better for us this way?"

"No, I think it's better for you."

Guilt surged through her as tears welled in her eyes. "Don't say that."

Miles stood and turned his back on her, staring out the window. "Ana, I love you, but I think it's best for now if you don't come visit me." His voice was muffled and hollow as it bounced off the glass.

She swallowed a sob. "Okay, if that's what you want."

"It is."

Wiping her eyes, Ana stood. She took a step forward, reaching out to touch his shoulder, but stopped when she saw Miles tense.

"I love you," she said.

Walking out of Miles's room, she noticed an unnaturally pale teenage girl watching her from an open doorway. She had been there the day Ana brought Miles to Longleaf. As Ana passed in front of her, the girl spoke.

"You must be Miles's wife. I'm Bethany." She flipped her hair out of her face, but it fell right back where it had been, obscuring her pale eyes.

"Nice to meet you," Ana said, although she did not mean it. She just wanted to get out of that place and back to the sanctuary of her car. Her eyes burned from holding back tears.

Bethany tilted her head to the side. "You're leaving awfully soon."

"Miles asked me to leave." Why was she telling this girl her private business?

"Can't say that I blame him. You were kind of a bitch sending him back here."

Ana's sadness switched to rage in an instant. "Excuse me, I don't think that's any of your business."

The girl shrugged. "Whatever. You're the one who has to live with yourself." Bethany turned on her heel and went back into her room.

Still fuming, Ana walked away as fast as she could. She cursed herself for wearing heels; running would be so much more cathartic. Her heels clicked and echoed down the long hallway, a rhythmic beat driving her forward. She was nearly to the door, and then she would be free. The waiting room was separated from the residential wing, and she would be safe. Safe from what, she wasn't sure. Just a few more steps.

"This place is hell, in case you were wondering." Bethany's voice echoed down the hallway after her. "And that's on you."

Ana surged forward; her hand slapped the edge of the door. When she was through, she closed it behind her and collapsed against its cold surface. She tried to catch her breath. The receptionist was on the phone and hadn't noticed her yet. Ana stood up straight and smoothed her skirt, dabbing the corners of her eyes with her knuckle. She held her head high as she traded her guest badge for her driver's license and made her way to her car. But when she got inside, she didn't fall apart as she thought she would. Instead, she dug her phone out of her purse and called Darius.

"Hey, it's me," she said. "I changed my mind. Can I come over tonight?"

MONDAY, SEPTEMBER 24, 2018 · 8:01 A.M.

"I'm sorry, Ana, but we have to let you go."

Numb and unfeeling, Ana nodded slowly as the senior partners outlined the terms of her severance and her final paycheck. They'd already cleaned out her desk. She'd known this was coming. After missing more than two months of work, she'd used up all her bereavement and personal leave. And when she'd stopped checking in, they'd locked out her email account. She didn't blame them.

"I think you'll find this is more than fair," Mr. Dagen said. His thick mustache twitched as he spoke.

"It is."

"Dominic will escort you out."

One of the interns, a tall, skinny guy with an ill-fitting suit, gave her a weak smile. She followed him down the hall and past reception, where she picked up a small box with her personal effects. Ana glanced in the box. It held a bottle of lotion, a box of tea bags, an engraved pen her mother had given her last Christmas and her framed law degree. She'd only been with the firm for a few months. So excited to land her first real job. And now here she was.

"You need any help with that?" Dominic asked.

Ana rolled her eyes. "I think I can manage."

She walked out the front door and into the blinding sunlight. The thick humidity hit her in the face, causing condensation to form on her cool skin. She shoved her sunglasses down onto the bridge of her nose. What now?

She had no savings, and her student loan payments would take most of what she did have in the bank. Without regular income, she'd be forced to move back home under her mother's scrutinizing gaze. Fat tears rolled down her cheeks, marking the box in her arms with haphazard polka dots of shame.

She put the box on the hood of her car while she fished out her keys, and her hands closed around a scrap of paper that had become tangled in her key chain. Ana uncrumpled it and read it.

"My offer still stands. – Miles."

She'd forgotten all about that. He'd slipped the note in her hand after the funeral service, and she'd blown him off, unable or unwilling to discuss it with him at the time. But now, well, now things were different. Could it really work? Could she marry Miles for his money?

They would only have to stay together long enough to get access to the trust, and then he'd split it with her and she'd be on her way. Simple.

Ana pulled out her phone and dialed Miles's number.

CHAPTER THIRTY
MILES

"I think I visited the future today," Bethany said, flopping down on the empty bed.

Miles had been back at Longleaf for a little over a week, and they'd already settled into a routine of sorts. Bethany had therapy in the morning, while Miles started out the day with Dr. Branagan, getting poked and prodded and digging up dirt on whatever he could about their experiments. In the afternoon they switched, and before dinner they met up to compare notes.

"You controlled it?"

"Kind of. I mean, I managed to initiate a time shift, but it didn't last."

"What do you mean?"

"Well, one minute I was there, watching TV, eating pizza, and then, like a slingshot, was thrown back to Thursday. Just THWACK smacked right into Thursday."

"How do you know it was the future?"

"I was in a place I've never been before. I'm not sure how far in the future it was, but the good news is I don't die here."

After the disastrous visit from Ana, Miles had become even more determined to get the hell out of Longleaf, and Bethany seemed more supportive than ever. Miles was beginning to feel normal. Whatever that was.

"At least not on the course we're currently on," he said. "You could step on a bug tomorrow and everything could change."

Bethany shrugged. "I'm not sure I believe in that theory. I think the future is more certain than that. If I saw myself living outside of this joint, then the universe will find a way to make it happen. Even if I decide to change something to manipulate that future, I will have already decided it as far as the future is concerned, so it still leads to that outcome."

"I guess I never thought of it that way. It's a theory we could test out. If you're right, then it should be impossible for you to kill yourself. At least not before we escape from here."

"As much as I'd love to prove myself right, let's stick to suicide as our absolute last possible option, okay?"

Bethany lay back on the bed. She now used the vacant bed in his room as if it were her own; Miles had even started to think of it as Bethany's bed. She still slept in her own room, but any time she was free, she'd be in Miles's room on the bed, reading.

"I almost forgot," Miles said, sitting across from her on his own bed. "I got a little more info from Kathy. It's not much, but man, it's fucked up." He opened his journal, which was now mostly a log of information he and Bethany had uncovered at Longleaf. He scanned his sloppy handwriting while he talked, looking for the exact entry he had made that morning. "John has been in care since two-thousand five, but he's actually a doctor, a pediatrician. When he started exhibiting signs of mental illness, his father had him committed. Sound familiar?"

She sat up. "He's not—?"

"I'm not certain, but from the way Kathy was sidestepping my questions, I think he may very well be one of us. When she walked away from the desk, I noticed she left his chart out. So I made a copy. He's in the lab right after I am every day." He turned the notebook so she could see it. "And look where he is when he's not in the lab. Right there, under room number."

"It says 'private residence.' What does that mean? Why isn't there a number?"

"Strange, isn't it? I think he has his own wing. Remember when you told me this place is a labyrinth? I'm guessing he got in here by mistake the other night. That's why we'd never seen him before. He doesn't live on the ward with the regular patients. Why would he if his dad runs the show?"

"No fucking way."

"Any idea where it might be?"

Bethany bit her bottom lip. "There's a door that's got a different keypad at the end of the research wing. Biometrics, fingerprints, something weird because there's no keypad like on the other private offices and labs. It just has this flat screen. I've also never seen anyone come or go from there, but if the security is that tight, there probably aren't a lot of staff members allowed back there. I always wondered where that door went."

"I think we should try to talk to John, find out what he knows."

Bethany looked skeptical. "You said he was rambling, though, and didn't we *just* discuss the top-secret security on the door?"

"I think he was sedated. As for the door, I have no idea how to get past it. Do you have any ideas?"

Bethany shook her head. "If only there was a way to know who has access."

"Didn't you say you swiped an ID badge once?"

"Yeah, but that was just a janitor. The nurses are more careful, and like I said, we don't know who has access."

"Well, that was kind of my point," Miles said. "We can use it to figure out who has access. The security upgrade requires the ID badge to log in, along with the password."

"Great, so we need to steal a badge *and* hack an account. Why didn't you just say so?"

"You got a better idea?"

Bethany glared at him, obviously uninspired by his suggestion but also without an idea of her own. After a few moments, though, she broke out in a crooked grin. "Dummy, why don't you just ask Kathy? You said she waited for you to ask her who he was. Maybe she's a disgruntled employee."

"Oh, come on. It can't be that simple."

Bethany looked at him as if he were crazy. "Why not?"

"It's too... simple. It won't work."

"What have we got to lose?" Bethany said. "We ask her and she says no. So what?"

"We ask her and she tells Dr. Branagan we've been snooping again. He'll strap us both to our beds for sure."

"But what if she doesn't? What if she's on our side and can't say? Someone had to let him out of that wing. What if it was Kathy? What if she did it on purpose so you'd ask about him and she's waiting for us to piece it all together?"

"Bethany, that's crazy."

"Of course it's crazy," she said. "We're in a nut house. So why wouldn't the crazy plan work?"

"I guess it's worth a try."

She sat up and bounced on the mattress. "Now you're seeing reason. So when are you going to talk to her?"

"Me? Why not you? It was your idea."

"Because I'm not a people person, and besides, Kathy actually likes you, though I can't imagine why." Bethany, laughing at her own joke, didn't notice that Miles had picked up a pillow, and so when he threw it at her, it hit her square in the face. "God, you're like the older brother I never wanted." She chucked the pillow back, but it landed in Miles's lap. She stuck out her tongue at him.

"Right back at ya," Miles said.

Miles went back to his notebook, and Bethany opened the novel she was reading, a ridiculous romance she had found in the lounge. It was easy being friends with Bethany. He knew he was going to miss her after they got out of there.

"Have you talked to Ana since she was here?" Bethany asked. She didn't look up from her book.

"No, she hasn't called, and I'm not interested in talking to her just yet."

"What about Adam? Have you heard from him?"

"I called him yesterday while you were still in the lab. I left a message, just to thank him for helping out."

"Did you say anything about the note?"

"Not yet. I figure he's got to come to that on his own. And anyway, I'm not leaving that on voicemail."

"Good point."

"Have you heard from your parents?"

"You know I haven't."

"Hey, things could change."

"And pigs might fly us to Mars on a bottle rocket. My parents are not going to call. They dumped me here to rot, and they're happy that way. I'm happy that way."

"Are you really?"

She lowered her book dramatically. "Really? The guy who kicked his totally smoking hot wife out of here the other day is asking me if I'm happy without a toxic relationship in my life? Get real."

"It's not the same, Bethany. They're your parents."

"Yeah, well, you wouldn't know it from their behavior." She turned a page so harshly it tore. "Look, can we just change the subject?"

"We don't even have to talk," Miles said.

"Good." Bethany rolled on her side, turning her back to Miles.

Miles went back to his notes, trying to makes sense of the scant details he had gathered. He noticed something on John's chart that he hadn't seen before. At the bottom of one of the pages, beneath an order for medication, was a signature: K. Bennett.

"Bethany, do you know Kathy's last name?"

"I'm trying to read."

"Bethany, please, this is important."

She dropped the book in her lap, looking annoyed. "Um, Barnett or something?"

"Could it be Bennett?"

She shrugged. "I suppose it could. Why?"

"I think she has access." He tossed the notebook on her bed and watched her eyes go wide as she saw what he had seen.

"Holy crap. Luck must be on our fucking side, Miles. We have to go talk to her."

Miles nodded. "After dinner, once Diane has gone home."

"I'll meet you back here before lights out, then. You can fill me in."

Now Miles just needed to figure out what to say to convince Kathy to let them talk to John.

ALL THROUGH DINNER MILES WATCHED Kathy out of the corner of his eye. She walked back and forth between the nurses' station and individual rooms, carrying charts, medication, trays for the patients who couldn't leave their rooms. He wanted to make sure that she didn't leave his sight. Once he heard Diane say goodnight, he knew it was time to make his move. Dropping his tray at the kitchen window, Miles made his way over to the nurses' station where Kathy sat reading a back issue of a gossip magazine with Halle Berry on the cover.

When she saw him approaching, she smiled. "Where's Bethany tonight? I thought you two were joined at the hip."

"I think she's still with Dr. Branagan."

They were under strict orders not to discuss their "treatment" with anyone other than Dr. Branagan, and Miles wasn't sure how much Kathy knew.

"Well, then she's in good hands." Kathy smiled and went back to her magazine.

"Kathy, where is John Branagan? I haven't seen him since the other night."

Kathy tensed at Miles's words, and he knew she had the answers he wanted. He just had to play his cards right.

"Why are you so interested in him?"

"I was worried about him. He seemed so out of it when I spoke to him. I guess I just wondered what happened to him."

"Nothing *happened* to him," Kathy said, feigning interest in the magazine.

"Then where is he?"

Kathy sighed. "Where he's always been, Miles. Why does it matter?"

"Where is he, Kathy?"

Her eyes shifted nervously. "I can't tell you that."

"Why not?"

"The same reason you can't tell me what goes on in the lab. Dr. Branagan has strict confidentiality policies."

"Why does he keep his son separate from the other patients? Is there something wrong with him?"

She dropped the magazine in her lap, visibly annoyed. "Miles, I don't have time for this. Why don't you ask Dr. Branagan all these questions?"

"Because you and I both know he won't answer them." He paused and leaned forward on the counter, catching her gaze. "And we both know this place is about more than mental health. Bethany and I are just trying to figure out what's going on with us. Surely you can understand that."

Kathy bit her lip. "I'm not supposed to say anything."

"That's okay. All you have to do is let me into John's room. I just want to talk to him, and if I get caught, I won't tell anyone you helped me."

Kathy remained uncertain, her sparse eyebrows furrowed together in thought.

"Please help us," Miles begged.

"I could lose my job."

"I won't let that happen. No matter what, I will never tell anyone, least of all Dr. Branagan, that you helped me get onto that wing. I swear."

She closed her eyes. "Okay," she muttered. "But you follow my lead, and if you get caught, you play dumb about how you got in there. Say you followed me in, anything but that I let you in."

"Cross my heart," Miles said. It seemed silly, but he couldn't think of anything else that would indicate his promise. Swearing on his mother's grave? She was still alive. "Can we go now?"

"Give me twenty minutes. I have a couple patients to check on and then usually I take John his evening medication. I'll meet you at the end of the hallway at eight-fifteen and you can follow me in. Once I give him his meds, you're on your own, though. I have to come back here and do meds for the rest of the patients and then bed checks. You have to be back in your bed by ten-thirty or both our asses are toast."

Miles nodded and ran off to tell Bethany the good news.

AT PRECISELY EIGHT-FIFTEEN, KATHY LED Miles down the darkened hallway, past the empty research labs and to the mysterious door that Bethany had told him about. Kathy pressed her palm to the flat screen to the right of the door, and it lit up bright blue. She typed in a four-digit code, and he heard the lock release. A simple turn of the door handle and they were through. As instructed, Miles kept close to her side once they were in the private residential wing.

"Does Dr. Branagan ever come to check on his son?" Miles whispered.

"Not usually, but he has been known to come back in the middle of the night and use the labs. You can't be seen, so be extra careful when you leave."

They passed several empty rooms, the beds stripped bare and the only light coming from the open blinds. They kept walking, following the signs for an emergency exit to the end of the hallway. As they neared the last room on the left, Miles heard loud, angry voices.

"Is someone here?" he whispered.

Kathy laughed at his moment of panic. "Relax, it's just the TV."

The door to John's room was propped open just enough so that Miles could see the flickering light from the television. Kathy knocked lightly, and a dull voice called out for them to come in.

Miles kept close to Kathy as he followed her into John's room. Sitting in an old blue recliner was the man Miles had seen the day before. He still wore the faded robe, but he had changed pajamas. Now that Miles knew who John was, he could see the resemblance between him and his father. They had the same watery hazel eyes and sharp, slanted nose, but something was different about him as well. He looked softer, less determined, and Miles found he wasn't scared of him at all.

"Good evening, John. This is my good friend Miles. I believe you two met the other night. He wanted to come sit with you and watch television. Is that okay?"

John glanced up from the TV and gave Miles the once-over. "Yeah, whatever," he said.

"Great, I'll leave you to it, then. I've got your sleeping pill, John. Do you need some water?"

Without looking up he said, "I have tea." He pointed to a table beside his recliner.

She set the plastic cup with his pill beside the glass and turned to Miles. "Remember, you have to be back in your room by ten-thirty." She looked at her watch. "It's almost eight-thirty now."

"Got it," Miles said.

"Will you two shut up? It's just getting to the good part."

Kathy rolled her eyes and squeezed Miles's shoulder. "Good luck," she whispered.

When she was gone, Miles pulled out the desk chair and turned it to face the TV.

"I hate these shows," John said. "They always try to make you think they know who the killer is in the first twenty minutes and they're never right. The show is an hour long, for Christ's sake. If they solve the case before the first commercial, then what's the point?"

"Then why do you watch it?"

"Because I get fucking sick of reading." He took a sip of his iced tea and returned his attention to the screen. "Oh, for Christ's sake, I've seen this one. The fucking mother did it. She's been poisoning the kid for years." He turned off the TV. "Now what am I going to do until this pill kicks in?" He grabbed the plastic cup from the table.

"We could talk," Miles said.

John stopped with the pill halfway to his mouth. "About what?"

Miles shrugged. "Time travel, maybe."

John laughed bitterly and threw the pill in his mouth. The ice cubes rattled in the glass as he drank. "That's all anyone around here wants to talk about."

"Really?" Miles said, trying to sound as friendly as he could. "Why don't you tell me about you then? How long have you been here at Longleaf?"

"Longleaf." John scoffed. "That's my father's idea of inviting. This used to be called Winter Haven Behavioral Health Clinic, but he thought it needed a friendlier name, so he picked a tree."

"You don't think trees are friendly?"

"I think trees are trees." He took another sip of his tea. "There's more tea in my fridge if you want some. I know the food on the residential wing is shit."

Miles glanced in the direction John had pointed and noticed the small refrigerator in the corner. He finally took in the whole room. It was at least twice as big as his and Bethany's rooms, and had much more homey-looking furniture. In addition to the recliner, John had a large flat-screen TV, a plush queen-sized bed and a private attached bathroom. Compared to where Miles had been living the past few weeks, John's room was a palace.

"Your father must really love you to give you all this." He gestured around the room.

"You've met my father, right?"

Miles nodded.

"The man doesn't know the meaning of the word love. You asked how long I've been here?" He set the glass on the table. "I've been a resident here for the last fifteen years. My wife thinks I left her for one of my nurses, and my kids think their father is a deadbeat. Although I'm sure they have children of their own by now."

Miles couldn't believe what he was hearing.

"See, that look on your face, it says, 'How could a father do that to his son?' Well, I'll tell you. He's got a one-track mind, my father. All he ever thinks about is unlocking the secret to time travel. That man has been researching time travel since before I was born, and when he realized I was capable of my own mental temporal displacement, he began studying me like a lab rat."

"You can time-travel?"

"Why? Can't *you*?" He said it as though everyone were capable of time travel.

"It's just... I never suspected..."

John held up a hand. "You have to understand something about my father. See, when he was a kid, his brother Harry claimed he could time-travel. Back then, if you so much as dressed the wrong way they put you in an asylum and threw away the key. So when my father was six, his older brother was sent away. The treatments back then were much more severe than they are now, and he was subjected to all sorts of inhumane experiments. He had a lobotomy when he was seventeen. Ever since then my father has been obsessed with time travel and mental health.

"When I began to exhibit similar symptoms around the age of five, my father was determined to keep my condition hidden because he knew what would happen if his colleagues found out I was a candidate for their studies. He studied me as best he could, and he taught me how to control it using breathing and meditation. Over time, I was able to prevent an unwanted episode, and my father was able to continue his research without involving his only son. Unfortunately, when my mother died a few years ago, I had a bit of a nervous breakdown and I became unable to control my temporal shifts—that's what he calls them—and I was sent to live here. Now that his investors and the other doctors know what I am capable of, they won't let me go home. I am part of the trials now, and there's nothing my father can do to stop it. Although, between you and me, he's happy about it. He's that much closer to realizing his dream."

"That's terrible," Miles said.

"I have all this, though," John said bitterly.

"Can I ask you something else?"

"Isn't that why you're here? To ask me questions? You know, I heard about you sneaking out. Pretty ballsy, kid. But you should know you have a tracking device in your arm."

"That's not possible." He'd never been sedated in the lab. He'd made sure of it.

"Remember your arm surgery when you were sixteen?"

"How do you know about that?"

"In my former life, I was a pediatric surgeon. I assisted on your surgery and my father had me insert the tracking device along with the metal pins that went into your arm."

Miles stared in disbelief at the scar that ran along his forearm near the elbow.

"My father has been tracking you since you were very young," he said. "Your uncle's brother used to be a researcher here, that is until my father found out about the breach when your parents tried to sue."

"How do you know all that?"

"Well, sometimes it pays to be the mad scientist's son."

"Is there any way to get rid of it?"

"Apart from having another surgery? No. But you can deactivate it."

"How?" Miles scooted forward on the edge of his seat.

"Well, I'm no engineer, mind you, but I think it works kind of like a credit card. If you demagnetize it, it should stop working. But you'd need a pretty heavy-duty magnet."

"So no matter what I do, they'll find me?" Miles felt sick to his stomach.

"Not right away," John said. "It needs to be scanned to track you. You have to go through scanners, like the ones found in airports or shopping malls. It registers on the system when you do. Sometimes cell phones can pick up the signal."

It was hardly reassuring, and realizing he was unlikely to find a giant magnet in John's room, Miles focused on why he was there in the first place: what John knew about all those experiments.

"How is it that we can time-travel?" Miles asked.

"Wow, you don't pull any punches, do you?" John finished off what was left of his tea. The glass made a dull thud when he set it on the table. "The thing you have to understand is, no one is one hundred percent sure how it works. They're trying to find a marker in our DNA—that's why all the blood tests—but most of this is still highly theoretical, you understand?"

"I just want to know what's wrong with me. Why is it that I have these 'temporal shifts' as you call them? Why am I so different?"

"Are you familiar with the theory of relativity?"

"Like Einstein and stuff?"

"Yes, well, to simplify, time is relative. Objects in space move faster than those on earth and as a result, clocks in space actually lose time relative to clocks on earth. It's fractional, but physicists have theorized if we could go fast enough, say near the speed of light, time would begin to speed up for the traveler and we should be able to time-travel."

"Okay, so what does that have to do with me?"

"The current theory is that our brains work differently because of our mental health conditions—you because of your dissociative disorder, Bethany because of her schizophrenia and me because of my chronic anxiety. My father thinks that our synapses fire faster than normal because of it, and in our extreme cases, faster than the speed of light. This is what allows us to shift our own personal timelines and visit different points in our lives."

"But you said you can control it. That you had the ability to keep from switching when you wanted to."

"Controlling it is an art," John said. "My father had been training me since I was a very small child to use my breathing to force my mind to slow and obey the natural order of time."

"He did that with me. The other day I was freaking out and started to switch and your father told me to focus on my breathing and it worked. I stopped the shift."

John rubbed his chin, the hint of stubble there making a sandpapery sound. "Well, that's impressive. You might have a natural gift."

"Do you think it's possible for us to stop these temporal shifts all together?"

"It might be, but your best bet is to work with my father. If you try to defy him, it will only make it harder on you."

"Is that what happened to Mary Dupree?"

John's eyes narrowed. "What do you know about her?"

"Only that she was a resident here and she died while in your father's care. What did he do to her?"

John cleared his throat and reached for his glass. When he found it empty, he sighed, kicking the footrest back under his chair. He shuffled over to the fridge. "Don't you want to know how I know about Bethany?" The ice clinked in the glass as he poured.

"I want to know what the hell is going on around here!" Miles knocked the chair back when he stood. "Why is everyone so cryptic?"

"Relax, Miles. All in due time." He placed the pitcher of tea back in the fridge. "I have soda if you don't like tea. Root beer?"

"Sure, whatever." Miles just wanted him to keep talking about his father's experiments. He took the bottle of soda from John's hand.

John sat down in his recliner with a grunt; the tea sloshed in the glass. "Damned sleeping pills make me clumsy." He sucked the spilled tea from his thumb and set the glass on the table. "Miles, I know you want answers, but trust me when I say you don't want to know everything that goes on here. You just don't."

"Just tell me something. Why me? Why Bethany?"

"That I couldn't tell you for sure. But I have a feeling it's just a matter of wrong place, wrong time. Unfortunately for you, a family member ended up working for ChronoCorp, and Bethany's psychiatrist used to be on staff here. Perfect storm, as they say." John began to blink slowly and he licked his lips. "My pill is kicking in."

"But you haven't told me anything."

"We can talk again," John said. "I'll come see you next time. In the int... inter... um..." He yawned. "Look up a government project from World War Two called Project Sphinx."

His eyes slipped closed and his jaw went slack.

Miles shook his arm. "John!"

The man's eyes shot open. "Sorry, it's the pleeping sill... sleeping pill. We'll talk again soon." He swatted at the air, and Miles couldn't tell if he was waving him off or trying to pat his shoulder.

Before long, John was snoring. Miles put the unopened root beer back in the fridge. He returned his chair to its original position and spared John a parting glance. He looked peaceful now with the tension gone from his features. Miles turned out the light and closed the door behind him. The hallway was dark and cold, a stark contrast to the cozy warmth of John's room. Miles shivered; he didn't want to linger, suddenly feeling out of place and in danger.

By the time he was back in his room, his heart was racing and his head was throbbing. Before he could register what that meant, he was slipping away, fading into the background as part of him from another time pushed through. He sat down on his bed and felt his legs turn to jelly. His vision grew cloudy and then went black.

THURSDAY, JULY 2, 2020 · 12:10 P.M.

Michaela and Adam managed to uncover some information about Tempus's history from the company files, but the connection to ChronoCorp was still a mystery. There was little evidence that the company existed, let alone that it was in bed with Adam and Michaela's employer. Under the guise of resurrecting old research, they had begun searching files in the storage locker for information on ChronoCorp. It was Michaela's idea. She told their supervisor that she found a notation in the computer system that she didn't understand and wanted to go back to the original research to determine if their new studies could benefit from it. She and Adam had been assigned to a special project, looking into a study from 1982 that outlined the effects of transcontinental travel on aging. Now that some years had passed, they thought revisiting the subject might tell them more about cell degeneration. Michaela said she thought the digitized records were incomplete and got the supervisor to grant them access to the original files.

After several unproductive days of searching, they were about to give up when Adam found a file box on the bottom shelf. It was buried behind stacks of old microfilm and a folio filled with newspaper clippings. The box was marked "CC Updates, 1995-2005."

"Michaela, look at this." He and Michaela sat on the floor and opened the box between them.

Most of it was filled with handwritten notes and various scraps of paper that looked like personal communications. Dozens of informal memos and "while you were out" messages that predated email covered two small file folders. One was labeled "M. Dupree" and the other "J. Branagan."

"A relation to Dr. Branagan?" Michaela looked intrigued.

"Could be. The Dupree file is dated much earlier, though. Let's look at that first."

Stapled to the first page, he found a typed memo from Dr. Tony Cavanaugh, president of Tempus Labs. Adam didn't recognize the name, and the memo was dated September 22, 1998. The line where the memo should have been addressed was blacked out, and no matter how he held it to the light, Adam couldn't make out the name beneath the black smudge. The subject line read "Investigation into Winter Haven Facility." He read the body of the memo aloud.

"According to company records, in 1971 a subject by the name of Mary Dupree achieved a brief period of time travel without the aid of a travel device. Throughout the course of our experiments, Miss Dupree exhibited a profound psychosis and multiple personalities. She would often switch between different ages at random, unable to control her own timeline. In 1976, she was moved to our facility in Winter Haven, Fla., where she underwent treatment for her mental disorders. However, she was also subjected to rigorous testing at the hands of the facility's doctors—blood work, electroshock therapy and hypnosis. She became a permanent resident of the facility and died in 1997 at the age of thirty-six. No cause of death was reported and her body was disposed of without notifying this office. She had no next of kin. It is the opinion of this office that Miss Dupree died as a direct result of the negligence of Dr. Emil Branagan and others working at the facility. I request permission to investigate further."

"Holy shit." Michaela slapped a hand over her mouth as if she couldn't believe the words had come out of it.

"Holy shit is right," Adam said.

He dropped the folder into his lap and reached for the second one. A similar memo was stapled to its cover.

"As previously reported, the research being conducted at our Winter Haven facility is morally abhorrent. We now know that Dr. Emil Branagan has moved his son John into this facility and is conducting experiments similar to those which led to the death of Mary Dupree in 1997. Dr. Branagan is non-communicative regarding his research and has ignored all requests from this office for updates. I respectfully request permission to form an oversight committee for the supervision of the facility in Winter Haven. To ignore this issue can only lead to legal action being taken against Tempus Labs."

When Adam looked up from the folder, Michaela looked pale. He was certain his expression reflected her terror as well.

"Miles," he said.

"And Bethany." Michaela's golden eyes were brimming with tears.

"This time we need a plan, though. I think we should go visit them and see what we can find out."

A loud bang made them both jump. They shared a terrified look.

"What was that?" Michaela mouthed.

Adam leaned forward, straining to see between the shelving units that surrounded them. He heard footsteps approaching. Adam stood, picking up a heavy file folder as a shield. He peered around the edge of the shelf and jumped back when a shadowy figure came into view. The figure was backlit and walking toward him. Adam lifted the folder, planning to strike if need be.

"There you two are." It was Jason, one of their colleagues from upstairs.

Adam lowered the folder. "Jesus, man, you scared the shit out us."

"Sorry, I just came to tell you a bunch of us are going to that sushi place for lunch. You guys wanna come?"

Behind him, Adam could hear Michaela laughing. He kicked in her direction, but he only caught air.

"Sure," he said. "Just let us clean up this mess here and we'll be right up."

"Don't take too long," Jason said. "You know how Gerard gets when it's time for lunch."

Michaela and Adam exchanged looks of relief.

"You know, I think we may have watched too many spy movies," Michaela said.

Adam tried to laugh, but his heart was still racing. His voice came out shaky and high-pitched between sharp breaths. "Well, with information like that, it's no wonder. This is some crazy, sci-fi thriller shit, here."

Michaela placed her hand on his arm. "You okay?"

"Fine." His voice was barely audible.

"I know you're worried about Miles. We'll go up there tomorrow, I swear."

Adam took a deep breath and closed his eyes. His heart rate was returning to normal, but he could feel tears welling up. He took another breath and opened his eyes. "Okay."

Michaela smiled. "Good. Can we get some lunch now? Because I am starving."

DRIVING HOME THAT NIGHT, ADAM let his mind wander to the two files he'd found at work. The truth about Longleaf and the knowledge of what had happened to Mary Dupree had distracted him all afternoon. Now more than ever, he wanted to get back to Winter Haven to find out if Miles was okay. When he pulled in the driveway, he realized he'd been on autopilot since leaving work. He barely remembered the drive.

Adam was still distracted when he walked into the kitchen, his nose buried in his phone as he looked for more information on Tempus Labs and ChronoCorp.

Anthony stood at the counter chopping vegetables, but Adam only registered it peripherally, walking past him and sitting down at the kitchen table.

"Hey," he said.

Anthony didn't respond, but Adam barely noticed, still engrossed in the article he was reading. The sound of the knife hitting the cutting board lingered on the edge of his attention. And then it stopped.

"When did you go to Kissimmee?"

Adam looked up from his phone, confused. "What?"

"I found a receipt from a gas station in Kissimmee."

"Oh, that," Adam said. "Well, I figured since Michaela drove us, I should pay for gas."

"I thought you said the conference was in Miami."

Oh shit.

"Uh, well, turns out I was wrong; it was in Tampa." Adam's heart fluttered the way it always did when he told a lie; he felt that unmistakable churning of his gut while he desperately hoped Anthony wouldn't see through his fabrication. He laughed nervously. "It was dumb of me, actually. When we were planning the trip, Michaela said she wanted to go to a restaurant in Ybor City. I thought that was a suburb of Miami or something and I just assumed."

"Uh huh." Anthony looked skeptical but went back to chopping veggies for the stir fry. "That's funny, though, because you and I went to Ybor when we drove out to Tampa for that Harper's Bell show last year. The whole band was there actually."

"Really?" Adam's voice was unnaturally high. "I must have been really drunk that night."

Anthony pursed his lips and nodded. "Except you were on antibiotics from that nasty ear infection. You weren't drinking."

"Anthony, I—"

He slammed the knife on the counter. "Just stop it, Adam. Just stop lying and tell me where you really were. Were you even with Michaela?"

"Of course I was with Michaela! What do you think, that I was with another guy?"

"Well, I don't know what to think because you said you were in Miami and I find this receipt—"

"What were you doing going through my pockets anyway?"

"I wasn't 'going through' your pockets, Adam. I was doing the fucking laundry." He went back to chopping. When he spoke again, his voice was calmer, but Adam could tell it held carefully concealed rage. "Just tell me where you were. Whatever it is, I'm sure that what I'm imagining is far worse."

Adam sighed and took off his glasses, setting them on the table. He scrubbed his hands across his face, as if he were trying to massage his fear out through his cheekbones. "I went to see Miles."

Anthony's grip on the knife tightened, but he kept chopping.

"He called me in a panic because Ana had him committed, and I knew you'd tell me to stay out of it, so I talked Michaela into taking me."

"Jesus Christ."

"I'm sorry I lied to you. I just didn't know how to tell you."

"Well, of course not." The rhythm of the knife on the cutting board sped up. "How could you possibly tell your fiancé that you'd gone to see your ex-boyfriend. I mean, what would he think?"

"That's not fair. You know it's not like that."

"Do I?" Anthony pointed the knife directly at him. "You take off for two days and lie to me about where you're going, and I find out that you've run off to rescue Miles from some argument with his wife, and I'm just supposed to *know* it's not like that?"

"It wasn't an argument. He's being held against his will! God, I can't believe you're not listening to me."

"Would you listen to yourself? You sound like a crazed teenager. 'It's not fair! You're being totally mean to me.'" Adam hated when Anthony used mocking, childlike tones to exaggerate his point.

"There is nothing going on with me and Miles. Nothing. He needs my help, that's all. When this is over and done with, he'll be out of our lives for good."

"When what's over and done with? You're not going back there?"

"I am. Michaela and I have to get him out of there. They're experimenting on him like a lab animal."

"Adam, this is none of our business. If his wife had him committed, I'm sure she had her reasons. You can't be releasing a mentally ill person while they're in the middle of treatment."

"It's not like that," Adam said. "That place is a nightmare. They're studying him because of the time travel."

Anthony stared at him slack-jawed and then he started to laugh. "Oh my God, you've been drinking that psycho's fruit punch. You actually believe him."

"It doesn't matter if I believe him. They're studying him, and he's terrified. I have to get him out."

Anthony closed his eyes, and Adam could see he was trying to control his temper.

"If you go back there and try to get him out, I swear—"

"What? Break up with me? Now who's acting childish?" Adam felt anger surge through him.

"Adam, don't test me. You've been lying to me for a week, and my patience is very thin. I've been more than understanding about this. When Miles showed up on our doorstep, I was nothing but supportive. When you told me he called you, I didn't bat an eye. But now you tell me you want to go break him out of a mental hospital, and I'm just supposed to roll over and let you?"

"*Let* me?"

"You know what I mean."

"Obviously I don't."

Anthony put the knife on the counter, and looked up at Adam. "I don't want to fight about this." His voice was calm, but Adam could sense the lingering anger underneath. "I just want to know why you lied to me."

Adam didn't know why he'd lied. At the time it had all seemed very rational, but now, faced with Anthony's hurt and anger, he couldn't remember his reasons.

"I didn't *want* to lie to you," he said. "I just didn't want to argue either. And I was worried you would think that I was choosing Miles over you or something. I don't know. It all sounds stupid now, but I promise you, there is nothing going on."

"I know you mean to reassure me when you say that, but there is something going on. It may not be romantic or sexual, but you don't just delete your feelings for someone because you broke up. You have a connection with him. I know that." Anthony lowered his head and when he spoke again, his voice sounded strained. "I just wish you trusted me enough to share it with me."

Adam stood up, the chair groaned as it skittered across the floor. He went to Anthony and put a hand on his shoulder. "I do trust you," he said. "I was being stupid. I'm sorry."

"Just tell me next time, okay? I hate feeling like you are hiding something from me."

Adam leaned forward and kissed his cheek. "I promise." He leaned his forehead against Anthony's temple. After a few seconds, he felt Anthony's hand reach up and squeeze his arm. They stayed in that awkward embrace, letting their anger subside. When Anthony finally let go and started chopping again, Adam stepped back.

"What are you making?" he said.

"Stir fry." Anthony's voice was clipped and still a little tense. "But it's not too late to turn this into a salad if you'd rather."

"No, stir fry sounds great." He kissed Anthony's cheek again. "I'm going to go get changed, and then I'll help, okay?"

Anthony nodded but didn't reply. The argument may have been over, but Adam knew it would resurface. And he still had to figure out a way to tell Anthony he was going back. And this time he was bringing Miles home with him.

THURSDAY, JULY 2, 2020 · 10:03 P.M.

Miles took a moment to let his eyes focus. He recognized the room, but couldn't place his location. The window he was facing looked out on an inky black night. Outside lights illuminated the blossoms of two crepe myrtles hanging voluptuously over the grass. When he saw the empty bed with a dog-eared copy of the third Harry Potter book on the stained mattress, he knew instantly where he was. It was the same book he'd seen Bethany hugging to her chest when he first saw her in this room a few months ago.

When he walked closer to the door, the citrus smell confirmed it. He was back at Longleaf. Adam hadn't come for him.

He sagged against the door frame, feeling betrayal wash over him. Adam had let him down in two different time lines. First Danny and now this. He felt so stupid now for calling Adam, who had known all along why they'd broken up. Adam had just been humoring him, trying to ease him into what he already knew: Adam didn't love him and probably never had. It hurt even more than finding out that Adam had kissed Danny Dubrow.

"You look like hell." Bethany pushed past him and flopped down on the empty bed. *Harry Potter* fell to the floor. "Did someone die?"

He blinked at her, studying her behavior. Why was she lounging on the bed as if she lived there? Did she know Adam hated him?

"I'm still here," he said.

"Of course you're still here. Did you expect to be somewhere el—? Holy shit!" She jumped up from the bed. "It's you." She rolled her eyes at herself. "Of course it's you. I mean... You're the younger one, right? The one I met the other day."

Miles nodded, wondering if Bethany felt this disoriented when she time-traveled. "How long have I been here?" he asked.

"Well, you came back about ten days ago. Before that it was only a few weeks, so maybe a month altogether."

"Came back?"

"Dude, we broke you out of here. Then, of course, your cunt of a wife sent you back. But your much-older self showed up and said to sit tight 'cause Adam's breaking you out again." She bounced on her toes. "This is so cool. Your time travel experiences are so much cooler than mine. I usually end up in math class or something. And it's always a day we're doing fractions or something equally stupid."

"He's coming back?"

"That's what the note said."

"What note?"

"It's in your top desk drawer if you want to see it."

Miles turned to look at the desk, but didn't open the drawer. He turned his attention back to Bethany. "How long do I have to stay here?"

Bethany shrugged. "No clue. The note didn't say. Regular Miles and I have been studying up on this place and trying to figure out how to control our time travel. We were supposed to meet back here to talk about what he found out from Dr. Branagan's son, but then you showed up."

"His son?"

Sighing, Bethany lay back down on the bed. "He lives here. He can time travel. You were going to sneak into his room to find out what he knows. That's all I know." She pulled a lock of hair up to her eyes and inspected it.

"Sorry." Miles sat facing her on his bed. "Did you say we're figuring out how to control our time travel?"

"Yep. Well, that's the plan anyway."

"And my much-older self visited."

"Is there an echo? Yes, and he left you a note. Top drawer." She kicked her feet out and stretched. "This time travel business sucks when shit gets complicated. I feel like I've had to repeat every conversation we've ever had because you keep changing on me."

"What I'm saying is, if we're currently learning to control it, and my older self visited to write me a note, wouldn't that mean I learn to control it at some point in the future?"

Bethany stopped playing with her hair and turned to face him. Her eyes were wide. "Look who finally blew my mind. You're absolutely right. Oh my God. This is huge!"

"Has your older self visited you?"

Her expression darkened. "I haven't experienced a shift in months. Dr. Branagan thinks my depression is messing with my abilities."

"You don't look depressed."

"You did not just say that."

"What?"

"I don't *look* depressed—like there's a tattoo or something that would mark me. Tell me, O wise one, what does depression look like?"

Miles stuttered trying to respond. He didn't know what to say.

"Never mind. The real you will be back eventually. At least he has some tact."

"Why do I get the feeling you hate me in every time line?"

"Only when you're obnoxious and say incredibly offensive things." Bethany scrunched her eyes closed and wrapped her hand over her forehead so that her fingers were gripping her temples. "Fuck me."

"Are you okay?"

"Migraine," she said. "Last time I had one this bad, I—Oh no."

"What?"

"Miles, just stay calm. I'll be right back. Don't freak out. I'll be fine."

Bethany's head fell back hard on the pillow; her face went slack as her eyes rolled back in her head.

"Bethany!" He shook her, but her head just flopped around on her shoulders like a rag doll. She was completely unconscious.

Miles tried to remain calm, but his own head was throbbing, and his vision was fading. He was leaving, and his older self would have no idea what he was walking into.

"I'm sorry," Miles said just as everything went black.

MILES WOKE UP TO FIND Bethany standing over him.

"Which one are you?"

"Regular Miles," he said. It was their shorthand code for being in the right body at the right time. Something about the way she looked at him made him think they'd both had a temporal shift. "What about you?"

Bethany looked down and shook her head.

Miles sat up. "How old are you?"

"Just a few days older," she said without looking up. Her hair fell across her face. "You just came back from seeing John, right?"

"Yeah, but then I had an episode. Well, John calls them temporal shifts." He wondered how much of this she already knew if she was from a few days in the future.

"I know. You'll tell me all about it when I come back." She looked around the room, as if she were looking for something. She picked up her book from the floor. "I find this in my room a couple days from now. I must have moved it there. *Will* put it there." She waved a hand in front of her face. "You know what I mean." She clutched the book to her chest. "Kind of ironic, isn't it? Us being time travelers and me reading this thing."

"I'd say it's more cliché than ironic," Miles said. "But I know what you mean. I think it helps me to feel less alone about the time travel thing to watch movies about time travel and stuff. Well, that and meeting you."

"You're a really good friend, Miles. I hope you won't forget me."

"Forget you?" Miles narrowed his eyes. "How could I? We're friends."

"Never mind. I should probably go back to my room, see if I can wait this out. We probably shouldn't be talking. We could mess up the entirety of space and time."

"I hardly think us talking sci-fi obsessions is going to mess with the fabric of reality. But if you want to be alone, I understand."

"I just think it's better if we don't have much interaction like this. Besides, I come out of it in my own room. You can't rewrite history."

"The future."

"Whatever."

FRIDAY, JULY 3, 2020 · 9:10 A.M.

"How long do you think he'll have to stay?" Ana switched the phone to her left ear and opened her office door. She waved Ellen into her office, half listening as Dr. Branagan told her he had decided to extend Miles's treatment. She pointed to the file on her desk and wrote a note to Ellen on a scrap of paper before sitting down.

"... so I can't say how long."

"You want me to leave him there indefinitely?"

Ana glanced up at Ellen, who was still standing in front of her desk. She waved her off and swiveled her chair so Ellen would get the hint. When she heard the door close, she relaxed.

"Not indefinitely," Dr. Branagan said. "Just until we can reevaluate his treatment. We'll stay on our current course and then reassess in a few weeks. I think we're on the verge of a breakthrough. He's been able to control his dissociative states a bit, and that's always a good sign."

Ana felt hope for the first time in weeks. "That's so good to hear."

"Now I know you had some concerns about cost, and I will have one of my staff call you about that. But I think because Miles is a special case, we can maybe work something out. His treatment could definitely aid me in my research."

"You mean, you'd treat him pro bono?"

"Well, there would still be some costs associated with residential care: food, medication, what have you. But I think we can cover a lot of the therapy and lab fees with grant money."

"Oh, that would be an enormous help," Ana said. "We've been using Miles's trust fund, but all the years of therapy and independent researchers have kind of worn our finances thin."

"I understand," Dr. Branagan said. "I'll make a note in Miles's file and have someone call you to work out the particulars."

"Wonderful. Thank you again, doctor."

"My pleasure, Mrs. Lawson."

As she hung up the phone, Ana couldn't help but think of Miles. Would he think this was good news? Probably not. He was so angry with her for sending him back to Longleaf. Darius seemed to think he'd get over it, but Ana knew her husband. He would carry that anger with him until the wrong was righted, or until time forced it to recede in his memory. That's what he'd done with Adam, and now he was doing it with her.

Her cell phone buzzed; the screen showed an unfamiliar number. Thinking it might be a client, she answered.

"Hello."

"Ana, it's Adam. We need to talk. It's about Miles."

"I think you should just stay out of this, Adam. This is between me and my husband."

"But you need to know what's going on at that place. He's in danger."

"You're being ridiculous. I just talked to his doctor, and he said Miles is improving. You need to stop listening to Miles's crazy stories and let me handle this."

"People have died at that place, Ana. That crazy doctor killed them."

"Just because people died, it doesn't mean the doctor had anything to do with it. I've spoken to Dr. Branagan on several occasions, and I assure you, he's perfectly normal."

"Really?"

"Okay, normal is a relative term, but he knows what he's doing. We need to trust him."

"Why are you so willing to trust a stranger over your own husband?"

"In case you haven't noticed, my husband is mentally ill. He's really not in a position to be making decisions for himself."

"Then why did you let him commit himself?"

"Because it was on the advice of his psychiatrist, who, by the way, is also a professional, unlike you or me. So I think she'd know better than either of us what's best for Miles."

Adam sighed. "Fine. I just wanted to let you know I'm getting him out of there. He wants out and I'm getting him out. I can't let him rot in that place."

The line went dead, and Ana looked at her phone in disbelief. It only took her a few seconds to regain her composure and then she dialed Longleaf to have them prevent Adam from visiting.

WEDNESDAY, OCTOBER 7, 2009 · 4:53 P.M.

They'd been running the same drill for an hour, and the heat was stifling. Sweat dripped from Ana's jaw and onto her chest, but she didn't even blink. She had to hold her position until the drum solo was over, and if any of them moved a muscle, they'd be running it all over again.

Four counts before she was to step off, Ana saw a drum stick go sailing past her face and land on the soggy grass in front of her. A giggle erupted from behind her and a few of the other clarinets groaned. "Stay still," she muttered through gritted teeth. But it was no good; the drum major had already blown the whistle and ordered them back to the start.

Ana fell out of line and swiped the back of her hand across her forehead. She jogged to the sideline to get some water.

"Hurry it up, Espinosa!" The drum major yelled.

"Yeah, hurry up," someone on the drum line called. It was that new kid, the scrawny Asian one that Miles had become obsessed with. Alan or something.

As she made her way back to her spot, she saw that he was wiping mud off one of his sticks with his shirt.

"You fucked up the run-through? And now you're telling me to hurry up? Jesus H. Christ, newbie, get it together. It's hotter than hell out here and your rookie mistake cost us another twenty minutes in this sauna."

"It was a joke, Ana." Miles was at the kid's side in a heartbeat. "And besides, Adam's not used to our marching style yet, and that drum solo is tricky."

"He needs to hold onto his equipment and shut his fucking mouth."

"Espinosa! Lawson! Get back to your spots!"

"This isn't over, new kid." Ana pointed an angry finger in his face.

"I don't think she likes me," she heard Adam say as she jogged away.

"Now whatever gave you that impression?" Miles said with a laugh.

FRIDAY, JULY 3, 2020 · 9:34 A.M.

Adam was shaking with rage after he hung up the phone. How could Ana not believe Miles about the atrocities at Longleaf? He considered copying the files he'd found at work and sending them to her, but something told him it wouldn't do any good. Michaela believed him, and for now that was enough.

He still hadn't figured out how to tell Anthony. So he was using the guise of a last-minute gig to go to Michaela's to talk strategy. There was a gig, but he'd told the band he was sick. The ruse reminded him of when he and Miles used to skip school to go to the movies and make out in the back row. This time the stakes were much higher and the consequences far more dire if they were caught.

Wondering if they'd ever uncover all of ChronoCorp's secrets, Adam spread out the files they'd managed to sneak from work. With the day off for the holiday weekend, they'd decided to spend Friday going over the papers.

"Where do you want to start?" Adam asked

"Why don't you look at Mary Dupree's file again. There might be more in there about what exact experiments she was subjected to. That might tell us what to look for with Miles and Bethany. We need to know what we're up against."

"Good idea." Adam picked up the thick folder, which sagged with age and the weight of the papers within. "And you can look at Branagan's file." He passed it to her. The folder was significantly lighter than Mary

Dupree's, but it too showed the weight of the years on its rust brown cover.

Michaela stood on one leg as she read, and Adam marveled at her balance. He turned his attention to the file in front of him, skipping the memo they had read in the storage locker and thumbing to a colored tab that caught his attention. It was an autopsy diagram, like they always showed in court on the cop shows. There were markings he couldn't decipher along her hips and upper arms and notations of abrasions on both wrists and ankles. The next page was a copy of her death certificate. Cause of death: asphyxiation.

"Michaela, look at this." He handed her the file. "If she suffocated, why would she have abrasions on her wrists?"

Michaela chewed on her lip as she read. She flipped to the autopsy diagram and back to the death certificate. "What if she was restrained?"

"Restrained? Like tied down?"

"Look at the marks," she said, leaning over him and laying the file on the table. "They're uniform in size and only at the wrists and ankles. She has other bruises, but they're not consistent with asphyxiation. Plus, the marks are old. But the report notes the wrist and ankle marks were fresh. So it's likely she was restrained at the time of death."

"She was murdered."

"Looks that way, yeah."

"But why? If she was restrained, why kill her? What threat could she possibly have posed at that point?"

"That must be what Cavanaugh was trying to figure out. I wonder if he ever got that far." Michaela rummaged through the files, checking the dates and labels one by one. "Nothing here. Do you think there's something back at the lab?"

"If Branagan is as evil as we think he is, that information may not even be in the company's possession anymore. I'd bet anything he has all the relevant files at Longleaf."

"Up for another road trip?"

Michaela grinned at him before jumping up to grab her keys from the counter. Then she threw her purse over her shoulder and said, "Let's go."

FRIDAY, JULY 3, 2020 · 9:12 A.M.

Bethany was back to her present-day self the next morning. For some reason, she kept apologizing to Miles for disappearing.

"It's not a big deal," Miles said. "We both experienced a temporal shift at the same time. Personally, I think it's kind of cool."

"You would." Bethany nudged him playfully.

Miles laid down on his bed and rolled over to face her. "So do you think you're comfortable confronting Dr. Branagan? I want to catch him off guard, and I don't think he'll suspect it coming from you."

"Honestly, if he doesn't know what we're up to by now, he's gotta be completely clueless."

"All I'm saying is we need to catch him off guard, and you ask fewer questions than I do. And I'm sure he knows I went to see his son by now."

"And what if something happens to me?" she asked.

It was something they had talked about—the danger they faced at Longleaf—but putting it so bluntly hit Miles harder than he expected. Anxiety twisted in his stomach.

"I don't think he'd hurt you for asking questions. I asked him about Mary Dupree and I lived to tell the tale."

"But she didn't."

"Well, then we're just going to have to take a chance. Remember, threatening suicide is our last option. I don't think he'll call our bluff."

"And if he does?"

"He won't."

Bethany sat on her bed and rolled onto her back. "Miles, I'm scared."

Her voice sounded childlike. Sometimes Miles forgot how young she was.

"If it's any consolation, I am too," Miles said.

"I don't find that comforting at all, but it's nice to know I'm not alone."

He saw the briefest hint of a smile at the corner of her mouth.

"How long until your appointment?"

Bethany looked at Miles's alarm clock. "About ten minutes."

"Not long now." He tried to think of something helpful to say. "The waiting's always the worst part." It wasn't helpful, but it filled the empty air.

"You don't have to make small talk, you know. This is a fucked up situation that's about to get more fucked up. Silence feels somewhat appropriate."

"Silence it is, then." Miles rolled onto his back, and he and Bethany waited out the remaining minutes trapped in their own thoughts. When it was time, she stood and, without saying a word, left Miles's room, leaving him to worry his way through his own morning.

"How are ya doing?" Jamie smiled as she plopped down in her chair opposite Miles. "Dr. Branagan says you're making some progress with your episodes."

"I've controlled it a couple of times," Miles said mechanically. "But it's kind of sporadic."

"It can be frustrating, I know," Jamie said. "But it's a process. You'll get there." She smiled again. "So, what's on your mind?"

Miles almost laughed. What wasn't on his mind? The weight of the last few weeks pressed in on him like a vice. He'd tried journaling, making notes of what he knew, ways to control his shifts, but his mind kept wandering, usually to Adam.

"Are you friends with any of your exes?" Miles asked.

"If you're asking me if it's normal to stay in contact with an ex, I think it depends on the situation."

Miles sighed. Jamie spoke in the same riddling way that Dr. Benson did, but she smiled more, which made her avoidance of personal questions seem less annoying.

"While I was in a dissociative state, I contacted an ex-boyfriend and now we've... been talking."

"And that is troubling you?"

"I wouldn't say it's troubling me so much as it's confusing."

"Confusing how?"

"I think I may still have feelings for him?"

Jamie hummed and nodded. "That sounds like it could be stressful." Miles rolled his eyes.

"What would you like to be the outcome of this resumed friendship?"

Miles shifted in his seat and turned to look out the window. "I'm not sure. I don't want to hurt Ana, but I like having Adam back in my life."

"So you'd like to keep this friendship?"

"I think so, yes."

"What about Ana? Have you told her that?"

Miles exhaled heavily. "We're not speaking right now. We had a fight on her last visit."

"Was it because of Adam?"

"In a way, yes. He's the one who helped me sneak out."

"And that's what you fought about?"

Miles nodded.

"Miles, you have a lot going on in your life right now. It's important for you to have supportive, loving relationships as you work on your mental health, but not to the detriment of your treatment." She waited for Miles to make eye contact. "Do you understand what I mean?"

"You think I should tread carefully?"

"I think you should protect yourself first and foremost. If a relationship is healthy and makes you feel good, it might be worth working on."

Miles nodded but wasn't quite sure what Jamie meant. Was she talking about Ana or Adam? He glanced at the clock.

Jamie's eyes followed his gaze. "Our time is almost up. Why don't you give our conversation some thought? Maybe journal about it, and we can talk more tomorrow."

AROUND MIDDAY, BETHANY RETURNED FROM the lab, ghostly pale and shaking. Her eyes darted around the lounge until she saw Miles. She motioned for him to follow her into his room. Miles noticed her steps were ambling and awkward, as if she were drunk.

"What's wrong?" he whispered when he was close enough to be heard.

She held a finger to her lips. "It's not safe out here," she whispered.

He followed her silently to his room, and when they were safely inside, Bethany closed the door. Miles saw that she was unable to stop her eyes from moving or her hands from shaking.

"What happened?" he asked, gripping her by the upper arms and forcing her to look at him.

"He called my bluff."

"Oh my God."

Bethany collapsed into his arms, and it took all of his strength to get her to the bed. He laid her back against the pillow, and unsure of what else to do, he sat down and waited.

Miles watched over her as if he were holding vigil. He barely blinked, waiting for her to wake up. As the minutes ticked by, he grew more and more worried. Should he call for Kathy? Bethany's breathing was shallow but steady. Her eyes fluttered wildly under her closed lids, as if she were dreaming. She began to mumble; her head lolled from side to side. Miles stood to lean closer, but her words were incoherent.

"Bethany," he whispered. "Are you all right? Please wake up." He shook her, trying to rouse her, but she remained unconscious.

Miles heard footsteps in the hall. Something told him he needed to keep Bethany's condition secret for now. He hurried to check the hallway, but when he opened the door, he came face to face with John Branagan. He was extraordinarily pale, and the dark circles under his eyes gave him the look of someone who hadn't slept in weeks.

"Is she okay?" he asked.

Miles stepped back and let him into the room, closing the door behind them. "She's unconscious, I think. She was acting kind of paranoid and then she just collapsed in my arms."

"I think she's experiencing a temporal shift."

"But last time it was like mine. She just sort of went to sleep. She wasn't like this."

"Remember what I told you about your mental illness influencing your ability to time-travel? Bethany has schizophrenia. Paranoia is not uncommon. Her temporal shifts have always been more violent than yours. Or mine."

They stood over her bed. She seemed calm, but her lips were still forming words that Miles couldn't understand.

"Will she be all right?"

"Well, there's no way to know for certain, but this is within the range of 'normal' for her condition."

"Do you know what happened? She was fine before she went to the lab this morning, and then she came back like this."

John nodded somberly. "She confronted my father. Told him if he didn't let you both out of here, she'd kill herself, destroy years of research."

Miles swallowed around a bitter lump. She'd gone through with it. "What did he say?"

"He laughed, and Bethany lost it. She started screaming and clawing at him, trying to rip his face off, but my father managed to restrain her. And then... " John scrubbed a hand over his unshaven face; his steely eyes watered as he glanced at Bethany. He didn't look at Miles.

"And then what, John?"

He closed his eyes and let out a harsh breath, burying his hands deep in the pockets of his blue bathrobe. "He injected her."

"He sedated her?" No wonder she was so freaked out. She hated being sedated almost as much as Miles did.

"No," John said. "He gave her an experimental drug to trigger a temporal shift. It acts on the brain's chemistry to speed up activity, kind of like Adderall, but much more powerful and targeted specifically to the portions of the brain he believes aid our ability to time-travel."

"You mean he *forced* her to time-travel?"

"He wasn't sure it would work," John said. He sagged against the wall next to Bethany's bed. "That son of a bitch gave her a drug that wasn't even out of the developmental stage. She could have died!"

Icy needles of fear shot across Miles's spine. "What happened?" he asked in a quavering voice.

"She switched timelines in rapid succession. Most times we couldn't tell what age she was, but some were definitely much younger or much older. After about an hour of that she passed out, and when she woke up, shaking like a leaf, my father sent her back here."

"What were you doing there?"

"Routine blood work. When that scene with Bethany started, everyone turned their attention to them, so I think they forgot I was still sitting there."

"Why didn't you try and stop it?"

"Miles, if I could have, I would. There were five other people in the lab. They would have easily overpowered me, and then both Bethany and I would be... Well, I wouldn't be here telling you what happened to her, that's for sure."

"We have to get her out of here." Frantic, Miles started to lift Bethany by the shoulders. "Grab her legs."

"Miles, be reasonable. We can't just walk out of here carrying an unconscious patient. We'd never get past security."

Miles let go of Bethany's arms and sat next to her on the bed. "Then what do we do?"

"Your friends who helped you escape before, can you get ahold of them?"

"If I had a phone, sure."

"There's a phone in my room. They used to monitor my calls, but I use it so rarely, I'm sure they've given up by now. It should be safe."

"Good, let's go." Miles headed for the door.

"No," John said, grabbing him by the arm. "I think you should stay here. Look after Bethany. I'll make the call. It will look less suspicious that way."

It made sense, and yet Miles desperately wanted to hear Adam's voice.

"Here, write the number down." John handed Miles his own notebook from the desk. "And anything else you want me to tell them. I'll make sure they get the message."

Miles hastily scribbled down Adam's name and phone number, but when it came time to write a personal message, he couldn't think of what to say. He looked from the paper to John's ashen face. "I don't know what to say. Could you just tell him to hurry? And tell him—Tell him *anything*. Just get him here." Miles ripped the page from the notebook and handed it to John.

"I'll make sure he understands the urgency. I promise." He took the paper. "I should go. If they find out that I'm not in my room, they'll sedate me again. I'll come back or send word as soon as I can."

The door clicked quietly shut behind John, and Miles was left in the cool quiet of his room with only Bethany's slow, steady breathing to keep him company.

MILES MUST HAVE DOZED OFF, because he awoke with a start to someone knocking on his door. "Come in," he called, his voice still carrying the raspy remnants of sleep.

It was Kathy.

"Hey," she said, peering around the door. "Dr. Branagan wanted me to tell you you're off the hook for the day. He doesn't want to see you in the lab."

Miles had forgotten about his usual schedule anyway, after what happened to Bethany. He glanced over at her. Kathy's gaze followed.

"Is she okay?"

"Oh, yeah," Miles said. "She had a headache, and I told her she could nap in here. I must have fallen asleep myself." He sat up and stretched; his spine let out a few ragged pops.

"Well, when she wakes up, could you tell her Dr. Branagan canceled her afternoon therapy as well."

"I guess he figured she had enough this morning." Miles rolled his eyes.

"He did mention that her morning session was intense," Kathy said. Miles still wasn't sure how much Kathy knew about what went on at Longleaf, but Dr. Branagan had made it perfectly clear that their visits to his lab were to be referred to as therapy when talking with the rest of the staff. And Kathy had never referred to them as anything else.

"She was pretty tired." It wasn't that far from the truth.

"Yeah, we should probably just let her sleep. I'll come check on you both later." Kathy smiled and turned to go. She stopped with the door open halfway. "Oh, I almost forgot." She took a folded sheet of paper out of her pocket and laid it on Miles's desk. Glancing over her shoulder, she smiled again and closed the door.

Miles was on his feet before the door clicked shut, unfolding the paper as he walked back to his bed. It was a note scrawled in shaky letters.

Adam on his way tonight. Don't do anything stupid. Stay put. --J

"Love note?"

Miles looked up to find Bethany lying on her side blinking at him through sleepy eyes.

"Oh, thank God you're awake. How do you feel?" He rushed over and put a hand on her forehead. Bethany swatted it away.

"I'm fine, creep. That ass Branagan drugged me with some fucked up shit. I feel like I have the worst hangover."

"Bethany, he used you like a lab rat. That stuff was a drug designed to induce temporal shifts."

"How do you know—?"

"John was here. He told me all about it. Did you really try to claw Dr. Branagan's eyes out?"

"Hell yeah I did. And I would've too if that linebacker of a lab tech hadn't pulled me off him." She tried to sit up, but stopped halfway and grabbed her head. "Ow."

"Headache?"

"Yeah, it feels like someone has vice grips on my brain." She leaned back and laid her arm across her eyes. "How long was I out?"

"I'd say two hours, give or take. But John says you were shifting pretty rapidly for about an hour before they sent you back here."

"Shit."

"Were you time-traveling just now?"

"I think so. It's hard to tell. The headaches are usually a dead giveaway, but if I moved around as much as you said, it could be from that instead."

Miles saw a tear fall along her cheek and hit the bare pillow.

"I'll see if I can get you some aspirin or something."

He stood up, but Bethany grabbed his elbow.

"Please stay," she said, both eyes rimmed in tears.

Miles sagged down on the mattress beside her and pushed her hair out of her eyes. "Okay."

"Who's the note from?" she asked after a few moments.

Miles smiled. "Oh, I almost forgot. It was from John. He called Adam for me, and help is on its way."

"So you're getting out then?"

"*We're* getting out," Miles said.

"You're taking me with you?" Bethany's eyes went wide.

"Of course I am. Do you think I would actually leave you here?"

"But the tracking de—"

Miles waved her off. "Michaela said we'll cut it out if we have to. You're coming."

Bethany flung herself into Miles's arms, hugging him so tight he could barely breathe. "Thank you, thank you, thank you," she cried.

When she finally pulled back, tears streaked her face. Miles used his sleeve to wipe under her eyes. He laughed. "I can't believe you thought I would leave you here."

Bethany gave him a gentle shove. "Shut up."

"No seriously, you have to be the biggest dummy on the planet."

"Shut up, Miles, or I swear to God I will punch you." She shoved harder. Miles had to put a foot on the floor to stop himself from falling over.

"Fine... fine. I give."

Bethany picked at the ragged edge of the bare mattress. "But seriously, thank you."

"You're welcome."

"So now what?"

"I guess we wait."

THE MINUTES CREPT BY; HOURS eased into what seemed like eternity. By dinner time, Bethany and Miles were beyond impatient. They had no way of knowing when Adam would come, and it was frustrating as hell.

Miles tried to eat, but the food tasted like sawdust. Even Bethany looked nervous, keeping her gaze trained on Miles though they sat at different tables. She said it would be best if they weren't seen in each other's company—she didn't want to give Dr. Branagan reason to interfere when they were so close to escaping—but right now, Miles wished he had someone to talk to.

He chewed the edge of a stale dinner roll and watched the other residents of Longleaf consume their dinners. What would it be like to share their ignorance? To not carry the burden of time travel. To be normal.

Miles had to laugh. These people were all here for inpatient treatment of a mental illness. Normal was what they hoped for as well. Still, he longed for the days when his condition seemed simpler, when there was still a possibility that he had a simple dissociative disorder. Whatever tiny hope he'd had that his time travels were just his own imagination evaporated the moment he found out that Bethany could also time-travel. What he'd experienced was real, and, ironically, he couldn't go back.

Attempting to look as normal as possible, Miles took another forkful of flavorless food. It was halfway to his mouth when a horrendous alarm began to sound, echoing off the walls and reverberating in Miles's ears. He immediately caught Bethany's eye and realized she had the same thought: Adam.

FRIDAY, JULY 3, 2020 · 7:13 P.M.

The alarm made an angry squawking noise that forced Adam to cover his ears with his hands.

"Well, that will certainly cause a distraction," Michaela yelled.

Adam led her along the corridor just beyond reception, where they'd been hiding until the security guard finally took a break. "Now let's just hope they evacuate the building."

"They will," Michaela said. "I don't know of a facility that would risk the liability if it were a real fire."

"If they have a smart system, though—"

"It could still take a while for them to figure out that it's a false alarm. That should give us enough time to sneak onto the ward."

He tugged Michaela's arm when he saw one of the nurses running in their direction. They ducked behind the reception desk.

"We need to evacuate," the nurse said.

Adam couldn't see who he was talking to, but a he heard a woman respond, "But if it's a false alarm—"

"We have to start evacuation procedures just in case," the male nurse replied.

"I bet it was a rez not wanting to take meds again."

"Probably. You want me to help you with Delaney?"

"Nah, he's still in his chair, but if you want..."

Their voices trailed off as they hurried down the hallway. When they were out of earshot, Michaela stood up. Adam chanced a look around the corner. A flurry of activity made the usually empty corridor of the residential wing look like a neighborhood block party.

"I think we can make it to Miles's room without drawing too much attention," he said. "I doubt they'll notice two more people wandering about with all that commotion."

"I sure hope you're right."

"Just act like you know what you're doing and stay close. Come on." He gave her arm a tug and she followed, but Adam knew it was with reluctance.

They passed a trio of staff members who were moving quickly, and he felt Michaela tense against his side. But they were too engrossed in doing their jobs to pay them any attention. Michaela released her death grip on Adam's arm, and he gave her a reassuring smile. "See?" he whispered.

A few more steps and he could see that the door to Miles's room was shut. All the other doors were wide open. He hoped that was a good sign. His hand closed around the handle and turned. Easing the door open, he could see that the room was entirely dark. His heart sank. "He's not here," Adam said.

"You two sure know how to make an entrance."

Michaela startled and covered her mouth to stifle a shriek. A light flickered on, revealing Miles and Bethany standing side by side, grinning.

Adam was so relieved to see them that he flung himself at Miles and wrapped him in a tight hug. "For a second there I thought we were screwed."

"Well, you did say to stay put," Miles said. His voice was close, and his breath tickled Adam's ear, sending shivers down his spine.

Adam backed away slowly, not wanting Miles to think he was rejecting him, but needing the space for his own sanity before he did something dumb like kiss him. The alarm suddenly stopped, enveloping the room in an eerie silence.

"We should probably get moving," Bethany said. "Do you have a plan?"

"There's a door on the east side of the building, away from the residential wing," Michaela said. "It didn't have the same high-tech locks on it as the rest of the doors. We should be able to get it open. Can you get us there?"

Adam tried to get his bearings as Miles murmured, "Which direction is east?"

Bethany groaned. "You guys are hopeless." She pointed to the windows and glanced from one to the other, looking at them as if it were obvious. "Seriously? East? Oh, come on, Miles. You only get sun through these windows in the afternoon. East has to be the opposite direction."

Adam looked at Miles and could tell he had no idea what Bethany meant.

"Oh, for crying out loud," Bethany said. "John's room is on the east side of the building. I'd bet anything that door is over there."

Miles's face lit up. "There was an exit sign near his room," he said.

"Glad you could join us," Bethany said, rolling her eyes.

"Could you two stop acting like bickering siblings for two seconds so we can get out of here? This place gives me the creeps." Michaela hugged her arms tight to her own body.

Adam rubbed her back. "Michaela's right. The longer we stand around, the less chance we have of getting out of here."

"Or we could wait until lights out," Bethany said.

"I'm not so sure that's a good idea," Miles said.

"Hear me out," she said. "If we go now, they'll still be on high alert. In fact, they might be looking for the person who pulled that alarm. But if we wait it out, we'd only have to worry about the security guard and the night nurse."

"That's not a bad idea," Adam said. He turned to Michaela. "You all right to hide out here for a bit?"

In the deep shadows cast by the desk lamp, Michaela's face looked paler than usual, but Adam saw the determination in her eyes. "I'll do whatever it takes to get them out of here." She took Bethany's hand in her own, squeezing it and lifting it waist high.

Bethany stared at their joined hands, eyes wide. When Michaela finally released her hand, Adam saw Bethany tuck her hair behind her ears. She kept glancing in Michaela's direction.

TIME TICKED BY AT ITS normal pace, but every second seemed an eternity. They turned out the light to give the illusion that Miles had already turned in for the night, but Adam kept stealing glances at Miles's worried face, which was shrouded in shadow.

"Won't they wonder where Bethany is?" Michaela whispered.

"They might, but they won't find it out of the ordinary if she's in here."

Adam could only see Miles's full bottom lip as he spoke.

"Miles, what if they do a head count?" Bethany leaned forward, her face glowing in the band of pale light coming in the window.

"That could be a problem."

"We could play checkers in the lounge or something; make sure someone sees us."

"What if they're searching for the culprit?" Michaela's voice sounded reedy and high pitched.

"It's been pretty quiet out there for a while," Miles said. "We could check it out."

Miles stretched out his legs and stood, tugged his shirt down and slid into flip flops. "Come on," he said to Bethany.

Adam stood. "Be careful," he said, pulling Miles into a loose hug.

When he pulled away, Miles looked at him in a way he couldn't identify, and the moment hung suspended between them. Something familiar sparked in Adam's mind. He squeezed his hands tight into fists to avoid reaching out and kissing Miles.

Bethany tugged on Miles's sleeve, and the two slipped into the hallway.

Michaela turned to Adam. "What was that?"

"What?"

"The googly-eyed 'please be careful' business. You could cut that tension with a knife."

"Oh, lay off it, Michaela. He's my oldest friend, and this place is a death trap. Aren't you worried for them, too?"

"Well, yeah, but I didn't practically drool all over myself to prove it."

"I'm pretty sure that was you holding hands with Bethany earlier," Adam said.

"I—That was..." Michaela blushed furiously. "I got caught up in the moment."

Adam raised his eyebrows. "Exactly."

"Fine. I'll stay out of your business if you stay out of mine."

"So there's business to get into?" Adam elbowed her playfully.

"She's cute. Maybe a little young for me, but she's cute."

Adam was about to argue, but something bumped against the door, causing them to jump. Bethany and Miles tumbled into the room. They were out of breath.

"Coast is clear," Bethany said. "They think one of the mouth breathers pulled the alarm."

Miles gave her a sideways glance. "Mouth breather? Really?"

"That guy literally breathes through his mouth. It's gross. You ever seen him eat potato salad?"

Michaela scrunched up her face. "Ew."

"See? Even the ginger agrees with me."

"Can we get back to the matter at hand?" Adam asked. "If we're safe, we can get you out of here."

"Everyone on the research wing has gone home for the night. We should be fine," Bethany said. "What about the keypad?"

"I gave Kathy a note for John," Miles said. "He should be waiting for us."

"Then let's go," Michaela said. "I don't want to be here any longer than we have to."

MILES LED THEM DOWN A dark hallway lined with eerie-looking labs and offices. The smell of disinfectant dissipated as they got farther from the residential section, but the air carried a sharp chill. Michaela huddled close; her hands were like ice on Adam's arm.

At the end of the hallway, they stopped at a closed door.

"Where is he?" Michaela asked.

"Be patient," Miles urged.

There was a commotion on the other side of the door, and Adam's heart thudded in his chest as his adrenaline spiked. He glanced over his shoulder to make sure they weren't followed.

"Should we hide?" Michaela whispered.

Bethany shushed her, holding up a finger. Michaela mouthed, "Sorry."

Adam took a deep breath as Miles knocked on the door. It opened a crack, and a middle-aged man with messy brown hair peered through the opening.

"It's us," Miles said.

The door swung wide, and the man beckoned them in. As they passed, Adam picked up the scent of sour milk. He suppressed a gag and tried to move as far away as possible. Michaela stuck close by his side, so she must have smelled it too.

"Michaela thinks she found a way out. Do you know of a door without the keypad locks on it?" Miles asked.

"Sure," the man replied. "Follow me."

"You must be John," Michaela said. "I'm pleased to meet you." She held out a hand as they walked side by side. John looked at it with a furrowed brow. Michaela began to play with her hair. She fell back to Adam's side.

"Just relax," he whispered.

"I can't relax. This place gives me the creeps. I feel like someone is going to pop out from one of these empty rooms and kidnap us or something."

"Not a bad guess, dear."

Michaela screamed and threw herself at Adam, ducking behind him as a gray-haired man with wire-rimmed glasses stepped out from a dark room to their left.

"Dr. Branagan," Miles said, his face ashen with fear. "How did you—?"

"Dad, just let them go," John said. "You've done enough."

"John, stay out of this."

"No, you can't do this to them. This is *your* obsession. They're just kids. Run all the tests you want on me; just let them go."

"We can't leave you here," Miles said. "You'll die."

"I'll be fine," John said. He turned back to his father. "They don't want to be here. Don't do this."

"I can't let twenty years of research just walk out that door."

Bethany moved toward the exterior door, but Dr. Branagan grabbed her arm.

"Let her go!" Michaela shouted, stomping on Dr. Branagan's foot with the edge of her heel.

He reeled back, releasing Bethany's arm.

"Run!" John shouted. He flung himself at his father, wrestling the man to ground.

Bethany and Michaela ran for the door, but Miles hesitated. Adam tugged on his sleeve.

"Miles, we've got to go."

"I can't leave him. He's the only one who knows about this place. Ana will have to believe me if—"

Adam gripped him by the shoulders and used all his strength to turn Miles to face him. "I can't lose you again. Please."

Something changed in Miles's eyes, a subtle shift from terrified determination to something softer, with the slightest hint of warmth, and he stopped resisting and let himself be led toward the door.

A crash behind them urged them forward, and as Adam chanced a last look over his shoulder, he could see that Dr. Branagan was holding an oxygen tank high over his head. He turned away just as he heard a sickening thunk. His hand hit the cross bar on the door and the humid night air fogged his glasses.

"I can't see!" he shouted. "Where's the car?"

"Over here!" Michaela's voice came from his right, and Adam changed directions, pulling Miles with him. He heard the engine start and a door close. By the time they got to the car, his glasses were clearing up. He could just find the handle to open the door. He dove into the back seat, and Miles followed close behind. They barely got the doors closed before Michaela pulled out, tires screeching.

"Headlights!" Bethany, her face white with terror, had braced herself against the door and dashboard.

"Shit, sorry." The headlights came to life and illuminated the empty parking lot.

Adam turned to look behind them and saw a disheveled Branagan standing in the open doorway. He held a phone to his ear.

"We need to get that tracking device out," Michaela said. "Or he's going to find Bethany no matter where we go."

"Me too," Miles said softly.

Adam whipped his head around and stared at him.

"John told me. The pins in my arm from that surgery when I was in high school. There's a tracking device embedded in one of them."

"We can't cut that out," Michaela said. "What are we going to do?"

"Did he tell you how it works?" Adam said.

"A little. It's older than Bethany's so it works more like a credit card. Basically we have to demagnetize it. Also it has to be regularly scanned in order to work. Security systems, airport scanners, some cell phones, that sort of thing."

"Well, that will at least buy us some time," Michaela said. "Bethany, do you know where your tracker is?"

"Yeah," she said, holding out her left arm. "Right here."

"Good. When we stop for gas, we're taking it out."

THEY DROVE ALL NIGHT, ADAM taking over when Michaela got too tired. They stopped at a gas station around midnight, and Michaela set about cutting the tracker out of Bethany's arm.

"How deep do you think it is?" Michaela asked as she poured rubbing alcohol over the blade of a knife.

"Can't be too deep. They inserted it with a syringe." Bethany was putting on a brave face, but Adam could tell she was scared by the way her eyes kept darting to the knife.

"Where did you get a knife anyway?" Bethany asked.

"Brought it from home," Michaela said. "I knew we'd have to get rid of that tracker so I snagged this from my kitchen." She tilted the blade, and it caught the glare of the overhead lights. The reflection flashed across Michaela's face.

Her sweet smile seemed creepy as she wielded the knife. No wonder Bethany looked terrified. Michaela must have noticed that, too, because she placed her hand on Bethany's arm and looked her square in the eye.

"It's going to be fine," she said, pushing Bethany's hair out of her eyes.

Bethany licked her lips and nodded. "Okay, I'm ready."

Michaela cut with precision where Bethany had indicated, and about a half inch from the surface she found it: a grain-sized tracker that she threw in the trash along with the knife and her gloves. She dressed Bethany's wound and settled them both into the back seat. Miles moved up front, and they were on the road again.

Soon, Bethany was sound asleep, her head in Michaela's lap. In the rearview mirror, Adam could see that Michaela was nodding off too, but beside him Miles was wide awake watching the lack of scenery fly by.

"You okay?"

"Hmm?" Miles turned his head. "Sorry. I guess I was sort of lost in my own thoughts."

"That's okay. I just wanted to make sure you're all right."

"I was just thinking about Ana. She's going to wonder what happened to me."

"We can call her when we get to the cabin. At least let her know you're alive."

"She's going to feel so betrayed."

Adam wondered if he meant because Miles had run away from treatment or because of him.

"You'll explain it," Adam said. He patted Miles's thigh with his right hand, leaving it there as reassurance. Miles turned to look out the window, but after a few seconds, his hand covered Adam's.

"You never said where we're going," Miles said. "Whose cabin?"

Adam felt his cheeks burn. "It belongs to Anthony's family," he said. "It's in Tennessee."

"You'll have to thank him for me. It's really cool that he'd let us use it like this."

Adam put his hand back on the steering wheel and tightened his grip. "Anthony doesn't know I came to get you." The confession felt cathartic, but Adam wasn't proud of lying to his fiancé. "He thought I should stay out of it, and I couldn't figure out a way to tell him."

"Shit."

"Looks like we're both in the dog house." Adam laughed, but he didn't feel cheerful, and Miles's responding laugh didn't sound happy either.

When they pulled up to the cabin, the sun was high in the sky; the early morning fog had burned off hours before. Michaela had awoken around dawn but remained quiet, stroking Bethany's hair as she continued to sleep. Miles had dozed off around six and he'd slept fitfully for the last couple of hours. Adam could feel exhaustion weighing on him, but he couldn't give in just yet. He needed to get everyone settled and call Anthony.

With only two bedrooms, the sleeping arrangements were going to be less than ideal no matter what they did, but ultimately Bethany decided when she wouldn't let Michaela leave her side. Adam showed the girls to the downstairs bedroom, leaving Miles sitting on the leather sofa in the living room. Bethany jumped into bed fully clothed and kicked her shoes onto the floor. She buried her head in the pillow and didn't say another word.

Michaela watched her with a smile. "Thank you for everything," she said, turning to Adam.

"No, thank you," he said. "I couldn't have done this without you."

"It was worth it to get them out of there."

Adam hugged her. When he returned to the living room, Miles was already asleep on the sofa with his arm draped across his forehead and a foot dangling over the side. Adam pulled a blanket from a nearby chair and covered him, then watched his slow, steady breathing.

With nothing left to do and everyone safe, he turned his attention to his own mess of a life. He took his phone out of his pocket and turned it on. He had a dozen texts from Anthony and two voicemails. He couldn't delay any longer. He tapped Anthony's number. He picked up after only one ring.

"You're alive. Thank God! Where the hell are you?"

SATURDAY, JULY 4, 2020 · 7:04 A.M.

Ana lay in bed, staring at the ceiling and listening to Darius's uneven snoring. This had to stop. She couldn't keep doing this to Miles, and yet something in her wouldn't let her do the right thing. The guilt nagged at her and made her bones ache. She hadn't slept in her own bed in days, preferring to avoid going home in favor of indulging in Darius's company. They hadn't talked about what they were doing. They ignored how they were betraying Miles, but Ana could sense that Darius felt the same guilt. And yet he did nothing about it either.

She rolled over, facing the wall. Shadows danced on the unpainted surface as wind shook the leaves on the trees. The forecast predicted storms overnight, but they hadn't arrived. Ana always hated that sense of foreboding as the sky grew dark and the trees began to sway. The waiting was the worst part, knowing a storm was coming without a definite arrival time.

Her phone buzzed on the night stand, and she hurried to answer it before it woke Darius. She got out of bed and went into the hallway, closing the bedroom door behind her.

"Hello?"

"Mrs. Lawson? This is Kathy Bennett. I'm a nurse at Longleaf Retreat. Do you have a moment?"

Ana's heartbeat accelerated immediately. "What's wrong?"

"Well, um... there's no easy way to say this, but Miles left last night. He's gone."

"*Gone*? What do you mean he's gone? A person just can't disappear!"

"Mrs. Lawson, please calm down. I'm sure—"

"No, you listen to me, you cut-rate piece of shit nurse. You get that quack Branagan on the phone. I want to know what happened to my husband."

"Mrs. Lawson, please don't yell at me. Dr. Branagan is with a patient, and he asked me to call you. I'm just doing my job."

"Your *job* was to take care of Miles, and now he's what? Just up and vanished? You tell Dr. Branagan that I'm coming down there, and he'd better be available to talk to me or I'm calling the police."

Ana seethed with anger as she disconnected the call. Her breathing was heavy as she turned to face a groggy Darius.

"What's going on?" he asked, rubbing sleep from his eyes.

"They let Miles escape from that place."

"He escaped? How?"

"They won't tell me anything. I need to get up there and find out what the hell they're doing to find him."

"Want me to go with you?"

"No, I don't think you should. I'll be fine. I need to call Miles's mom, though. In case he shows up there."

"I don't think he'd go see his parents. What about that Adam dude?"

Ana's stomach dropped. Suddenly she knew, in every fiber of her being she knew. Miles was with Adam.

She ran back into Darius's room and grabbed her clothes from the floor. Without giving Darius a second glance, she headed for the bathroom, washed her face and threw on yesterday's clothes. She called in sick to work and had Ellen reschedule her appointments before she went to her house to change and pack a bag. She'd call Miles's mom on the way.

INSTEAD OF MILES'S MOM, THOUGH, Ana dialed her own mother. She would have said she didn't know why, but when her mother answered, she immediately knew.

"Ana, what's wrong? You sound sad, *mija*."

"*Mamí*," she cried, using an endearment she rarely invoked anymore. "Miles is missing."

"He cheat on you? I will chop off his *huevos* and feed them to my cat."

"No, *he* didn't cheat. You remember I told you about his broken arm?"

"*Sí*."

"Well, that wasn't the whole truth. He did break his arm, but it's because of his other condition. He's actually been... well, he was in a mental hospital, and last night he took off."

"Mental hospital? *¿Está loco?*"

"Don't call him crazy. Lots of people seek treatment. It doesn't mean they're crazy. And anyway, that's not the point."

"Fine, you call and tell me Miles is in a mental hospital and you make me worry, but I will ignore it. Because that is so easy."

"Mama, please. I don't need a lecture right now. I just need my mother to comfort me."

"Ana, you don't need comfort. You need a divorce."

Ana opened her mouth to protest, but the words died on her tongue.

"See, you don't say anything because you know I am right. He is no good for you."

"No, Mama, it's me who's not good for him."

Her mother snorted.

"No, really. I'm the one who's been cheating. I didn't mean for it to happen, but when I met with Miles's boss a few weeks ago he was so sweet and caring and he understood what I was going through. I needed someone to take care of me, Mama. Miles has been gone for so long, and even when he was here, he wasn't himself."

"You cannot make it okay by telling yourself you had reasons. You cheated on your husband, *mija*."

"I know. But Mama, I can't do this anymore. Miles isn't the same man I married, and I'm afraid if I tell him that I don't want to be with him anymore he'll go off the deep end."

"You cannot take responsibility for his actions, only your own."

Ana sighed. "Yeah, well, first I've got to find him."

"You will, *mija*, and when you do, you tell him the truth."

"Okay, Mama."

The Bluetooth beeped as she disconnected, and the car was filled with silence. She hadn't expected her mother to be so direct and level-headed, but it was just what she needed. Miles could get better without her, but she needed to help find him, and then she'd worry about the end of their marriage.

It was the first time Ana had allowed herself to think of it that way. She had found refuge in Darius's bed, but she'd always thought she'd go back to her own when Miles came home. Now that she knew that wasn't a possibility, she felt relieved and sad all at once. She loved Miles, but she was exhausted from the emotional roller coaster of the past few years. At least he had Adam. There was solace in that.

WHEN ANA ARRIVED IN WINTER Haven, she realized she'd been on autopilot since talking with her mom and she'd forgotten to call Miles's parents. Now she wondered if she should.

She decided to figure that out later and headed for the lobby. The receptionist greeted her as usual, but instead of stopping and turning over her license in exchange for the visitor's badge, she pushed right past the desk and barged through the door leading to the residential wing.

"Ma'am, you have to check in," the receptionist shouted.

Ana, focused on the nurses' station, broke into a run. The receptionist attempted to catch up, but her short, stubby legs were no match for Ana's longer ones. She got to the desk while the receptionist was still waddling down the hallway.

"Hi, I'm looking for Kathy," Ana said.

"I'm sorry, Kath, she just pushed past." The receptionist, panting as she tried to catch her breath, was now standing beside Ana. "Want me to call security?"

"No, it's okay, Heather. This is Mrs. Lawson. She's here about her husband, Miles."

Heather's eyebrows shot up. "Yes, of course." She waddled off toward the lobby.

Ana reeled around to face Kathy. "Where is Dr. Branagan? I demand to speak with him immediately."

"Let me call the lab and see if he's free."

"You *tell* him he's free."

Kathy winced, but Ana couldn't find it in her to care that she had hurt the woman's feelings. These people had lost her husband.

"Ana, you must be so worried."

She turned to see Dr. Benson sauntering in her direction, looking carefree and relaxed.

"Where the hell is my husband?" Ana cried.

"Kathy, I'll take Mrs. Lawson to Dr. Branagan's office. He's expecting me." She placed her hand on the small of Ana's back and led her around the corner from the nurses' station into a hallway she hadn't seen before. "Relax, Miles is going to be just fine. Emil and I have a plan."

Ana clutched her purse close to her side and simply nodded. She was too nervous now to speak. She had no idea Dr. Benson was on a first-name basis with Dr. Branagan, and for some reason that made her uneasy.

They passed labs where researchers in white coats seemed to be examining vials of blood and then took a right turn into a shorter hallway with just two doors: one was marked "stairs" and the other "Dr. Emil Branagan." Dr. Benson rapped lightly on the office door.

"Come in."

Dr. Branagan's office was bright and cheery compared to the hallway. An orderly desk was flanked by large bay windows that faced the courtyard. Twin potted palms framed the view. When Dr. Branagan looked up, Ana gasped. A deep purple bruise bloomed under one eye, and his glasses on that side were held together by tape.

"Jesus, Emil, did you get in a fight?" Dr. Benson sat in one of the chairs facing his desk.

"Ah, this?" he said, gesturing to his cheek. "It was stupid. Tripped over some equipment in the lab and took the corner of a table to the eye."

"Looks like the table won." Dr. Benson laughed at her own joke.

"Mrs. Lawson, won't you have a seat?"

"Not until you tell me what happened to my husband," Ana demanded. She stood, arms crossed, staring down Dr. Branagan. He looked small and weak, not to mention very, very old. Why hadn't she noticed that before?

"Mrs. Lawson, please have a seat. We'll explain everything." Dr. Branagan gestured to the chair next to Dr. Benson.

Ana sat, perching on the edge of the chair and keeping her purse in her lap.

SATURDAY, JULY 4, 2020 · 8:56 A.M.

Miles woke to the sound of someone yelling. Adam's voice was muffled, but it echoed through the cabin. Miles followed its sound to the master bedroom, where he found Adam sitting facing away from him on the bed. His shoulders sagged and his hair was disheveled as if he'd been pulling on it.

"Don't say that." Adam dropped his head and listened as the person on the other end of the line talked. Suddenly his head jerked up. "Well, I don't know if I want to get married anymore either!" Adam threw his phone on the bed, and it bounced under a pillow.

Miles knocked and Adam turned around with a start. When he saw it was Miles, he stood.

"Everything okay?"

"That was Anthony," Adam said, shoving his hands in his pockets. "He's, uh, not happy I rescued you. Jesus, he said he wanted to break up!" Adam ran his hand through his hair and began pacing.

Miles walked toward him, hoping to calm him. "I'm sorry my problems caused all this mess," he said.

Adam stopped pacing and looked at him; his expression softened. "No, it's not your fault. I lied to him. He's angry about that, not you."

"Still, if it hadn't been for me—"

"No," Adam said, stepping closer. He placed his hands on Miles's shoulders. "This is my fault. Don't you dare blame yourself. You have enough going on; you don't need to add my drama to the list."

Miles's arms broke out in gooseflesh. He'd always loved when Adam had looked into his eyes like this: his bit of extra height forcing Miles to look up at him, the strength of his arms bearing down on him. His gaze shifted to Adam's lips and then back to his eyes. Even shrouded in the glare of his glasses, what Miles saw there gave him the courage to act. He leaned forward, pressing his lips to Adam's, closing his eyes and drinking in a scent he'd thought he'd forgotten.

Adam responded immediately, his hands coming up to frame Miles's face and his mouth opening as their kiss deepened. Miles snaked a hand around Adam's back, resting it just above his waistband, feeling the heat of Adam's body through his thin T-shirt.

Suddenly Adam pulled away. "We can't do this," he said.

Miles wiped his bottom lip with the edge of his hand; the taste of Adam lingered on his tongue. He knew Adam was right, but his body was aching for more.

"I'm sorry," Miles said, stepping back. "I just wanted to comfort you, but I think I got caught up in the fairy tale of it all. Handsome guy rescues you, you're supposed to kiss him, right?"

Adam laughed. "I guess so, yeah." His expression turned serious. "But it can't happen again."

"No, of course not. I was just caught up in the moment."

"It's okay. I got caught up too." Adam sat on the edge of the bed and patted the space next to him. "I don't want you to think I'm leading you on. I have a fiancé, and you're married."

"I know," Miles said, although at the moment he didn't feel married anymore. He felt fourteen and back in high school with the same butterflies in his stomach he felt the first time Adam. "For a moment there, I thought... Never mind."

Adam lifted his chin and looked at Miles, his eyes narrowed. "What?"

"Sometimes, and don't get me wrong, I loved my life with Ana. Until this crazy shit started, that is. But sometimes I just want to go back to a simpler time." He paused and took a deep breath. "A time where I'm with you."

Adam remained silent, staring at the floor. The cherrywood blurred as Miles stared at it too.

"I remember the first time I saw you," Adam said.

"In the bathroom? Yeah, I remember that too," Miles said. He smiled at the memory.

"No," Adam said, shaking his head. "I saw you in the hall. I *followed* you into that bathroom."

"You what?"

"It's so creepy, I know, and I can't believe I never told you, but I saw you from behind. I was watching you because I thought you had a nice ass." He looked up and laughed. "I know. I was a horny teenager, okay? But then you turned your head, and I saw your gorgeous eyes and that smile that lit up the fucking room. Of course, you were smiling because you saw that kid from the basketball team walk by, and I knew you were into him, so I followed you. You were so determined and trying to be discreet following him into the bathroom. I don't even think you saw me duck into a stall the same time you did."

"I didn't."

"Anyway, I waited for you to come out, and the rest, as they say, is history."

"I thought you were into Dahlia at first, you know."

"You did not."

"Well, you were always laughing at her jokes and telling me how great she was. I thought you wanted me to tell her you liked her."

Adam threw back his head and laughed. "I was using her as an excuse to talk to you."

"Well, I know that *now*." He gave Adam a playful shove.

Miles studied his profile. He'd always found Adam's narrow eyes and stick-straight hair so intriguing, so different from his own.

"I was into you right away, too," Miles said.

Adam looked shocked. "But you kept going on and on about that basketball guy."

"I wanted to make sure you knew I dug guys, and I was trying to get a read on you. I couldn't tell if you cared about that sort of thing or not. I never even imagined you might be gay. I mean, you were from Texas after all. You could have been a Bush for all I knew."

"We sure wasted a lot of time, didn't we?" Adam said.

"Not as much time as I wasted being mad at you all these years. I'm glad to finally have you back in my life. I missed this. I missed us."

"We do make a pretty good fucking team," Adam said wistfully.

Miles smiled, his whole body aching with desire to kiss Adam again. He bit his lip and clenched his fists to stop himself. "Adam, I'm not sorry I kissed you."

"Miles, I—"

"BETHANY!"

They both turned at the sound of Michaela's voice coming from downstairs. She was running through the house shouting for Bethany and it grew louder as she got closer to the bedroom. "Have either of you seen Bethany?" she asked. "I got up to take a shower, and when I came out, Bethany was gone. My stuff was all strewn over the bed, and this was lying on the floor." She held up an ID badge. "I think she misunderstood."

A green sphinx in the corner of the badge looked just like the logo he'd seen on the researchers at Longleaf but facing the other direction. "What the hell is that?" Miles said.

"It's her work ID."

"You work for ChronoCorp?"

"Not exactly," Michaela said. "But if you think that, then I'm sure that's what Bethany thought too. We have to find her!"

"Not until you tell me what's going on," Miles said, crossing his arms across his chest.

Michaela rolled her eyes. "Can you fill him in while I check outside? Maybe she just went for a walk." She handed Adam her badge.

Miles stared Adam down, his eyes lingering on the sphinx. If he had been working with Dr. Branagan this whole time....

"Don't look at me like that. I didn't know about ChronoCorp until you did. We work for a company called Tempus Labs. We study the effects of aging. I thought our research was being used by the cosmetics companies or maybe the pharmaceutical industry. I had no way of knowing it went this deep. Tempus Labs owns ChronoCorp or they're affiliated or something, but we had *nothing* to do with that place, I swear. I'm just as much a pawn in this as you are."

"What do you mean a pawn?"

"They recruited me, Miles. They must have known about us, and they sought me out. I had no idea. You have to believe me. If I'd have known, I swear I would have warned you."

Adam's eyes brimmed with tears, but he didn't break Miles's gaze. He was telling the truth.

"I believe you," Miles said. "But Bethany has no reason to trust you guys. I'd bet money she saw that ID and took off. She barely trusts me, so I doubt she'd hang around for an explanation from Michaela if she felt betrayed."

An out-of-breath Michaela appeared in the doorway. "She's gone. But she couldn't have gotten too far. I'm going to take the car and look for her. Will you two be all right here?"

"Sure," Adam said. "Call if you find her."

"Want me to come along?" Miles asked.

"No, you need to rest, and anyway, this is my fault. I'll find her. Don't worry." Michaela patted him on the arm and left. They heard the car engine and the sound of tires on the gravel and then silence.

"I'm sorry I didn't tell you sooner," Adam said. He flung the badge on the nightstand.

Miles picked it up.

"Oh my God," he said. "The sphinx."

"What about it?"

"Didn't you ever read *The Time Machine*? The white sphinx is where the Morlocks hide the time machine from the traveler. How could I have missed that? It's been right under my nose the whole time. If I'd realized, I'd never have let Ana check me into that place."

"You couldn't have known," Adam said. "That place is called Longleaf Retreat and it's got a pretty good cover. Did you even see those ID badges when you first checked in?"

Miles thought about it. "No, I guess not until the first session with Dr. Branagan." John had mentioned a Project Sphinx. Miles wondered if they were related.

"Exactly. Stop blaming yourself... and Ana. This is all Branagan's fault."

A different kind of guilt crept in. "Speaking of Ana, I should probably call her."

"Here, take my phone," Adam said. "I'll wait out there for you."

MILES SAT ON THE BED and turned Adam's phone over in his hand as he tried to think of what to say. In a strange way, he didn't care if she was angry, only that she might be hurt by his actions. He couldn't go back to his old life, not after everything he'd learned. Ana would be heartbroken, but he needed a clean break. He'd give her what was left of his trust fund; he could get a job now that he could control his temporal shifts. Or at least he hoped so. Perhaps it was best if he just blurted it out. Ana must know he'd disappeared from Longleaf, so he wouldn't have to explain that.

Resolved, he tapped the contact in Adam's phone for Ana. It rang far longer than he expected, and when Ana finally picked up, her voice sounded strange.

"Oh, Miles, I was so worried. Are you okay?"

"I'm fine," he muttered.

"Where are you, sweetie? I'll come get you."

Miles cleared his throat. "Um, I'm with Adam."

Ana's breath caught, but when she spoke her voice was even. "You know I don't care about that," she said.

Miles heard mumbling in the background. "Where are you?"

"I'm just worried about you. Why won't you tell me where you are? I can help you."

"No, you can't."

"Well, of course *I* can't. But you can get help at Longleaf with Dr. Branagan."

"I'm not going back there."

More mumbling, this time it was louder. "Who's with you?"

A scratchy sound filled his ears, as if Ana were covering the receiver.

"I'm here with Dr. Branagan and Dr. Benson, Miles. We all want you to get better."

Miles's blood ran cold. "Ana, get out of there."

"Now, don't be silly. They want to help you just like I do."

He heard voices in the background again; the sound was garbled, but it sounded as though someone said, "Find out where he is."

"I'm sorry, Ana, but they can't." He paused and took a deep breath. "I love you."

"We're coming to get you, Miles. Where are you?" When he didn't respond she shouted his name into the phone. In the background he heard Dr. Branagan say, "I can track him. Don't worry."

Miles hung up. His hands were shaking.

He'd have to stay on the move until he figured out a way to remove his tracker or disable it. Maybe Adam could give him a ride to a bus station. He didn't know where he would go, but he couldn't risk Adam's safety. He had to get away.

MILES APPROACHED ADAM CAUTIOUSLY. HE was staring out the large bay window at the mountains. A low, misty fog had begun to creep in. It was beautiful, and so was Adam. Even so, Miles could read the tension in Adam's body language, and it hurt him to see it.

"Is Michaela back yet?" he said softly.

Adam turned his head. The light from the window bathed him in a golden halo of perfect light. "Not yet. I'm worried she won't be able to find Bethany."

"Bethany is a fighter. She'll get by." Miles laid his hand on Adam's shoulder. Adam's hand came up to rest on top of it. He squeezed.

"I need to go, too," Miles said after a moment. "Ana was with Dr. Branagan, and they're coming for me."

Adam spun around; their joined hands fell from his shoulder. The separation startled Miles.

"Then we have to go," Adam said. He patted his pockets. "Where the hell are the car keys?"

"Michaela has the car, remember? And anyway, I need to go alone."

"No, I'm going with you."

"I have to stay on the move. I'll be constantly running and looking over my shoulder. I can't do that to you. What about Anthony? Your job? The band?"

"Miles, it doesn't matter—not if you're not safe."

"I'll be fine. I can't let you uproot your life for this."

"It already is uprooted." Adam held up a piece of paper with an unmistakable red sphinx logo. "I found this in a desk drawer. It's a check stub from ChronoCorp made out to Anthony."

Miles grabbed the stub from Adam's hand. "Anthony's part of this?"

Adam shrugged. "Maybe he is; maybe he's not. He could be a pawn like you and me. But he knows more than he's saying. So you see, I can't go back to him."

"You don't know that. Maybe it's a misunderstanding."

Adam lowered his head. "It's more than that. I don't think I want to be with Anthony anymore."

Miles couldn't think of what to say. He stared openmouthed at Adam, trying to figure out what he was feeling. Adam took a couple of steps forward, so close that their toes were touching. Miles shifted on his feet.

"What are you saying?" he said.

"I'm saying I have feelings for you. I don't think I ever stopped."

Miles's heart soared, and then crashed to earth when he remembered the obstacles in their path. "You're engaged, and I'm still married to Ana."

"I'm not saying it's not complicated, but we'll figure it out," Adam said, smiling. "All I know is that I want to figure it out with you."

Fighting the urge to kiss him, Miles stepped back. He definitely had feelings for Adam too, but this was too much. "You can't just spring this on me!"

"I know it's sudden and I'm sorry. But after you kissed me, it all came flooding back. You can't tell me you don't feel it too." He stepped closer. "While you were on the phone I was thinking, and it all came back to one thing: you. I love Anthony, but it's not the same. I never felt about him the way I felt about you, and now we have this second chance—a chance to make it all right, and I want to take it. I think it's fate."

Miles's heart was racing; his breathing was uneven.

"Tell me you don't love me, and I'll let it go. Tell me you don't feel it, and I'll let you walk out that door and never bother you again."

"I—" Miles's head began to throb at the temples; his vision swirled into a mass of blurry color. "Oh God, no." He swayed on his feet and fell into Adam's arms. He struggled to control his breathing, but it was no use; he was time-traveling.

SATURDAY, JULY 12, 2040 · 8:22 P.M.

Miles found himself in an unfamiliar place, a warmly lit room filled with comfortable furniture. A plush sofa cushioned his back, and a thick, deep-pile area rug welcomed his feet when he stood. A large, flat-screen TV faced him and opposite that was a high-end kitchen where a delicious smell wafted toward him.

"You're awake," a voice said from behind him. "Dinner's almost ready."

Miles spun on his heel and saw... well, it looked like Adam, but he was significantly older. His hair was still black as ink, but there were subtle laugh lines around his eyes and he was thicker around the middle. Looking at his own hands, Miles was stunned to see they were coarser and rugged with age. He didn't recognize the clothes he wore.

"You okay?" Adam asked.

"I think I'm in the wrong place." Miles looked around trying to find a clue as to the year, but he didn't even see a cell phone nearby.

"Or the wrong time, perhaps?" Adam said with a knowing smile. "How old are you?"

Not this again. "Twenty-six?" Miles said hesitantly.

"Are we at the cabin?"

"How did you—?"

"I remember it well."

Miles took a few steps closer, noticing that his neck and back ached in an unfamiliar way. "What happens with us?" he asked, massaging the back of his neck.

Adam laughed as he wiped his hands on a dish towel. He crossed the room to where Miles stood. "You know I can't tell you that."

"But obviously we end up together. Do I let you go with me?"

"Let's just say you follow your heart." Adam wrapped his arms around Miles's waist and pulled him in for a kiss.

Unable to help himself, Miles opened his mouth and returned the kiss with fervor. It seemed safer than kissing Adam in his own time, as if it were less a betrayal of Ana and Anthony and more the way it was meant to be.

Miles pulled back and rested his forehead on Adam's, keeping his eyes closed. His head was throbbing again. "I think it's time for me to go."

Adam's strong arms supported him. "Let's get you to the couch."

Miles let himself be led by the arm, leaning on Adam for support. He rested on a cushion and closed his eyes, waiting for the blackness to take him.

"I'll see you soon," Adam said.

Almost like a reflex, Miles replied. "I love you." And then he slipped away.

SATURDAY, JULY 4, 2020 · 10:31 A.M.

Miles jolted back to consciousness in the cabin. Disoriented, he flailed his arms as he came to, but Adam cradled him in his arms and stroked his forehead. It instantly soothed him.

"Hi," Adam said.

"Hey. Was I gone long?"

"Just a few minutes. Do you feel all right? I can get you some water."

"Could you just hold me for a bit?"

"Of course."

"I saw you," he said. "I time-traveled and you were there."

"From high school?"

Miles shook his head. "No, this was the future. We lived together, I think."

Adam's eyebrows shot up, and the side of his mouth turned up. "Really?"

Sitting up, Miles made sure to look him square in the eye. He needed to be certain Adam understood him. "Adam, I'm not ready to say I love you, because I'm not sure how I feel just yet. But right now you're the only one I can trust. If you come with me, I can't promise anything."

Adam bit his lip and nodded. Then he kissed Miles's lips. "I can work with a maybe," he murmured.

Miles couldn't help himself. He returned the kiss, a little firmer than Adam had been, and slipped his arms around Adam's neck.

"That's one heck of a maybe," Adam said when he finally pulled away.

"We should get going," Miles said.

"I'll call us a cab. We can go into town and rent a car."

"Okay. I'll leave Michaela and Bethany a note in case they come back." He stood up and went to the kitchen for a pad of paper.

"Miles?"

He stopped, turned.

"I love you," Adam said. "And I'm going to figure out a way to make everything up to you."

"You already have," Miles said. He smiled and left Adam sitting there with tears shining in his eyes. Something told him he was following his heart.

THE END

ACKNOWLEDGMENTS

FIRST OF ALL, I WOULD like to thank my editor and good friend Annie Harper. This book would literally not exist if she hadn't keep pushing me to get back to writing, and it would be far more disjointed if she hadn't edited it. The sophomore slump is real, guys. I also want to thank my editors Nicki and Cameron. I promise to use the word "really" far less in my next book.

I also owe a huge thanks to everyone else at Interlude Press— CL Miller, CB Messer, and, of course, Lex Huffman. I dedicated this book to you, Lex, because I know you would have loved it, and I'm forever sad that you'll never get to read it. I hope that you're among the stars rolling your eyes at my liberal interpretation of science. CB, this cover art is amazing. I hope the inside lives up to the outside. To Brian Brewer, thanks for being my dearest friend and the Blanche to my Dorothy. To Knits, our Rose, for encouraging me and being inappropriate as frequently as possible. To Laura Stone for being rad and supportive and an all-around awesome friend.

I'd also like to thank my mother for reading through this novel in its early stages and calling me out on creating a confusing timeline and for not developing characters enough. It really helped even though I complained a lot at the time. You're also a pretty great mom and, most importantly, my best friend. So thanks for allowing me to become an adult on my own terms. Well, except for that time you threatened to sell my car if I moved out.

Thank you to anyone who has ever encouraged, read or reviewed my writing, especially Heidi, Lalli and my fellow Interlude authors.

You make it easier to keep going when my own inner demons are telling me I suck. I hope you enjoy this tale as much as you did my other stuff.

And to my husband, Josh, I never seem to find the right words to say how I feel about you, which is odd for a writer. But I want you to know I'll never be sorry I answered that email all those years ago, even though on our first date, my car got locked in a parking lot and I saw your sketchy apartment. You're the best guy I could have trusted with my heart, and I'm so lucky you love and support me unconditionally. I'm still going to make sure everyone knows that I'm not the crazy cat lady, though. It's definitely you. And I wouldn't have it any other way.

ABOUT THE AUTHOR

CARRIE PACK IS AN AUTHOR of books in multiple genres, including *Designs on You* (2014), *In the Present Tense* (2016), *Grrrls on the Side* (2017), and *Past Imperfect* (2018). She is a recipient of two Foreword INDIES Book of the Year Bronze Awards for *In the Present Tense* and *Grrrls on the Side*, which has also been named a Bisexual Book Award Finalist. She lives in Florida, or as she likes to call it, "America's Wang."

interlude**press**™

 interludepress.com
 @InterludePress
 interludepress
 store.interludepress.com

interlude press

also by **carrie pack**...

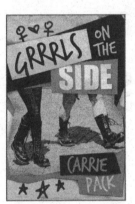